THE LION OF INDIA

"Injustice exists in abundance, but evil can never succeed in the long run."
—Vizier Ptah-Hotep under Pharaoh Djedkare Isesi

A Novel by Rafael Morillo

ISBN: 0692062386
ISBN-13: 978-0692062388 (Caribbean Lion Publishing)

LCCN: 2018902550

I would like to dedicate this novel to the members of the Indo-Caribbean and Indian communities that introduced me to their beautiful culture. I also dedicate this to my friends and family who have helped and inspired me to write this novel. A special thank you to my father who taught me about hard work and determination and completing what you start. Writing this has been a long but satisfying experience throughout some significant periods of my younger life.

CONTENTS

Statue of Chandragupta Maurya

PROLOGUE:
A SHIFT IN GLOBAL POWER
"Thought gives rise to desire."
—Rig Veda

The Land of Punt or Ta Netjer (meaning the land of God) was an early civilization possibly existing in modern day Somalia, Djibouti, Eritrea, and the coast of Sudan. The Ancient Egyptians traded with the Land of Punt and led expeditions as early as the fourth Egyptian Dynasty under Pharaoh Khufu earlier than 2600 B.C. Civilizations such as the Olmec and later the Mayas, Incas, and Aztecs existed in the Americas. In modern day Iraq, in Ancient Sumer, developing Sumerian cuneiform writing and a civilization around two rivers named the Tigris and Euphrates began to emerge. This was named Beth Nahrain (meaning House of Rivers) by the Persians and Mesopotamia (meaning land between rivers) in the Greek language.

Ancient Egypt was a world power where many of the surrounding people would come to work and learn, later influencing Ancient Greece. Under the Nubian Pharaohs of the twenty-sixth Dynasty, Egypt would regain its glory and engage the Assyrians, based in Mesopotamia, in war. Egypt would secure Palestine and its other territories from Assyrian invasion. The Medes made an alliance with the Babylonians, Scythians, Chaldeans, and Cimmerians and later captured Nineveh in 612 B.C. and defeated the Neo-Assyrians. King Astyages of the Median Empire would be overthrown by his own grandson, a client king named Cyrus II of Persia, who would later be called Cyrus the Great. Cyrus the Great was the King of Kings of the Persian Achaemenid Empire in 559 B.C. He liberated the Jewish slaves from Babylonian rule and allowed them to practice their religion freely in Babylonia, leading him to be referred to as the Messiah by the Jewish people. Cyrus the Great would be recorded in *Isaiah 45:1-7*, which reads, "This is what the Lord says to his anointed to Cyrus, whose right hand I take hold of to subdue nations before him and to strip kings of their armor to open doors before him so that gates will not be shut."

Cyrus the Great's son, Cambyses II, expanded the empire by conquering Egypt, Nubia, and Cyrenaica during his short rule. The Persian Empire later expanded into the Punjab region of Northern India during the reign of Darius I in 516 B.C. India was famed for its gold and various resources that had been exploited by the Persians. The Persian King Xerxes recruited Indian soldiers into the Persian army during his invasions into Greece. The Persians had introduced a highly-centralized administration system in the Punjab, but by 380 B.C. Persian control of the satrapy of Gandhara began weakening and would fall to the Macedonian leader Alexander the Great. India was divided into many kingdoms at this time and the rise of Alexander the Great would bring about a new global shift in power. The Indian people would form alliances against their enemies during this time. One such man was Rishan Ramankrishna, who would serve a pivotal role during this important age in Indian history.

CHAPTER 1:
HOUSE OF RAMANKRISHNA
"A journey of a thousand miles begins with a single step."
—Laozi (Tao Te Ching, Chapter 64)

It was not always as it is now (304 B.C.). Old men know of a time devoid of hopes of a new beginning. The youth are ignorant of the past, yet full of hope of what might be. Rishan Ramankrishna had become a man of the people. A man followed by others from the lowest to the highest castes. The wealthy and poor both saw inspiration within Rishan's leadership as he embarked on one of the most important battles in his life. This was a battle within a larger war for the peace and survival of the Mauryan Empire. Amazing how a land and people with so much history and knowledge had previously succumbed to these foreigners and their different customs. Some men felt satisfied in their high positions but recent events threatened their status; others were comfortable. The lower castes had hard lives and didn't involve themselves with political issues as they rarely changed their social standing, while the politically motivated, powerful families had the most to gain or lose. These thoughts were not expressed or discussed with the fortunate children of the House of Ramankrishna—the house that raised Rishan. One of the young men yearned to know the story of Rishan the man he admired, and Rishan explained as the men prepared to initiate a military offensive that would change the tide of war against the Greeks.

It was almost thirty-four years ago (338 B.C.) that Rishan, the youngest son of the Ramankrishna clan, was born—thirteen years before the strong, stocky man with dark brown hair who they called Iskander or Alexander the Destroyer arrived. Alexander had piercing eyes and was feared as his legend grew after the defeat of King Darius III, the Supreme Ruler of the Persian Empire. Rishan's older brother Rajesh was ten years his senior and received the best education and military training that his warrior caste affiliation afforded him. The youngest of the family was Priya and she was two years younger than Rishan. The father was Manish Ramankrishna, who was a strong, moral man who had worked hard to get to his current position in life. Manish was respected by his children and dearly loved by his wife Lakshmi. He was a tall, slender man who was stronger than he appeared, admired for his great intelligence. This, along with Manish's reliability and perseverance, allowed him to rise from the lower levels of his caste to the very heights of his caste within Punjabi Society. Manish had recently become a lower level adviser to King Porus, which gave him access to greater social mobility within the Kingdom of Pauravas.

Manish studied mathematics and architecture and began his career with small building projects in the kingdom. He was multi-lingual and was involved in civil affairs—a specimen of physical prowess. His reputation for loyalty, his ability to stay calm and make deals even in the most hostile situations, and his skills in predicting events yet to occur caught the attention of the Royal House. Manish was subsequently employed to supervise construction projects outside of the kingdom as well as serve diplomatic functions. His rise in position happened rapidly, elevating his social standing along with his family.

The Ramankrishnas were very dark in appearance with straight, matted hair. Even as the family rose in social standing and influence, they were still seen as outsiders by others in high society. Manish was a great father who taught his children morality, mathematics, architecture, and allowed them to explore and form their own perspectives. Manish's children also learned the Hindu religion from a young age and the *Bhagavad Gita* was a personal favorite of his youngest son Rishan. The Mahabharata and Ramayana were celebrated within the household, but Manish also spoke against blind devotion and belief in leaders who sometimes claimed godly ancestry in order to legitimize their rule. Manish taught his children the importance of self-reliance and the errors of blind devotion, which would impact Rishan.

Manish's eldest Son Rajesh was also astute but was mostly involved in physical competition like his father during his youth. Rajesh was expressive and outgoing and enjoyed a large social circle. He was the first Ramankrishna family member to join King Porus' army and he would become a great tactician. Manish's position in the king's court was the determining factor in Rajesh's recent appointment as a young officer. He would soon leave his father's house while he pondered which young lady to pursue for marriage—a luxury of choice that many other young men did not have. In contrast, Rishan was shy and reclusive but greatly admired Rajesh and wanted to also serve in the military against his mother's wishes. Rishan was a small child and his introverted condition convinced his family that he was better suited away from the battlefield and in a profession which made full use of his mental abilities. Rishan was already multi-lingual before the age of ten and possessed a solid grasp of religious texts with a curiosity for mathematics and the diplomatic work of his father.

Priya Ramankrishna was a sweet young girl who had hair like midnight and dark brown skin the color of the rich earth near the ancient lands of the Punjabi Rivers. Priya's eyes were wide, loving, and full of wonder. She played with small figurines her father had crafted for her and she was closely watched and guarded by her parents and older brothers. Priya was artistic and loved to draw the

Hindu God Vishnu and his various forms as well as Lord Ganesha, who she hoped would bring her family good fortune. Priya was the joy of the Ramankrishna household and she was almost identical in personality to her mother. Mother and daughter spent most of their time with each other as Manish spent most of his days at the Royal Court. Rajesh was currently establishing his new home and studying strategy as a young officer and Rishan was frequently at his school and secretly beginning to think about studying military strategy like his brother.

Manish and Lakshmi came from more humble origins. Manish's father Mahesh was smart and spent most of his life as a laborer building houses. Mahesh saved enough wealth to provide Manish with a great education in architecture, which Manish used to provide a good standing for himself and his family. Manish was great at his craft; he built an estate of three floors for his family with additional rooms used to house his extended family. The bricks were cut precisely and the floors were made of rocks with polished surfaces. Lakshmi was a good housewife who did not have to work outside the home as she once did in her younger years. She was a hard worker who kept all aspects of the home running smoothly. She was also intelligent and a strict disciplinarian who taught her children how to behave within and outside the home.

The city of Kausambi had been around for many centuries and was mentioned in the Ancient Vedic texts of the *Rigvedas*. It held significance and pride in the hearts and minds of the people of this city. However, the lower caste people in society were exposed to steadily increasing hardships. Taxes were getting harsher for the lower castes and the Royal Court was dealing with increasing tensions from regional kingdoms from both the east and west. Manish's career offered a high level of luxury but it was also coupled with increasing stress. In these last few years Manish's career began to cause him anxiety and stress as the Royal Court was now involved with increasing political threats from regions of Punjab.

CHAPTER 2:
THE PUNJAB AND THE KINGDOM OF PAURAVAS
"Peace comes from within. Do not seek it without."
—Gautama Buddha

The Pauravas Kingdom was established in ancient lands which predated many of the ancient religious writings. These lands were identified as the Trigarta Kingdom in the Mahabharata and would later be named the Punjab by Persian invaders (meaning the land between the five major rivers). These rivers were named the Sutlej, Beas, Ravi, Chenab, and Jhelum. The Kingdom of Pauravas was led by King Porus, who claimed to be a descendant of the Chandravansha Lunar Dynasty depicted in the *Rigvedas*. King Porus belonged to the ancient Puru Clan, rivals of the Yadavas Clan. Hastinapur was the ancient capital in the stories of the *Mahabharata* and the second and current capital was built in the city of Kausambi, which was the seat of power of King Porus in the Kingdom of Pauravas.

The kingdom was strong but comparatively weaker than it had been in previous centuries. Pauravas maintained some diplomatic relations with the much larger Magadha Kingdom to the east, whose current leader was the older King Mahapadma Nanda, the first ruler of the Nanda Dynasty. Mahapadma had defeated his family and rivals belonging to the former Shishunaga dynasty to ascend to the throne. King Mahapadma was immensely powerful, and so was his son Dhana Nanda, who would later take over the empire. Manish had previously visited the Nanda Royal Palace at the Magadha capital of Pataliputra during his diplomatic assignments. He had informed King Porus that he did not need to fear King Mahapadma, although he felt different about Dhana, who was unstable and about to take power of the House of Nanda and the Magadha Empire. The Magadha Empire had internal issues within the Royal House, their subjects, and the state of Kalinga, which was southeast of Magadha.

King Porus had a strained relationship with King Ambhi Kumar of the Kingdom of Gandhara (north of King Porus' territory). Takshashila was a major city in the Kingdom of Gandhara, which was the location of the famous University of Takshashila where Manish desired his youngest son Rishan would later attend. However, he understood that the current political tensions between the territories would make that goal hard to achieve. Manish debated with other advisers regarding the issue of King Ambhi's Gandhara Kingdom and the position King Porus should take against King Ambhi's increasing military power.

These kingdoms shared ancient lands with lovely architecture and a rich cultural history. The people spoke Punjabi and other languages with various dialects, sharing a common culture. The earth was dark like the shades of brown and black skin of the people who inhabited them, and rains and rivers kept the earth fertile, producing much of the harvest for the entire region. This was a bountiful region with the ability to support entire civilizations. Lamb and various meats were seasoned to perfection created a dance of flavors similar to the music the people would enjoy. There were spices of all different colors mixed together like a rainbow and there was a vibrancy in the clothing and faces of the people partaking in the festivities that were a joy to the young Rishan.

Rishan was a reserved boy who only recently had begun to play with other children. Rishan usually loved to go out on his own adventures after his studies and like his father, Rishan loved and saw the beauty of numbers. Rishan's mother Lakshmi rarely had to discipline him as he was dutiful and obedient—unlike the grief that his older brother Rajesh had caused during his own youth. Manish always reminded Rishan that they belonged to the warrior caste and that even if he was not involved in direct combat he could serve as a military strategist, so he encouraged his youngest son to begin socializing with boys his age and engaging in physical competition. Manish understood Rishan's passion for religious study and his love of numbers and nature, but he also knew that Rishan needed to learn how to communicate with others and develop healthy relationships.

The Punjabi land was a majestic sight with large plains, the eastern snow-covered mountain range, the northwestern salt range, and the semi-desert in the south; one bathed in the rivers during the hot months, the two most famous being the now known Jhelum and Chenab Rivers. The other main river was the Indus, for which these ancient people were named and referred to by foreigners. The Ramankrishnas had a nice house with a recently completed third floor which afforded extra accommodations for extended family. The floor had smooth polished stones fitted tightly together and was cleaned weekly by Rishan— Manish did not employ cleaners as he felt it was a person's duty to take care of his own home. He took pride in his home and his garden and he loved to instill pride and hard work in his son Rishan. Manish was impressed with Rishan's education and the rapid pace in which Rishan was absorbing information. He wanted Rishan to embark on a career as an adviser or follow in his footsteps as an architect.

Manish was not a strict follower of Hinduism, although his wife Lakshmi certainly was. Every now and then when father and youngest son were together, Manish would advise Rishan that it was important that he learn the *Vedas* and the other spiritual books and also stressed that Rishan pursue an education in practical subjects that could offer him a good livelihood. The ancient writings served a purpose in shaping morality and offered life lessons, but a man also had to use his body and mind to provide for himself and his family. Whenever he managed some time for himself, Rishan would usually take these religious writings with him and read the adventures of the *Bhagavad Gita* and the conversations between his favorite Gods, Lord Vishnu and Arjuna. Rishan would get lost within his imagination, sitting beneath trees in an oasis of shade during hot summer afternoons.

Manish finally convinced his wife that it was important for Rishan to start going out on his own and playing with the children of his caste. Perhaps he could make new relationships—especially with children from the prominent families in the kingdom. It would help Rishan develop essential relationships during his schooling and help him form social circles that could later help him in a successful career. He also encouraged Rishan to engage in physical contests to improve his physical health. Manish was a confident man who rose beyond his initial standing in life and he felt that an early start for his shy young son would be a great benefit for Rishan.

Rishan's family had enrolled him into a Gurukula (or school) under a good local Guru named Rampal. The school was within the Pauravas capital of Kausambi and within a few miles of the Ramankrishna House. Rishan was nervous the first few weeks and would stay to himself most of the time. Although many of the questions did not have a wrong or right answer, Rishan was anxious that he might be incorrect. Guru Rampal attempted to expand the minds of his students and guide them towards a certain understanding of the world, where each idea was nurtured and given a certain level of respect. Many times, Rishan would have an idea on the moral decisions made by Arjuna in the *Bhagavad Gita* when Krishna would pose certain questions and although his thoughts on the subject were well thought out, Rishan would remain silent. After about a month, Rishan began speaking and when Rishan did all the other students listened. Some felt a little jealous of how easily the answers flowed out of Rishan like a waterfall while other students enjoyed his perspective and the knowledge he presented far above his age group. Many of the students were also impressed at Rishan's intelligence and humility that many of the lesser talented students usually displayed. As time progressed, Rishan became more confident and his rapid rise in school began.

Rishan had already mastered much of the *Mahabharata* and the *Ramayana*. Although reserved at first, Rishan was able to make friends quickly—with boys and girls—despite their respective wealth or caste. Rishan did not place importance on caste differences due to the fact that his father rarely discussed such issues. Rishan embraced his studies as a fish embraces the sea and his first few years of education were fun; he was passionate about learning with little complaints and much praise from his guru Rampal. Some of the boys were envious at the ease with which Rishan learned his lessons and the eloquence that he displayed when expressing his views about the ancient scriptures. Rishan was not overtly proud of his own success and although it was hard for him to share his thoughts, he was amicable when approached by others, no matter their background or caste.

Most students lived at the school and Rishan began to devote more time to staying there, mostly improving his writing. All students had their own responsibility at the school and Rishan's included washing the garments of his fellow students. Rishan also cleaned around the school and later with the help of a young female classmate named Anupa Jhingan, he would learn how to prepare a variety of meals. Anupa Jhingan was from a respected family of Brahmin caste. Anupa was not the first girl Rishan liked but it was the first girl he was intrigued by and they would spend a lot of time together.

Anupa showed just as much thirst for the classic works of the *Vedas* as Rishan. Her family was very prominent and respected in the Punjab and she was attractive with a medium brown complexion and long black hair the color of a moonless night. Anupa's eyes were wondrous to look into and hid deep knowledge. Her relatives were involved with religious work while some concerned themselves with military affairs of the kingdom. The Jhingan Family heavily stressed education and instilled a deep love of learning in their daughter. They raised Anupa to have self respect, empathy, and spirituality. Rishan would speak to Anupa about various concepts regarding a just life and Dharma. Anupa was not like most girls; she was smart and had a strong sense of self that one could simply see emanating from her person when she engaged in conversation. Many of the boys sought out her attentions, but she never gave them any. She only cared for Rishan. This angered some of the higher caste boys, who looked down on Rishan's family. Undoubtedly there were rumors within the upper caste households that Rishan's family was out of place or did not belong to the position to which they had arisen. It was easier to ridicule and believe these rumors about Rishan's family than admit that the object of their affections was directing her attentions to the young intelligent boy.

Some of the children began to openly mock Rishan and although he felt uncomfortable, he would laugh it off to diffuse the situation. Rishan's non-confrontational nature fueled the other boys more; they perceived this as a weakness—an irony in the minds of the other boys because Rishan belonged to the warrior caste—which caused them to physically intimidate him whenever they had the opportunity. Rishan did not fear the other boys and just wanted to blend in. Rishan usually answered some questions although he knew the majority of the answers and would remain silent but attentive during lectures, absorbing all the wisdom Guru Rampal would impart. Rishan preferred to have private discourse with Guru Rampal. Rishan only talked with a few of the other students, preferring to mostly converse with Anupa. Rishan began to pursue athletics in order to build more self-confidence and perhaps fuel the interest of Anupa. Most importantly, Rishan felt that with more exercise he could assert himself during school and in physical competition. Rishan sought to compete with other boys and improve not only his mental ability but also with physical activities, which would legitimize his standing within the warrior caste.

At home, Rishan and his father would talk about classic writings, mathematics, and history. Manish also began to teach Rishan the importance of exercise, physical endurance, and discipline. He instructed his son to run once every few days to develop his breathing and told him that it would make it easier for Rishan to reach the same distances at a faster pace. Rishan was also instructed to steadily increase the distance once he got comfortable. At first Rishan was frustrated with how quickly he would tire and he complained to his father about how much of a bore it was to partake in this seemingly fruitless activity. Rishan would often get exhausted just leaving his immediate upscale neighborhood. However, as time went on, Rishan was able to take shorter breaks and run farther and faster Rishan and he was also able to maintain a full run through his entire circuit back towards his home. Rishan even began to increase the distance of his routes. Rishan loved the improvement and also began to exercise, which increased his confidence— especially because he understood that a member of the warrior caste should have a strong body to go along with a strong mind. Rishan

During some songs and dances, Rishan approached a few of the boys in class. Rishan desired to join in a speed contest after they set down some sticks to mark off a starting point and placed another at an endpoint to see which boys were the fastest. To everyone's amazement, the shy and unassuming Rishan was the victor. A little laugh was heard from a distance—it was Anupa, who had sneaked away to see what the secret activity was, and she was delighted her friend Rishan had won. At first Rishan was full of anxiety, but it helped him run even faster than usual. Previously, he had not stood out in physical competition but his daily training had helped develop his legs and speed. After he won a few times, his confidence increased and he became more comfortable around the other boys. Rishan's reputation as a fast runner quickly circulated throughout the community and the boys would search for the fastest runners to compete against Rishan would promptly defeat them all. Finally, one day they were able to find the fastest boy in the community.

He arrived with a lot of fanfare. He was a little older than Rishan and much stronger. He was tall and light brown in complexion and he was accompanied by young ladies far prettier than Rishan had ever seen—with exception to his dearest Anupa. He seemed calm but slightly excited to test his ability in a physical contest, knowing that it would only elevate his already high position among the boys of his age group. Rishan overheard the name "Karna Mehra" between shouts and pockets of conversation that began to swell as the boys clamored for this anticipated contest. One of Karna's female friends was striking and beautiful with a level of experience in matters that Rishan and his schoolmates lacked, and she was the main supporter of her champion. They set up markers and were ready to begin the race after a brief countdown. At once, the boys were off running swiftly as a gust of wind. Rishan ran hard, amazed at how fast he was as energy pulsed inside of him in waves, further increased by the loud cheering that was now becoming muted. As he lifted his head, his face was hit by an onslaught of dirt and as he gasped for air, his throat immediately dried as he noticed the champion was far ahead. Exhausted as he approached the end, he tripped on something and fell head first into the hot summer ground. Everyone laughed, including the boy who tripped him. Embarrassed, Rishan lifted himself up and was angered by the apparent perpetrator: a strong boy named Anand Agrawal. Anand threatened him but it was overshadowed by the cheers dedicated to the champion.

"Mehra! Mehra! Mehra!" the children yelled with glee.

Afterwards, Mehra called on his main female companion Anjali. Mehra approached Rishan and was impressed with his speed but still added a little fun at the expense of Rishan's ego, as most boys do when they are victorious. Everyone laughed as they walked away.

Anand Agrawal was a strong boy with a stocky frame. He appeared jovial at most times but would poke fun at Rishan whenever he could. He was not like many of the other students and he appeared to be from a lower position—perhaps the Vaishya caste. It was possible that Anand's family were merchants, however they had gained some wealth and they also stressed education which was apparent the rare times Anand spoke during school.

Anand was also a good fighter; he had learned from having to fight others who thought less of him growing up. Rishan, who had seemed to turn down a direct challenge from Anand, was seen as weak by the other boys and like all young boys when sensing a weaker male, they intensified their mocking.

Rishan, who had walked away from possible conflict with Anand, was met by Anupa. As she approached, he desperately tried to calm his hot spirit and hide his embarrassment. Anupa cheered Rishan up when she mentioned how surprised she was that he could run so fast. They walked together and Rishan spoke to her about his family and the work that his father did—something he never told the other kids. Rishan and Anupa enjoyed the afternoon as the sun began to fall on the horizon and the sky turned shades of orange and red.

The next day after a break in school, Rishan witnessed some of the boys wrestling and fighting. Rishan also wanted to fight like he ran, but when he was approached the other boys encouraging him to join in the competition, some of those in Anand's group openly mocked him. Rishan joined in the competition and was nervous at first but as soon as the fighting started he felt a sudden rush of energy and a competitive spirit. There were kicks, punches, grapples, and although Rishan was fast and strong, he understood he needed to improve his vigor and determination. Anand was ferocious and to say that Rishan did not have some fear about the possibility of a confrontation with him would be dishonest. After a few competitive matches where Rishan won and lost, Anand shouted at Rishan to face him, to which Rishan made his exhaustion known to everyone. Anand's friends erupted in laughter and mocked Rishan even more. Rishan was nervous but the pain he would feel upon Anupa learning that he turned down a challenge now competed with this emotion. Anand walked towards Rishan and looked at him with disdain; it was clear that he was bothered by Rishan's relationship with Anupa. At once Anand struck Rishan in the stomach, inflicting pain so powerful that Rishan gasped for breath. Anand then pushed him to the ground, causing the dirt to soil Rishan's clean clothing. Rishan felt like running away but his pride wouldn't let him and he got up and swung with all his might at Anand. With tears welling in his eyes, Rishan managed a few strikes at Anand, who landed more blows. Rishan was now in a full fight the likes of which he'd never experienced. Anand's fists felt like two of Rishan's, making quick work of the weaker boy. Rishan fell to the ground and wanted to continue but some girls who were looking on saved him from further punishment.

"I will tell my older brother Rajesh," Rishan yelled, and Anand responded by stating that his own brother would beat Rajesh just as soundly as he defeated Rishan. Anand did receive some blows and the other boys were a little surprised that Rishan put up that much of a fight. Rishan was too embarrassed to notice the other boys' reactions, however he realize some of Anand's friends were mocking him. Rishan was going home for a few days and wondered how he would hide the bruises.

Leaving the school, Rishan quickly gathered his clothes and said his goodbyes from far away as he began his brisk walk home. Rishan did not want to inform his guru about the fight, wishing to take care of his own problems and avoid spreading the information regarding his defeat to a wider audience like a forest fire during a drought. Rishan's elation of being one of the fastest boys just one day prior was deflated by the resounding defeat he just endured. Rishan felt miniscule and was embarrassed by just the thought of his failure. Rishan resolved that he would learn how to fight and beat the others not only in running, but in fighting and other forms of competition. Rage swelled inside him as he heard the familiar, pleasant voice of Anupa as she ran to catch up to him.

Rishan quickly wiped away a few tears that had managed to escape his prideful grasp. "Hello, Anupa," he said. "I forgot to say goodbye."

Anupa smiled but her curiosity and shock manifested as she touched Rishan's face. She asked him about his bruises. Forcing a smile, he managed a laugh, stating that he was just having fun with the other boys. Anupa was surprised, saying that he did not seem like the type who enjoyed wrestling and fighting.

"Well now I do!" Rishan explained, slightly annoyed.

"Oh, okay. Just wanted to make sure you were all right," Anupa responded.

As time passed, the sun began its slow descent, also lowering Rishan's rage. Rishan Eventually, he was able to enjoy his walk home along with the girl with whom he enjoyed spending time. Rishan loved the capital city of Kausambi and he barely remembered when his father moved their family from outside the kingdom into the heart of the capital.

Sometimes Rishan would ask his dad why some people seemed to always struggle more than others. Rishan often asked why some did the hard work considered dirty by others, and how come they never interacted with them during extensive holiday celebrations. Manish would avoid the questions when Rishan was very young but later he explained that certain people worked certain jobs in their lives but that everyone who worked hard deserved respect. Rishan noticed these people of lower standing as he walked home with Anupa and he realized how fortunate he was compared to others who seemed to have a lower lot in life. Anupa asked Rishan about his thoughts and Rishan shared them with her. Anupa informed him that she believed every spirit was unique and special and was to be watered like a flower. Rishan agreed, but also understood that that some flowers were watered while others were left to wither in the sun.

CHAPTER 3:
KEMET, PERSIA, AND PALESTINE (330 B.C.)
"You have a right to perform your prescribed duties, but you are not entitled to the fruits of your actions. Never consider yourself to be the cause of the results of your activities, nor be attached to inaction."
—The Bhagavad Gita, 2:47

The Ramankrishna Family was currently in a great position. Manish was rising quickly in society as an established architect and junior adviser to King Porus, his family was doing well, and his eldest son Rajesh was excelling as a young officer in the military. Manish's wife enjoyed his success and was happy managing the family's finances and home. Rishan advanced in his studies at a rapid pace and the youngest, Priya, was healthy, happy, full of potential, and had her entire life ahead of her. Manish, who had worked so hard to rise in his caste and finally put his family in great standing, now felt the pressure of the unknown. He looked back on how his own father sacrificed so much to give him security and opportunity in the land of Pauravas, and now the future of this powerful kingdom was uncertain. As adviser, Manish had advanced knowledge of foreign activities. In the east the Nanda Dynasty appeared strong, but it was rotten at its core and the enormous might of the Magadha Kingdom seemed unbalanced and ominous with instability. This was an area of concern for Manish as there was nothing that he loved more than stability when it came to politics, diplomacy, and economics—especially now that he had a family for which he was responsible.

Manish understood that there was a climate of urgency and he needed to initiate new proposals for King Porus' review. His position as a military adviser and diplomat afforded him access to various relationships King Porus had with the surrounding kingdoms and there was a possibility of major wars on the horizon that could influence their dynamics. Manish was also a realist and a pragmatist; his youngest son Rishan was taking on some of the same qualities. However, Rajesh was extremely loyal to Porus and the kingdom and although his father disagreed with him on certain matters, he at the very least felt assured that a strong kingdom led by the strong King Porus would ensure Rajesh's future.

Manish pondered these latest occurrences as a naval captain ponders the most efficient routes amidst a turbulent ocean. In a few days Manish would write an official report on his ideas and submit it to King Porus. Other voices in the king's court carried more weight than his, however Manish had begun thinking deeply of a few options that perhaps the other advisers had not thought about. Manish understood Nanda politics very well and he reflected on possible actions the future King Nanda would take; he also reflected on King Ambhi in the northern kingdom, who was hostile towards King Porus.

Rishan had arrived home and his mother Lakshmi welcomed him with a dinner of curry lamb and fruit juices to wash it down. Lakshmi was happy to see her youngest son home now that Rajesh was starting his own life and career. She was an educated woman and was impressed by Rishan's progress, which was far ahead of her eldest son at the same age of eight years old. Lakshmi was also happy to find that Rishan had gained a close friend in Anupa Jhingan. She knew of the Jhingan family and thought it was a great relationship for her youngest son Rishan to develop. Rishan did not mention Mehra or his trouble in school to his mother due to his embarrassment on this issue, but he would seek to ask his father for advice in private.

This was a fascinating time for young Rishan. He had learned many things in school but having a father who was involved in the inner workings of the Pauravas Kingdom granted him extensive access and knowledge not available to most people. Rishan was not interested in politics but he loved to hear about the history of his people as well as learning about faraway civilizations. His uncle Manu would always talk about distant lands he saw during his travels as a merchant. Although he was also from the warrior caste, he was good at business and he wondered about the rest of the world and his profession allowed him travel. Manu would be visiting his family soon and Rishan was overflowing with anticipation.

Rishan enjoyed being at home because he enjoyed playing with his little sister Priya. She was now six years old and she had the most beautiful long black hair. Priya enjoyed hearing stories of Rishan and his stay at school and she would often ask Rishan about his guru Rampal and what he taught the students. Priya was also about to start school and her nerves were somewhat eased by her brother's stories. Rishan sensed his little sister's fears and did not mention the negative experiences that he had begun to face with some of the school boys. Their father would arrive home tomorrow from his involvement in a series of important meetings at the Royal Palace and Rishan was excited to see him.

Manish came home as the sun began its descent. His family was there to welcome him with open arms and he was overjoyed to see his youngest son Rishan and hear about his time under Guru Rampal. Manish had spent a lot of time with his eldest son Rajesh while he was in school to learn battle tactics and leadership skills. Rajesh was a natural and confident leader and Manish was comfortable with the direction Rajesh was taking in his life. He now focused his time in the guidance of his two youngest children. Manish was aware of Rishan's success and mental capabilities, but he was also curious to learn about his youngest son's social growth—specifically, who his new friends were.

The next day began as the sun shone new light upon the land. Rishan washed his body with the water which was kept in his family's house; daily showers were important in the Ramankrishna household for cleanliness and to mitigate the summer heat. Afterwards, Rishan enjoyed a breakfast of lamb with mild spices and breads, which he washed down with fruit juices from his mother's garden. Manish expected his son to excel in school and improve his physical health through martial arts as part of the duties of his caste, although secretly Manish never desired his children to be involved in combat—particularly Rishan.

Manish worked hard as adviser to King Porus with the objective of maintaining the strength of Pauravas, whose main threat came from King Ambhi in the north. The Nanda Dynasty of the Kingdom of Magadha controlled the most powerful military in the region but the Nanda Royal Family was like a rotting fruit: a beautiful on the exterior but breaking apart from within. Manish feared that their internal turmoil and unfavorable view with their own subjects would soon cause a collapse in that society. Instability with a nearby empire might negatively impact the Pauravas Kingdom. Also, news from faraway lands weighed Manish down and he wanted to discuss this with his guests before his major meeting at the Royal Palace in a few days.

These affairs all would be discussed soon but for now, Manish was interested in learning about Rishan's experiences with Guru Rampal and he sat his son down before dinner to talk with him privately. Manish was excited to learn of Rishan's continued academic success in his historical, mathematical, and religious studies. Guru Rampal had spoken with Manish and had only good things to say. The only thing troubling Manish was his youngest son's shyness but he was happily informed by Rishan that he had formed a friendship with Anupa Jhingan. Manish respected Anupa's father Daha Jhingan, who was an important Brahmin in his community, and his lovely wife Surina Jhingan. Anupa's brother Nakesh also showed great promise and was expecting to follow his father's footsteps as a knowledgeable and influential Hindu priest. Manish enjoyed Rishan's friendship with Anupa because she was smart and of good moral character and she would uplift his son.

Rishan also informed his father of the trouble he had with some of the boys, but he did not describe the full extent; he felt it was his responsibility to correct the situation. Rishan told Manish that he engaged in physical contests such as races and wrestling and he had done better than most, which elated his father. Manish advised his son to begin learning how to fight but also said that fighting should be used as a last resort. "One must always aim to resolve conflict through words," was Manish's advice. Rishan also informed him of the older boy he had met at school with the last name of Mehra. When his son described Mehra's features, Manish quickly recognized the boy and his prominent family. Manish identified the young man as Karna Mehra, who had been named after a celebrated warrior of the *Mahabharata*. The Mehra family was prominent in the Royal Court and in the Pauravas army. The Patriarch of the Mehra clan was Kali Mehra, a high-level adviser to King Porus whose opinion usually overruled that of Manish and other lower level advisers.

The next day began with an early shower and breakfast. Manish woke up as the sun's rays splashed the rich Punjabi soil then roused his youngest son to surprise him with the news that his uncle Manu would be visiting later in the day. Rishan could not help but betray his anxiety and anticipation as this would only be the second time in his young life that Rishan would see his uncle Manu since Rishan was four. Rishan's excitement grew as he wondered what adventures Manu would reveal to him and his family.

The Ramankrishnas gathered around the main entrance of their house as they waited to welcome Manu. He was tall like his older brother with a slightly wider build, and his trimmed beard and hair was dark as opposed to his older brother Manish, whose hair was already sprinkled with growing patches of grey. Manu appeared exhausted but his eyes burned like the sun itself; he was eager to inform Manish regarding the information he had personally gathered.

"Hello, family!" Manu loudly announced as they welcomed him back to Kausambi in the Kingdom of Pauravas.

Dinner was served earlier than usual and the smell of curry and various spices filled the Ramankrishna home. Manu ate peacefully and savored his meal; it was a pleasure he had sacrificed during his long travels. Manu desired to eat faster due to his hunger but he mitigated his urges for the purpose of maintaining proper manners. Manu also waited for everyone to finish and entertain second helpings before he himself would eat more of the tasty curry lamb Lakshmi had prepared. He had no wife or household of his own, as his main goal was to enrich himself with gold, wisdom, and adventure. Manu's travels also benefited him with significant levels of understanding in business, trade, and culture. He was one of the most knowledgeable people Rishan knew and more informative than the politicians Manish worked with at the Royal Palace.

Manish was not very religious and Manu was far less so. Although Manu knew the lessons and stories of Vedic Literature, he did not necessarily believe in the existence of all of the beings mentioned. Manish kept his honest opinions from Manish's wife Lakshmi, who was a conservative Hindu. After dinner, the family asked Manu about his business and the lands he had traveled to. Manu's answers were interesting and his adventures were remarkable but vague when compared to the level of detail in which he would privately describe his last four years away to his older brother Manish. The discussion regarding Manish's career created a visible tension; Rishan had gradually seen stress increase in his father—particularly within the last two years—but Rishan rarely asked him about his lengthy meetings at the Royal Palace. Manish disregarded Manu's questions and simply stated that he was trying to provide a stable environment for his family and that required a stable government and peace.

Rishan asked his uncle about his job in the distant regions outside of the Punjab. Manu sold spices and other goods from the Punjab abroad and his occupation allowed him to meet merchants from all over the known world. Manu's business and location helped him meet with people from all walks of life—including people who held high positions in their respective lands. Rishan asked his uncle regarding the extent of his travels and Manu revealed that he had been as far west as an area called Palestine. Manu described the people of Palestine who lived under Persian leadership—t he same Persian leadership the Punjabi Kingdoms were under. The authority of the Persian leader, King Darius III and the hegemony of the Persian Empire was weakening as the Punjabi kingdoms were entering a changing and uncertain future.

As the sun was beginning its downward retreat towards the horizon, Rishan's interest in his uncle's tales continued. Lakshmi had put Priya to bed and beckoned Rishan to sleep. Always the obedient child, Rishan asked his mother if he could stay with his father and uncle and listen to their conversation. Manish felt it was time for Rishan to participate in an adult male conversation and told his wife that Rishan could stay up with him and his brother as long as he wished. Manish was reluctant but felt it was time for Rishan to understand the ways of men and the world. His intelligence was like a body of water breaking a dam during monsoon rains, pouring forth whenever he spoke. Manish understood that world events would eventually come crashing down on Punjabi society, breaking the chains of ignorance even among the most uninformed.

Rishan had numerous questions for his young uncle, which his uncle was happy and eager to answer. Manu spoke about his travels and how he sought adventure different from the difficult and arduous life of study in which his older brother Manish excelled. Manish would become financially successful and Manu himself would be less so, however he would travel more extensively and learn directly about foreign cultures. Manu revealed that he had traveled northwest far beyond the Indus River towards the civilizations of the Thamud (later the Thamud people would be called the Arabic peoples of Arabia). These people traded various perfumes that eased the natural smell of a person even at the end of a laborious day. Manu had forgotten to give these gifts to the family earlier but now handed a few aromas to Rishan and Manish. Manu reserved some lighter smelling resins for Lakshmi.

Manu reached into a travel bag and showed Rishan some of the frankincense and myrrh he had also collected. He explained that the Arab people cut this from the bark of a special tree and it flowed like the blood of cut skin. This fluid was commonly called "tears" by the locals and it was sold far and wide to meet rising demand. Rishan had never seen hardened frankincense. Manish had some of these oils applied by the local doctor—the Ramankrishna family now had access to some of the best Ayurvedic Doctors in Pauravas. Many of the families in the Brahmin and warrior castes that Manish worked with also used these doctors for cosmetic purposes including nose enhancements and other facial features. Rishan Manish reminded Rishan that doctors should heal illnesses originating from within the body as well as physical injuries and deformities; they should not be used to fuel a person's vanity because a person's true characteristics and appeal came from within. The two men and the young boy shared a small laugh as Manu asked to burn his resins. Manish rarely burned these aromatic stones but for a rare occasion with the Ramankrishna men, he welcomed it.

These "tears" were traded all over the land of the Arabs. The ruling Persian Empire had special interest in these aromatic luxuries that the Royal Achaemenid Persian House enjoyed. Rishan had heard of the new Emperor Darius III from some of Manish's conversations with fellow advisers. The details regarding Emperor Darius were known by some within Pauravas but these powerful men that controlled the world were lesser known to the lower castes. Global Affairs were rarely discussed by people who were struggling in poverty. Rishan burned with curiosity about this powerful Persian monarch but before he could finish his question, his father interrupted, asking Manu to talk about another mysterious land he was able to visit.

The people in Palestine were dark like the color of the people of the Indus River. The lightest appeared as wet sand mixed with dirt and the darkest approached the darkest Dravidian people far south of the Punjab. The Palestinian people had hair that was coarse like Rishan's and at times matted to the extent that it could be twisted as the people of the Indus civilization often wore. Manu's interest in language and culture also increased his vocabulary to include Aramaic, which highly interested his nephew Rishan. Manu explained how many of these languages were related in that region, including across a slim waterway where the people were black as onyx—a place the Greeks called Ethiopia. These Hebrew people practiced a religion which worshiped only one God named Yahweh, and this intrigued Rishan. Rishan

He asked, "Do they not have other Gods they pray to involved with other aspects of life?"

Manu explained that they believed there was only one God but that they were respectful of other points of view and other faiths. This land had passed through many hands: the Babylonians, Assyrians, and many others. Cyrus II or "The Great" was a ruler that the people of Palestine respected because he allowed them to settle back into their lands as well as enacted laws affording them the freedom to worship as they pleased. Compared to earlier rulers, this was a great relief to the people. Rishan wanted to learn more and asked about the people with the dark skin.

Manu continued, stating that there was a massive land that was so large that much of it remained to be explored—a land believed to be much bigger than those of the Indus River, Persia, and eastern lands combined. This amazed Rishan and he hungered to learn more. Manu said they were darker than the Palestinians and the people south of the Indus River, yet these Aksumites also included hues of beautiful dark and light browns. This amazed Rishan, for in his mind the Dravidian people were the darkest only to be surpassed by Lord Krishna himself. Manu believed these darker people were among the oldest people.

Rishan's ideas on man's origins and civilization were primarily derived from ancient Vedic texts. For him, life was cyclical, but perhaps his uncle was correct, as his favorite God was Lord Krishna who was black like the night sky. Perhaps there was an origin and time flowed in one direction or perhaps both schools of thought were intertwined or far too complex for simple beings such as man to comprehend.

Manu conversed with these people who were called Nubians, who taught him of a history even older than this own. Perhaps they were related to the black pygmy people who lived in their own island communities far off the eastern coast of the Punjab lands in the exotic east. These discussions with the Nubians impacted Manu's perspective and he eagerly shared this with his family. The furthest reaches of Manu's travels led him to the civilization adjacent to the Nubian people in an ancient and glorious place named Kemet. Kemet was the land that Manu most desired to share with his family and his kids if he found a wife and married in his later years.

Manu had traveled by camel in a caravan with a group of Nubians who had previously made the trip themselves many times for business. Originally, these Nubians of the Kingdom of Kush contributed to the development of Kemet, which they came to rule, creating several Royal Dynasties including an expanded Kushite and Egyptian Dynasty. Manu was astonished at the sight of the major centers within Kemet and the people were hard working with a sense of purpose and also enjoyed life. Manu noticed various styles of clothing the people wore as they lived simply in small housing and worked on their farms as well as those who were more financially comfortable. Many wore the Persian style of dress and it was explained to Manu that the ruler of Kemet was Sabaces, who ruled in place of Darius III. Sabaces had been away at Issus in a battle against the Greek upstarts, so the temporary ruler in place was Mazaces. There were already grumblings about Mazaces and Manu told his brother and Rishan how he decided to leave the area and travel back to Palestine, as he felt the situation there had grown unstable.

Rishan had learned about Persia from his father but Rishan had limited knowledge of the power of the Persian Empire and how they indirectly ruled the Indus Valley civilizations. Manu also explained to Rishan that the people of Kemet enjoyed an ancient history stretching thousands of years and that they were the original black Nubians of that society. "Kemet" was a term used for the black rich soil of the land, which was enriched by the flooding of the Nile. The word Kemet was also reflected in the beautiful complexions of the people that inhabited that land. Manu explained that other peoples had migrated back into Kemet in search of better opportunities. These people had long before engaged in wars against aggressors but had fallen victim now to the Persians.

The Persians ruled under the Achaemenid Empire, beginning with Cyrus The Great who had conquered Babylon, making Babylon a regional center of education and power. Cambyses II of Persia was the first Persian ruler to conquer Kemet at the battle of Pelusium, making it a satrapy and naming himself Pharaoh a few hundred years prior (525B.C.-402B.C.). Kemet was able to recover but Kemet was re-conquered by Artaxerxes III in 343 B.C. Rishan was attentive and interested; he asked his uncle if he had brought anything back from his journey to Kemet. Manu remembered he had a few records and revealed a papyrus with hieroglyphics he managed to keep in his travels. Manu had limited knowledge of the writing system but managed to learn how to read it at a basic level.

It was now very late and Manish advised his son to sleep, as he would be attending school again in several days, but Rishan wanted to know about the Greek people. Manu said they were interesting and had been in the area. He had encountered a few who were students and merchants; they had an unfamiliar language and called the people of the region different names due to their physical features or cultural peculiarities. They referred to the people of Kemet as "Egyptians" and their land as "Egypt" and the Greeks also referred to the lands of Aksum and Kush as "Ethiopia", which referenced the dark skin of its inhabitants who appeared as if they had been scorched by heat. These ancient people had a language which was similar to those spoken in Palestine and they referred to themselves as "Habesh" or "Habesha". Rishan asked his well-traveled uncle the reason for his hasty retreat, which was met by an angry exclamation by Manish towards his curious son to go to sleep. Rishan obeyed his father. Besides, there was much for Manish and Manu to discuss in the morning and Rishan could possibly learn of his uncle's travels at a more opportune time.

The next day, Manish awakened before sunrise and prepared for a morning walk with his younger brother. Manu was already awake and ready to divulge the real reason for his return to Pauravas. Manish sensed great trouble in his brother's face—a skill of discernment he executed with extreme ease from their childhood years. "What sorrow befalls you, brother?" Manish asked.
"Let us converse with the coolness of the morning wind," Manu replied.
Manish awakened Rishan and Priya for a bath and breakfast. Lakshmi would take Rishan to school and their daughter out to the market. Rishan had been a smart and obedient son and was a joy to his father. All the hard work that Rishan had done would be rewarded now, as Manish would have him go train in the ancient martial arts of their people. Rishan had been appealing to his father in order to learn wrestling and martial arts and Manish also believed it would strengthen his son physically and enhance his discipline. As the sun began to appear rise, he kissed his wife and kids and began his walk with his brother, whose insight involving foreign affairs would be most beneficial. In just several days, Manish would attend a meeting at the Royal Palace with King Porus, top advisers, and military leaders where they would discuss foreign affairs as well as

secret information that would be made available to him and the other lower officials.

Manu was impressed with the home his older brother had created and the great family he sheltered and inspired. Manu also began to yearn for these things himself and he expressed this to his older brother for the first time. Manish asked once again what troubled him and Manu replied that the reason for his rapid departure was the astonishing pace of advancing destruction and submission that Alexander of Macedon was inflicting on the once mighty Persian Empire. Manish had already heard reports of this Alexander of Macedon and his father Philip II, but now the situation within the ruling Persian Empire seemed perilous. The Persian Empire and its Royal House had suffered from inner turmoil while experiencing setbacks at the peripheries of their empire with Egypt and Greece before, but now the empire seemed a hollow power living atop the crumbling edifice of its past glory. The Greek city-states in constant quarrel with themselves had managed small temporary victories against Persia in the past—as Sparta proved in their brief success against King Xerxes—but this Macedonian son of Philip II was now leading the unified Greek city-states and had taken power in Egypt, threatening to overtake the Palestinian areas.

Manish continued to ask his brother questions about Alexander's conquest across Egypt and the lands around Palestine. He also desired to learn about the pace of Alexander's forward advance and the state of the Persian military. The intelligence that the Royal Advisers had access to stated that there was a significant event roughly two years prior (332 B.C.) which had seen the young Alexander as victorious. The status of King Darius III was not clear and his specific activities in that battle remained just as unclear. Manu stated that Alexander was particularly vicious and vengeful at times, which sparked Manu's speedy return to the Punjab after Alexander crossed the Hellespontus (Dardanelles). Alexander's actions in his Siege of Tyre was particularly brutal, however Manu explained that the Persian general, Batis of Gaza, seemed unfazed by this and was confident he would contain Alexander's advance awaiting King Darius' reinforcements. During Manu's travel back to Pauravas, he also heard that Batis of Gaza had suffered a horrific end at the hands of Alexander. These events were common knowledge at the Royal Palace, but little attention was given to this information. Alexander's crossing of the Hellespont was significant, as this was the same point which King Xerxes had crossed to subjugate the Greek city-states over 100 years prior. Now Alexander had solidified his power, unified Greece, crossed into Asia, and taken the battle to Darius. Alexander's entrance into Egypt was greatly welcomed as the Egyptians sought to free themselves from Persian rule while the Macedonians sought to continue east.

King Porus had a distant but mildly cordial relationship with the Royal House in Babylon. King Darius held control of the Punjab areas—a control passed down through multiple generations from the Persian King Cyrus the Great before him. This relationship with Persia had not always been friendly, but it had been amicable. At various times, the people of the Punjab areas had sent troops to fight for the glory of Persia. Some of these Indian troops were recruited by the Persian kings of the past to fight battles in foreign lands to include the suppression of uprisings by the Greeks as well as the upstart Spartans over 100 years prior—a fight which the mighty Persian King Xerxes eventually won. Some Punjabi fighters were recruited to fight a few years ago against the Macedonian Alexander, but many of them perished, alerting Porus and the other rulers of the region regarding the strength of this foe. King Darius had fallen mysteriously silent in the last two years and many speculations as to why arose. Many believed it was a change inside the Royal Family that caused the silence while others thought Darius had met his fate on the battlefield. Manish believed it was a combination of both. Persia perfected the art of propaganda and in dire situations, information would seldom reach the ears of even the current kings governing their respective territories, however now the rumors were beginning to swell within the palace of Porus and even into the streets of the capital.

The morning was cool with a soft but steady wind that eased the tense conversation. The sun would soon rise and the heat would scorch the skin of the people once again. Many thoughts swirled like monsoon rains in Manish's head, but his walk with his brother helped temper his spirit. For this reason, Manish loved to go out for walks before the sunrise to ponder aspects of his life. The brothers walked the streets of the capital city commenting on the early morning calm and observing people of the Sudra caste, who were already busy and involved in their duties. They cleaned the streets and made up various levels of manual labor. Some of these people were on their way to their duty of brick making—something that demanded long, hard days of labor and mental strength. There were more laborers in the streets before sunrise who worked until sundown, especially because there was an overall increase in new building construction in the capital of Kausambi. Manish loved seeing the laborers at work and he highly respected them no matter their caste. As an architect, he appreciated these workers who received his ideas and and made them manifest in great physical projects readily available for public use.

Manish remembered when he received his promotion to adviser and amazed the court with his knowledge of foreign affairs. His work was of a quality seldom rivaled and his forward thinking and vision for architecture and mathematics translated well into his observations of people, which helped the rulers maintain peace and order among their subjects. King Porus trusted Manish and respected his honesty, directness, hard work, discipline, and calm demeanor. King Porus was also impressed with Manish's physical abilities and his love for Pauravas and its populace. These qualities made it easier for Porus to promote him to higher levels of his advisery body, prompting celebration by Manish's supporters and family but a slight contempt from others in high places who felt he did not belong. Manish's conversation with his brother and his new insight would helped create different perspectives that he would discuss with King Porus during his meeting at the Royal Palace.

Manu explained to his older brother everything he had seen and the rush of the people out of the lands to avoid Alexander's wrath. He had seen very little and was able to flee just as he heard reports of the Macedonian king crossing into Asia a little over four years ago. Manish already knew of these things obviously, but the personal experiences of his brother gave him new insight on the situation and it surprised him to find out the relative ease with which Alexander walked into Egypt declaring himself pharaoh. Alexander had overthrown the second Persian Dynasty from their regional seat of power in Egypt and did so surprisingly easily and with the support of the majority of the Egyptian people—or so it seemed. The Persian ambassadors and advisers to Porus did not reveal the ease with which Alexander became pharaoh, which robbed King Porus of an accurate analysis and weakened his foreign policy.

Manish and his brother paused by the ancient Jamuna River just as the sun began to kiss the dark rich soil of the Punjab. Manu then revealed the reasons for his personal anguish: he had finally found love. This woman was named Saba, a Habesha Aksumite from the lands close to Kush. The Greeks referred to her as an Ethiopian because of her lovely dark skin. Saba was young, smart, and taught Manu about her history and her people. Manu also noted the ancient relationship between Saba's lands and Gaza. He was intrigued by Saba; he had never met a woman that fulfilled him in such a way. He loved her strength, loyalty, hard work, and selflessness and spent time with her as he also taught her about the Indus lands and his ancient Hindu religion and Vedic traditions. Manu felt he had finally met a woman he could start a family with and in her he saw his own future. Manu had discussed marriage with Saba and they both agreed they would live their days together. They made plans as questions arose as to whether they would remain in Gaza, go to Aksum, or return to the Punjab. Persia had control of Palestinian lands and Egypt, however news of Alexander reached the populace and with each of his conquests fear was sparked in the hearts of the people, making the choice to go back to Pauravas seemingly the best course of action for the two lovers. As Alexander's success increased, the logical progression was for Alexander to conquer Egypt, and the way to Egypt was through Palestine. Saba believed her lands would be next and she felt it was necessary to go back and part ways, leaving an anguished Manu alone to depart to Pauravas, distraught that perhaps his duty was to follow and protect Saba. Manu did not know Saba's fate and felt he had failed at his duties as a man towards the woman he cherished.

The two men began the walk back to the Ramankrishna household and Manish comforted his brother's decision and advised that he should join him at the Royal Palace in order to share his personal experiences. Winter was coming and Manu thought just as the winter was fast approaching, perhaps Alexander and his army would soon follow.

CHAPTER 4:
PORUS AND THE ROYAL PALACE OF PAURAVAS
(330 B.C.)

"Do not be led by others, awaken your own mind, amass your own experience, and decide for yourself your own path."
—The Atharva Veda

Manish prepared his thoughts and with the help of his brother, formulated domestic and foreign policies for King Porus' review. Manish convinced his younger brother to travel with him to the Royal Palace and advised Manu to seek employment there so Manu could set a solid financial foundation and perhaps create a future for himself and start a family of his own. Manish dressed in his finest clothing and adorned himself with gold jewelry and gems. He never wore excessive jewelry like the others at the Royal Palace; he was a humble man and did not wish to rub his increased wealth in the faces of the less fortunate. After the brothers were dressed, Manish went to his stable where he had bought a selection of personal horses of high quality. He fed and maintained clean drinking water for his horses and picked his favorite—which he secretly named after his oldest son Rajesh because of the horse's initial stubbornness—and chose another for Manu. Manish reviewed his prepared speech and then both brothers set off for the Royal Palace.

The sun began to rise as they rode and caught up on

old stories pertaining to their childhood. Although usually tempered and cerebral, Manish would at times get involved in mischief like his brother. Mahesh was the family patriarch and he and his wife Seeta brought up Manish and Manu in a strict household where education and physical exercise was stressed. Manish excelled in academic studies but Manu yearned to explore the world, preferring the life of a merchant. Although they belonged to the warrior caste, the Ramankrishna men engaged in various trades during times of peace. Manu had debated selling iron—a trade that his people were known for—or spices and eventually chose the latter. Manu sometimes wished that he had learned the business of shaping and combining heated metals to sell as weaponry abroad, as it was a more lucrative business, but in his thirst for exploration he learned the easier business of selling goods including exotic spices abroad.

Manish excelled in his academics and was invited to the famous university at Takshashila, where he studied architecture. Manish's intelligence, hard work, and fame had brought him to the inner circle of King Porus and the Royal Family, where he also showed a talent for foreign affairs, which propelled him to his rapid rise and his current position.

The brothers laughed at some of the mischief they got involved in and the girls they liked as boys. They pondered the locations and the current situations of their childhood friends. Manish was more reserved around the ladies and kept the majority of his relationships private, while Manu was more outspoken and carefree and was not a stranger in receiving the affections of many a young lady no matter the caste. Manu had good business sense and eased the minds of others with his ability to find humor during life's many challenges, even making light of his sudden flight from Palestine. The brothers laughed and Manish found temporary relief from the increasing stress in his life. As they reached the Royal Palace, Manu's excitement began to grow. This would be his first visit inside the main hall.

The air began to heat up as the sun rose above the

horizon. Both men pondered their own journeys in life as well as each other's. They were satisfied but yearned for more and were nervous about what the future held for them and their people. For a long time their world was balanced and relatively stable under Persian leadership and the strength of Porus. The Ramankrisha men were aware of their ancestral lands to the south but they were confident and identified in the strength and stability of King Porus and the Kingdom of Pauravas.

Rishan was excited to start his new martial arts training and had already improved his athletic skills and some wrestling. These new abilities lifted his confidence, which he had been severely lacking for most of his young life. Rishan pondered why he had been given great gifts yet suffered from low self-confidence. Why did he have trouble talking with the girls—especially the object of his desire, Anupa Jhingan? How was it that others who were not as privileged as he was, like Anand Agrawal, still managed to have confidence? Now Rishan slowly grasped the answers to these questions. Rishan's athleticism and increased competitiveness allowed him to gain new friendships and social elevation. Rishan's high level of intelligence, which garnered praise from his teachers like Guru Rampal, also fueled jealousy from his lesser performing peers but his athleticism began to give him a different kind of praise. Rishan "Better to learn as a child than as an adult," Rishan would repeat to himself.

Rishan had fought Anand many times but now had begun to equal him as the frequency of their fights decreased. Perhaps Anand respected Rishan's spirit and had begun to seek Rishan as a possible ally, although Rishan did not like having a legitimate rival. Rishan would have another encounter with Anand as he sought to finally establish himself as a boy who knew how to protect himself.

Both boys found themselves below the popular Karna Mehra, who was slightly older than Rishan but more involved in the world of adults than that of children. Karna also excelled socially, especially with girls and even women older than him. Rishan was in awe as well as a little jealous of Karna's popularity. For most of Rishan's his life he never sought to be the center of attention, preferring to blend in.

Rishan had arrived at Guru Rampal's school complex and began to clean his personal quarters when he was interrupted by Anand. Rishan became defensive as his rival approached but he did not fear Anand anymore and felt as strong as him. Anand and the others began to mock Rishan's relationship with Anupa.

Rishan, who had held his own in previous fights, found his confidence, stating, "You mock me because she fancies me over the lot of you!"

This angered Anand and he approached Rishan, who quickly took the offensive by striking Anand with a blow to his face and upper chest. A fight ensued and a small crowd gathered with some boys openly cheering Rishan as if they also found their voices in his bravery. The much faster Rishan frustrated Anand, who rushed at him, tossing him to the ground as he began striking Rishan, who was able to get to his feet and trip Anand. As he stumbled, Rishan struck him on his head, making Anand fall like a rock. Another boy tried to attack Rishan and he struck him hard on his head, sending him to the floor. When the other boys approached, Rishan picked up a stone and hit another boy in the leg. As Rishan turned around, he sidestepped the charging Anand, kicking him into the wall. When Anand turned around he was met by a powerful body blow and a punch to his head. One of the other boys stopped Rishan for fear that Guru Rampal would see this behavior. Anand held his stomach and had a small gash on the side of the head while two of his friends writhed on the floor. The rest of the boys were silent with surprise and then a loud cheer erupted in favor of Rishan's victory. Despite his bruised ego, Anand respected Rishan and apologized for his previous hostilities towards him. Anupa had witnessed the later portion of the fight and rushed to help clean Rishan's cut, commenting that she was happy that Rishan had defended himself but he did not want him to get involved in any more fighting.

Manish and his brother were entering the Royal region of the inner city of Kausambi. The roads were made of stone polished down as much as possible and maintained carefully under the leadership of King Porus. This was Manish's first time entering the Imperial Zone of Kausambi, although he had seen the palace from afar. The palace was large with a main entrance at the front and large gardens surrounding the sides and back, a steady stream of water for plants which added color and beauty. The palace had several floors with water running to the higher levels as well. At the main entrance as well as within the palace courtyards, many people of importance had gathered. The architecture was a marvel to behold and the palace was large with immense open spaces filled with gardens and water controlled to manipulate the rate of flow and direction. It was also elevated to higher levels of the palace with the usage of power from various beasts of labor which belonged to King Porus. The beasts were generally well treated with regular rest periods—an observation which Manu found ironic when comparing it to the harsher treatment of the lower members of society occupying the Sudra caste. As they approached the main entrance, Manish identified himself and his position as adviser to the king and stated that Manu was his brother who had an important message.

Manu was allowed entry but was limited to a private courtyard. He was amazed at the sight of so many beautiful women in the most colorful saris of the highest quality fabrics. The women all belonged to wealthy families and wore excessive amounts of gold and precious stones. They had their faces and bodies pierced in some of the most decorative and best cut pieces of gold Manu had ever seen. Manu had been all over the world and he believed only women from Puaravas wore jewelry with such intricate beauty.

The Persian loss of Egypt brought about celebration

among a portion of the Egyptian populace—at least publicly. Perhaps they were a fabrication to appease Alexander. Manu and Manish felt that these celebrations would not be repeated in Pauravas. The people of Pauravas and the surrounding kingdoms had a friendlier and less direct relationship with the Persian Empire. These dynamics would be discussed at the meeting with the aid of Manu's observations.

Manish approached the entrance towards the central quarters of the palace where the Royal Affairs took place. After walking through various courtyards, he arrived to the main hallway. The hallway was broad and long with large depictions of the gods of the region and the warring clans. King Porus was believed to have descended from these gods, but he rarely discussed this belief held by many in his kingdom. Before entering the Royal conference hall, Manish asked the Royal security if he could let his brother join him in the proceedings due to the fact that Manu had a different perspective about the Greek invasion and the preparations of regions in Palestine and Kemet. Usually important Royal meetings were limited to the Royal advisers and military leadership, but today's meeting was less restrictive, allowing for lower advisery staff. Manish awaited the decision by Porus to include his younger brother as the other advisers began to arrive.

Manish was concentrating on his personal statement and how and when to express it to King Porus and the rest of the advisers. He was slightly anxious because he knew the gravity of the geo-political situation as well as the importance his statement had on the future progression of his career. He also contemplated how he would present his ideas without possibly alienating segments of the Persian advisers and guests as well as the senior advisers. His relationship with some of the military members was favorable, however Manish understood his statements would be favorable with the military. As the food for the morning feast was almost completed and most of the advisers were beginning to enter the main hall, a member of the Royal guard informed Manish that Manu would be allowed to enter the meeting.

Manu was escorted into the main hall and Manish could see the amazement in his brother's eyes. Manish informed him that he would relate his personal story to the king—particularly what he thought of the various populations and their reactions to Greek aggression. Darius had fled towards the east to regroup and amass a final attack to destroy the Greek upstarts, but Manish understood that this was misleading information and that the Royal Achaemenid Persian Empire was in serious disarray. Manish was also aware of the possible misinformation that the Persian ambassadors and advisers might be providing King Porus with in private. Manish did not know what new information would be made public today or what official position the king might take. He understood that he could make a conservative analysis to solidify his current position or advise Porus more in accordance with his ideals, potentially impacting the course of his career along with his family and his people.

Manish's rise in politics caught the attention of the third most powerful adviser to King Porus—a man named Kali, leader of the Mehra family and one of the most powerful and wealthiest families in the Punjab. Kali Mehra was a skilled orator, adviser, and politician who could exploit a person's weaknesses and disarm someone with language alone. Kali would be Manish's challenge today but he felt the time had arrived where the world would experience drastic changes and he believed his advice would be pivotal. Manish and Manu sat down with all the advisers who had arrived as their meal was brought to their table. The day's event would begin shortly.

The cooks left and palace staff exited the main halls as soon as the food and drinks were served, closing the doors behind them. The Royal party now entered the hall through the other main door which provided access to the Royal Family's personal quarters. Everyone rose, including Manu, who was particularly anxious as he witnessed the king himself for the first time. Some senior generals and Persian officials entered the palace as a senior minister shouted, "Here enters King Porus, the living descendant of the Puru tribe, who were victorious in the ancient battle of the ten kings as depicted in our *Rig Veda* and the ruler of Pauravas!"

King Porus' eldest son—also named Porus—entered along with a cousin and was then followed by Kali Mehra, who was dressed in expensive official clothing in the Persian style. Kali Mehra was an Aryan of the highest standing within the warrior caste and a man measuring over six feet tall, but even he was dwarfed by King Porus, who entered last. King Porus was a sight to behold, dressed in red and blue clothing over seven feet tall. King Porus had a determined and focused look in his eye that reflected urgency and paralleled the dire state of foreign affairs. King Porus sat at the front of the table and everyone seated themselves soon after. First the meal would begin and then the important discussions on foreign and domestic affairs would subsequently start.

The meal was an assortment of meats and spices served with various juices extracted from different fruits that had been harvested from the Royal garden. The lamb was the best Manu had enjoyed in many moons and he made frequent commentary regarding the meal to his brother Manish. There was a low rumbling throughout the hall as the food was consumed and washed down. King Porus stood up at the front of the table, announcing that he welcomed new ideas on domestic and foreign affairs.

"I have continued progress in our kingdom and have spoken on our system of taxation and overall economy. I have increased building projects and have used the knowledge of my architects, including my junior adviser Manish Ramankrishna, who has proven that his knowledge on foreign affairs equals his exemplary aptitude in the realms of mathematics and architecture. Manish's projects have also increased the available work for all castes in Pauravas and have given our society economic strength. I also want to congratulate the members of our warrior caste, who have fought valiantly for the Persian Empire abroad in long battles against Greek aggression in the western parts of Asia and maintaining our kingdom's position of strength to our rivals: the Nanda Dynasty of the Magadha Kingdom in the east and our enemies to the northwest—Takshashila-Gandhara—whose ruler Ambhi has rejected diplomacy and has insulted me and our kingdom. However, today we will explore the new developments that I have been discussing with our Persian diplomats and our senior advisers for the last few months."

King Porus seated himself as the conversation finally began. Manish understood the importance of this meeting to the kingdom, his career, and his family and in the back of his mind as he felt war would arrive within a few years if not sooner.

Manish began to organize his thoughts when Kali Mehra stood up to address the ministers. Kali Mehra had a loud, confident voice he used to state his opinions as if they were factual statements voiced by Lord Krishna himself.

Kali Mehra said, "Esteemed ministers, advisers, and military leaders, today is a very important day! I recently was informed of developments in the eastern Magadha Empire pertaining to the Royal House of Nanda. As most of you already know, the usurpers who reside in Pataliputra, following the example of King Mahapanda Nanda, have internal economic turmoil within their empire. These usurpers belong to the lowest Sudra caste and are not legitimate. Prince Dhana Nanda has essentially taken control of day to day affairs and we have reports stating that his father has become severely ill. King Mahapanda is a corrupt king predicted by the gods as a sign that we are currently living in the age of Kali Yuga—the Dark Age we find ourselves living in after our Lord Krishna left our material world. At the very least, with King Mahapanda we were able to maintain some diplomatic ties with his prime minister Amatya Shaktar, but Dhana Nanda is the least capable in the Nanda House and unfortunately it appears he will soon become king. This news coupled with other information arriving from the western borders of the Persian Empire is very troubling. The Greeks are advancing, harming the perfect balance in the world and between our kingdoms. The supreme leader Darius III is in far more serious trouble than we previously imagined."

There was silence in the hall when King Porus stood.

An obvious tension in the entire hall intensified with the nervous appearances of some of the Persian officials. Some Persian advisers observed closely as they anticipated the words of King Porus.

"There are many developments involving the battles in the western edge of the Persian Empire," he said, "and it seems the young upstart—Alexander, son of Philip II—has advanced further into Persian territory. The King of Kings, Darius III, lost a battle at Issus three years ago and again at Gaugamela just last year. The Royal Family was captured by Alexander and his officers and we are ignorant regarding the exact whereabouts of the Royal Family and King Darius III. We have provided Persia with many resources during their war, including goods and iron weaponry. We have also provided manpower to the service of Darius III, but now we must come together with our Persian advisers and friends to find a way to end Alexander's advancement. We must remember we have stood with the Persians just as they have stood with us and we can all agree that the Alexander menace will not advance further with our strong military!" King Porus shook with determination, which was received with a loud roar from the dignitaries.

Kali Mehra stood and stated that they should speak with the Persian generals and negotiate a deal with the Macedonian general and king, as he believed that Alexander had suffered great losses and did not wish to continue his efforts against greater Persia and Pauravas. Manish was angered by the suggestion of diplomatic avenues with Alexander, who had all the momentum on his side, and pondered the way he would best navigate through the various opinions already shared at this meeting. Manish felt slightly vexed regarding the advice of Kali Mehra, but thought the best way to introduce his point of view was to ask his little brother to relate his travels abroad as far as

Egypt, Meroe in the Kingdom of Kush, and Palestine.

Manu nervously rose to his feet and began to address the Great Hall as he bowed in the custom of Pranama. "Namaste, my king and honorable ministers in this hall. I am a guest invited by my older brother Manish and I am here to share my story abroad in the western regions of the Persian Empire. I traveled as far as Kush and Egypt and settled mostly in Palestine. Through my journey and through my business I have met people of all class and culture from all over the Persian Empire and I have gained different perspectives on Alexander of Macedon's advancements into these territories. In fear, I left Palestine and came back here to Pauravas when I received information on specific brutalities committed by Alexander and his Macedonian generals. After Alexander crossed the Hellespont four years ago, I began to make preparations to leave the fortified city of Gaza."

Manu further explained how the cities along the route to Egypt quickly surrendered for fear of Alexander, except for Gaza led by the Persian commander Batis. Batis was a great commander who understood, as Manu also did, that he was the only man standing in the way of Egypt—which Alexander wanted most. In an electrifying cry, Batis rallied his troops towards a major confrontation with Alexander of Macedon. Manu, with sadness in his voice, stated how he had left his "future" in Gaza but that it was necessary to come back to stand with his family in Pauravas.

There was silence as Manu recounted that on his return journey he was informed of the destruction of Gaza, paralleling the horror that previously occurred at the Battle of Issus and Tyre and revealing the fear that occurred in the surrounding lands after Alexander killed the men and sold the women and children into slavery. Manu described the stubbornness of Alexander and how it fueled his unquenchable march forward. Much of this information King Porus already had partial knowledge of, however he had little knowledge regarding the ease of Alexander's conquests of Egypt and the fate that befell Batis, the

Persian commander of Gaza. What amazed Porus was the reaction of the Egyptians, who welcomed Alexander as a savior delivering them from the occupation of the supreme leader Shah Darius III. In a tale which mirrored the story of Achilles and Hector, Alexander tied Commander Batis by the legs and dragged him while he was still alive. Alexander's rendition was all the more horrendous as he had dragged Batis while he was still alive as opposed to Achilles, who dragged Hector only after his death.

Manu detailed the infamy of Alexander after he defeated the powerful Greek mercenary Commander Memnon. Memnon was a valuable asset to Darius III and a powerful ally against Alexander's initial advancement into Asia. The skilled Greek battle strategist was the first major test for Alexander after he gained control of the Greek city-states. Memnon understood that Alexander's existing financial troubles in Macedonia and the Greek states coupled with a scorched earth policy would cripple Alexander's army by destroying his chances of victory. Memnon was also a skilled politician who understood Greece better than the Persians who employed him. He sought to enlarge the fire of rebellion among Sparta and Athens against their new leader. However, the distrust that the Persians had for Memnon's true intentions and loyalties along with with his scorched earth strategy led the Persians to disregard his plan. The fate of the Greek mercenaries under the leadership of the great Memnon ended on the tip of Alexander's sword, in chains of bondage back to Macedonia and the Greek lands, and the eventual death of Memnon himself. It was during this period that Alexander made his mark in Asia, which led to Manu's preparation to flee Gaza.

Alexander had accomplished something that no Athenian or Spartan commander ever had: a decisive defeat of Persia deep within their own territory. King Porus listened carefully and he was most interested in the reactions of the respective populations within different foreign lands. King Porus also wanted to learn the tactics Alexander had employed in his march towards eastern

Persia. The mention of Memnon and the consecutive successes of Alexander brought about a noticeable rumbling among all the high officials.

The personality of Memnon the Greek and his service to the Persian Empire was legendary—a testament to Persian loyalty. Memnon was a pivotal character in the greater conflict between Persia and Greece and was publicly praised within the Persian Empire while privately looked upon with uncertainty regarding his intentions due to Memnon being of Greek origin. It was also a lesson in loyalty and war strategy. In Pauravas, the advisers of King Porus were very careful in their public statements regarding the death of Memnon and now the conversation was causing a noticeable tension in the Great Hall.

Manu shared his own personal story and gave King Porus a different perspective on a conflict that had now erupted into a major war that saw King Darius III in fear of his life and in a position where he could not control the fate of his own house and family. This particular information was kept from the people of Pauravas, higher level ministers, and King Porus himself.

Kali Mehra rose from his seat, breaking the silence that had ensued. "The relationship between our King Porus and Persia has been strong and mutually beneficial. The association between our people and the Persians has existed for generations, resulting in stability and peace. King Darius III has suffered some setbacks and we should await any further information on potential agreements between King Darius III and Alexander and his united Greek armies."

King Porus looked on as many in the Great Hall began to show their support.

Manish felt his heart racing ever faster as he formulated his thoughts. He could choose to remain conservative in his advice for King Porus or convey his honest thoughts.

Finally, he addressed the ministers. "King Porus, what you require is a stronger military and better diplomacy with the Kingdoms of Magadha and the soon-to-be emperor Dhana Nanda, as well as King Ambhi in Takshashila."

Kali objected by stating the obvious fact of the bitter relationship between Porus and Ambhi as well as questioning the stability of Prince Dhana Nanda.

Manish quickly replied, "We all understand that Prince Dhana Nanda is of questionable character, but we must send our smartest negotiators to their capital in Pataliputra and speak with him, as he is set to inherit a large, powerful army that can be a major benefit for you King Porus in a temporary union against possible Greek invasion. We can also use this leverage against King Ambhi if he chooses not to join our union."

Some of the Persian advisers liked the ideas that Manish put forward, including Haxamanis. Other Persian ministers in the Great Hall seemed slightly bothered by the statements, perhaps feeling that Persian support among the various kings would dissolve a Persia that was now weakened.

King Porus agreed with the advice of Kali Mehra and Manish Ramankrishna. He was particularly taken by Manish's opinion, although he did not agree with him completely, stating that he would take Kali's advice but he would ask for Manish's more often. Other Persian advisers, led by Jahangir, stated that Porus should be wary of the Nanda family and Ambhi and focus on the continuous supply of troops for the Persian Empire's efforts against Alexander of Macedon. Rahim, who was usually outspoken, was ironically silent on this particular topic of conversation. Rahim was focused upon Manu's personal revelations of life in Gaza. Kali Mehra added that Prince Dhana Nanda was irresponsible and dangerous, for he was soon to inherit the largest army in the region while displaying a lack of self-control. His politics with others in the region were abrasive and slightly aloof while containing an element of superiority. The Nanda Dynasty had a problematic relationship with their closest neighbor to the south, Kalinga, and enjoyed only a brief peace when Prince Shauryananda wed Damyanti of Kalinga that dissolved as quickly as the marriage.

There was considerable conversation in the Great Hall and everyone believed there would be a major shift in the world hierarchy. Manish understood that his actions would impact not only his own family but the Royal House and ultimately the future of the Kingdom of Pauravas and surrounding civilizations. This created a weight to his thoughts and an overall importance to every decision he and other advisers made from now through the upcoming years. King Porus disagreed with some of the statements made by Manish but others in the Royal Family would take greater heed to those same words. The first of many conversations on Greek aggression and surrounding civilizations had now commenced and the Great Hall was cleared, leaving only the highest advisers, military officials, and Persian advisers.

Manish felt at ease with his statements; he avoided politics and spoke ideally and for the purpose of the advancement and general safety of the people of Pauravas. Manish had a personal stake in the military and in Pauravas and he wanted to elevate the way of life for all people despite caste. All these issues he felt would be brought up at a future date as he gained more influence in Porus' court.

Manish and Manu exited the Great Hall through the long elaborate hallways into other rooms filled with beautiful artwork depicting Lord Krishna and other gods and their involvement with mankind as depicted in the Vedic Tradition. Outside in the main courtyard, members of the military had gathered, including the future leaders of the Pauravas military. Among several young leaders, Manish identified his eldest son Rajesh and called to him. Father, son, and uncle were now reunited after several long years and they would have a lot to talk about.

Rajesh embraced his uncle Manu and Manu was excited to see Rajesh, who was a full grown young man now with a promising future. He was a younger version of his father with great nobility about him, as if he was born of the highest caste though he did not have the aggressive questioning mind of his father. Rajesh was strong, tall, and dark and appeared like Manish in his younger days. Manu was pleasantly surprised at the young man Rajesh had turned out to be. Rajesh was smart, valiant, and had a sense of purpose and drive; he was looking forward to his life as a military leader for the Pauravas army.

The three Ramankrishna men were glad to finally be together. Manish was proud of his son and his exemplary service so far but closely guarded thoughts of war, hiding behind the horizon and threatening to overtake their lives like a stampede of elephants. Pauravas was a strong civilization which stood just as strong as their enemy to the north, Gandhara led by King Ambhi, and garnered respect from the civilization to the east soon to be headed by Prince Dhana Nanda. Manish had family members who were already serving the Persian Empire, defending the now receding western Persian borders against the might of the Macedonian led Greek military. He had already lost family abroad and although his thoughts on war were nuanced, Manish was prepared to defend Pauravas and his home bravely and to the death. Manish believed that a temporary unity with the surrounding kingdoms could finally defeat an exhausted Greek military if they made it to the Punjab. Although he was rising steadily in influence, Manish understood that not only did he have to contend with the bad relationships between the surrounding kingdoms but also with the Persian advisers to Porus, who he saw was draining the military to fight the Greeks abroad as they continued to push back Persian borders. Rajesh asked for his little brother, who he had not seen in quite some time. Rajesh always worried for Rishan, who seemed to have inherited mainly their father's questioning mind and intelligence. However, the family worried that the young Rishan, although he excelled in mathematics and science, was at a disadvantage when it came to social intelligence. Manish eased their thoughts by stating that Rishan was now involved in activities of the body to include speed, endurance, and now fighting. The Ramankrishna men laughed with excitement at the news and Manish also proudly shared that his son had a new female friend named Anupa Jhingan and they were all happy; the Jhingan family was respected in the higher levels of society.

Rajesh brought up the idea to his father about visiting the military elephants which were near the palace grounds. He was excited to parade the new war elephants Porus had obtained for the military in front of his family, however the ominous clouds betrayed the incoming rain so the elephant exhibition would be brief. The men got on their horses and rode down to the Royal elephant pen that had many laborers who were skilled in taking care of every need the animals had. The laborers made sure the elephants were clean, healthy, and well fed as well as maintained a strict exercise schedule to enhance and maintain their strength. Manu joked that these elephants lived a better life than the poor people who populated the lower castes and Manish told him that even the people of lower castes should be respected because when they were neglected they could unite and hurt general society.

"Just like the elephant is respected and treated well for the enhancement of the fighting force," he said, "if they are neglected it will only serve to hinder and degrade the entire military body."

Manu particularly enjoyed seeing these mighty beasts of battle. This was the first time he was allowed to be this close to the Royal elephants and he touched some of them. Porus was sending more of the elephants to satisfy the needs of the Persian military, but now with no direct order from Darius III or his Royal House, fewer elephants were sent north. Manish assumed the situation was far worse than was originally discussed at the Royal meeting earlier in the day and felt the Persian Empire was on the verge of breaking into several centers of power. He requested that his eldest son come home and Rajesh agreed, as Rajesh was eager to see his family and younger brother Rishan. The three men got on their horses. As they began their ride home, the sky began to turn a dark grey.

As they rode back east towards the Royal Palace and then south towards their home, they noticed many of the officials in the main palace courtyard also leaving to their various destinations by way of the Royal Road. Manish did not wish to stop to entertain conversation so he greeted some people as they rode by. A voice loudly called for Manish and he turned to discover that the origin was Kali Mehra walking towards him in his Persian style dress.

"Great speech, Manish," he said, "but why did you advocate for the establishment of diplomatic relations with Prince Dhana Nanda and his father? They are pretenders on the throne and descendants of a barber."

Manish responded, "It is because that descendant of a barber Dhana Nanda will soon be king of Magadha and control a vast army of over 200,000 fighters, around 60,000 cavalry, over 4,000 war chariots, and over 6,000 war elephants. It is better to establish diplomatic ties to understand how they operate their kingdom and to observe how their population regards their king. Sometimes enemies become friends, Kali, when confronting a powerful and common foe."

Kali laughed a little while looking directly at Manish who resumed his journey home with Manu and Rajesh. As they neared home, a light rain began to fall. Manish sighed with the relief as he was now free to concentrate on the affairs of his household. Just as the Ramankrishna men arrived, a torrential rain storm began.

CHAPTER 5:
HOUSE OF MEHRA (329 B.C.)

"There are three gates to self-destructive hell: lust, anger, and greed."
—The Bhagavad Gita, 16:21

The rains were especially heavy and remained steady for a longer duration than usual, as the monsoon period had lasted longer than usual. The monsoon rains caused damage to the poor sections of the city, but later improved soil fertility and crop production in the kingdom. This proved to be a good occurrence for the Kingdom of Pauravas, as the previous years had been particularly dry. Kali believed his caste was naturally gifted to rule over and provide for those of lower castes. He focused on the survival of Pauravas and the continued power and stability of those of upper society to include himself, his family, and those of his caste. He was a man of extraordinary wealth which he felt he earned through hard work and his mental abilities. Kali also believed he was the best adviser to King Porus, who he respected but believed would be led astray by other advisers such as Manish Ramankrishna.

Kali paced outside his large estate comparable to those of the Royal Family. This estate was large and one of several owned by the Mehra family. Kali Mehra was in deep thought about recent developments in the great Magadha Empire to the east. The latest news was that

Dhana Nanda had become the king and his father was believed to have passed away. Perhaps Manish was correct! King Porus should extend diplomatic relations with that despicable monarch. Kali was beginning to see the importance of reaching out to Dhana, with the increasing threat of the great Greek Army continuously marching through Persian territory. Kali believed King Dhana Nanda was unworthy for the position of king but he respected the power of the army Dhana now possessed.

The clouds were dark grey and appeared swollen and ready to unleash a large deluge, as flashes of light illuminated the darkening in bursts and the sky happily anticipating the coming rains. Kali Mehra did not care if the rains began falling on his expensive Persian clothes as he anxiously paced outside his estate thinking of events yet to come. Would Alexander continue to remain victorious throughout his continuing expedition into Persian territory? The answer to that question was uncertain just a few years ago but the question was becoming a clearer. Alexander honored agreements although at times he seemed possessed by uncontrollable fits of rage just as one of his favorite heroes Achilles was. Perhaps Manish Ramankrishna was correct in his solution to counter the potential Greek invading force. However, Kali felt that Rishan's growing influence with King Porus coupled with what he believed were his idealistic yet naïve views would plunge Pauravas into a long, dreadful war with the Greeks and even if Pauravas was victorious they would be weakened and left almost defenseless against the competing surrounding kingdoms. Without the watchful eye of a Persian king, these animals, like King Dhana Nanda or Ambhi, would consume what was left of the Kingdom of Pauravas and possibly topple the elite Mehra family.

The occupation of Babylon, the most powerful city and symbol of Persian power, continued under Alexander of Macedon. The closely guarded secret of Alexander traveling with the family of the dethroned Darius III was now beginning to spread throughout the lower level Palace officials and among the people of Pauravas. Kali Mehra feared a battle with Alexander and particularly the complete destruction of the social order that would lead to chaos caused by the lower castes. Kali felt it was his duty to keep the peace of the kingdom and his place as their superior for the greater good of society. Why trouble lowly people and their happiness with the immense duties of maintaining society and social order? It was becoming clear that Manish was given responsibilities far above his place in society. Kali believed Manish's advocacy of greater inclusion of the common people in the affairs of the state would create instability. Kali Mehra, a man who claimed Persian and Aryan descent, was now rivaled by the newcomer Manish Ramankrishna. Kali scowled and grunted as rain began to drop rapidly, soaking his expensive garments. His responsibilities were not only devoted to his powerful position but also in the leadership of his family. His father had suffered a massive heart attack not long ago, leaving a power vacuum in the Mehra family, which left Kali in a position to become the patriarch and wrest control of the massive wealth and most of the houses and land, leaving some enemies within his own family. Kali shook his head and drank the remaining wine in the cup he had carried with him in what was initially supposed to be a long walk and entered the main Mehra estate where he and his family resided.

Kali entered his three-floor house; his surrounding estate far dwarfed the house of Manish Ramankrishna. It was large with an enclosure for his horses, a small farm area with fruits and vegetables, and there were several artificial streams. There was a sewage system draining the four major restrooms in the large house. The main house was a large T-shaped structure with several annexes and separate living quarters for the servants. Most of the house was built using rocks of various sizes rubbed down and smoothed along with wood in the inner areas of the house. Unlike Manish, Kali employed many servants to tend to his household as well as personal servants for himself.

Kali's Persian pants and blue shirt were now wet with rain. He was slightly angered that his personal time had been cut short and he reluctantly walked into his house right before the rain fell with extreme force typical of monsoon season. Kali was greeted by one of his personal servants, who gave him some comfortable dry clothes as he retired for the day.

Dinner was being prepared by his wife Sanjeeta with the aid of the servants. Kali enjoyed a fresh meal from the finest cuts of meats and the most expensive spices—a luxury few outside the Royal Family enjoyed. Kali's eldest two sons were respected young leaders in the military. Randeep was the oldest and was supremely calculating, self-confident, and at times boastful. He was now twenty-one years of age and was over six feet in height with a muscular physique. Randeep had already created a solid reputation in the military and had potential to rise to the highest levels. Kali's second son was Janeesh, the most cerebral of his kids and showing promise of a future in politics, which his father encouraged him to seek. Janeesh was now nineteen years old, of average height with a stocky but strong muscular form, and had more of a reserved personality; he preferred to study the arts of war and philosophy, making him an outlier among his father and siblings. The youngest of Kali's sons was Karna Mehra, a smart and athletically gifted young boy eleven years of age. He was almost as intelligent as Janeesh and he would grow to have the strength of his eldest brother Randeep. Karna was already exceptionally strong for his age and had the potential of rising to the top in martial arts in the kingdom. His cunning, intelligence, and overall strength would culminate to provide him the life that he pleased and a life that others only yearned to have. These qualities would help Karna Mehra surpass even the political success of his father. Kali's youngest son was self-confident and competitive, but at times his temper would overrule his judgment, which was cause for concern. Karna Mehra was the only son to still reside in the family estate—the two eldest boys had already begun progressing in their respective military careers. Kali Mehra did not have a daughter and at times boasted that if he had any more children they would all be boys.

Kali went to greet and kiss his wife Sanjeeta, a beautiful woman with light brown skin and large dark eyes. She had long black hair which flowed beautifully in the wind. Kali was a man of importance who had all the attention from other women but he still believed his wife remained among the most beautiful in the land. Like everything else in his life, when choosing a wife, Kali approached the practice as a business move and a long-term investment. His wife was five years younger than him but appeared even younger. Sanjeeta came from a highly respected family with a large amount of wealth; she was surrounded by wealthy people of her caste, never knowing what a hard day of labor was. She had a good education but only learned the basics as her life was already set since she was young: Sanjeeta would go to school and later a man would be chosen out of her many wealthy suitors. Her parents felt that the statesman Kali Mehra would be the best choice for their daughter. Sanjeeta liked Kali's determination and rising position as a state official and so the marriage was solidified.

Sanjeeta was a housewife who did not get involved in politics and was oblivious to the lives of who she referred to as "commoners." Sanjeeta was not particularly religious are absorbed in self-thought. She was mostly interested in trips to exotic locations and events with other wealthy people. Her sons were her pride and glory and she loved to parade their successes and expected potential which were most assuredly to be fulfilled. Most of Sanjeeta's duties were taken care of by servants all her life, allowing her to spend time with her three sons or join in gossip with other wealthy women. When she was in need of excitement she was able to enjoy trips to the Royal Palace to gossip with the other wives of important men. She was also able to travel outside the kingdom to and meet other rulers and famous statesmen. Stories of the lands in the orient intrigued her most, but now times were changing and travel outside of Pauravas was strongly discouraged by her husband. Sanjeeta did not ask many questions but thought that this was simply a temporary setback. Eventually, life would continue just as she had always known.

Kali Mehra asked his wife for the location of his youngest son Karna; apparently, he was with his friends. All of Kali's sons were excelling in their own ways. He encouraged a household full of competition and athletic excellence. They needed to achieve their expected warrior caste roles to satisfy their standing as a man born into one of the twice-born castes. They had to live a life of responsibility, but if those duties were fulfilled, many entitlements and honors were ready to be bestowed on them. The boys understood this from a young age and they performed well in school and especially athletically in various forms of combat and ancient martial arts. Their physical features did not go unnoticed by beautiful young ladies from affluent means and even the mild mannered Janeesh attracted their attention due to the powerful Mehra family name and a reputation that preceded him.

Rain hit the ground at a furious pace, the wind howling and lightning breaking the air like a hot whip. Usually Kali would sit and enjoy the rains at home with his family but the last few years, full of threats on the horizon, had brought stressors. Kali had to use his mental abilities to maneuver through the incoming waves breaking through the calm fabric of Pauravas society while competing with the intelligence and idealism of Manish Ramankrishna. Darius III, King of Persia, was rumored dead and Bessus, the regional governor of Bactria, had declared himself king and renamed himself Artaxerxes V. Kali was also angered that the population of Pauravas was learning about the events in Persia; he believed they should be tamed and their raw emotions and short sightedness would create chaos. Kali also secretly believed that Manish could win over the masses and gain more influence.

Kali's blank stare only served to anger his wife but Kali couldn't care less for Sanjeeta's mindless ramblings and aimless thoughts——especially at a time like this. Women like his wife thrived during peaceful, stable times but during potential societal instability she would be a wingless bird. Kali responded to Sanjeeta's anger with the intended purpose to cease her talking. He did not have a specific ideology like Manish, however he was more politically astute and pragmatic. Although Kali was not a Royal, his immense wealth and position afforded him levels of influence and power to rival that of a king—a power he felt was being challenged by Manish. Kali ate but could not taste and enjoy his food, however he continued the cold, mechanical process of finishing his dinner, thinking tomorrow could not come soon enough.

Kali awakened before sunrise, tired from lack of adequate sleep yet anxious but determined in his ability to influence foreign policy through the action of his superior King Porus. Initially, he stayed awake waiting for the arrival of his youngest son but once he was home, uncertainty flooded his mind, causing disturbances in the delicate balance of sleep. Kali's wife and Karna were asleep; only a female servant was outside the house tending to Kali's personal horses, which were fed and maintained better than the poor men, women, and children in Pauravas. Kali picked his favorite horse—a majestic brown horse as swift as the wind—and instructed his servant to inform his wife and son that he had left for the Royal Palace to see his other sons and have an audience with the king.

Kali was a proud Aryan Punjabi with partial ancestry from the ancient Persian lands and he often boasted about the advances the Aryans had brought to the Punjab. Kali believed that he and King Porus came from an ancient people of the ruling class. He was not a religious person in his private life, although he always made sure to state his king's rightful place as ruler through these ancient tales. Kali believed that religion served a purpose in the day to day life of lower people because it further solidified the caste system as an efficient organizational tool. As a politician and an opportunist, he understood religion was malleable in the hands of someone like him and could be used as a tool to manipulate society. King Porus acknowledged the importance of a man like Kali as an ally to strengthen his position as a monarch, but now he welcomed Manish's new perspectives regarding the developing foreign events as well as a few Persian members of his court.

Riding fast towards a military annex close to the Royal Palace, Kali was anxious to see his two sons who awaited him. Kali's main estate was very close to the Royal Palace and its placement was important to Kali so he could work every day with the king. Randeep and Janeesh were allowed some time away from training to see their father— a luxury afforded to the Mehra family. Kali wanted to meet with them shortly before his meeting with King Porus and take advantage of valuable time before Manish and the other advisers arrived. The rain was light and the air was cool and crisp as Kali rode closer to the military complex. In the distance, he caught sight of his sons and a rare smile appeared upon his face. Kali wanted to question his sons pertaining to the discussions that the military leadership was engaging in and the new military training. As he approached, the rain had stopped and the sun began to appear.

Kali greeted his sons. "Namaste, mighty warriors. What new intelligence are they teaching the young leadership in the army these days?"

Randeep replied that the military was planning extensive exercises and new tactics in the near future. Janeesh asked his father if there were any new developments in the ongoing drama in the now collapsing Persian Empire. Kali stated the numerous Royal advisers was ready to denounce the self-proclaimed king of Persia Bessus, who renamed himself Artaxerxes V, and was illegitimate to numerous Persian and Punjabi advisers. Kali believed that the invading Greeks would soon have to negotiate peace treaties with Persia and King Porus. It was imperative that King Porus propose a treaty with Alexander to position himself ahead of his rivals and solidify himself as monarch and maintain the upper class.

Kali looked at his sons and said, "Janeesh, one day

you will make a great politician but you and Randeep have to focus on your military training while I focus on foreign affairs." Soon after, Kali said his goodbyes and rode a short distance towards the Royal Palace.

He entered the Royal Grand Hall where King Porus was waiting along with his younger brother Amar and his son Prince Porus. Kali was surprised to see Amar present as he had not been present in many of the recent meetings. King Porus welcomed Kali and they began to discuss the state of foreign affairs.

Kali stated, "A deal from a position of power is best, ""but as it looks now, Alexander will only seek a deal if he is writing it himself!"

The king's son also named Porus smiled with approval. King Porus continued to pace, his immense seven-foot frame dwarfing all men he was near, and stated that he understood the importance of a deal and the politics involving the balance of power between the three civilizations. For the first time, Kali felt he was losing his influence and soon his new rival would make his proposals and threaten to weaken his arguments. Kali felt the future safety of the kingdom sat upon a fragile balance, and his pragmatic, political approach was being successfully countered by the honest conviction and idealism of Manish Ramankrishna. King Porus and his brother shared a private conversation as the advisers and senior military members arrived for another discussion on the future of Pauravas.

The morning's affairs began in earnest, as the situation had become serious and unpredictable. Manish was now accepted as an equal and was one of the first to arrive followed by a select few others. Some of the Persians within the court were saddened and embarrassed by the usurper on the Persian throne and many of them referred to him as Bessus and not his self-proclaimed name of Artaxerxes V. Intelligence was now showing that Artaxerxes V himself would not survive against Alexander because of further desperation and internal turmoil within the Persian leadership in the face of an approaching Alexander. The Persian Royal Family was now publicly supporting

Alexander, regarding him as the true leader of the Persian Empire and causing the would-be adversaries of the Macedonian leader to give up the fight against Alexander and turn against themselves.

Haxamanis, the great Persian adviser in the court of Porus, greeted and exchanged words with Manish. The conversation had begun with King Porus stating that the new king of Persia Artaxerxes V was now surrounded with his brief reign in jeopardy. In the last few years, the Persian ability of withholding information had suffered and now it was clear that King Porus should begin taking initiative for the safety of Pauravas.

Kali stood up and greeted everyone in the hall. "Namaste, my king and esteemed colleagues. We remain unaware regarding the fate of King Artaxerxes V, but I advocate for an agreement if Alexander reaches our lands. I doubt he will want to face our forces and I can't imagine that Alexander or his Greek army will have any interest in the invasion of the Indus region. Alexander has proven that he can be negotiated with if given a fair deal and a deal is what we should seek. A treaty between you and Alexander will be mutually beneficial and put us in a position of power over our regional rivals. I have served honorably for King Porus throughout my life and have served my warrior caste as best as I can. We will fight if we must, however we must first try to seek stability and strength—not only for ourselves, but also for the benefit of the Persian Empire. Did you not observe the actions of the people of Kemet? They have an ancient, marvelous history just like we do and they maintained their way of life with minor changes to their leadership. They exist today and their children and grandchildren will also exist in peace and harmony."

Numerous people in the chamber congratulated Kali for his speech while King Porus looked on.

Others spoke briefly, including some of the Persian advisers who advocated for a peaceful resolution and a search for more access of materials in the Persian effort against the Greeks. King Porus now asked Manish to speak and the entire hall fell silent in anticipation. Manish was an astute man but he did not have the political experience of the great Kali Mehra and did not wish to directly engage Kali.

"Namaste, my king and all the esteemed guests present today," Manish said. "We are witnessing many events that are going to impact the world and create new alliances and enemies, so we must act with haste. I and many others here believe Alexander's army is currently suffering numerous human losses and possible financial strain and that should encourage us to remain on the offensive to counter their weakened forces. We can only make a deal from a position of power because the pattern of Greek conquests reveals treaties only benefitting the Greeks and at times punishing the conquered populations. We should decrease or cease all our material and human resources that are currently provided to Persia due to the fact that Persia has lost its leadership. We should dedicate all our resources and manpower to this kingdom under the full control of King Porus and increase and strengthen our military in preparation for a possible confrontation. We should also attempt to unify with King Ambhi and Dhana Nanda. Together our combined military and intelligence will outmatch the Greeks. We should study our potential enemy and learn the Greek language, religion, customs, culture, and most importantly their military. This is the key to your victory, King Porus, and you will negotiate with Alexander from a position of strength and not weakness."

With that statement, many in the Great Hall stood to agree. The king's brother Amar appeared overjoyed at Manish's statement and made it known to everyone that he agreed with his perspective.

Some of the Persians—particularly Argus—felt slightly angered at Manish's statements, feeling Manish and his new supporters were pushing for the abandonment of the Persians during a time of need. Argus objected, stating that Manish's refusal to help Persia would result in the increased success of the Greeks and a stronger army when they reached the Indus Valley.

Argus angrily exclaimed, "You now wish to end our

bond and friendship with Persia to selfishly protect your own borders? The Persians have kept order among the kingdoms of this region. Manish, your advice will only encourage the Greek savages and when they have consumed all of Persia they will consume the Punjab as well!"

Some Persians agreed with Argus while King Porus appeared slightly annoyed. The hall fell into a low grumble as each man was involved in private conversation discussing the best solutions for the Kingdom of Pauravas and secretly plotting what direction would be best for their respective personal lives.

Sensing doubt in King Porus' mind, Kali stated, "We should continue our unity with Persia as long as they can make a deal with Alexander in order to halt his advance. Manish's advice is unwise— I seriously doubt that unity among Pauravas and King Ambhi of Takshashila will occur. King Ambhi holds tremendous anger and jealousy towards our King Porus, and King Dhana Nanda of the Magadha Empire is unpredictable and despised by his own people. King Dhana Nanda has a large army but his reign might be short-lived! Look at those dark people of Kemet whom the Greeks refer to as Egyptians and their acceptance and peaceful coexistence with the Greeks. They were able to maintain their political system and way of life without the destruction of their monuments and have preserved their culture."

Manish directly answered Kali. "I apologize to the Persian advisers, however I must speak to the problems facing Pauravas. In the past when the Royal Family of Persia had gone through tumultuous infighting involving the Eunuch Vizier Bagoas, it never impacted the affairs of Pauravas in the degree that it does now. Bagoas is said to have killed members of the Persian Royal Family until Darius the Great killed Bagoas. The Persian Empire had a bad relationship with the people of Kemet due to their historical struggle with Persian occupation, which was further aggravated by Bagoas and his theft of Egyptian scrolls and property that increased his personal wealth. Kali, this is the reason the Egyptian people readily accepted the Macedonian and Greek defeat of the Persians and welcomed them into their ancient lands, but this peaceful coexistence between them will be temporary. The native Egyptians might very well develop anger towards their new conquerors as time goes on. Kali, you praise the Egyptians now but previously had condemned their hostility towards the Persians, and you might criticize the Egyptians in the future. The Greeks have had their own tumultuous history with the Persians regarding various Persian aggressions—particularly Xerxes and his invasions into Greek lands. Our own Punjabi people have supported Persia with troops throughout many generations in an effort to suppress the Persians' Greek territories. My distant relatives have died in generations past in those famous battles of antiquity involving Persia and the Greek city-states in numerous tales that will never be told. Even now I have a young cousin who fights in distant lands and I do not know of his fate. Gentlemen, we have always been great Persian subjects. However, we must be realistic and observe that they themselves are in disarray and Persia has fragmented. We are now aware of the reported capture of Artaxerxes V and we should expect his death at the hands of Alexander very soon! Just last year Cyrus the Great's famed city of Persepolis was looted and burned to the ground by Alexander. Should we wait until our capital of Kausambi is burned to ashes as well?"

Manish paused momentarily as he observed the approval on many of the faces in the Great Hall as he concluded his speech. " It is time to change our tactics and keep all of our assets in Pauravas under King Porus and seek unification with other regional kingdoms. We will vastly improve, increase, and strengthen our fighting force. If the Persians seek to help us here in our territory then we will welcome them because we will need them. I'm sure our combined forces will stop Alexander's tired and resource-less armies by the time they reach here in a few years. Then and only then will we negotiate a compromise."

The Great Hall erupted in cheers, including King Porus and his brother Amar.

Kali disagreed with Manish and was angered that he was winning the audience. "I applaud you Manish, but your emotions impact logical reasoning. Ambhi will never join Porus and Dhana Nanda. Although he boasts a large and formidable army, he is unreliable—a man of low character who is unpredictable, hated by his own people, and might face a revolution. We will possibly be alone in a bitter war with Alexander, rendering us weak and vulnerable even if we defeat him. If we are victorious but weaker and our regional enemies grow stronger, they will defeat us and finish what Alexander started."

Some Persians agreed with Kali except for Haxamanis, who stated that it was understandable to seek unification against the Greeks as he stated, "I am a proud Persian but I understand my land is now fractured. It is not the same great empire of generations' past. The Punjabi people have served the Persians well but I expect that you should take your destiny in your own hands and build your own future."

The other Persians were angered as they were coming to terms with the irony that they were now protected by the people they once ruled over—a reality Haxamanis had revealed.

"Thank you," replied Manish. "I advise King Porus to begin reaching out to the regional kingdoms to seek unification to counter a possible invasion by the Greeks. We should set our differences aside and try to reach an agreement and unification. We should also anticipate a possible attack by a combined force of Ambhi and Alexander. If we have information that he will do this, we can have people planted within his kingdom to antagonize the Greeks and thwart any potential agreement between Alexander and the Gandhara Kingdom. If King Ambhi unites with us, we may get Dhana Nanda to do the same and our combined forces will defeat Alexander's army. If Ambhi rejects and conspires against us, then we can spark a battle among Alexander and Ambhi. This will weaken both Ambhi and Alexander's armies and will give us time to organize and send our military to engage the Greeks before they get near our borders. These developments might encourage other regional powers to join us and will make Alexander retreat, giving us an upperhand in any future agreements."

King Porus and Prince Porus seemed satisfied with this plan and even some of the Persians agreed.

Kali was losing influence while Manish's popularity continued to rise. Persian power had severely degraded in the last year and would continue to do so as time went on, giving King Porus increased power and control over Pauravas. Kali realized that his battle with Manish was a battle to define the foreign policy.

"Manish, what makes you so sure that your ideas will come to fruition if implemented?" Kali asked.

Manish replied, "I am not sure, but how are you so certain that if we sit passively awaiting the advancing Greek force that they will consider any compromise with us?"

The Great Hall seemed to shift in support for Manish and for the first time in his career, Kali had made a decisive error as Manish's plans gained the support of King Porus. Some of the Persians to include Haxamanis were now openly supporting him.

A man named Harbir Marawar questioned Manish's call to learn from the Greek enemy as he exclaimed, "Manish, I am with you and I will not quake in fear in the face of these barbarian Greeks. Our land and people are magnificent and rich in culture, science, philosophy, and our own gods! We should not learn their inferior ways!"

Manish looked at Harbir and answered, "I welcome your support, Harbir, but these inferiors and barbarians as you call them are defeating the Persians and have even burned down Persepolis. At least in matters of war, they have displayed superior intelligence. We will not fall victim to false superiority as others do. Learning from our enemy is a weapon that we must sharpen in our efforts to defeat our enemy. We will learn their culture and language from their written materials that the Persians have collected."

King Porus was pleased. "Manish, I wish for you to

join me and my closest advisers so we can discuss the best way to proceed. My Persian friends, it is time for you now to draw up the best ways we can fight these Greeks. Darius would not have invaded our lands and burned down our cities like what has been done to many of your own cities and I simply cannot let that happen to my own cities while I am king. Although I do not like Ambhi, I should negotiate terms for possible unification with him in hopes of defeating this Greek menace. I will welcome Persian support for the greater good of Pauravas and will wait to observe developments this year to see if I should use Manish's advice. Thank you all for this great conversation—and military leaders, you will at once begin to strengthen our military and report back to me personally. As for Manish, I will need your advice in the future and will bestow upon you greater responsibility."

Prince Porus looked at Manish with approval while Kali, usually masterful in hiding emotion, now appeared impacted by Manish's growing influence.

Rajesh and some other young military members had gathered in the Royal courtyard in the early afternoon as they conversed with many of the young ladies from the various important families of Pauravas. Rajesh talked with several ladies but they were jealous of his growing interest in one woman named Divya Marawar. Rajesh was previously romantically involved with some of these women but he loved Divya. They had known each other for a few years and in the past year they had become seriously involved. Divya was smart and reserved but vocal when her convictions were challenged; in this aspect she was similar to her father, the strong and proud Harbir Marawar. However, she would not make her opinions known as often or as loudly as her powerful father. Divya was the only child of Harbir and her dear mother had passed away during childbirth. Harbir loved women and women loved him but he always made sure to treat them with respect and he kept his private relationships away from his daughter and public view. He did not have handsome features but his aggressive style, fighting ability, moral character, and strong convictions made him attractive to many women old and young. Rajesh had recently discussed the possibility of marriage with Divya with her father and the families were very excited for this potential union.

Rajesh excused himself from the company of the beautiful ladies to privately talk and walk with Divya, showing her the Royal Palace grounds.

In another corner of the Royal grounds stood a large crowd of women around the young Mehra men and a few members of the Royal Family. The attention lavished upon the Mehras was almost comparable to the level of attention given to the Royal sons of King Porus. The Mehra men were also close friends with some of the young Royals, including the heir apparent to the throne of Pauravas and leader of the military, Prince Porus. They would enjoy festivities and drink with the Royal children at parties that only the privileged would attend—which excluded outside families like the Ramankrishnas. However, exclusive festivities and fame did not heavily interest Rajesh; only a future family with Divya and a secure, successful career in the military. The Mehras loved festivities, fame, and power with the exception of Janeesh, who was more reserved.

Kali approached his sons, stating that Manish's course of action was not thoroughly planned and had a high probability of failing. With that, he got on his horse and quickly rode away, angry and disgusted.

The eldest son Randeep agreed with his father's sentiments, stating that Manish's recent actions were erroneous and idealistic. Randeep did not believe the military would accept any action largely influenced by Manish's ideas. Randeep would look down on anyone he felt was beneath him and sometimes his brother Janeesh, who he felt did not take full advantage of the social standing his family name afforded him. Although Randeep had many pretty ladies to choose from, he held some affection for Divya and secretly envied Rajesh and their relationship. Divya was a smart young woman and she was not swayed by Randeep's popularity; she did not care for the powerful

Mehra family. Divya honored the hardworking, honest qualities Rajesh had and the family from which he came from. Randeep, who rarely went without, had previously been rejected by Divya, which angered him.

Randeep continued to speak ill of the possible decisions Manish might be taking and the advice that could negatively impact the kingdom. Prince Porus was within earshot and joined the conversation. Randeep was slightly irritated as the young prince joked about the anger Kali had shown against Manish and the silliness of the political friction the Mehras had displayed against the Ramankrishna family.

"For such a powerful and self-confident family," Prince Porus said, "you and your father seem very insecure about the Ramankrishna family who just seek the well-being of my father and the direction of this kingdom. I may not agree fully with Manish, but I heard some of the details that you are not privy to and I personally believe Manish's ideas are ingenious! Your brother Janeesh understands this, yet you cannot understand that ideas can be integrated. I trust in my father to listen to all advice and decide the best possible solution for Pauravas. As your leader in battle, whatever decision is made, we must follow through as best as we can."

The prince's statement annoyed the emotionally invested Randeep and he decided to focus on a different topic concerning his youngest brother to let his anger subside and to prevent the prince's enjoyment at his expense.

Randeep was particularly proud of his brother Karna; he saw him as a younger version of himself and the continuance of the greatness that was the Mehra family. This was not lost on the middle child Janeesh, who internalized his resentment. The young Karna was performing better than his elder brothers in each of life's stages and was intelligent, a great athlete, and self-confident at an early age. Compared to his older brothers, Karna received the most attention and care from the otherwise cold and calculating Kali. Even Karna's mother, who was more in love with material items than the day to day care of her family, managed to show most of her affections to her youngest son. Karna also garnered the attention of many girls his age and was soon to become popular as he got older. Karna's main friend was a beautiful girl by the name of Anjali who followed him everywhere. Anjali's parents were strict but gave her a little more freedom when it came to Karna Mehra, as the Mehra were part of high society. The young Karna already had gathered some attention from the Royal Palace who anticipated the young man's entry into the military in the near future.

Harbir noticed his daughter Divya walking alone with Rajesh and smiled to himself. Harbir was very protective of his daughter but he enjoyed the prospect of having Rajesh as a son-in-law. Harbir saw a loyal, intelligent, and moral young man in Rajesh. He displayed a discipline lacking in the other young men of high positions in the kingdom. Harbir enjoyed Rajesh's warrior spirit and combat abilities and although he admired Rajesh's self-control, he was only disappointed that he was too cautious in the face of his enemies like Randeep Mehra, who would sometimes indirectly tease Rajesh. Harbir Marawar was a man who did not hesitate in responding to an idea or person he did not like. He respected Manish Ramankrishna and was his most vocal supporter, overjoyed in the assertiveness Manish had displayed in the Great Hall and wishing that his future son-in-law would begin to follow his father's lead. Harbir approached Divya and Rajesh and invited them to his house for a big feast with the Marawar extended family and to discuss future wedding arrangements. Harbir and his daughter then departed to their home, leaving Rajesh to wait for his father.

Manish spoke with several of his colleagues as he was leaving the Royal Palace. He was relieved that he had delivered his advice in a calm, intelligent, and comprehensive manner. Manish truly believed in his advice and felt that time would prove him correct. He was not a confrontational man but he didn't hesitate when he felt strong in his convictions. A potential war in Pauravas was a possibility that would involve the safety of his friends and family. Therefore, Manish disposed of previous caution to make sure his opinion was acknowledged as a possible course of action for King Porus to take. Outside of the palace, he met up with his eldest son and rode home with him. Having his entire family under one roof was a rarity now and he intended to take full advantage of this opportunity to catch up on family affairs. Manish and Rajesh spoke about the young man's career and his general attitude on several issues including his possible marriage to Divya. Manish liked the idea of his son and Harbir's daughter getting married; he respected Harbir for his honesty. The sun was beginning to set as the two men arrived at their homes.

Lakshmi happily greeted her eldest son along with the young Rishan and Priya. Rishan had not seen his older brother in many moons and was excited to hear his stories about being in the military and show him how he had gotten involved with martial arts and running. Rishan was also secretly interested in joining the military after he completed his advanced schooling—against his parents' wishes. Rishan informed his older brother about Anupa and his new friends. Rishan had also developed a close friendship with his former school rival, Anand Agrawal. Rishan respected and looked up to his older brother and was saddened that he was always away fulfilling his duties as a young military member.

By now the public was aware of a possible external threat that might possibly befall Pauravas and Manish emphasized the need to learn about the enemy in all facets of life and without revealing too much information, he stated the need to learn the Greek language and general culture. The family understood the reasoning for learning this but the young Rishan, who was shunned by his father from joining the military and engaging in military combat, took his advice seriously and began to learn the language with vigor. Rishan's family seemed to not care about his recent athletic accomplishments so he reasoned he would also continue to build his mental capability to contribute towards a possible war against the Greeks.

As summer arrived and left the Kingdom of Pauravas, new developments in the war between Persia and the Greeks came to be known. The unceremonious assassination of Darius III and the dumping of his body in a cart only to be discovered by a Greek soldier infuriated Alexander as he painted the new Persian Ruler Artaxerxes V as a usurper. Alexander was energized and received support from his troops to press further into Persian territory. After Artaxerxes V crossed the River Oxus, his own men abandoned him to be captured by Ptolemy, a trusted general who made up Alexander's vanguard. Alexander finally caught up to the shamed usurper and he was stripped naked to be displayed for the Greek infantry; he was questioned and later tried in military court. Another fellow conspirator against the former King of Persia, Satibarzanes satrap of Aria, had been pardoned by Alexander because he did not seek the Persian throne for himself. Later, Alexander punished Artaxerxes V, stripping him of his titles and torturing the man formerly known as Bessus.

This information was relayed to the Royal Court of King Porus but was not disclosed to the public in an effort to avoid further disruption in the day to day activities of the kingdom.

Alexander had Bessus' nose and ears cut off to imitate the punishment Persians had reserved for usurpers and it was said Bessus was subsequently decapitated. Other reports stated that he was tied to two trees bent towards each other which were released, ripping apart his body in a slow and painful death. These acts against the last known leader of the Persian Empire shook the sense of security of the Royal Palace but King Porus remained resolute in the face of a possible clash with Alexander. The balance of power had officially shifted from the Persian Empire to Alexander's growing Greek Empire. King Porus would begin seeking Manish Ramankrishna's advice as Manish's influence steadily increased.

CHAPTER 6:
KING OF GREECE, SHAH OF PERSIA, PHARAOH
OF EGYPT, AND SON OF ZEUS (327 B.C.)

"The bravest are surely those who have the clearest vision of what is before them, glory and danger alike, and yet notwithstanding go out to meet it."
—Thucydides (460 B.C.—395 B.C.)

As a way to solidify the diplomatic bonds between the east and west, the weddings were a success in his eyes. Alexander wished for a cultural unification between the Greeks and Persians and he believed the best way was to have a mass wedding involving his military leadership and general army with the Persian women. Roxana was a beautiful Bactrian princess who had just become his wife. Alexander remained privately insecure despite the fact that he had a string of successes dating back to the unification of Greece. In his mind, his successes were still overshadowed by Cyrus the Great, who built the first Empire in the region and created a land of laws and tolerance encapsulated by his famous Cyrus Cylinder. Alexander's insecurity and the need to prove his worth fueled him to surpass his father and all previous Greek rulers—even the legendary Greek heroes Achilles and Heracles—that he idolized. Alexander projected himself as the son of Zeus to legitimize his family and himself as ruler; his successes further solidified these claims.

Alexander's father, Philip II, initiated the rise of Macedonia—a land considered backwards by the rest of Greece. Macedonia had risen to a level of prominence comparable to the cultures of Athens and the legendary warriors of Sparta. Alexander's mother Olympias was secretly referred to as a barbarian in some circles and all these rumors called into question the legitimacy of Alexander's ascension to the Macedonian throne. Furthermore, Olympias' mechanizations and long term designs caused friction among the upper levels of the Macedonian-led Greek military.

King Philip had many lovers who competed for his affections and this created a conflict which intensified with political rivalries and other motivations that led to deadly consequences. Philip had married another younger wife named Cleopatra Eurydice, who was the niece of a prominent general named Attalus. Attalus desired that the future child of Cleopatra and Philip would become the future heir of the Macedonian throne, alienating and infuriating the young Alexander, who was rumored to be a bastard. The drama further unfolded as a love triangle between the former lover of Philip named Pausanius of Orestis and a new lover also named Pausanius came to light. The new lover was publicly embarrassed by Pausanius of Orestis—much to everyone's amusement—causing the new lover Pausanius to recklessly put himself in danger while protecting King Philip during a minor battle which ended in his death. This enraged Attalus, who mourned his friend's death and in retaliation got Pausanius of Orestis drunk at a party and allowed him to be sexually violated by the other men.

King Philip II was angered with Attalus but did not punish him due to their close friendship. Philip II promoted Pausanius of Orestis with haste to become a member of his Somatophylakes, Philip II's elite bodyguard. This promotion proved to be the end of Philip's life.

Philip II, who in 337 B.C. created the League of Corinth which set the stage for a unified Greece and Hellenic power structure, the king who set the stage for the invasion of Persia by a united Greek force, was now at the mercy of Pausanius of Orestis and those within his house who wanted to see his end. In October of 336 B.C., in the capital of Macedonia at Aegae, Philip II was attending the wedding celebrations of his daughter Cleopatra of Macedon and Alexander I of Epirus, who was also the brother of Olympias and uncle of Cleopatra of Macedon. Olympias was angered with her husband Philip II for previously trying to start a war between him and her brother, Alexander I of Epirus. Philip II's answer was to form a political union with a marriage between Alexander I of Epirus and his daughter. However, Philip II was unaware of the clandestine plan against his life involving his own bodyguard.

With a heart pounding with anger and a mind drenched in revenge, Pausanius of Orestis stabbed Philip multiple times. Sensing the crowd would soon notice his actions, he fled, leaving Philip II gasping on the floor near a gateway of the main stage. Pausanius made it close to the gate of the city before tripping on a vine root just out of reach of awaiting horses and meeting his death when a spear met his torso.

Philip's assassination by the hands of his smitten lover had given rise to a plethora of conspiracy theories that threatened to unravel Alexander's claims of legitimacy to the throne as well as his personal honor. Alexander had spent several years trying to solidify his support among the elder members of the military as well as with his overall military, but it had proven to be a continuous battle. It did not help that Alexander's mother honored his father's killer indirectly after Alexander crucified his body. Alexander's conflicts with Attalus before and after his father's assassination also did not help reduce conspiracies of his own involvement in his father's assassination.

A trial was held where Heromenes and his brother Arrhabaeus were found guilty and executed. Leonnatus, who helped kill the fleeing Pausanias of Orestis, was suspected of killing Pausanius to prevent his capture.

Subsequent testimony possibly implicating him in the conspiracy resulted in his demotion. Alexander was fond of Leonnatus and his widowed sister Cleopatra sought his hand in marriage. Alexander's uncle, Alexander I of Epirus, had perished in the Battle of Pandosia in 331 B.C. after his peace treaty with the Roman Republic. Alexander I of Epirus had previously defeated several Italic Tribes including the Lucanians, Samnites, and Bruttii. Many believed Alexander of Macedon would march against the Latin tribes and the Roman Republic but that was not the primary mission Alexander of Macedon had in mind.

Alexander was now the most powerful man in the world, but with great power he had also inherited a lot of responsibility. His success in battle was comparable to Cyrus the Great and now he planned to surpass Cyrus and his legendary mark upon history. It was not enough to conquer and unify Greece, Palestine, the ancient lands of Egypt, and the rival Persians; now Alexander wished to go further east to other territories of Persia where the Greek army never ventured. Some of the older generals did not approve of Alexander's wedding to Princess Roxana of Bactria. Many of the Greeks believed it was below their king to marry a barbarian and have a barbarian as their queen; they reflected on the dreaded idea of having a future barbarian king who would rule Greece after Alexander's death and its future implication to the Greek Empire. They believed all the blood, sweat, and tears shed to create a great Greek Empire would be in vain if the barbarians eventually ruled Greece again.

Alexander had previously faced rebellions across lands that he controlled. Most notably, he had to quell several revolts after his father's death. The Greek city-states sought to revolt while the young leader was beginning his rule. In 333 B.C., the Spartan King Agis III met with the Persian Commanders Pharnabazus and Autophradates in the Aegean Sea. Alexander noticed the irony of the great Spartans who fought fiercely against Xerxes and the Persian Empire now plotting with the commanders of Darius III against him. Alexander also understood the divisions between the Spartans and the Athenians, who had formed alliances with various rival factions within the Persian leadership in order to gain an advantage over their mutual enemies. In 331 B.C., Alexander faced a revolt from Sparta—a city whose history he respected. Alexander sent his regent Antipater to face King Agis III and his force of over 20,000 infantry and 2,000 cavalry. Antipater unleashed Alexander's wrath of over 40,000 mostly Macedonian troops and some barbarians to subdue the Spartans and bring them back under Alexander's control—a feat made more impressive as it came after Alexander's defeat at Memnon's rebellion.

Alexander encountered his most recent rebellion within his new empire at Sogdian Rock the previous year. The leader was a baron named Oxyartes. The Bactrians, believing they were safe from Alexander's army, told Alexander that he needed winged soldiers to be able to win the battle. Alexander offered his most experienced climbers and others a reward to use long hooks fastened with linen to climb the peak. Approximately thirty men met their deaths attempting to climb the summit until a few succeeded, causing King Alexander to proclaim, "I have found my winged soldiers!"

Psychologically, the Bactrians were defeated and quickly surrendered to Alexander. Upon first sight of Oxyartes' daughter Roxana, Alexander thought she was even more beautiful than the women of the Royal House of Persia and spoke to Oxyartes regarding his intentions of marriage, which he later accepted. This marriage further solidified Alexander's Empire and provided Alexander a queen who would rule his Greek Empire alongside him.

The wedding ceremonies were ongoing for several days—a good alleviation from the constant fighting and marching of his troops, Alexander thought. Roxana was now resting as she spent many days among her new subjects and in conversation with Alexander's vanguard. As the sun was beginning to set, Alexander drank wine. He spent a brief period of time without the warm embraces of wine after an unfortunate incident just the previous year involving the now deceased Cleitus the Black. Recently, Alexander had begun to drink again, at times even before the midday sun illuminated his vast empire. Wine and specifically its intoxicating impact was at the center of many unfortunate events that Alexander rarely spoke of. Alexander realized that he should temper his indulgences but he believed they were part of his success. His risk-taking had served him well in his campaign but at times he felt his emotions were uncontrollable—a reality he battled his entire life.

Alexander felt he had surpassed Philip II during his conquest and establishment of a Greek Empire, but this self-assessment was not shared by many of his generals who served under his father. Philip II had planned the Asian invasion but it was Alexander who took Greek conquest further than anyone expected. Alexander's biggest enemy was himself and now he was exhibiting some of the same negative behaviors which he had criticized his father for, most notably during a party celebrating his marriage to Cleopatra Eurydice. Growing tensions between Alexander and Attalus caused Alexander to strike him with a cup, creating a larger fight between Alexander's friends and the party who had arrived with Attalus. In an alcohol-fueled rage, Philip II had reprimanded his son and accused him and Olympias of political maneuvering. Philip II lunged at Alexander but drunkenly collapsed, prompting Alexander to mock him as he stated, "This is the man who wishes to conquer Asia but he is unable to simply cross one seat to the other."

After the death of his father, Alexander never forgave Attalus, who was now serving with Parmenion as a commander in the invasion of Persia in the Macedonian advance army. Attalus revealed a plan for Athenian revolt by the intelligent orator and legal expert Demosthenes of Athens. Despite the revelation of Demosthenes' designs to use Attalus and Athens to rebel against Alexander, Alexander conveniently had Attalus assassinated along with his two children (who were also Alexander's cousins), after which Cleopatra Eurydice committed suicide.

Demosthenes survived, causing more trouble for Alexander, who planned to resolve the issue upon his return to Macedon.

"Alas!" Hyphaestion said as he entered Alexander's chamber, "drinking alone, Alexander. You look rather pensive and gloomy once again. Perhaps you should not be left alone; come join us in the festivities. You are now finally married to a beautiful wife and you can begin to create an heir and legacy for this marvelous empire you have worked hard for. Join me and our friends because idleness and solitude have proven a much greater foe for you."

The sun was beginning to set and some of Alexander's closest friends were wondering where he had gone since he was not with his new bride. Hyphaestion was the closest friend Alexander had and the only friend who had almost full access to his most private thoughts. Alexander replied, "It is the recent actions on my behalf, my dear friend. I have alienated even my supporters with my loss of self-control and now there is a rift forming between my Persian subjects and our Greek military. Did Cyrus the Great suffer the same divisions among his subjects? Am I not advocating for religious freedom within my empire?" Alexander was at first vexed but now his frustrations had turned to sadness.

Always supportive, Hyphaestion replied, "Must you continuously mourn these unfortunate incidents? You have made important decisions against those who seek to destroy what you have built—including your own family. Family is usually the downfall of a powerful man because your senses are lowered regarding potential conspiracies. I suspect your sadness is focused primarily on your incident with Cleitus, which was an unfortunate accident. You should focus on your next mission and the rallying of your troops."

Alexander had some tears flowing from his eyes and he wiped them away, surprised he had tears left as he had cried privately for many months and thought he had no more to shed. He had revealed his plans to go further into the territories that the Persians controlled in the Indus Valley to Hyphaestion as well as his desire to surpass the total territory of Darius III. Hyphaestion respected his close friend's aspirations but he believed it would be a tough prospect to convince Alexander's military to comply with. These were uncharted areas for the Greeks and the recent events between Alexander and Cleitus would make this endeavor hard to sell. Alexander's troops had a tough winter where their march was slowed down by heavy snow and resilient forces that countered their advance and they felt they had completed their original mission set in place by Philip II. Some in the older generation also felt unease as Alexander was eliminating everyone belonging to the previous generation and they did not see an end to his plotting and politics. The underlying tensions finally exploded to the surface in an alcohol-fueled tirade between Alexander and Cleitus witnessed by Alexander's Vanguard and members of his military. This incident had become one of the lowest points in Alexander's life.

The tension had been building since the young Alexander's assumption to the throne of Macedonia. It was a tension between Alexander and those of his father's generation who sought to keep the original plans Philip II had created with his top military advisers and generals who were now Alexander's subordinates. The killings of members of the previous generation and Alexander's aggressive campaigns in Asia were seen as overreaching; many felt Alexander had completed the original mission of unifying Macedonia and Greece as well as the successful defeat of the Persians. For over 480 years, Alexander's Royal House, the Argead Dynasty, had ruled since 808 B.C. and already Alexander had bested his ancestors and brought Macedonia and Greece to a level never before seen. Alexander's success did not mitigate the growing tension beginning to spread like a sickness, intensified by his claims of godly birth—an opinion echoed by his mother Olympias in an effort to place her son next in line to the throne. The mythical founder of the Royal House of Argead was Caranus, who was claimed to be a descendant of Zeus.

Alexander further solidified his godliness by implying a direct relationship with Zeus as his son. Alexander's increasing adoption of Persian culture and dress further alienated many of the Macedonian upper class, most notably Cleitus the Black.

Persian satrap Artabazos II, who had formed many alliances with various Greek city-states and later fled to Macedonia under the protection of Alexander's father Philip II, was no stranger to the Greek and Persian political strategy. He had learned from political moves by his family and brother-in-law, Mentor of Rhodes, who sided with him and the Athenian Charidemus against the Persian King Artaxerxes III Ochus. While Artabazos II was in Macedonia, his brother-in-law betrayed the last native Pharaoh of Egypt, Nectanebo II, who had sought Mentor's help against the Persian Empire. He had concentrated his efforts on amplifying the importance of the Egyptian religion in order to strengthen the Egyptian culture and the shutting down of the rock quarry at Abdju, or Abydos as the Greeks referred to it. Nectanebo II barely held onto power after experiencing early success supporting Phoenician revolts against the Persian Empire. Nectanebo II relied on Greek mercenaries led by Mentor to initially fight Persian aggression. Pharaoh Nectanebo II's plans backfired when Mentor betrayed him, effectively ending the rule of the last native Egyptian pharaoh as he fled towards Nubia. Later, Artabazos II fought for the next Persian leader, King Darius III, and after Alexander's victory over King Darius III, Alexander honored Artabazos II's bravery by awarding him the satrapy of Bactria. Alexander had originally offered the satrapy of Bactria to Cleitus the Black, but he would never live to assume this position.

It was a festive mood that fateful night as they had effectively conquered the furthermost reaches of the Persian Empire—a resounding defeat that echoed throughout the known world and made Alexander the owner of the largest unified territory. Alexander had far surpassed his father's initial plans and wished to share his success with his most loyal men. Among them was the person he had admired all his life: Cleitus. Cleitus had been one of his father's closest friends; he had fought hard and was loyal to Alexander. However, Alexander had sensed some tension between himself and Cleitus and wished to reward him with the position of satrap of Bactria in an effort to mitigate any potential hostility. Alexander had previously discussed his plans with Cleitus and decided to publicly announce it at a large banquet he was holding at the Sogdian satrapy capital palace at Maracanda. There were a few more battles remaining to be fought and seated at one end of the room, Alexander began announcing changes in his political and military structure. As the sun began to set, more wine flowed and it became a festive atmosphere with women and men dancing and kissing each other. Alexander, who had begun to drink earlier but stopped in the early afternoon, decided he too should join. Some of Alexander's Persian subjects were in attendance and conversed with him regarding the affairs of the state. Alexander enjoyed this time to talk with his subjects directly and as they completed their questions, they bowed down to him in their Persian custom. Alexander had spoken to his men regarding the importance of maintaining the customs of his Persian subjects just as Cyrus the Great once upheld religious freedom in his vast empire, however the Persians were looked upon with disdain by the Macedonian upper class.

Alexander did not notice Cleitus' hateful stare as he gulped down the remaining wine in his cup. Alexander was laughing, making various exclamations as the continuous flow of wine into his system made his voice carry farther than he intended. "I have to reexamine this section of my Greek infantry that were bested in battle by the so-called feminine Persians. Perhaps it is these Greeks who are feminine."

Cleitus drank some more wine and stated, "Why is that humorous to you, Alexander? You mock your own troops in front of these Persians, or have you forgotten your great teacher Aristotle? We are civilized people and they are barbarians who fight and break bread alongside us and now laugh at us while we sit here silent."

Sensing Cleitus' growing frustration, Alexander tried to mitigate the tension. "Cleitus, I did not mean any insult. We are a wider empire and now control the roads that Cyrus established. We all learn from each other; Greeks, Persians, and Egyptians have been forming alliances for centuries long before any of us in this room existed. Part of establishing order is to have the respect of your subjects and for them to respect you in their way. We will establish a system of integration of all peoples in my dominion and you and some of my most trusted men can advise me on the best course of action I should take for me to accomplish this goal."

Cleitus stood, asking for more wine to be poured into his cup. "I have always respected you Alexander, but your emotions have the best of you at times. You say you will blend our cultures but you do not see the potential rift this will cause in your empire among the people and this is the very reason there needs to be a hierarchy implemented. It also seems you are adopting more of the Persian customs while forgetting your Macedonian roots. Are the Persian customs more important than ours? You are even wearing their feminine pants and clothing and allow them to bow to you as if you are a god instead of a man!" Cleitus was now slurring his words and shouting.

Alexander felt slightly embarrassed and was trying to make light of the situation and while wearing a forced smile, he responded, "As I said previously Cleitus, if they wish to respect me in their custom as their Shah or their Supreme Leader then let them do so! Do I ask my Greek or Macedonian subjects to do the same? And you, Cleitus. You should get used to these customs, for you are to become the new satrap of Bactria! I am tasking you with the power to command these 16,000 Greek mercenaries against the nomadic mountain Asian tribes. I believe you can instill confidence in these troops and drive out any signs of cowardice. But the way in which you speak now makes me believe you are unsure of yourself." Alexander was making light and some understood the joke and laughed to themselves while the rest of the room cheered for Cleitus, the new satrap of Bactria.

However, this statement further infuriated Cleitus, who was increasingly emboldened by his anger and the wine. Cleitus responded angrily, not caring about his new promotion. "Ironic you call me a coward while you claim to be a god. Shall I remind you I saved your little life at the Battle of Granicus six years ago when you were attacked by Rhoesaces and Spithridates?" The latter would have cut Alexander down from behind in the heat of the battle if not for Cleitus, who at the key moment delivered a massive blow as he separated Spithridates' arm from his body while the second blow killed him, allowing Alexander to continue the battle.

Some of the Persian subjects began to leave the main chamber and the chatter almost fell silent as everyone sensed the anger between the two men.

Alexander replied, "I have fought alongside you and my army and have proven myself as a worthy king, general, and soldier. Although I thank you for your help in battle, you cannot disrespect me. I am still your king and you will respect my position just as you respected my father Philip II!"

Cleitus wobbled and now spoke very loudly. "Yes, your father. The man who would never adopt Persian customs and think of blending our cultures. What is next, Alexander? Will you marry a barbarian woman from among these conquered people as well? We once talked as equals and as men with your father but you sit here saying you are the son of Zeus and you have people bow down to you. You can shower me with eastern pomp but I'd rather live in Macedonia as a commoner! What is worse is that you insult me and banish me to a land far away with mercenary Greeks who have yet to experience a major victory. Is your plan to slowly erase me from influence because you cannot directly kill me like you did Philotas and his father Parmenion? Did you not think you would alert me and others to your wickedness and machinations even when you involved us in your foulest of deeds?"

Alexander was annoyed and raised his voice. "I have surpassed my father and have conquered more land than he ever imagined. I have taken the Greeks to the ends of the world yet you still compare me to him? What else do I have to do? Heracles was a mortal but a son of Zeus and so was Achilles so why can't I be as well? I have traveled as far or farther than my father or Heracles! Be careful with your words as you are now openly insulting your king!"

Cleitus, who was advised to sit down, ignored his friends' pleas and yelled back, "I am not a sycophant like Nearchus, Perdiccas, and your friend Hephaestion who grovel at your feet and cater to your whims. I believe I am correct in stating that you have become delusional! Who do you think you are? You disrespect your army, your people, your blood. I saw you grow up while my sister Lanike was your nurse spanking your spoiled bottom! You had siblings yet you and your mother plotted and caused disgrace to come to your father Philip II, the true unifier of Macedonia and Greece and the true originator of the Persian invasion. Perhaps it was your effort to mask you and your mother's barbarian past and illegitimacy that caused you to plot against your own siblings in your quest for power. Perhaps that is why you call yourself the direct son of Zeus!"

Alexander yelled "Enough!" and threw an apple at Cleitus' head while asking for a spear.

The Hypaspists, the trusted infantry men, removed themselves from the area near Alexander; he was drunk and unpredictable. They believed a man who burned down Persepolis and was known for cruel punishments should not get hold of a weapon. Alexander called out for his trumpeter to summon his army to arrest Cleitus but the army respected Cleitus and did not want to get involved in a quarrel between close friends.

"I am your king! Arrest him and whoever is with him!" Alexander burned with rage. "Cleitus, you no longer serve the purposes of this expedition and are relieved of your command. Remove yourself from my sight before I kill you!"

Alexander's bodyguard held Alexander down and a group of other men took Cleitus away as they hoped to clear up the misunderstanding the following day. Cleitus, who momentarily was led away, had slipped from the grasp of his friends, screaming, "Come kill me yourself! You are a barbarian and an illegitimate usurper who lost his way! You are a despot, false king, and tyrant!"

Alexander blacked out as he lost control and tripped over a guard's foot. He managed to grab a long spear and his insecurity, rage, and frustration, exploded into a single throw of the javelin which found Cleitus' chest and a portion of his heart and lungs. Cleitus stumbled back, falling to his side, eyes wide with surprise and his breathing rapid and shallow as others rushed to his aide. Blind with rage, Alexander continued to proclaim that if anyone else shared Cleitus' negative feelings of him and his mission in Asia they should remove themselves from his army or face imprisonment and execution. Many men denied any involvement in plots out of fear that Alexander would target them. A short time later, Alexander's anger subsided and he regained his full senses, allowing him the ability to see the consequences of his actions. Alexander cut through the crowd gathered around Cleitus' body and as he knelt down, Cleitus' eyes rolled back in his head and his heart stopped beating. Alexander held Cleitus' body realizing what he had done and the grave mistake he committed which left his standing as king in question. The impact of Alexander's tragic act would have consequences which would resonate in his future and in the way he was viewed and portrayed. The thought of this weighed heavily upon the young ruler.

Alexander was still thinking of that fateful night last year when he had struck Cleitus down. Thankfully the words of his closest confidant and childhood friend Hephaestion helped ease his worries on the matter. Alexander continued to drink, asking his friend for advice as to how to progress with the final phases of his eastern campaign and into the Indus Valley region. Alexander was intrigued with moving forward and gaining more resources for his new empire. One way was to maintain the former economic ties in the Indus region that the Persian Empire had. Several times during his early battles with the Persian Empire he ran the risk of running out of money and resources to continue his march. Alexander understood the importance of keeping his military fed and paid in order to ensure their success on the battlefield. Thanks to his father Philip II, the Macedonian and united Greek army had a core military membership of professional soldiers. Hephaestion aided Alexander in crafting speeches and an overall message to motivate Alexander's army from generals all the way to regular infantry members as well as contributed his engineering and logistic skills.

Hephaestion knew the importance of incorporating Greek and Persian traditions to craft a united empire as the Persians had when Cyrus the Great rose against the Median Empire over 300 years prior. Cyrus the Great, a client-king, revolted against the Medians and battled the Babylonians, who held Hebrew slaves from Palestine after the Babylonian King Nebuchadnezzar II conquered the Palestinian lands. Draining the waters of the city during the night, Cyrus' soldiers were able to breach the lowered water levels, surprising their military and incorporating Babylon into one of Persia's main cities.

Alexander had enslaved thousands of people, usually when they angered him, and Hephaestion reminded him of the importance of freedom for his subjects. However, Alexander needed the free labor to fuel his ongoing conquests despite all the riches he had already plundered. Alexander would enact new laws upon his return to his new capital in Babylon after he completed his war in the Indus Valley then march back to Greece and Macedonia to solidify his strength at home.

With the upcoming battle against the Indus civilizations approaching, Alexander was now discussing war strategies with his military advisers and generals. He also asked Hephaestion to deploy diplomats to learn the relationship between their kings and see if they could form alliances or expose any weaknesses. Alexander was thinking of sending scouts to observe the tribes at a forward location, or perhaps diplomats would be sent ahead as the war preparations would begin in just a few months after the wedding and festivities concluded. This would also give Alexander some time to inform his general army of his plans and measure the overall mood and reaction.

Alexander exited his personal quarters and entered the central room where everyone else was busy drinking and sharing war stories. Alexander's top generals were enjoying wine and the Persian women among them, engaging in carnal desires of various degrees. They needed this time to relax and unload a lot of their stress. The sun was setting below the beautiful mountainous landscape in the distance as they observed the Khyber Pass where they would soon cross on their journey towards the Indus Valley. Lands awaited that were not well known in Greece, which made Alexander question his Persian companions. Alexander's most trusted men shouted with glee as they caught sight of their friend and king. In addition to Hephaiston, there were six other men: Aristonous, Lysimachus, Peithon, Leonnatus, Perdiccas, and Ptolemy I Soter. In Alexander's opinion, Ptolemy was one of the most intelligent and observant of his lieutenants. He often said that Ptolemy was a friend of quiet thought and solitude.

Alexander began discussing war preparations with his personal bodyguards; many of whom were in agreement with their leader. The fiercest supporter was Hephaiston, who encouraged Alexander to continue in an intelligent and measured manner into this uncharted territory. Ptolemy also advocated for the use of intelligence gathering to understand the capabilities of the enemy or diplomacy. Opinions varied among Alexander's generals as some questioned his intentions in going so far into this region.

Alexander replied, "My closest brothers in arms, we will have an ambitious offense after crossing the Khyber Pass in the next few months. To legitimize our empire, we must not only conquer and control the Persian Empire's primary land, but also gain the Persian's territorial holdings so we can extract taxes and their materials and manufacturing. Basically, we will gain the same weapons and materials used against us by the Persians for hundreds of years and finally use them for ourselves. We will have everyone learn Greek within our empire under my guidance and we have the option of learning the various languages of these new territories. We have not ventured into that unknown land but throughout history we came into contact with some of these men and some of you may have faced them in battle as they served the Persian Empire. They are the people whose king was under agreement with King Darius the Great. We shall cut off all rebellions and solidify our people by fusing our cultures."

A particularly resilient Memnon of Rhodes and his Greek mercenaries frustrated the young Alexander by land and sea through the usage of Darius' own fleet to take over the Aegean Islands. This fueled the other Greek city-states to rebel, including Athens and Sparta, who were enemies themselves but united in their hatred against Macedonian control. The initial battle was a tough one in its brutality and a strategic and mentally grueling contest where the young Alexander, eager to prove himself, was pushed to the outer bounds of his limits. Alexander was plagued with economic trouble and lack of supplies and Memnon exploited this weakness by unleashing a scorched earth policy and subsequently capturing the islands of Chios and Lesbos. Memnon then attacked Macedonia, shocking Alexander and his generals. The terror of Memnon was finally extinguished when Memnon died. Memnon of Rhodes was a famous, perhaps infamous Greek depending on one's perspective and to Alexander he was a menace who needed to be stopped.

Alexander found it ironic that Memnon's brother was Mentor of Rhodes, the man who would take down the last native Pharaoh of Egypt, Nectanebo II. Alexander's strength was that he learned from his victories as well as his failures and the adversaries who would fall under the might of his army.

Many of Alexander's top generals applauded in appreciation for the determination their king displayed but more importantly, they were happy because the endless campaigns were seemingly coming to a conclusion. The initial mission had been completed and many of the Greeks wished to return home and find relief in their wives, children, family, and fame. Many in the infantry fought long and bravely and wanted to be rewarded for their service. Perhaps their families should be rewarded as well, but mostly they wanted what all men did: peace and stability. The veterans had suffered many years of battle and tough, agonizing hand to hand combat along with the gore and anguish of war. This caused a profound change in the minds of these men, however their leader was fueled by the search for further glory and land. Something within Alexander propelled him forward. He had begun to believe in his own destiny and the idea that he was divine and who could say no to him?

Hephaestion was one of the few generals that understood the value of a solidified blended army under a unified law. He also supported Alexander's ambitious plans for the Indus Valley and had begun to speak with the generals on tactics regarding this endeavor. Alexander also added the fact that this Indus region contained large riches. Why else would the Royal Persian House hold an agreement with the rulers of the Punjab with such interest? Also, the goods and metals of the region could be used to economically strengthen his new empire. Craterus, one of the most respected officers, added that it was risky to go into the Indus Valley without further intelligence of the terrain, to which Hephaestion disagreed; they only needed to reestablish relations with the former rulers who were under Persian influence and he suggested that if they were hostile but remained divided among themselves, the Indus Valley could become an easy conquest. Both were partially right but tensions rose once again. Craterus held some frustration over Hephaestion's recent promotion to Chiliarch and second in command. In fact, Hephaestion now invoked jealousy and envy in the hearts of some of the high generals, causing some of them to say that Alexander was closer to Hephaestion than the women he was intimate with. Hephaestion was not involved in many of the most important battles—a glaring observation that made the situation in particular between him and Craterus unbearable for Alexander.

Alexander said, "This is a discussion between my best strategic minds, not a simple quarrel between two men! We must resolve our differences in our strategies in conquering this foreign land, properly motivate our army, and understand the vital importance of this expedition."

The leader of the elite cavalry of the companions, General Perdiccas, responded by stating that Alexander should give a speech within the next few days advocating for this expedition. Perdiccas had risen in prominence during Philip II's war against Thebes and Alexander's complete destruction of the same city. Thebes was the most powerful Greek state, comprising of elite units made up of lovers who fought to the death for their beloved. Destroying them in 335 B.C. was a major boost of confidence for Alexander and his troops. Alexander respected the persuasive abilities of Perdiccas and suggested that he make a separate speech of his own.

"Even Aristotle encourages us to keep on exploring new lands, although he wishes to see the new ruler of the world," Hephaestion said.

Alexander looked at his former classmates, Hephaestion, Ptolemy, and Lysimachus and stated, "We have come a long way from school under Aristotle and now we are the conquerors of the world, my old friends!"

The invasion plans was settled, and Alexander assigned Hephaestion to travel through the Khyber Pass and set up a trail, taking care of the supply lines and building bases along the way. Alexander needed additional time to plan a method of attack which needed to be swift but smart.

The generals departed with the exception of Hephaestion; Alexander wanted time alone with him before retiring to bed with his new bride Roxana. Alexander picked up the *Iliad* and the *Odyssey;* these were the stories he enjoyed because he always thought of himself as Achilles and Hephaestion as Patroclus. Sometimes in jest he would compare the pensive Ptolemy to Odysseus. Alexander and Hephaestion reminisced of earlier days. Hephaestion was so respected by Philip II that when Alexander and his friends were briefly exiled due to Alexander's rivalry with Attalus, Hephaestion was spared the humiliation—something Alexander internalized for many years. While reading some of his favorite parts of the *Iliad*, Alexander remarked on their previous trip to Troy where he poured libations for Goddess Athena and then poured oil on his body. After which, he stripped naked and raced along with his companions as was the tradition. Alexander and Hephaestion then paid respects to Achilles and Patroclus.

On another trip Alexander visited Phrygia, once a part of the Greek Delian League a hundred years prior that had become a Persian satrapy. Here Alexander encountered the Gordian knot. Prophecy stated that he who untied this knot would come to rule the land. Previously it had been put there by a peasant turned king named Gordias, father of King Midas, and this knot still remained in place during Alexander's arrival. It was important for Alexander to conquer all physical and mental tests to solidify the purpose of his mission as well as to strengthen his legitimacy in his own eyes and the eyes of his subjects. Thinking long and hard after several attempts to untie the knot, Alexander unfastened it by removing the pin that secured the yoke to the chariot. The next day, Alexander's prophet Aristander declared a heavy lightning storm to be a sign of Zeus confirming Alexander's claim as the ruler of Asia.

On another trip during their time in Ancient Egypt, Alexander and Hephaestion traveled to the Oasis of Ammon (or Zeus Ammon), where Alexander claimed that the oracle stated that he was the next Pharaoh of Egypt.

The oracle at Ammon was an important stop for Alexander, evidenced by the long journey of roughly six weeks taking him away from his eventual confrontation between himself and Darius III and traversing a sea of desert while fighting hunger and thirst during February of 332 B.C. As the long, hazardous journey lengthened, Alexander and his men were welcomed by cool and light rains which comforted the eager leader on his quest to seek the oracle the same his heroes and ancestors Heracles and

Perseus once did. Finally, Alexander reached the small oasis only several miles around and filled with plants and animals. He entered the inner center of the sanctuary where only the high priests were allowed alone.

The oracle who did not have a solid grasp of the Greek language greeted the conqueror, stating, "Oh, my son." But in the oracle's poor handling of Greek, he had uttered what resembled "Son of God" which caused confusion among the men waiting outside the temple. The men had reserved their respective interpretations to themselves as to not offend Alexander. Now inside the temple, Alexander asked several important questions, the first of which being whether he had captured all the conspirators in his father's death.

The oracle replied, "Why ask questions about your father who is not a mere mortal?" Not satisfied, Alexander rephrased his question, asking if he avenged his father, and the oracle responded, "Yes, Alexander avenged his father."

Alexander, the new Pharaoh of Egypt who was welcomed as a hero, now asked if it was his fate to conquer Asia and the oracle confirmed this fact. Upon his exit, Alexander stated that he had brought everyone to justice who conspired against his father, which personally helped ease his mind and strengthen his case of innocence regarding that tragic ordeal. Alexander then stated his ancestry and legitimacy as the son of Zues or son of Ammon and king of Asia, but this created friction among some of his Greek generals and subjects.

Alexander took the error in the oracle's language to mean that he was the legitimate king. A convenient error confirming Alexander's claims of legitimacy and a great political move, thought Hephaestion, although these details were not discussed even between the two close friends. They both sat drinking wine remembering their adventures together as the sun began to set.

Alexander carried Hebrew Holy Scriptures and Egyptian teachings in law and the sciences to go along with his Homeric works like the *Iliad*. Hephaestion reminded Alexander of a new letter sent by their teacher Aristotle.

Alexander and his friends of upper class Macedonian society had the luxury of having one of the most famous minds in all of Greece as a teacher. Aristotle taught the importance of Greek government and culture above all others and why they should protect them from outside intrusion and corruption. Hephaestion was probably the best of his students and he kept frequent correspondence with both him and Alexander. Aristotle, who at first was disappointed with Alexander adopting Persian customs, now began to understand the purpose of these undertakings which he expressed in this latest letter. He also wished for the quick return of Alexander to Macedonia to solidify his new empire and to reign from his seat of power.

Alexander created his own city in Egypt west of the Nile Delta, naming it Alexandria. He planned to create more Alexandrias throughout his new empire. Aristotle lived among the Macedonian Royals for most of his life and his connections were deeply entrenched as his own father Nicomachus was the personal doctor of Alexander's grandfather, King Amyntas III of Macedon. Aristotle previously attended Plato's Academy in Athens, where he remained for many years. There he studied Plato's ideas of the failure of the senses and its ability to only observe the copy of pure forms of objects which formed the general concepts of Plato's cave. According to Plato, humans only witnessed reflections and could not see the direct pure objects as revealed by the sun. Aristotle later stressed observation in obtaining true knowledge regarding a wide range of scientific pursuits.

Alexander, who was greatly influenced by Aristotle, viewed the Hebrew religion as sharing principles more along the lines of Plato and his philosophy. Gods could not be observed directly, Alexander thought, but they were an ideal never reached in our own world. Alexander also loved to compare and contrast Hebrew and Greek religious beliefs. Privately he admitted to Hephaestion that the Egyptians and their long history and practices were hardly below that of the Greeks. Perhaps they surpassed the Greeks as they had existed prior and the Greeks had learned much from the

Egyptians. However, Alexander would not share these observations in general as to not offend his Greek subjects, but he could not wait to share them with Aristotle at a later date when he could better summarize and present his ever-growing education.

Alexander kept many of the native Egyptians in administrative positions while appointing Macedonians, Greeks, and native Egyptians into military and financial positions as well. He ordered cultural festivities celebrating Greek and Egyptian customs all in an effort to avoid a native Egyptian revolt. Alexander understood that Aristotle's positions on Greek supremacy could not be applied when governing a foreign people and practiced extreme care in his governance of Egypt.

Alexander asked Hephaestion to plan the logistics and economics of the next major mission. Hephaestion was to present Alexander with the details in a few days before Alexander would publicly address his military. As for now, Alexander would go to his Royal quarters where his new bride Roxana waited for her husband. He took the letter with him and left Hephaestion to rejoin the others in the continuing wedding festivities. Alexander went to his bed and found Roxana with a pensive look upon her face.

Roxana's name meant "little star" and her beauty was like the beautiful stars that lit up the night sky. Many of Alexander's men opposed his marriage to Roxana and many resented him for advocating mass marriages of Greeks and Persians. Roxana was supportive of her new husband and Alexander loved her dark hair and dark eyes. Her skin was slightly tanned by the sun and smooth to the touch. Roxana's hair was long and dark and she always combed it. She had a small waist with a pronounced young female figure standing just slightly shorter than Alexander. Being a politician's daughter, Roxana was able to gain political skills and knowledge. She understood that her Greek subjects would have trouble accepting her as their queen so she made an effort with the encouragement of Alexander to learn Greek and Macedonian as fast as possible and also adopt some of the Greek customs. Roxana also helped

Alexander learn the Avestan language, which was also spoken by the Zoroaster, the founder of the Persian official state religion. Roxana learned and improved the Greek and Macedonian languages at a rapid pace due to her intelligence and determination to solidify her position.

"You are very pensive, my love," Alexander said.

Roxana was slightly annoyed and preoccupied with her own thoughts. "You spend so much time away from me. Perhaps you devote more time to Stateira, Parysatis, or perhaps Hephaestion. You need to spend time with your queen and help bring a true heir to your throne."

Alexander was stressed over the fact that he had no legitimate sons and his involvement with a previous woman was rumored to have produced a bastard son which Alexander never publicly acknowledged. As time passed, Alexander also received direct pressure from his mother Olympias and indirect pressure from his closest generals to produce an heir and an ending to the constant warfare—perhaps to solidify and create stability in the Greek Empire. Alexander was irritated by Roxana's jealousy but she had correctly identified his love for these Persian Royal women Stateira II and Parysatis II. Alexander sought to marry these women in the future in a plan to further solidify his empire which he thought would re-energize his unified subjects in his plans of further conquest. These Royal women traveled with Alexander along with the rest of Darius' immediate family. Bagoas, the Persian Eunuch who belonged to Darius the Great, also traveled with Alexander and had reached substantial fame within the Greek army.

Alexander reassured his wife by stating her importance and after reading Aristotle's latest letter advocating his quick return to Macedonia, he kissed his wife. Alexander ended the conversation by announcing his deep love for her and spending a long night of passion with his new bride.

A few months passed until Hephaestion's logistical plans were presented and reviewed by Alexander, who then spoke to his most trusted men for advice. Alexander planned on building alliances with rulers who wished to side with him; perhaps these subjects who operated under Persian rule could easily shift their allegiance for Alexander. He made it clear that this was just an aid for further conquest and if they did not cooperate they would suffer. Many of Alexander's troops were increasingly agitated at their new orders and only wished for a brief expedition, hopefully with little military conflict. Personally, Alexander wished to unify the entire unexplored lands in a peaceful manner, but he would use aggression if need be.

Alexander began his march through the Khyber Pass and into the northern edge of this strange territory. It was late 327 B.C. and the season of snowfall would be arriving soon, so he made the trip as quickly as possible to avoid the bulk of it. Ptolemy and other generals advised Alexander regarding his strained supply lines as he extended them through the Khyber Pass. Alexander had immense self-confidence and determination, however he understood the importance of strengthening this. Alexander was eager to visit the university at Takshashila and read and study the ancient writings. As he and his men approached, he received intelligence from his scouts regarding a large army led by a man named Ambhi Kumar who controlled a powerful kingdom named Gandhara from the city of Takshashila. Strategies were discussed and ready to be implemented as Alexander prepared for a possible hostile confrontation. Alexander did not underestimate the strategies of his potential enemies in war, as opposed to many soldiers who would see these people as below the Persians in intelligence and military capability. The events which would unfold would test Alexander's army, the Greeks, and Alexander himself.

CHAPTER 7:
A SAGE AT THE WEDDING OF RAJESH (327 B.C.)
"Rhetoric is the art of ruling the minds of men."
—Plato

This was Rishan's first wedding and he was thoroughly savoring the food, the colors of the women's attire, the music, and the dancing. It was a time for enjoyment and laughter; a time for the adults to release stress. Rishan was now eleven years old and he was enjoying the festivities, singing and dancing along with the children of family, friends, and relatives. Rishan At age twenty one, Rajesh had formed an official union with a woman of high quality and intelligence who would strengthen his family and provide a secure home for his future children—a valuable asset that was not easily secured even for the men of the highest wealth.

Several years earlier, Rajesh's parents met with Divya and her father privately to make sure all parties agreed to this union. Harbir Marawar greatly respected Manish and his family and he held a special regard for his eldest son. Harbir felt Rajesh had his warrior spirit but also held a certain reserve that he didn't possess and perhaps this was the best combination of qualities that would provide a good house for his daughter and future grandchildren.

The wedding was small compared to the other lavish weddings held by families of Manish's warrior caste who worked at the Royal Court. King Porus asked Manish to hold his son's wedding in the Royal courtyard of his palace or any of his numerous estates if he so desired. However, Manish favored a smaller wedding and Rajesh echoed his father's opinion on the matter. Rajesh wanted the wedding to occur with his family and closest friends; he did not wish for members of the Mehra family to be present.

The eldest son of the Mehra family, Randeep Mehra, was developing an animosity towards Rajesh most likely because Divya and her father preferred Rajesh. Randeep was desired by the most beautiful women in the land, yet he felt jealousy over the one woman he could not have. Randeep flaunted his wealth and power more often in the last year and sometimes made it a point to disagree with Rajesh even in the most trivial of matters regarding their military studies. Manish nonetheless invited the Mehra family mostly because a non-invitation would cause further tension. This was an animosity that began in the wake of the heated discussions on diplomacy and strategy in the previous year about foreign policy. Manish was trying to form a bond even with his biggest rival as he felt that unity among members of the advisery body would serve to strengthen them as they stood behind their king in anticipation of the potential clash with Alexander.

The wedding ceremonies were held in the Ramankrishna family house and Rishan's grandparents had arrived a few days prior in preparation. After weeks of ceremonies, Rajesh and Divya were officially husband and wife. Some extended family arrived from the outer areas of the Pauravas Kingdom, including close friends of Manish and Lakshmi. Everyone was clothed in an array of bright colors and jewelry—especially the bride. Wearing large quantities of jewelry on her body—almost as much as the Royals themselves—Divya was a wonder to behold. She was reticent but very intelligent and was a great addition to the Ramankrishna family. The father Harbir gave his daughter away to Rajesh and they made their union official among all their family and most esteemed friends. It was a successful union built upon mutual attraction and they both supplemented each other, which made them a good pair.

The Ramankrishna grandparents, Mahesh and Seeta, were excited to see their first grandchild wed a beautiful woman and possibly grant them the rare gift of welcoming great-grandchildren into the family. They had made the long journey from the northern borders of the Assaka Kingdom (or the Asmaka Kingdom as Mahesh usually referred to this land) and were happy to partake in the festivities and learn of new family developments, including the youngest grandchildren Rishan and Priya. Both grandparents had seen Rishan's birth and helped raised him during his first few years, however this was the first time they were able to speak to the youngest child Priya and see how beautiful and smart she had become. Priya was now nine years old and a smart, obedient daughter with a natural curiosity which her father and grandparents urged her to explore.

Rishan was making positive developments in his social life but had felt his relationship with Anupa Jhingan had distanced. Rishan had explored his attraction towards her but she did not reciprocate the same feelings. This had a slight negative impact on Rishan, who had noticed that this situation was not experienced by others—especially his new friend Karna Mehra. Karna had befriended Rishan soon after he and Anand became friends. This new friendship surprised Rishan; Karna was his senior by a couple of years and had an entirely different social circle. However, as quickly as this friendship with Karna began, it soured. Karna would sometimes make indirect remarks pertaining to Rishan's friendship with Anand and his family. Rishan admired and respected Karna's physical abilities and recent entry into schools for the military arts. Rishan also wished to improve his social abilities with others, especially the opposite sex—something that came naturally to Karna.

On one occasion just a few days prior, Rishan had approached Anupa in the presence of Karna and several of his friends. They were at a school gathering where students participated in music and games and some students were completing their studies. Anupa's family was not able to attend Rajesh's wedding but he had expressed how it would fill him with joy if she could; what a pleasure it would have been, enjoying the festivities with a girl whom he thought was special and unique. Rishan Anupa's reply was a swift and heartless rejection, leaving Rishan in an awkward situation in front of Karna and the other boys. Rishan was embarrassed at this unexpected outcome and all the excitement he felt about academic success and a possible trip to Takshashila to study was momentarily forgotten. Anupa gave her apologies, stating that perhaps she would join him at a future occasion, but she had to focus on her studies and other family functions. Karna made light of the situation and chuckled while some of his friends laughed. *What kind of friends were these?* Rishan thought. Perhaps that was how older boys like Karna handled unexpected outcomes relating to the opposite sex. What was certain was that the response of Karna and his friends angered and mortified Rishan.

Karna approached the disappointed Rishan, stating with a smile, "You are a good person Rishan but perhaps you are mistaking her friendship with compatibility. You must understand that Anupa is Brahmin and they only prefer men of the Brahmin caste. It would be hard even for a person like myself of Aryan blood and of high standing in the warrior caste to gain her attention. You are from a respectable family who has attained much and you have reached a high status. Perhaps a woman who is Dravidian or of lower standing is more suitable for you. This is the way of life, or has your father not explained this to you? Surely a man must know his place in the world. Very few Brahmin women will marry a Kshatriya man unless your family is well established. Your friend Anand for example, is of lower caste and although he is a good man sometimes it's best that castes do not mix and that Anand only associate with others of his caste. It is of benefit to us and our society."

Rishan appreciated the advice, however he had conflicting thoughts. Rishan felt slightly angered at Karna for speaking negatively about Anand because Anand was becoming more of a second brother to him. Rishan would seek to keep private questions between him and his father and not reveal them to Karna.

Words are a powerful tool and more invasive and powerful than physical force. Rishan began to find that the aforementioned was true, but his lesson in this regard was only beginning. Karna' words were in Rishan's head for the next several days during Rajesh's wedding ceremonies. Perhaps certain girls like Anupa were not in Rishan's future and perhaps he would not achieve success like his peers, let alone his father or the popular Karna Mehra. These thoughts crept into Rishan's mind like an oncoming sickness and he would momentarily forget his successes in academics and athletics. A strange impact this is in a boy's mind that one negative aspect in life could be powerful enough to cloud the many more achievements. Rishan's biggest enemy was self-doubt. It was an issue that Rishan needed to correct soon or else it could be his biggest obstacle as he grew into adulthood.

Rishan's mood was uplifted during his brother's wedding. There was music, games, and other activities. The presence of another young female named Priyanka Kumari helped Rishan forget the absence of Anupa Jhingan. Priyanka Kumari was the daughter of a lady named Padma who was a dear friend of Rishan's mother. Priyanka belonged to the warrior caste and was one of the young ladies Rishan's parents encouraged him to couple with; Priyanka's parents had begun to speak with Rishan's parents about the possibility of a future union. Rishan overheard his parents speaking on the matter, but he remained uncertain as no formal conversations had taken place. Rishan thought it was nice to converse with the pretty young lady and get to know her better. And what a lovely distraction she was!

Priyanka Kumari was a slender girl with medium brown skin and long, jet black hair. Her beauty was simple but her overall personality was rivaled only by Anupa, especially in Rishan's eyes. Other young ladies in the community were beautiful but these two were the ones that suited Rishan the most. Priyanka's father was a smart, quiet man named Padmesh, who also worked in the Royal Palace as a physician. Priyanka's older brother was an intelligent, reserved young man named Kulvir; he was pursuing a career in architecture and looked up to Manish from afar. He generally admired and respected Rishan as a potential husband for his sister. Rishan had a good character that was shared by the Ramankrishna family—a family Kulvir looked forward to joining.

"Hello, Rishan! I am so happy for your brother and family," exclaimed Priyanka.

Rishan responded, "Yes, I am happy for my brother. He is a great man and my sister-in-law is so beautiful and kind to me; I wish for the same for myself when I get older."

Priyanka laughed and asked about Anupa, letting Rishan know she was aware of his close bond with her.

Rishan replied, "Anupa is busy with her studies and her family now, and she made me aware that she and her family would not be in attendance." Rishan felt naturally at ease around Priyanka—more than he did with Anupa. Perhaps it was that he did not have an initial overwhelming attraction towards Priyanka as he did with Anupa, perhaps it was that Priyanka reciprocated Rishan's feelings, or perhaps it was a combination of both. Whatever it was, Rishan began to like Priyanka and her simple, unique personality, and she also enjoyed talking about interests that Rishan shared, including the Greek language.

Lakshmi and Padma were conversing about the wedding, delighted with how the events were turning out and the enjoyment of their guests at this important, festive occasion. The clothes worn by the bride and groom as well as all the guests were pleasing to the eye and the music was soothing to the ear. Lakshmi and Padma also noticed their children Rishan and Priyanka sharing a conversation and they both were pleased. Padma and her husband Padmesh were both overprotective of Priyanka but Padma was generally pleased with Rishan and the new growing friendship. Padma also vocalized her sentiment with Lakshmi that perhaps at a future date both families could spend more time together. However, both women understood a growing uncertainty in the near future. Their husbands were discussing foreign affairs and now the possibility that these foreign affairs would soon become immediate domestic affairs began to steadily weigh on everyone. Foreign developments never had a direct impact on the people of Pauravas but the recent circumstances threatened to change this fact.

Manish was happy with the growth of his family and especially Rishan's social development. Rishan was soon to become a young man and he also had become best friends with the former cause of his anguish, Anand Agrawal. Anand grew to respect Rishan which also caused Anand to reevaluate his previous actions. Never the conversationalist, Anand simply did what other kids do when making new friends and joined in play and mischief with Rishan. Some of the other students also followed Anand's change in behavior and befriended Rishan; Rishan was now free of enemies in his school and any potential enemies now had to contend with Rishan's friends. In the last few months the bond between Rishan and Anand had strengthened and Anand would come and stay at the Ramankrishna household and spend time with Rishan's family. They also spent much of their time in streams and other bodies of water fishing and talking about a range of topics that young boys talk about—usually girls, games, studies, and what they would like to do when they got older. Manish grew to like Anand and began to view him as a nephew.

The relationship between the boys blossomed and each benefited from the other's character and personality. Rishan enjoyed his newfound confidence and curiosity for exploration, while Anand improved in his academic studies which were reinforced by Manish, who began inquiring about Anand's school work and general well-being. Anand enjoyed having an older father figure who cared about him and his studies; his academics and social relationships improved drastically because of this. Anand came from dire circumstances, the complete details which he kept to himself and dared not let any of his peers learn—except for

Manish, who carefully, gradually, and respectfully gathered information. Manish began to naturally learn about Anand's life and family as he became best friends with his youngest son and a close part of the Ramankrishna family. Anand began to be an important part of the Ramankrishna household as time progressed.

Anand Agrawal was of a lower caste—which was not lost on Manish, but it was never of major importance; caste was not a large part of conversation in the Ramankrishna household and it was a rare environment within the Ramankrishna family as far as Anand was concerned. Anand received positive influence from Manish and began to gain self-confidence and hope. Anand had support from his parents but their labors were hard and time consuming, leaving little time to take care of Anand. Perhaps one day he too could rise above his social status and caste and aspire to something more. These were the positive thoughts of a young man who now saw a bright future ahead of him.

Anand Agrawal was from the Vaishya caste and only Rishan and his father Manish had knowledge of who Anand's parents were. Anand's father was a brick maker named Abichal Agrawal and his mother was named Anahat, a street cleaner and laborer who sometimes worked alongside her husband. Both parents worked endlessly but they were fulfilled that their only son had an opportunity for an education—something that was denied to them in their younger years. Skeptical at first, they had grown to love the Ramankrishna family, especially now that they had taken in their son as one of their own. The benefits of this new relationship showed in their son's rise in self-esteem and academic performance; it was also seen in the overall decrease in Anand's troublemaking ways. Anand's self-control and confidence translated in an overall peace in the Agrawal household.

The relationship Anand had with Manish's youngest son was mutually beneficial. Rishan Due to his friendship to Anand, Rishan's social skills also received a noticeable improvement on par with his rising academic intelligence, putting Manish's mind at ease. Thus, Anand's presence at

Rajesh's wedding was appropriate and welcomed by the Ramankrishna family. Manish smiled as he spoke with his parents, remarking on all the progress Rishan had made with his new friend. Rahesh and Seeta were pleased since they were aware of how solitary and shy Rishan had always been and they did not want that to be his personality as he grew older.

As the newlyweds walked around the Ramankrishna estate greeting and speaking to all the guests, Manish talked to his parents about the positive happenings in their family. Rajesh and his marriage to Diyva and the beautiful blossoming of Priya delighted Rahesh and Seeta but Manish could not conceal his overwhelming happiness when talking about Rishan. Rishan was multi-lingual but the amazement of his father was due to the progress in his learning of the Greek language. Manish had access to Greek writings through the Persian advisers at the Royal Court which Rishan read as a personal hobby. Manish had discussed that the future would be hard with his sons and his family, causing Rishan to study Greek as much as he could and to take his physical education more seriously. Rishan even requested to join the military as a warrior—something Manish did not want for his youngest son this soon. Manish felt that Rishan was not suited for battle like his eldest son, even though Rishan had made such impressive physical gains in the last few years. Manish discussed this with his parents, who were alarmed as it finally dawned on them how dire the future might be. As Manish was in the middle of conversation, an unexpected guest arrived.

His features were unique and he stood out from far away; some of the guests recognized him despite his attempts to blend in. His mostly bald head, medium brown skin, piercing dark eyes, single bundle of hair flowing down from a single point behind his head, and the manner of his walk clearly identified him. As he swiftly walked towards Manish, his earrings reflected the setting sun in the distance and a slight smile struggled to appear on his usually stoic face. Manish had offered an invitation to him for his son's wedding but he had been informed of his busy schedule in the mighty Magadha Empire led by Dhana Nanda. His name was Vishnu Gupta (or Kautilya and widely known as Chanakya) and he warmly embraced Manish.

Chanakya was not a remarkable man at first glance but upon closer inspection, that initial opinion was easily reversed. He was of average stature with physical definition of strong character. Chanakya's eyes were sharp and focused and he rarely smiled or betrayed his pure inner emotions. When in the middle of conversation, Chanakya would listen carefully and pause before sharing his response, taking special care to formulate his ideas before he verbalized them. He was an extremely disciplined man and had a strong sense of purpose and his place in society. A scholar and philosopher, Chanakya was a highly regarded teacher in a range of topics such as politics and socio-economics at the highly regarded university in Takshashila. Chanakya had left the famous learning center and had not returned due to the approaching march of the massive Greek army. Chanakya's relationship with Ambhi had previously been strained and the animosity between the two had increased recently.

Chanakya's arrival caught Kali Mehra's eye and his gaze remained fixed upon the man as he conversed with Manish. Manish did not wish to invite Kali but he wanted to defuse some of the growing strain between them. Manish understood his rise in importance in the eyes of King Porus was received as a direct threat to Kali's influence and he wanted to avoid tension in his career. The most important issue in Manish's mind was the successful plan set in motion to stop Alexander from reaching King Ambhi's kingdom.

If King Ambhi would not put aside his differences with King Porus, then the operatives sent by King Porus would initiate an offensive which would encourage some or all of King Ambhi's men to attack the Greeks. This plan would initiate a first strike upon Alexander's battle-weary troops whether Ambhi liked it or not; at the very least, it would prepare King Porus' forces to meet a further weakened Greek army. This was Manish's main focus as well as keeping his family safe, therefore he anxiously waited for the events to unfold abroad.

Manish did not want additional stressors in his career and within the Royal Palace; it would only serve to hurt him and distract other advisers and military leaders from the main task. Manish also did not want to have a dispute with the politically astute and dangerous Kali Mehra. However, the presence of Chanakya would cause further friction.

Manish was curious to know if Chanakya had met with anyone else from the Royal Palace. Chanakya replied, "Yes, some members of the Royal Family already know of my presence in Pauravas and of my attendance to your son's wedding. I met personally with King Porus' younger brother Amar, who was interested to know of the situation at the Magadha Capital of Pataliputra. King Porus understands that I embrace unification between our kingdoms but I am sure that won't happen now. The situation has become serious and the only king who is willing to agree with unification is your King Porus. I don't know the full details of your plans but I hope for the safety and strength of your kingdom that you remain unified at least within your palace and borders because. This fight will either be a monumental success or a monumental failure. I had to leave my post as teacher at Takshashila not too long ago because King Ambhi has grown unreasonable. So many talented people have come to learn there, including the personal physician of Siddhartha Gautama—or the Buddha as his followers call him today. Amazing that one man with a simple message can gain a following long after his death."

Manish called for Lakshmi to bring their guest some food and drink. Now that Chanakya was here, Manish would use his knowledge to his full advantage.

Manish's brother greeted Chanakya as he joined the conversation. Manu talked about his travels to the west in Egypt and Palestine while Chanakya listened carefully, interested in the details. Manu's travels coincided with the march eastward of the Greek army. The ferociousness of

Alexander's army concerned Chanakya but he remained confident in Alexander's defeat and believed victory for Alexander was certain only if unification occurred between the Punjabi Kingdoms.

Chanakya stated, "Your story is interesting. I am very surprised Alexander has been able to progress as far as he did with his financial troubles and the rebellions between the Greek city-states."

Manish added, "We have had a relatively peaceful relationship with the Persians for hundreds of years while the Greeks have had a tumultuous relationship with the Persian Empire and Persian interference in their lands has also divided the Greeks for countless generations. The Greeks have proved strong when united and now they have overthrown the pharaoh of Egypt and conquered major portions of Persian territory. Now they area threatening to overtake the Punjab."

Chanakya agreed. "Yes, you are correct. They have a history of internal conflicts and so do we. We should take the positive aspects of the Greeks' history and society and turn our internal conflicts into political unity. We should set aside our minor differences and focus on our similar traditions and culture to unify against the Greek Empire and not repeat the mistakes that allowed us to be conquered by the Persians. I am surprised Alexander has been so successful and perhaps the financing of his continuous war has been aided by taking the Persian treasury. But even with his war machine financed by Persian wealth, his troops will become war-weary and our combined forces should be able to defeat Alexander or at least bring him towards negotiations on our terms quickly. The key, however, is King Ambhi in Takshashila. It is my belief that he would rather fight against your King Porus than get into a costly battle with Alexander. My sources tell me Alexander is already within the northern borders of Takshashila, perhaps even using the old Uttarapatha Road. Whatever your plans were, Manish, I hope it is regarding the unification of Punjabi Kingdoms against this Greek menace or a unified first attack on the Greek army. I personally cannot influence Dhana Nanda in Magadha; he is oblivious and indifferent to foreign affairs. Dhana is of low caste and has grown rich while overtaxing his subjects. The upper castes don't accept Dhana Nanda as their King, who view him to be of lower caste and the lower caste people do not like him because they grow poorer while Dhana Nanda grows drunk with power and wealth. Dhana is like a rotting fruit waiting to get picked and discarded."

Manish began to understand the dangerous possibilities that the near future held as unity would more than likely not be achieved. He did not reveal the actual plans of inciting a battle against Alexander within Ambhi's military using agents sent by King Porus. This plan Manish believed might backfire and would leave Pauravas vulnerable because Dhana Nanda did not seem interested in joining King Porus despite his formidable military.

"What will you do, Chanakya?" Manish asked.

Chanakya responded, "I cannot persuade Dhana Nanda and I am in a very dangerous situation there. I will not be able to help you in your fight, Manish. Dhana Nanda will fall but it will take some time. I will receive help mostly from King Dhana Nanda's subjects who grow tired with the never-ending burdens of increasing taxation and societal decay. I also have a young student who is smart and will help us achieve our goals. The time for change is rapidly approaching. I have taught many exceptional students in my lifetime, Manish, but now I have found and one who he has taught me more than I have ever learned in my lifetime. Imagine the old teacher learning something new from a young student. Life is mysterious in these ways."

The men laughed at the irony.

Chanakya reminded the men that the Greeks who were employed by the Persian kings over 200 years ago explored these ancient waterways and recorded their explorations, including the most famous account of Scylax of Caryanda. Scylax's works were well known and other Greeks had added to that work. The men agreed that Alexander and his standing as an upper class member of

Macedonian society would easily allow him access to material regarding the Indus Valley and potentially the regions south of the Punjab. However, it was agreed Ambhi possibly could be the first obstacle against Alexander and this possibility would be of utmost importance. Manish observed his eldest son Rajesh and desired to include him in the conversation but saw him in an important exchange with his new father-in-law Harbir and did not wish to interrupt. Manish then turned to see his youngest son Rishan talking with Priyanka and a big smile came over his face; his son was now seemingly over his shyness. Rishan impressed Manish with his academic progress and his remarkably speedy rise in his athletic skills, but he was now socially maturing and this pleased Manish above everything else.

"Rishan my son!" Manish called. "Come here. I would like you to meet someone!"

Rishan excused himself from his conversation with Priyanka and he approached Chanakya, who was seated with his father and uncle.

Manish announced, "Rishan, my son! This is Chanakya, the great teacher at the school in Takshashila that I have mentioned. Perhaps in the future you may build upon your talents with the aid of Chanakya or a teacher like him."

Rishan was excited to meet Chanakya, whose intelligence he admired. Chanakya was informed of Rishan's academic success, his interest in pursuing more intense levels of study, and his recent rise of athletic abilities in competition. Chanakya was particularly impressed with Rishan's language abilities. Chanakya explained to Manish that Rishan's abilities were remarkable and that he had met very few children with comparable abilities. Chanakya mentioned the similarities between Rishan and his most prized student who had made remarkable progress and displayed a potential for greatness rarely seen, motivating Chanakya to adopt this young student. Chanakya stated his desire to help Manish but also explained that his help could be a threat to Manish's rivals. Manish made it a point to state that he had no rivals and that his desire was to find unity even through differences.

Chanakya smiled and said, "Manish, it does not matter how correct and righteous your cause is. It is natural that as you gain political influence that your success will create rivals just as rain creates puddles. Be careful, Manish. You might get mud on yourself no matter how carefully you tread."

As Chanakya made his way to congratulate Rajesh and Divya before leaving, Kali Mehra tried to intercept him. Manish looked on with his brother Manu and became alarmed as Harbir, who was nearby, might make his displeasure of Kali into a public spectacle. Harbir, known for his unapologetic honesty and his unpolished delivery of his opinions, was a potential threat to the general peace of the wedding. Although Harbir was Manish's most vocal supporter, Manish felt Harbir should reserve political conversation for a more appropriate time.

Kali greeted Chanakya carefully, observing his body language before he even initiated his approach. Chanakya received Kali with a smile, stating his purpose at the wedding was to enjoy a brief celebration of the new husband and wife. Harbir joined the conversation, slightly inebriated, which further alarmed Manish.

Kali exclaimed, "Well then it's been so long since you have been in Pauravas. Did you also meet with the Royal Family, or was the visit a surprise for your dear friend Manish?"

Chanakya replied, "Yes, I came to enjoy the wedding festivities and I am not on official business. I have arrived from the east near the city of Pataliputra. I really wish you and the other advisers reach a consensus and advise your King Porus so he can successfully lead his military against this Greek menace."

Kali asked him for any information he might have on the Greek advancing force.

Chanakya responded, "A united force will be ready for war against Alexander and I support that. Ideally, unification with King Ambhi of Gandhara would be best but I seriously doubt he will lend you his support so King Porus must act swiftly."

Kali paused momentarily then added, "Perhaps you expect King Porus to fight such a large Greek force on his own. May I ask what your motivations in Pataliputra are? I still have influence and will not let the stability of Pauravas wither away needlessly and let our fate be determined by King Ambhi and Dhana Nanda who is a low caste ruler and descendant of a lowly barber who you have served! A man who is led by his love of wine and whores? Are you fulfilling his desires or are you seeking our destruction and his gain?"

Chanakya laughed and replied, "Kali, your reputation as an astute politician is in serious question. The more you speak the more your tongue reveals how little understanding of political matters you have. I am not personally fond of Dhana Nanda, who you criticize so passionately, ironically like Dhana Nanda you also worship your own god of greed and material objects!"

The tension was high and Harbir's dislike of Kali took form. "This is the wedding of my daughter Divya! What political deceptions are you creating now, Kali? We should be united with Manish, who is a man of great morals and character. Chanakya has accomplished more than most—including you, Kali. Chanakya is the builder of minds while you are in the business of tearing minds down for your selfish gains!"

Kali was visibly angered, but Manish stepped in, giving Chanakya an avenue of escape from Kali and diffusing the rising tension.

Chanakya wished Rajesh the very best in his military career and gave him valuable advice to aid him in possible battle. The leader remarked on the beauty and intelligence of Lakshmi as he departed. Chanakya was succinct and sincere. "Manish, protect your family by helping to protect King Porus and his kingdom. I am proud of your success and I am proud of your children and the lives they are making for themselves. You must fight these Greeks bravely. The truth is that King Ambhi is not to be trusted and whatever your plan was to initiate a war against Alexander at Takshashila, it will be very difficult to successfully control. Nevertheless, I will do my very best to help you but it will not be soon. We can discuss plans to maintain the safety of your family if the unfortunate happens in battle. I will depart now, Manish, and remember that your worst enemy might not be Alexander."

With that, Chanakya departed, leaving Manish with more questions than answers. Kali Mehra also began preparations to leave, calling on his wife and sons while saying goodbye to Manish and giving him thanks for his invitation. As the Mehra family began their departure, Kali stated, "Manish, this was a fun affair and I wish you continued success. You have a great family. I also see you have enlisted the help of that lower caste boy. Additional help in household duties are always needed, especially when you have a large property and are continuously busy with your career. I have to say, it was nice seeing him partake in these ceremonies away from his household duties."

Manish laughed and responded, "Kali, this young man is named Anand Agrawal. He is a good friend of my son and we consider him part of the family. Anand is of good character and is a young man who understands the importance of hard work."

Kali added, "Well I understand, but I have been informed that Anand and your son had fought and were at odds previously. I simply believe that it is best our children socialize within our own warrior caste. This is of vital importance because throughout our lives we socialize with our families from our own caste and work within our own caste, so it is of utmost importance that we train our kids to excel and develop good relationships with people of our caste so they can make a better future for themselves. This is our tradition, Manish."

As Kali turned to leave, Manish said, "Yes, my son Rishan and Anand were at odds but what children are not? It is just the simple play that most boys are involved in just like us when we were children. The important thing is that their friendship has strengthened, and they have learned from each other and this boy Anand has been a true blessing for my son. Safe travels, Kali."

The guests were leaving now, including Priyanka. Rajesh and his new bride retired inside the Ramankrishna home. Manish decided to shorten the wedding ceremonies and would only enjoy a brief one tomorrow. As the guests took leave, Manish talked with Rishan; they had not spoken alone in quite some time. He asked Rishan about his academics and personal affairs as well as Anupa's absence, the current situation between the two, and about his relationship with Priyanka.

"Don't despair, my son. This is the way of life. As a man you will be disappointed in women and women may be disappointed in you. When you are young you will make foolish decisions and so will the young ladies you encounter. As a man you will have to first respect yourself and be confident in yourself and develop your mind, spirit, and body. As a father I will recommend a good woman for you as you get older and I will give you the opportunity to have the final say in the wife you eventually choose. Do not let someone control your mind, alter your perspective on life, and let you fail to see your own value."

Rishan felt relieved and happy that his father understood his sadness.

Manish also explained how difficult it was to find love with a woman of a higher caste—a social paradigm that Manish never fully accepted and one that his son Rishan would also not accept; they did not see it as a static station in life but a nature which one could transcend. Manish made Rishan understand that it was always possible to create fluidity between the castes in all aspects of life as long as a man continued to strive and develop his mind and body. Rishan was aware that life would not be as simple as his father's as war was on the horizon—a fact that had become public knowledge and led Rishan to seek the life of a military man. Reluctantly, Manish accepted. Perhaps it would serve the boy good to protect himself in case of his death. Manish could not protect his son's innocence any longer. Reality would come crashing down on the kingdom of Pauravas very soon and Rishan's boyhood would soon come to an end.

Several months had passed and Manish was anxious to learn new details on the plans he helped create against the advancing Greek forces. He was now in the Royal Palace awaiting intelligence on the outcome with the highest Royal advisers, including an eager Kali Mehra. In attendance by special permission were Manish's sons, Rajesh and Rishan. Rishan had joined martial education and Manish reasoned it was better for his youngest son to learn the art or warfare than be completely defenseless and fall victim to the Greeks. Everyone stood still and silent as King Porus and his younger brother arrived along with his sons. It was rare to see the most important members of the Royal Family together and this display further cemented the idea that major events were unfolding.

The first matter was to analyze how effective Manish's plan was and if Alexander's forces were weakened or if he was defeated, but no one was sure of the status of Ambhi and his military and if his entire force were involved in the initial clash.

The Royal Family was now seated in the Great Hall at the Royal Palace; in attendance were also the most senior leaders of the Pauravas military. The king rose and began to speak of the recent events taking place in Gandhara to the north. He read the reports which were promising at first, involving the secret agents under direction of King Porus who had infiltrated Ambhi's kingdom and managed to disguise themselves as members of military. A major disappointment to Manish's plan was revealed: although these agents convinced some troops to fight the Greeks, King Ambhi had made the decision to become an ally of Alexander. An agent was captured and now everyone was certain that Manish's plans were uncovered by King Ambhi and would be used against Pauravas. Some of the troops who turned against Ambhi had fled to join hostile forces determined to defeat Alexander in a valiant effort further north in the first battle against Alexander in the region.

In the winter of 327 B.C., the fighters fled into a mountain fortress to draw Alexander into a long, fierce battle. Alexander's reputation as a besieger had grown and preceded him and now his reputation would be tested at Aornos. Alexander's supply lines stretched dangerously thin over the Hindu-Kush and this battle threatened to cut the life blood of his army. Alexander was well read in the legendary exploits of Heracles and he was also aware that his hero was unable to reach a place in this region called Pir-Sar. This was his chance to surpass Heracles and cement his place in history. The mountain was fortified and stood at a bend in the Indus River with men guarding all sides of the mountain. The top was almost flat with natural water flows and crop growth which provided food and water for the men within the fortress. Alexander understood the importance of victory in this siege for the improvement of morale in his troops. He was pained by thoughts of his most recent purge which included the death of Callisthenes of Olynthus, the great nephew of his teacher Aristotle. Callisthenes was Alexander's historian who resided with his closest friends and family. His initial praise of Alexander ceased when he began questioning Alexander's adoption of Persian customs, echoing the opinions of Aristotle. This angered Alexander as Callisthenes began displaying Cleitus in a positive light; Alexander felt this made him seem as a most negative character, leading to Callisthenes' eventual torture and death. With this victory, Alexander would try to distance himself from these unfortunate events and set himself up for further glory and spoils of war in the southern areas of the Indus Valley.

Heavy snows had stopped falling, clearing a path as Alexander approached the mountain fortress at Aornos. Alexander was determined to keep his supply line intact and complete a swift victory. He split his forces as he took the right flank of the mountain path. General Craterus was left in charge of the supply line while General Ptolemy led the left flank. Ptolemy held an advance position and signaled Alexander with burning stacks of wood to alert the enemy. Alexander had completed the creation of an artificial level surface that allowed his catapults to be moved closer while withstanding endless efforts to kill his men with the use of large boulders thrown from above. After about four days, Alexander reached the summit with many of his enemies fleeing and subsequently intercepted. Reports stated that a large number were massacred by Alexander's soldiers. The path was clear for the march on the Indus Valley and Alexander began to approach King Ambhi's empire.

News of the alleged massacre at the hand of Alexander and his previous massacres after the siege at Tyre years earlier—among others—only served to strengthen King Porus' resolve. The information of Alexander's progress into Gandhara was now being discussed as the entire court received this information with careful analysis, confirming the worst fears of many.

With a powerful military, King Ambhi had met Alexander to offer peace and aid against King Porus. In fact, King Ambhi had already sent his diplomats to meet with Alexander when he was in Sogdonia, however Alexander's nervous nature was apparent upon witnessing King Ambhi's large force and thousands of men, cavalry, and horses. Ambhi escorted Alexander to their capital of Takshashila and promised to aid him in their advance into the kingdom of Pauravas, erasing any previous questions Alexander had regarding Ambhi's intentions. King Porus' advisers and military leaders remained quiet, not so much surprised but finally realizing their worst thoughts becoming a grim reality. This information was also provided by an official letter from Alexander himself, read aloud for everyone within the Great Hall. Kali Mehra glared at Manish as if the events unfolding were his doing.

King Ambhi Kumari, the descendant of the legendary figure Bharata of *The Ramayana* Holy Scriptures and the legendary Shakuni of the *Mahabharata*, had now openly invited Alexander to Takshashila—the center of learning and an important center of Hindu and Buddhist learning—without a fight. A letter written by a close aid of Alexander confirmed the union between Alexander and King Ambhi and although Alexander made no mention of the number of his combined force, everyone understood that King Ambhi would only serve to motivate Alexander to crush King Porus and Pauravas. However, Alexander stated that the forces of King Ambhi were now under his influence and the end of the letter also advised that King Porus should follow the example of his enemy King Ambhi and receive Alexander in peace.

Kali Mehra arose in anger, barely able to control the level of his voice. "My king, now you see that Manish's plans were a resounding failure. Witness the predicament your kingdom now confronts with a confident Alexander encouraged by your most vile enemy Ambhi supporting him with an additional 5,000 troops of his own army. Will he raise another Nike altar in our own capital just as he erected one for Athena Nike, their goddess of victory in war and wisdom, at Aornos?"

The Persian adviser Jahangir joined Kali in his cries against Manish, adding, "I agree with Kali. Although it pains me to go against my Persian people, it is vital that we ally ourselves to maintain the basic functions of this society."

Some in the court agreed with the objections against Manish. Rahim, another prominent Persian adviser, disagreed with Kali and Jahangir as he felt loyalty to King Porus and his decision.

Rajesh and Rishan were incensed at the accusations launched by Kali but were signaled by Manish to keep their emotions under control. The Persian Haxamanis rose from his seat and took to Manish's defense. "You accuse Manish of this failure but you do not have an alternative to his plans and did not enhance his initial plans whatsoever. You sit here and only offer negativity. You offend our agents that perished at Aornos by the hand of Ambhi, you offend King Porus, and most importantly you offend yourselves as members of the advisery body."

Manish stood and spoke. "It is easy to accuse me, but I tried to gain an alliance for King Porus with King Ambhi. I understood this was a losing proposition, therefore I tried to initiate a conflict between Alexander and King Ambhi. That conflict would have weakened both leaders and we could easily have beaten them."

Rishan stood, unable to control his temper; he yelled at Kali, accusing him of jealousy towards his father's character, sincerity, and rise in position.

Kali laughed. "You invite your child into this hall so he can show how weak these Ramankrishna men are! Why don't you mention your invitation of your ally Chanakya at the wedding of your eldest son Rajesh? Was the Royal Family aware of this? What conspiracies has that plotter Chanakya involved you in, Manish? Is Chanakya a member of your family as well? These Dravidian people should not be trusted and I question their status as high members of our warrior caste!"

Harbir answered Kali swiftly, "You are a pain and an internal sickness to this body and always have been. You do not have the courage to fight alongside Manish and for our King Porus who already agreed to Manish's plans so you disagree with him as well! Now you personally insult my friend and the family of my new son-in-law and the husband of my daughter! Shame on you. What about the outside connections and money you have collected for many years outside of the territory of Pauravas? What influence have you bought abroad and within this kingdom? Has that been disclosed to our king?"

Kali responded, "And what do you accuse me of, Harbir? Speak and make your opinions public!"

"Enough!" King Porus interceded. "The petty infighting between all of you offends me. Manish advised me well and his plans were partially successful as our agents encouraged the clash at Aornos. Our clash with Alexander was destined to be before Manish formulated his plans. We have been training and growing our powerful military for several years and have increased our war elephants to aid our military. I support and thank the advice that Manish has given me and continues to give me. Whether he is right or wrong, I know Manish's advice is sincere and I believe he is of sound moral character. I also respect his son Rajesh and his character and will support him in his efforts within our military. I look forward in

Rishan's growth and his future in our military in whatever capacity he chooses as well."

The legendary warrior General Spitakes was in attendance. Spitakes was a middle-aged man with a strong body, broad chest, and stood six feet tall. He was King Porus' cousin and a legendary fighter and leader. The young troops aspired to be all the warrior Spitakes was and young leaders aspired to have his leadership abilities. Spitakes had trained his other cousins—the children of King Porus—in the arts of war and one-on-one combat. The only generals higher than Spitakes in power were the king's sons, who he had trained since they were boys. Both sons were intelligent and the eldest Prince Porus was valiant while the younger son Parikshit was a slave to wine and the smoking of hemp plants possibly to shield his feelings of inadequacy and perhaps cowardliness in the face of battle and leadership. Spitakes was honorable in his bravery and controlled focus in battle also helped to improve the negative aspects of the Royal Family. Rishan

Spitakes finally voiced his opinions, stating, "I applaud Manish's bravery and his intelligence. We should cease this political infighting and unite towards one goal. It is time for our military to collaborate under a common cause and provide our military with a combined front, starting with our leadership among you, the advisers, the leaders within Pauravas, our military leadership, and our supreme leader King Porus and the Royal Family. Kali Mehra, you and your family have served long and faithfully but it does not serve you or us to insult the Ramankrishna family, for they have provided much help to our king. It will not help your politics and it surely doesn't help us militarily as we are now at war!"

King Porus now exclaimed, "Alexander sent me a letter advising me to follow the example of King Ambhi the coward. King Ambhi, my enemy who is more concerned with defeating me than fighting our common enemy and their allies. Alexander will have to fight us! If he does not the other people in the Punjab region will once again regain their bravery against him, but we already have this bravery within us. As your king, I will lead you into battle and crush Alexander once and for all! Alexander asked if I, your king, will receive him as my Ambhi already has and I will write to him and send him this message today saying I will meet him with the full might of my will and military!"

The entire hall cheered in thunderous agreement with their king. Kali, always politically astute, joined, showering praises upon his king. There was a new war on the horizon and life and death were uncertain. The only certainty was that there would be a change in Pauravas and that change was coming soon.

CHAPTER 8:
CLASH AT THE HYDASPES (326 B.C.)

"Water shapes its course according to the nature of the ground over which it flows; the soldier works out his victory in relation to the foe whom he is facing."
—Sun Tzu (*The Art of War*, 6:31)

Using King Ambhi's capital Takshashila as a base of operations, Alexander crossed the Indus River and approached the edge of the Hydaspes River where King Porus waited with a massive army. Roughly two months had passed since Alexander had arrived at his current destination. The Greeks had small boats which they used to cross the Indus and were ordered to break them into parts to be easily carried and used at the Hydaspes. Alexander led a 23,000-man infantry and over 9,000-man cavalry, the bulk which fought for roughly a decade and had improved their skills. Alexander's force was also supplemented by Persians and a segment of King Ambhi's army. King Ambhi decided to use his alliance with Alexander to decisively defeat King Porus.

King Porus commanded over 30,000 men with an additional 2,000 men in his cavalry and over 300 chariots. He also commanded experienced and trained war elephants numbering over 200 and personally kept a couple of them for himself.

Manish was relieved that his parents were safely south of the Magadha border in their home in the Ashmaka Kingdom. He also instructed his father to take some of their family wealth with them as well as important records for safekeeping. For several months he had argued with Lakshmi to take Rishan and Priya and stay safely outside of Puaravas in his parents' home, but she refused to leave. Manish and his eldest son were the only members of the family who were supposed to be involved in this war and although Manish was confident King Porus would be the victor, he also understood that one never truly knew the outcome until the battle ended. What made things worse was that his youngest son Rishan had recently snuck away to join the king and his vanguard. Rishan had been learning about warfare at military school, but was not ready to fight. However, he feared for his father's safety. At the young age of just twelve, Rishan was now in the forefront of a war against a man seeking to become the world's most powerful ruler. Manish was alerted to Rishan's presence just the previous day. He demanded that his wife remain at the family home along with Priya and they were instructed to abandon the house and flee south to join Manish's parents at the first sign of defeat.

It was a hot day and the sun was directly above, drenching all the men in sweat. Grey clouds began to group together—an ominous sign of things to come. Kali Mehra was dispatched to a unit under the leadership of King Porus' eldest son, much to the dismay of Kali, who wished to stay near the king. This was a decision made by the king to help ease tensions between Kali and Manish especially during battle, but the decision to have Manish close to himself only served to increase the strained relationship. However, that was not the immediate concern of King Porus and the military leadership. The main problem would be who would make the first strike. Porus' military force was on one side of the Hydaspes River and Alexander's had been gathered on the opposite side for nearly two months. Even with the supplemental force provided by Ambhi, King Porus' was still the superior in numbers. The

Greek army was well trained and battle hardened but Porus believed the fierceness and loyalty of his forces would prevail.

This potential war would serve to unify his people and provide a boost in his economy if he was successful. These thoughts as well as leading his men in victory in a potential battle invigorated King Porus. Alexander's cavalry had traveled up and down repeatedly with Alexander clearly in view, but recently Alexander was not visible—probably falling back to calculate his logistics and supply line aided by Ambhi and some of his new allies. The archers were still preparing and practicing their skills in preparation for the Greeks' potential river crossing. They were to position themselves on the river bank and launch a hail of arrows, sending the Greeks to an early death as they were defenseless and partially submerged. Some elephants were previously paraded in full view of the Greeks and King Porus observed the fear of some of their faces as they witnessed the powerful beasts of war. Perhaps the combination of the river crossing, facing King Porus' full military might, and his war elephants would dishearten the Macedonian Alexander and he would conclude his advance and agree to terms.

"No sight of Alexander," King Porus said, observing the opposite bank.

Alexander's troops had to cross this river eventually and King Porus was enjoying his advantage. King Porus had inherited an economically declining kingdom from his father, whom he had worked hard to slow down and was somewhat successful. In the last few weeks, a segment of the Greek army would mobilize and move parallel to the river bank. Manish made sure to keep his king alerted to every enemy troop movement and a segment of Porus' force would move parallel to the Greeks as they stood in front of each other on both sides of the Hydaspes River. King Porus equipped his additional archers with long arrows and long bows. The bottom end of the bow apparatus would rest on the earth and a press of the foot would launch arrows with devastating, armor-piercing force. After the first week of similar Greek troop movements, King Porus called on his eldest son Prince Porus to take command of the force whose responsibility was to counter this forward section of the current Greek force.

"There will be no surprises," King Porus exclaimed.

King Porus' other younger brother—also named Porus and nicknamed Porus Balarama—had recently joined the formations, supplementing his own contingent of fighters which he had personally overseen and led into King Porus' infantry units. Porus was nicknamed Balarama after God Balarama, who was Lord Krishna's elder brother. He wore his image on his shield and clothing and appeared as Balarama, shorter and heavily built as opposed to the towering seven-foot figure of his older brother. King Porus' elite warriors also wore Balarama's image on their shields.

Kali and his son Janeesh were placed under direct order of Prince Porus. Harbir and some of the Persians to include Haxamanis and Jahangir were also under the command of Porus' eldest son. Randeep had received a promotion to a high leadership position in King Porus' reserve forces and the Persian Raheem was serving as a member of the Royal archers. A large segment of the Royal cavalry was commanded by King Porus' cousin and legendary chieftain and commander Spitakes. The right flank was to be commanded by Porus' younger son Parikshit. Manish was to remain with King Porus, advising him on battle tactics as well as offering new ideas. Manish also held a weapon just in case the fight progressed towards the king. These were the current orders given but were subject to change if the battle was to take place after the rainy season.

King Porus previously gave specific general orders for his military, but now he grew complacent. Alexander was not initiating a cross and King Porus believed it would be another few months before he would. King Porus thought Alexander would wait because only after the rainy season would the river's water lower, making Alexander's crossing more feasible. This idea was further cemented by the fact that King Porus witnessed Alexander's logistics apparatus bring large supplies of grain for a long stay at their position. With the advice of Manish, the king would try to gain additional alliances for battle to cease Alexander's advances. King Porus gathered that Alexander would now wait until a new season, as he did not have additional forces or any clear strategy on how he would overcome his disadvantage. Manish speculated that perhaps Alexander had additional forces waiting to join him. To counter this potential threat, Manish advised King Porus to amplify his call on other regional kingdoms for supplemental forces. His plans were only countered by Kali Mehra, who was cynical of Manish'sidea of unity, reminding everyone of the long history of fighting between the kingdoms. However, King Porus viewed Manish's plan as the best counter. If Alexander's force did not increase it would make the battle even more favorable for King Porus.

The sun was beginning to set and the hot muggy air gave way to winds, cooling the unbearable heat from the last few weeks. The Greeks had ceased their usual parallel movements on their side of the river bank and now dark grey clouds increased, grew, and merged above. Perhaps the rains would come early; more time to possibly recruit from other regional armies against Alexander.

By late afternoon, the clouds had turned the sky dark while the winds began to increase in ferocity. Raindrops fell on the warriors, momentarily comforting their sun burnt skin. Manish advised the king to send his eldest son up river to make sure the Greeks would not move throughout the night. King Porus commented that rains would make the task of crossing hard and that it would place the Greeks in a vulnerable situation. However, he ordered his son to march his men about ten miles upstream.

Alexander was not currently visible. Perhaps he had fallen towards a rear position as he waited for other supplies from King Ambhi. The young Porus marched his troops as his father ordered and all throughout Kali and Jahangir detested the events that had led up to this clash while Janeesh remained silent and confident. They were statesmen but also warriors and had to carry out their duties along with the military in the ways of combat; only the older statesmen were allowed to remain absent from the initial combat.

Prince Porus halted his over 2,000-man cavalry and some infantry close to six miles from his father as lightning lit up the darkening skies and the thunder separated the lengthy silence. The men had stopped their idle chatter as they began to set up cover using parasols or articles of clothing to shield themselves from the rain. The sky was almost dark as Prince Porus stated the need to remain vigilant and prepared for any surprises . The rain was now beginning to come down hard, the sky was enveloped by darkness, and clouds covered the heavenly bodies which usually offered some light. Prince Porus stated they would march farther upstream in the morning. Many began to get some vital sleep while others remained awake conversing about their friends and family to take their minds away from the upcoming battle.

Unbeknownst to King Porus, Alexander had divided his forces, moving them upstream roughly eighteen miles of the Hydaspes River. There was a downpour of rain during the last six miles, but Alexander studied his enemy, restructured his military, and emphasized the use of light infantry to move and counter the war elephants. Alexander was still unaware of the number of these beasts of war but he anticipated a larger amount. There was a sizeable island near the middle of the Hydaspes and Alexander ordered his troops to wade through the river while it was swollen by steady rains. The skies were dark and ominous and some of his men feared crossing. Losing his patience, Alexander screamed the importance of moving forward to prevent trouble for the men behind them.

Alexander was now leading over 10,000 Greek infantry, 6,000 heavy cavalry, and 1,000 Persian and other Asian archers across the Hydaspes. The crossing generated noise, but it was muted by the storm. Some troops had crossed with inflated bags filled with straw which they used for flotation aids while some drowned because of the panic that overtook them. They reached the larger island and after a brief rest, Alexander ordered his other troops to also cross. This left a small portion of his forces behind to keep a central position between his main forces eighteen miles south. Alexander then crossed through the river, reaching a second smaller island. Many troops became hesitant to know they had to get in the raging waters once again. Alexander pointed to the other bank, keeping his hands fixed to train his soldiers' eyes to the destination, which finally came into view through multiple lightning strikes. Screaming at the full capacity of his tired lungs, Alexander encouraged his army of Greeks, Persians, and Asians across the final banks and finally split his entire force into three positions with him leading the advancing third position towards Prince Porus' direction.

Scouts on horseback arrived from the north at full gallop, catching the attention of some of the military and awakening some who had taken temporary rest. His heart racing, the scout quickly informed Prince Porus of the news. "The Greeks have made it across the river. I'm not sure of the number but they have many thousands of men and I have reason to believe that Alexander himself is now advancing towards you!"

Prince Porus at once sent his messengers towards his father's camp to inform him of these events as he told his men about the upcoming battle. The men put on their wool clothing between which was outfitted with raw, unprocessed cotton, and wrapped turbans around their heads. As Prince Porus rallied his men, the messengers returned with direct orders from his father to confront the Greeks as the king prepared to send reinforcements. Prince Porus moved his men with furious speed as soon as he received his father's orders.

With the rain still coming down with unrelenting ferocity, Prince Porus continued to lead his men up river. Even as the sun rose, the rain continued to fall; he took a moment to observe the sun when Kali and some of the others informed their commander regarding the first sighting of the Greek troops. Kali yelled for his son Janeesh to fight hard and with honor as a Greek line formed. Alexander had repositioned his light cavalry in the front and they began a fast advance. Prince Porus matched their speed when an arrow ripped through the neck of one of his troops and he observed him let out a scream as blood rushed out of his mouth while he reached for the arrow to no avail. While he perished, choking on his own blood, more arrows showered down on the front lines, killing a few and injuring many. Prince Porus called for formation and a unified advance to cut down the archers. As soon as he did this, Alexander ordered the advance of his heavy cavalry, barreling directly toward the center of Prince Porus' men. The battle was now raging on the southern bank of the Hydaspes.

Prince Porus encouraged his men to fight as hard as they could, and they plunged forward, fighting and killing, but the Greeks delivered massive strikes to the front line. The Greek kopis sword with their forward curving ends were now butchering the men, separating arms and legs from bodies. The Persian adviser Jahangir turned to run from the slaughter to no avail as a Greek soldier ripped a devastating wound across his neck and nearly decapitated him, causing Jahangir to fall forward, his eyes rolling back. Another Greek soldier struck him again, completely severing his head as his body continued to writhe on the muddy, blood-soaked ground. Within a short time, half of the troops under Prince Porus's leadership were dead. Prince Porus, with bow in one hand, shot at the Greek soldiers. He yelled for a messenger to let his father know of his devastating losses as he continued to fight bravely as he knew his father would.

The heavy chariots were rendered useless in the mud. They were bogged down, becoming easy targets for Greek arrows. Some men used their chariots to shield themselves while others abandoned them altogether. The Punjabis who remained fought a fierce battle but were eventually cut down themselves. The mud was now flooded with blood, vomit, and feces as some of the men lost their internal organs in the contest. Some Greeks and most of the forces led by Prince Porus were defeated and now lay dead. After a hard fought but disastrous battle throughout the night, the life of King Porus' son and heir to his throne was in danger.

Kali Mehra called for Prince Porus to temporarily retreat as they were overwhelmed by the surging Greeks and Prince Porus responded, "We should make a stand here until reinforcements arrive. I will not dishonor my father with cowardice. They will cut us down as we face them or they will cut us down with our backs turned. I choose to fight with bravery!"

Harbir called to his commander, stating his support of his orders and continuing his brave fight alongside Janeesh. Harbir killed some of the Greeks who were forming around Janeesh but was not able to give him full support; he was also outnumbered and had to fight for his own survival. Janeesh Mehra lunged forward through the Greek line, killing one Greek with a bamboo spear through the chest. Another Greek tried to kill Janeesh with a swing of his sword but he blocked the attempt, taking the sword from him and cutting off his arm as another Greek ran a sword through Janeesh's stomach, spilling his blood as he pulled the weapon out.

Kali joined, suffering an injury while killing a Greek solider in an effort to save his son. The loud screams of anguish of the battle muted his attempts to ask his son to retreat. Kali witnessed his son fall to the ground as he stabbed the Greek with an upward thrust. Janeesh finally took his last breath as another Greek ripped a sword through his chest.

Prince Porus now had less than half his original force with a few hundred men under his command now breaking their battle lines in a full retreat, yet he still called for his troops to keep fighting. The Persian Haxamanis fought bravely for his commander; seeing his men retreating, Prince Porus yelled orders to Harbir, his best warrior, to retreat and aid his father in the battle if he was to get killed. The rains had now slowed and the sun was rising, lighting up the battlefield and revealing thousands of troops continuing their advance. In the distance they witnessed Alexander himself coming towards them while motioning for the rest of his troops to cross the waters. Harbir expressed his desire to cut Alexander down but it would be hard to reach him. Prince Porus was overwhelmed by Greek opponents and Alexander tried to advance towards his position as a Greek soldier finally cut through his chest, killing the king's son. More men began to run in a frenzy as Harbir took a horse and reluctantly began to retreat. Haxamanis, who was sliced on his thigh and lying on the ground, was saved from a death blow by Harbir who carried the injured Persian on his horse. They rode away, leaving a few hundred fighting while another hundred retreating Punjabis perished under a hail of Greek arrows.

Kali Mehra retreated towards the king's position as Harbir and Haxamanis caught up to him. Harbir exclaimed his wish to cut Kali down himself if it wasn't for his importance in the king's court.

King Porus was advised of Alexander's advancement and he was informed by returning scouts that his reinforcements had been lost with some now retreating to his position. King Porus was also informed that the battle was now lost and that his son and potential heir was one of the victims. A segment of Alexander's army was still across the river—a tactic that kept King Porus fixed in his current position. King Porus realized that he had lost his advantage and decided to reposition his forces and advance towards a secondary position. The king learned about the initial clash that took the life of his son and to make full use of his chariots and Royal archers, he commanded his men to stop at the first sign of relatively dry, solid ground. They were to face Alexander and defeat him then deal with the rest of his army wherever they crossed. To successfully accomplish this, he had to have full use of his military. King Porus understood that he would have to defeat Alexander quickly and decisively.

King Porus left a reserve position at his rear in case the army still stationed across the river bank chose that location to cross instead. As King Porus reorganized his forces, his younger son Parikshit remained in command of the right flank. King Porus' young brother Amar remained at his side, ready to confront the Greeks. Harbir was stationed in the reserve forces both to give him much needed rest and to help Manish and Kali's sons in battle. Randeep Mehra had a large leadership role while Rajesh Ramankrishna had a minor one. The king's younger brother, Porus Balarama, supplemented his brother's infantry. The Royal archers were placed at the far left and right flanks and over 200 war elephants were positioned in the front of the infantry with a few reserved for the king.

King Porus left Manish's youngest son Rishan behind the reserve line and although it was too late now for his escape, he was relatively safe and ready to flee in case the battle was lost. However, the king felt quite confident as he witnessed Alexander and his army arriving. King Porus waited for Alexander with a combined force of 30,000 infantry and his roughly 2,000-man cavalry were divided in half into 1,000 each, occupying King Porus' extreme left and right flank.

Alexander approached at a distance on top of a beautiful black horse with a large head—a majestic creature, King Porus thought. As he began to organize his archers, the king observed that a small portion of Alexander's men were marching upstream, leaving a sizeable portion on the opposite bank of the Hydaspes. This did not bother Porus; his combined force outnumbered Alexander's by more than two to one. Howeveer,he observed that Alexander's roughly 6,000-man cavalry outnumbered his own by roughly four to one. How would Alexander make use of this specific advantage? Alexander's 16,000-man infantry were tired and slow to reach their leader. With his men in position, King Porus wondered if he should take the offensive or let Alexander lead himself into a devastating battle with his infantry and elite units.

After a slow but steady movement of Porus'

military for around three hours, King Porus found that the mud had somewhat dried and the rains had slowed to a drizzle while the grey clouds began to disperse. King Porus rallied his military and prepared them for what would be a brutal last clash. He would use his Royal archers and his war elephants to shock and destroy his enemies.

He noticed Kali Mehra desperately trying to guide his horse through the muddy river bank and trying to hide his anger and despair. King Porus asked Kali about his last strategic position and Kali described the slaughter and the loss of his son Janeesh. He also relayed how he almost lost his own life, to which King Porus replied with the need to prepare for the possible loss of his life once again. This would be a ferocious fight and the king was not prepared to lose. Alexander's army was now rapidly approaching and many of the soldiers who were fleeing the initial clash were cut down by arrows and swords while some escaped from the battlefield. In the distance, some men were seen fleeing and an injured Haxamanis was hunched over on the back of Harbir's horse. Not far behind them was the Macedonian led Greek military.

As Harbir made it safely to the king, he was given a position in the rear reserve unit to rest and aid both Randeep Mehra and his son-in-law Rajesh Ramankrishna. Haxamanis crawled to a rear position with inexperienced young troops that were the last option in battle. General Spitakes was mounted on horseback on the right flank awaiting orders from King Porus while holding his military in formation. Manish advised his king to attack the Greeks and take the offensive; if they moved quickly they could crush Alexander's force.

King Porus replied, "We have the superior troops and they will not outmaneuver us. It will come down to our infantry and our archers will hit their cavalry if they dare charge."

Manish advised King Porus to move his position towards the left near the bank of the Hydaspes to deny any flanking option, but King Porus felt it would pin his troops in a dangerous position near the swollen waters. The rain had stopped, and the sky was now devoid of clouds. Alexander's archers riding on horseback launched their arrows towards the Punjabi forces, killing several Punjabis and nearly hitting General Spitakes in the head. Reluctant to break his line, King Porus held his position as Alexander unleashed his entire cavalry directly towards the left flank.

Mud was kicked up by the horses moving at break-neck speed. King Porus ordered General Spitakes to lead his thousand men behind his units to join his cavalry on the left flank. It was then that Alexander and Coenus, along with 2,000 of his cavalry, turned the opposite way into King Porus' now defenseless right flank. Coenus swept behind the king's lines and it was then that Alexander led his own 2,000-man cavalry to the extreme left. Alexander's archers opened a relentless barrage of arrows on King Porus' cavalry with deadly results. King Porus asked everyone to maintain the line as he went to join the main infantry. Avoiding arrows, King Porus mounted his elephant as the Greeks stood in awe of the over seven foot tall king atop his war beast with a menacing look upon his face. Amar joined King Porus on top of an elephant of his own. King Porus and his elephants pulled Alexander away from his cavalry and in front of his infantry.

Some Greeks were frightened as the elephants charged; their horses had lost control, killing many of them as the elephants let out triumphant cries. King Porus ordered his archers to begin shooting. Haxamanis and the other archers could not gain their footing and were not able to find stable ground in the mud to anchor their powerful six foot bows; they could not launch a consistent number of arrows towards the Greeks. Haxamanis killed several Greeks but it took a lot of effort to release just one arrow, which also tired the few that continued to be successful in this endeavor.

Haxamanis and his fellow archers were still trying to shoot but were hindered by the loss of stability and the swirling winds did not help matters. A few archers launched errant arrows, finding their targets among their fellow brothers in battle. The Greeks crashed into the archers as they reached for their swords. The Greeks smashed them with their shields then began to cut them down. Haxamanis jumped back at the initial onslaught but received a blow by a Greek shield, sending him on his side, his face landing in the blood-soaked mud. Trying to gain a breath, he swallowed other men's blood and filth, causing him to cough as he reached for his sword and slashed a Greek soldier in the leg. As he managed to get back to his feet, another Greek soldier swung his kopis sword at Haxamanis and he bent to avoid the blow, causing the offending Greek to fall on his face. Haxamanis kicked the soldier as he struggled to stand. Noticing his own sword beyond reach, he took one of his arrows and stabbed the Greek through his heart. More Greeks were coming and he took a horse to flee as the archers faced overwhelming odds. Haxamanis decided to join the fight alongside the infantry.

The war elephants dealt massive blows. Fearing these giant beasts of war, the Greeks' horses trampled their own men. King Porus ordered unused arrows to be salvaged and used from the relative safety atop the elephants. The mighty weight of over 200 of these animals snapped at legs, arms, heads, and chests as they tore through the Greek infantry.

Alexander momentarily galloped behind his infantry questioning the availability of his own war elephants—he only possessed twenty. Alexander had taken them in his war against Persia at Gaugamela, however he now faced the very same people who supplied Persia with these beasts and he learned quickly how effectively they were used by Porus. Alexander realized he could not compete with King Porus' larger and better trained war elephants, deciding that his troops should blind them if they managed to get close. This was no easy task; each elephant was surrounded by Porus' infantry and had archers launching arrows at the advancing Greeks.

Mud and blood filled the air in an ugly mist and the smell of death combined with the deafening sounds of elephants and men. A few Greeks, injured by arrows, were able to blind some of the elephants. This caused the animals to panic, tossing some of Porus' men. General Spitakes took charge of his men, racing behind Alexander's cavalry which was now surrounding King Porus' infantry. Spitakes ferociously advanced towards the right side of Alexander's cavalry units, delivering devastating blows and commanding his men to crash into the cavalry so as to draw them away. An arrow hit Spitakes' horse, causing the animal to suddenly change direction and buck upwards. Spitakes fell into the mud surrounded by Greek cavalry and he rose as the approaching enemy sought to take their prize. Spitakes fought two Greeks, landing blows to his opponents and using a Greek sword to make a swift end to the contest. Taking a horse and witnessing the rapid losses of the troops he personally commanded, Spitakes raced to the rear to join the reserve forces led by Randeep Mehra.

The Greek Phalanx, initially devastated by Porus' war elephants, now managed to blind many of the beasts. This caused them to panic and many of the men on top were no longer able to control them, plummeting to the ground. Many of the elephants trampled their former handlers as they fled the carnage. The Greek infantry gained confidence where before they were occupied with fear. King Porus continued to launch arrows from atop his elephant but as the Greeks began to surround him, he circled back to encourage his other men.

King Porus' younger brother, Porus Balarama, continued to fight himself atop his own elephant. In the distance, he saw the Greek King Alexander heading straight at him. It was an opportunity to deal a devastating blow to the enemy's army even as they were beginning to turn the tide of battle.

Randeep Mehra was leading the charge to join the main infantry unit along with Rajesh Ramankrishna. Harbir rode his own horse alongside them with his son-in-law Rajesh. Some of the non-combatants left behind were Rishan Ramankrisha and some female members of King Porus' family along with family members of other men who were fighting. Karna Mehra, who at fourteen was two years older than Rishan, was available to fight as a reservist. However, his powerful father had advocated for his absence from the main infantry forces, believing the fight would end in an agreement of a victory. But now the Greeks were outnumbering King Porus' forces and threatening to overrun them. The Persian adviser Raheem, who had been critically injured, writhed in pain on the muddy ground as he received treatment from some of the ladies and Royal Palace doctors.

Rajesh instructed his little brother Rishan to begin to flee with the rest of the non-combatants but Rishan and Karna both remained as the carnage continued. Manish followed behind Rajesh to make a last stand along with their king.

Alexander rapidly approached Porus Balarama. His infantry was led by a strong, charismatic general named Seleucus, and sensing victory, Alexander charged towards King Porus' younger brother. Crushing several Greeks, Porus Balarama delivered an arrow to Alexander's majestic black horse Bucephalus. Alexander's favorite horse was in critical condition, causing the animal to reduce his speed. King Porus, who had joined his last remaining reserve forces, now made his way back towards the rear of the battle. Leading his remaining men into the thick of the battle, Randeep Mehra clashed with Greeks who had broken through the rear of the main infantry and was knocked off his horse. However, he was able to defeat some of the Greek soldiers.

Randeep ordered his men to approach the center of the conflict with Harbir advising they should concentrate on defeating the incoming Greeks who had cut through King Porus' main infantry. Rajesh also recommended this, however Randeep cursed them both, encouraging his men to press on. Randeep's ride was halted by Greeks who had crashed into his flank, sending Randeep into the ground. Desperately trying to get up, he received a slash across his right leg and another reached his face on his left side. Blood rushed into his eye, nose, and mouth and he struggled for air; he began to panic as he feared the same fate of his brother. Randeep tried to scream for a retreat but the blood cut his voice short as he crawled on all fours in view of his men. only Rajesh was able to fight his way through, saving Randeep Mehra's life by killing the Greek soldier who was about to deliver the death strike.

"We should call a tactical retreat and continue the fight by regrouping," Randeep exclaimed, his voice trembling with fear. Rajesh carried Randeep to the rear, stating his need to help his father.

Alexander's horse Bucephalus was wounded as Alexander attempted to circle towards King Porus as Porus Balarama approached with his elephant. One of Porus' elite guards shot a poisoned arrow, glancing Alexander as he fell off his horse. Commander Spitakes, who had survived overwhelming odds, raced towards King Porus as the Greeks advanced. Just as Porus Balarama tried to trample Alexander beneath his elephant, Greek infantrymen blinded the animal, jolting him and his men off their perch and his men fell to their deaths under the same elephants they commanded. Porus Balarama plummeted to the ground, injured but still able to fight. King Porus trampled his enemies in an attempt to approach Alexander, observing most of Alexander's military was crossing the Hydaspes and would soon join the battle. Greek soldiers had managed to climb onto King Porus' elephant, pulling him down. Amar was knocked from his elephant; he broke his leg and was killed by Greek soldiers while on the ground. King Porus fought valiantly, looming over his opponents; his over seven foot height was sight to behold. Alexander was wounded but safe under the protection of his troops as his general Seleucus approached him along with a large segment of his infantry.

Spitakes continued to fight, invoking fear in the Greeks. Running to aid King Porus, Spitakes stumbled over a mud-covered rock and injured his foot. As he got up, he grappled with a Greek soldier who managed to land a blow to his leg. Spitakes then received a critical injury across his stomach, spilling out its contents onto the ground. Trying to gather his entrails, he managed to stab his enemy when another Greek brought a sword straight down the middle of his neck and right shoulder. Spitakes the legendary warrior had perished in battle with Alexander's army encircling King Porus.

Rajesh Mehra joined his father Manish, now fighting against overwhelming odds. Surrounded by his loyal fighters, Porus Balarama was able to defend his brothers. King Porus' young son Parikshit was now in danger as he was pinned in the middle of the infantry he was leading.

Parikshit continued to fight as Seleucus led a bloody charge against the young prince. Seleucus sought to personally kill him but had trouble getting to the center of King Porus' main infantry. More Greek commanders encircled King Porus' infantry while Greek commander Craterus actively pursued retreating men who gave up the fight to save their own lives. Commander Seleucus wanted to set himself apart from the other Greek commanders and he believed defeating Prince Parikshit was the best way to achieve this. Seleucus was near the young prince when Parikshit was finally cut down and trampled by his own men in the confusion.

The death of the young prince and King Porus' younger brother Amar was a devastating setback for the morale of the king's infantry. Alexander's horse Bucephalus lay dead on the ground and he asked for another horse at a safe distance from the rear battle where King Porus was surrounded. He viewed King Porus and his perseverance as he continued to fight and faced overwhelming devastation. Alexander was also tired and battle-weary and his men were exhausted. Alexander understood that the weather also aided him in the battle as King Porus' military was severely limited by the heavy rains. He was not aware of how many more armies he had to face and felt he could negotiate a peace treaty with King Porus.

Manish was injured but continued to fight alongside his king. Rajesh entered the battle but suffered a blow to his left knee and Manish now had to aid his oldest son who was now limited in movement. Seeing this from afar, Rishan Ramankrishna was motivated to aid his father despite others advising him against this—including Karna Mehra, who stated he was not prepared for battle. Raheem also asked Rishan to avoid the battle in an effort to save Rishan's mother the anguish of losing all the men in her family. Porus Balarama received a strike to his right arm, hindering his ability to wield weapons, but continued to fight on with his brother. Rishan stated his need to help his father and upon seeing his determination, Kali who was with the boys in the rear advised his son and Rishan not to join the battle. However, Raheem stated, "Be valiant, young one," as his eyes rolled back in his head.

Raheem had drawn his last breath and was now dead on the ground, finally succumbing to his wounds.

Rishan took a horse and sword and rode towards the battle with trepidation and air seeming to escape his lungs. As he approached, he witnessed his father on the ground wrestling a Greek soldier. Rishan slowed his horse and jumped off. Raising his sword with fear in his heart, he closed his eyes and brought down the sword towards the Greek man with all the strength his body could muster, landing in the center of the Greek man's back. Manish yelled at his son to strike him again and Rishan brought the sword down once more, hitting the Greek man's head and causing him to fall forward. Manish was able to get up and help defend his son from approaching Greek infantry. They were surrounded when the Greek leader Commander Coenus exclaimed that Alexander was ready to come to an agreement with King Porus.

A Greek man was rushing towards Rishan's brother who lay defenseless on the ground when Rishan picked up a stone, throwing it at the Greek and hitting his head and causing him to fall back to the ground. Coenus again ordered the Greeks to stop their aggression until Alexander arrived to meet King Porus.

The Greek army was now almost completely across the Hydaspes River and were about to start crossing at a third crossing point closer to where the main battle had been. With no other allies aiding him in the battle and the loss of roughly sixty-five percent of his military, King Porus decided to discuss terms with Alexander. He had received various wounds in the midst of battle including one in the shoulder he did not initially notice. As the battle was coming to a close, the realization of the great losses to his military coupled with the information of King Ambhi's presence in his territory changed King Porus' perspective from a victorious leader to a man subject to his enemy's whims. King Porus was also informed of his devastating personal losses including the death of the potential heir to his throne as well as his son Parikshit and his younger brother Amar. King Porus had also witnessed the death of his cousin, chief, and commander Spitakes and many of his advisers and elite military soldiers. King Porus did not want further losses to his military and wanted to gain some time to analyze the response of other kings in the Punjab, including Dhana Nanda, who had the largest military in the region. Porus Balarama however, wanted to keep the battle raging as he felt that despite their losses the Greeks were on the verge of losing their morale.

A light rain began to fall again as some clouds drifted overhead, peppering the living and wounded alike, falsely advertising a possible torrential rainstorm common of monsoon season. The Greek soldier injured by Rishan now ceased to writhe in the mud, succumbing to internal injuries and blood loss as Manish comforted Rishan and explained to him the realities of war. Rishan actively participated in the battle despite his young age, innocence, and his father's wishes. However, Manish would not punish Rishan. Instead, he would devote his time to comforting him and he asked his king if he could accompany his youngest son away from the battlefield and home to his worried mother. As Manish prepared to escort Rishan away, Alexander and his commanders approached King Porus.

Alexander's tanned light skin was covered with blood and mud and although his body appeared worn, the fire in his eyes was enough to light a starless night. Manish and Rishan noticed this iron will in Alexander—a feature Rishan would rarely see in others throughout his life. Alexander approached with some senior leadership of King

Ambhi's military to help with the translation to ease communication between the two leaders. King Porus asked for the young Rishan to be his own translator to help confirm that the correct information was conveyed, much to the dismay of Manish.

Alexander was impressed to find such a young intellectual warrior that was fluent in the Greek language. He was also informed that the actions of this young warrior brought about the death of one of is elite men; surely this boy would mature to become a great sage and warrior. Perhaps he would be an asset to Alexander when he established his borders and unified his new kingdom.

Rishan Alexander was also impressed with King Porus' courage and determination and saw a reflection of himself and how he wished to behave in battle in victory or defeat. This battle was particularly brutal and tiring for Alexander's men. Alexander's scouts also talked of other kingdoms with much larger armies and fearsome fighters, specifically mentioning Dhana Nanda. Alexander was interested in continuing his progression and hoped to create new alliances and strengthen his forces in order to conquer the kingdoms of the east and south. Alexander understood the importance of creating an alliance with King Porus, who could have easily continued to wage war or perhaps form his own alliances against him. A prompt and comprehensive agreement with King Porus was ideal for strategic purposes in his future battles as well as to assuage the undercurrent of anger and fear growing within the hearts of Alexander's military.

Surrounded by the top leadership of the former combatants, Alexander finally met King Porus. Light rain fell as King Porus approached Alexander. Alexander set up an operations center and was seated with many of his commanders. A towering figure, King Porus dwarfed Alexander and the rest of the Greeks.

Through translators, Alexander asked, "And how do you wish to be treated?"

King Porus responded, "As a king to be respected with honors bestowed on me as a descendant of my ancient

Royal Dynasty."

The two leaders began negotiations as Rishan confirmed the accuracy of the interpretations by the translators. Expressing his continued satisfaction with Rishan, Alexander said it would be his honor if he could meet with the young man at a future date. Manish agreed with Alexander and asked to be excused from the battlefield so that he could return his son Rishan to their family home to comfort the women in their household who were anxiously waiting for them. Manish and Rishan hurried home, much to the relief of Lakshmi and Priya.

Both King Ambhi and King Porus were to retain their territories and rule as client kings under Alexander's rule to represent Alexander in the Punjab. King Ambhi became angered with this agreement; he felt his aid to Alexander was not reciprocated. King Ambhi was a bitter rival to King Porus and he expressed his animosity to Alexander and felt he would be given a larger kingdom, which also belonged to King Porus. Alexander would find political avenues to help resolve the rivalry between these two enemies.

As the sun began to set, Alexander proclaimed new cities in the very location of the battle he fought, naming it Nicaea to honor the Greek goddess of victory. On the other opposite bank of the Hydaspes where Alexander had stood with his anxious military for roughly two months fighting a mental battle with King Porus and fighting the River Hydaspes itself, he founded another city called Alexandria Bucephalus in honor of his majestic steed who had succumbed to injuries just hours before. The rains ceased once again as the wounded were treated by doctors and the dead gathered for quick burial by their friends and brothers in war.

Alexander had secured the main territories formerly belonging to the Persian Empire for his own and now he sought to expand the boundaries further. There was no major celebration after Alexander's victory—he was aware of the rising tension within his army. Hephaestion stated that perhaps it was time for Alexander to return to Babylon and solidify his empire. From there, Alexander could easily travel to Macedonia and increase his ability to suppress rebellions that were constantly fomenting. Alexander agreed, but he felt that he should march east and asked Hephaestion for advice on how to motivate his military. Alexander was eager to continue east before turning back west where he would initiate the invasion of the Thamud people of Arabia as well as possibly go west of Macedonia in an effort to perhaps lend support to the Samnites against the Romans. But first Alexander had to find a way to unify all the people and religions of his new empire and encouraged the Greeks to take Persian women for marriage. Alexander continued his conversations with Hephaestion about his ideas for the future of his new empire until the Macedonian leader fell asleep.

CHAPTER 9:
HYPHASIS (326 B.C.)
"Selfish desires and animosity obscure the purpose of leadership."
—The Bhagavad Gita

In his great wisdom, Hephaestion was busy reorganizing the logistics for the Greek army, leaving Alexander available to host gatherings in an effort to improve his cultural understanding of his new subjects. Roughly a month after the battle at the Hydaspes, Hephaestion had completed a majority of his duties while Alexander positioned and stabilized his new territories. Alexander also invited his new allies to several gatherings to solidify his territories before proceeding with further conquests. What was seen as a weakness by his fellow Greeks and Macedonians was viewed as vital by Alexander in the construction and stabilization of his new kingdom. Alexander's new subjects were no longer limited to Macedonians and Greeks, but Asians as well and just as King Cyrus did hundreds of years prior, Alexander would work to unite his subjects. These gatherings were also an occasion to create and reaffirm certain political appointments, designate responsibilities, and for an uplifting of morale. Alexander also invited local wise men of the region as he previously had enjoyed conversations with them along his march and between battles. Alexander loved intellectual conversations and learning from other perspectives which added to the rich knowledge base he had attained in Macedonia under Aristotle. The Greeks had trouble conquering the exotic languages of these sages and would often rename them by physical features they had or statements they heard them make.

The Greeks also began to rename many of the regions, mountains, and bodies of water. They gave these areas Greek names to show their dominion as well as changing the original exotic names of these regions into a Greek alternative that rolled easier from the Greek tongue. Alexander himself renamed areas, marking important events or to respect his favorite gods. He also sought to create more Alexandrian cities that he sought to build as important financial and political centers throughout his empire. These philosophers that Alexander met were referred to as "gymnosophists" due to their lack of clothing or at times full nudity. Many of these wise men were also behind several successful rebellions against the Greek forces and had been captured by Alexander.

Alexander was excited to relate some of his favorite stories to his guests. Several of these stories were the favorites of some of his commanders and personal guards, including Nearchus, Hephaestion, and Ptolemy. It was late afternoon and Alexander was dressed in his comfortable Persian clothing. The day was coming to an end and a cool breeze blew through the court. King Porus and other important dignitaries sat beside Alexander. Kali Mehra, still mourning his son Janeesh's death, was in attendance. Kali's eldest son Randeep was still nursing his wounds and after insisting he accompany his father to this occasion, his youngest son Karna was there as well.

Manish had been personally invited by Alexander who was intrigued by the actions of the young Rishan on the battlefield. Rajesh had trouble walking due to his leg injuries but his father asked him to come. King Ambhi was not in attendance as Alexander felt it was unwise to have him and King Porus share words at this time; he would have to find a way to create political stability between these two men if they were to retain their leadership of their respective regions and maintain peace within Alexander's dominion.

Alexander was also accompanied by a wise sage from Takshashila named Sphínēs, but renamed Kalanos due to the fact that he greeted the Greeks in his language saying, "kallāṇa." Kalanos was a follower of the great teacher named Siddhartha Gautama. Alexander also eagerly awaited the arrival of the wise Chanakya.

The Macedonian leader asked for some wine as he began to feel comfortable with his guests. Food was plentiful and music was played for the enjoyment of all. Alexander introduced his translators and asked for Rishan to join the conversation as he wanted to display Rishan's command of the Greek language. After a few drinks, Alexander began his story of his conversations with these philosophers. Alexander had previously imprisoned ten philosophers who opposed him and had motivated a rebel named Sabbas to revolt against him. He had sat them down, asking them difficult questions and decided that the oldest sage would judge and rank the answers. Alexander would hold a trial and question these sages.

Alexander asked the first sage, "Which is more numerous: the living or the dead?"

The sage responded, "The living, for the dead are not among us anymore."

Alexander asked the second sage, "Which contains more animals and larger animals: the land or sea?"

Responded the thinker, "The land has more animals, for the sea is but part of the land."

Alexander asked the third astute man, "Which is the smartest of all creatures and what has more power: life or death?"

The man responded, "The animal who remains hidden from man is the smartest, and life, like the rising sun, is more powerful than death, like the setting sun, for the sun's rays are more powerful and significant as the sun rises."

Amazed at the answers, Alexander a asked the fourth sage, "Why did you encourage Sabbas to revolt against me?"

The sage responded, "I asked him to live nobly or to die nobly."

Alexander asked the fifth man of wisdom, "Which came first or is older: day or night?"

The sage responded, "The day after the night by one day."

Alexander momentarily stopped the questioning, stating he had forgotten the order of the answers and causing laughter among some of the listeners. Alexander asked the sixth wise man, "What should a man do to receive the greatest love or admiration?"

He replied, "To be powerful, fearless, yet know how to rule without causing fear in others."

The Greek king then asked the seventh man of wisdom, "How can you become god-like or a god?"

The seventh wise man responded, "A man cannot do the impossible."

Alexander asked the eighth man, "Who can't we lie to?"

To which the sage responded, "To god, for He is all-knowing."

Alexander asked the ninth sage, "How long should a man live?"

The sage laughed. "When that man feels he is more useful dead than alive."

Alexander asked the last philosopher, "What is better: the right or left side?"

The last wise man answered, "The left because even the sun wanders from the left to the right and even the baby suckles the mothers left breast."

Rishan listened carefully. Rishan had an interest in religious and philosophical discussions and felt intellectual conversation and debate were more intriguing than the physical competition he thoroughly enjoyed.

The other guests laughed as Alexander shared his story, then King Porus asked, "So Alexander, who provided you the worst answer and who did you kill?"

Alexander previously designated the oldest sage as

a judge to rank the answers in the order of worst to best so as to put the men to death in order depending on their answers.

The sage responded, "All have answered worse than another."

Alexander rejected the answer as it failed to rank the quality of responses and the sage responded, "You also reject your own guidelines, for you stated that you would kill he who provided the worst answer."

Alexander smiled and let out a small laugh although he tried to remain serious. Alexander rewarded the men with gifts, interested to learn more of their ways of life and perspectives.

A slender Greek man seated near Alexander was busy in conversation with Alexander's commanders. This man's name was Onesicritus and he was documenting Alexander's conversations and travels for future generations. Some members of the military regarded Onesicritus as disingenuous in his duties and disliked his appointment of leader of Alexander's ships, but Onesicritus and Alexander had a great relationship and the commanders kept their opinions to themselves. Onesicritus stated how Alexander loved to converse with men of high mental capacity and recalled how his own famous teacher Diogenes of Sinope had intrigued Alexander upon their first meeting. While everyone had labored in preparation for the Macedonian king's arrival, Diogenes carried his tub up and down a short pass, stating that he would also appear to be occupied with a task. Alexander sought out Diogenes and asked him what he could do, to which Diogenes responded, "You can move. Stay away from my sunlight."

Everyone laughed loudly, including Alexander.

Rajesh also joined the conversation, attracted by the laughter as the wine continued to flow. Kali stood silently at a distance, rarely sharing a word with others. Rajesh asked about this man Diogenes and events related to this interesting thinker. Onesicritus stated how he disliked the great Plato and regarded a man by the name of Antisthenes as the true heir to the great Socrates. Diogenes did not like the abstract thinking of Plato and challenged his ideas frequently, once bringing a featherless chicken to Plato's Academy to challenge Plato's description of man as a featherless biped. Plato subsequently included nails to his definition of a man. Alexander stated that his childhood teacher was Aristotle who was himself a student of Plato and everyone laughed once again.

Alexander stated, "Once Diogenes announced he was cosmopolitan, a man of the world; he did not limit himself to a Greek city-state. That is another reason I seek to create a large society where people are free to practice their beliefs and share with each other their perspectives and knowledge. An empire where man and woman can join and create a family without regard to where they were born or other devices that divide."

The guests enjoyed hearing of this Greek philosopher Diogenes and his actions. Onesicritus also mentioned how Diogenes would urinate on people he disliked, defecate in public, and even pleasure himself in front of others, causing them to question his behavior, to which he responded, "If only I can relieve my hunger by rubbing my belly."

Another story depicted Diogenes visiting a rich man's home and he was warned not to spit within the house. Diogenes chose to resolve the issue by spitting into the face of the man who had initially warned him, stating he could not find a "meaner receptacle." The laughter continued and Rishan was amazed a man could behave in such a way and still be considered a man of wisdom. King Porus then stated the similarities between Greek thinkers like Diogenes and the followers of Siddhartha Gautama or Gautama Buddha who had lived in the northern regions over a hundred years earlier. Upon learning that this great sage known as the Buddha taught in various locations to include Takshashila, Alexander became excited and introduced a sage he had encountered during his stay with King Ambhi in Takshashila.

Alexander beckoned his new friend who the Greeks called Kalanos. Kalanos was an old slender man in his early seventies who possessed great knowledge. Manish relished this opportunity for Rishan to have access to minds like that of this man. Onesicritus spoke about Alexander's first encounter with Kalanos—a meeting which occurred when Alexander was interested in meeting Kalanos' teacher Dandamis. Alexander was told to strip naked because Kalanos believed that all people were the children of gods and they must meet as equals. After Alexander spoke with Kalanos, he was informed of Dandamis' continued refusal to meet him. After some time, Alexander met Dandamis after threatening to decapitate the great leader. Kalanos now spoke through a translator of what Dandamis said. Dandamis sent Alexander the message: "You cannot be a living god, for God the Creator is a source of water, food, light, and life. You are not a god, Alexander, for you love violence and are mortal. Even if you take my head you cannot take my soul, which will depart this mortal vehicle. We Brahmins do not fear death or lust for gold so King Alexander has nothing of value to offer me. If he needs me he will come to me!"

Kalanos now spoke about how Alexander met with Dandamis for roughly an hour and upon meeting Alexander, Dandamis stated, "I have nothing to offer you; we have no want of treasure or gold. God is not a source of violence but provider of water, food, light and life. We love our God and do not fear death, whereas you love pleasure, gold, and violence. You fear death and despise God or try to falsely represent him on earth." Alexander stated he simply wanted to learn from Dandamis and did not wish harm upon him.

In his thirst for knowledge, Alexander sat in the forest with Dandi-Swami, as his followers referred to him, and learned much from the old sage. Alexander learned about the power of freedom from materialism and responsibility. He had inherited his position from his father Philip II and he was to live life as any king. Alexander respected great kings just as he respected great thinkers. The standard Alexander continued to hold was that of King Cyrus the Great who he actively sought to surpass.

Alexander often read *Kúrou paideía* or *Cyropaedia* which meant *"The Education of Cyrus"*, written by a student of Socrates named Xenophon of Athens. He also respected his contemporaries such as King Porus; he understood the importance of forming this alliance as his military was fragile and these territories east of the Hydaspes would be difficult to administer. As he was pondering his future actions, he met Kali Mehra's eyes and called him over to join them in conversation. Alexander was curious to learn the status of Kali's eldest son Randeep, who had suffered significant injuries during their battle just over a month before.

King Porus was the first to greet Kali as he sat down, giving his condolences for the loss of his son Janeesh and showing concern for the continuing recovery of Randeep. Karna sat silently next to his father. Manish was the next to offer his condolences, making it known to everyone how the death of Janeesh weighed heavily on his mind, as Alexander embraced Kali, speaking of Randeep's bravery. Kali acknowledged the various guests but showed little appreciation for Manish's words—an act that did not go unnoticed by Manish. Kali expressed unwavering support for King Porus and his respect for the compromises made between him and Alexander. Kali also advocated for peace and stability for the people of Pauravas under the new agreements set forth.

Trying to ease Kali's spirits, Manish mentioned the topics of the previous conversation regarding philosophy. Kali agreed that religion and philosophy were a vital part of society and a necessity to maintain order, however he viewed the Kshatriya caste of kings and warriors as more important in preserving society than the Brahmin caste of religious and philosophical teachers. Kali was dismissive regarding Diogenes, who he saw as operating outside of proper society. "With all due respect, my King Porus and King Alexander, we are all from the warrior caste. We are the warriors of our respective societies and you and your military are the warriors of Greece. Men like Diogenes stand outside of society and in doing so they mock society and the rules set forth by men which are important for the benefit of all. If there are many like Diogenes then society and order fall apart. Why should we champion men like Diogenes and those who share his perspectives or behave like an animal?"

Manish responded, "Every person has received the ability to reason by our Creator and a spirit we all share and can use to advance the world of men. We do this by looking at our life in different ways. This gives us our own personal, unique meaning of life. Why should we compartmentalize sections of society simply because we are born into a specific family or specific region? Why can't we be both warriors *and* thinkers? Great warriors and leaders are also great thinkers."

Kali interrupted Manish, failing to hide his frustrations. "Well, Manish, we are born into certain stations in life for the benefit of greater society. Our kingdom needs stability in order to function and men such as Diogenes lead a way of life that many of these sages in our jungles lead. If these sages wish to share their knowledge they should help the leadership and abide by our laws. This also sets an example of what a true sage represents."

Alexander responded, "Well obviously these wise men, whatever perspective they hold, influence people and their disciples. I believe we can all learn from these men or at least understand their perspectives. Kalanos is a wise man who follows the teachings of Siddhartha Buddha and he has imparted his wisdom on me and will serve as my teacher. It only helps a man to understand another's perspective even if he disagrees with him." As Alexander finished his statement, another guest arrived who was well known by everyone in attendance.

As darkness began to envelop the land, Chanakya the great teacher arrived with a young man about the same age as Rishan who had fire in his eyes and appeared as eager to meet Alexander and his guests as much as his protector. Chanakya spoke with some of the Greek commanders, spending most of his time with Ptolemy, who had first approached him for conversation.

Ptolemy always regarded himself as a man of learning and wisdom and therefore he sought out those he viewed as intellectuals. Ptolemy did not have the personality and social abilities that Alexander naturally possessed, but he had self-discipline and a hunger for learning. Ptolemy enjoyed the study of nature and the art of numbers and although he was of high intelligence, he would at times feel self-conscious when his intellectual limits were exposed—particularly for the entertainment of the other Macedonian generals. Ptolemy would feel insecure about his level of intelligence and would lash out in anger at those he commanded and shrink away whenever Alexander used his insecurities against him which he dreaded more than physical danger in battle. Chanakya was a brilliant man who could understand the inner mechanisms of the people he interacted with, even if the interactions were of the brief variety. Chanakya easily deduced Ptolemy's character flaws and insecurities after a brief observation, as Ptolemy followed Chanakya and his young student as they greeted many of Alexander's guests.

Many of the guests were now comfortable, talking loudly and drinking wine. Music and dancing were enjoyed by the majority. The Royal Family were also present, including some of Porus' consorts who were conversing with some of the Persian and Asian women to include Alexander's young bride Roxana, who had just arrived to join the festivities. Alexander's adopted Persian family, including Stateira II, the daughter of Darius III, and Parysatis, the daughter of the deceased Artaxerxes III Ochus who had previously re-conquered Egypt for Persia, were also in attendance. Alexander and his treatment of the Persian Royal Family helped increase his support from the Persian populace but it did not gain any significant support from the Greek people—even from his closest and most important commanders.

Roxana did not enjoy the intimate relationships Alexander maintained with the Persian Royal women who formed part of his Royal Court. Alexander's marriage with

Roxana was also suffering from allegations pertaining to Alexander's rumored bastard son—a subject Alexander only rarely discussed with Hephaiston. Heracles was a baby barely one year of age who was believed to be under the care of his mother Barsine. Alexander was raised and taught in the ways of war and leadership but now he was learning how to maneuver the politics of his own household much like his father Philip II before him. This was a time of celebration and Alexander would not involve himself in domestic matters, especially with esteemed guests in his presence. This occasion would be devoted to conversations between leaders and great intellectuals; it was a rare occasion that Alexander enjoyed while drinking wine with his guests and friends.

King Porus was expecting Chanakya and his young guest and was aware that Chanakya had met with his younger brother the day before. King Porus had sent word to Chanakya that he should not speak in detail regarding his meeting with Porus Balarama and his son Parvateshwara (King Porus' nephew). Porus Balarama, who previously fought valiantly in the Hydaspes battle, was noticeably absent from tonight's feast and King Porus wished to not make his younger brother the topic of conversation. Weeks before, King Porus' younger brother and his son Parvateshwara had been angered at the outcome of the Hydaspes battle and the current political alignment between King Porus and Alexander. Alexander's army was strained and weakened and although the Punjabis could not gather more forces against Alexander at the time of the battle, they were able to notice weaknesses. King Porus sought to maintain his kingdom and parts of his military; he desired to take back power with the further weakening of Alexander's army as he marched back towards Babylon. King Porus' younger brother and his son expected Alexander to march farther east and take control of more lands unless he was defeated and forced to turn back. These details King Porus wished to keep private from Alexander and most importantly his minister Kali Mehra. Although he was a brilliant politician and minister who served him well,

King Porus did not fully trust Kali. These new political alignments would create friction between King Porus' ministers and he understood that Kali's brilliance could be used against him in the future. King Porus would remain vigilant this night as his position as king was still protected but was now dependent on Alexander or until he was able to secure full power once again—diplomatically or through battle.

Chanakya made his way towards Alexander as everyone stood to greet him and his new student. Only Kali Mehra remained unimpressed. Manu, who had spoken sporadically throughout the evening, became visibly excited to see Chanakya. Rishan was thrilled as well.

Alexander rose from his seat to greet them as his Persian clothes flowed in the light breeze. "Welcome, Chanakya. I am glad to finally meet such an esteemed man of wisdom and discipline. I am enjoying a great conversation among great minds and I am happy that you will include your wisdom in this conversation. May I ask, who is this young man who accompanies you?"

Chanakya greeted Alexander as well as the other guests. "Thank you, Alexander. Your strategic mind in the battlefield has proven superior! I am curious to know your designs for this region and your plans for the governance of your outermost territories. I also want to introduce this young man who has joined me for this special occasion; his name is Chandragupta. He is a strong, smart young man and one of my most gifted students I have been blessed to teach. When a young student has a thirst for knowledge combined with natural talents it makes the duty of imparting wisdom very easy and enjoyable."

Many of the guests were curious of this young man around thirteen years old named Chandragupta and asked questions about his origins.

Chanakya briefly explained that Chandragupta was from the Maurya tribe from the northern regions of the Nanda Empire. He also mentioned the current hardships of life under King Dhana Nanda and Dhana Nanda's taxation policies which were stressing the lower castes that had very little food to eat or means to take care of their families. Dhana Nanda would be a formidable foe for Alexander and his large military was dangerous. However, Alexander was encouraged by the information of internal problems threatening to topple Dhana Nanda. Perhaps the difficult task of defeating Dhana Nanda would be completed from within his own empire and perhaps this man Chanakya was the man to do it. Chanakya explained the embarrassment he faced at Dhana Nanda's court when he was introduced to the king by a disenchanted minister named Sakatala. Alexander smiled thinking of a possible march on Dhana Nanda's empire while the leader faced a potential revolution, but he did not reveal his intentions. Despite instability in the region, Chanakya believed Alexander's weakened forces could not reach far enough into India. Chanakya informed Alexander that King Dhana Nanda faced anger from his subjects of all castes including the merchant Vaishya caste and the working poor Shudra caste who were overtaxed as well as the Brahmin philosopher-teachers and Kshatriya warrior caste who never accepted the Nanda family's occupation of the throne.

Chanakya stressed the importance of all people no matter their position in the Varna System. As a member of the Brahmin caste, Chanakya explained to Alexander how his status was similar to his own famous teacher Aristotle.

"Perhaps this young Chandragupta Maurya will be another Alexander someday with a teacher like Chanakya just as I benefited by having Aristotle as my teacher," Alexander exclaimed.

"Chandragupta is one of my best students and a natural leader. Perhaps he will be greater than Alexander," replied Chanakya, creating laughter among the guests.

Alexander respected Chanakya's confidence in his student and directed his attention to Rishan, comparing both as strong, smart, and potential future leaders. Alexander was impressed with the young warriors as well as Rishan's knowledge of Greek language, religion, and culture. Alexander asked, "How did you learn so much about Greece, Rishan?"

Rishan replied, "My uncle Manu was involved in selling merchandise from our wonderful land and his business led him to Palestine and farther west. Manu taught me about your gods and my father introduced me to Greek literature, which I studied every day and found very interesting."

Chandragupta was interested in Rishan's knowledge and asked if he could speak regarding these topics.

Alexander stated he was of the lineage of the great warriors Achilles and Heracles and how his Royal line was legitimized through his ancestry. Alexander talked about the heroism of Achilles in his fight against Troy and the valiant battle between Achilles and Hector the son of Priam. Alexander also mentioned the wisdom of Odysseus and the manifestation of his intelligence in his idea of the Trojan Horse which brought about the destruction of the once impregnable Troy. Alexander proudly described his adventures in Troy and his belief of surpassing his hero Heracles in his most recent siege at Aornos. Alexander spoke of Zeus, the king of the gods as his father, which made him a representative of the gods on earth and an equal to the heroes in Greek culture who also had godly bloodlines. Alexander called these heroes demigods—a collection of heroic men like Theseus who slayed the Minotaur and Perseus who beheaded Medusa.

The story intrigued Rishan, who listened to the fate of Medusa, a beautiful woman with long flowing hair who incited envy and jealousy among the women who failed to match her beauty. Many men pursued Medusa, including Poseidon, the older brother of Zeus. In a later version it was said Poseidon raped her in Athena's temple, leading to an enraged Athena punishing Medusa. Medusa's hair was tragically turned into living poisonous snakes and her gaze turned others to stone. Medusa's place of banishment was a garden of lifeless stone blocks resulting from her gaze, isolating her from humanity and creating an intense hatred in Medusa towards men. Rishan pondered about the gods of the Greeks who possessed the same strengths and weaknesses as the humans they ruled over.

Chanakya spoke about the infinite beings that were his own gods who ruled from a distance but could also be intimate, occasionally interacting with the world of mortal men and within the individual. Chanakya referred to the Vedic traditions and the *Upanishads*, that were a collection of writings and traditions passed down orally for the purposes of instructing a person towards an overall improvement of mind, soul, and body. The concept of the ultimate reality— or Brahman—encompassed all worlds, the source of life and energy which was unchanging but the cause of all things. Brahman is the belief in a single binding unity behind everything in the universe. The ancient recitations of the *Upanishads* also helped one to reach moksha, or a release from samsara, the cycle of reincarnation. Chanakya explained that the spirit was eternal and the body was a vehicle where the spirit was temporarily housed. A person's life was a short period of time where their actions determined the next physical embodiment, leading to the goal of freedom from this cycle or a perpetual rebirth. Dharma, a virtuous and moral life, was important along with artha, the encompassing material wealth or security for oneself and property. Kama was the healthy expression of love and desire, encompassing sexual and other relationships or the desire to reach a goal or improve a craft. Alexander was impressed with Chanakya's definition regarding the different facets of a healthy life. Alexander was disciplined in many aspects of life, including war, politics, and to a certain extent, romantic love, but he was not disciplined in other activities involving Kama. At a young age, Alexander understood that even his great father Philip II suffered from a lack of discipline in many aspects of his life. Alexander also realized that he suffered from a lack of self-control. He laughed. "Chanakya, even the great Achilles, Heracles, the gods, and Zeus himself suffer from lack of self-control and improper pursuits of Kama." The guests laughed at Alexander's exclamation.

Chanakya stated the importance of culture and the belief systems of his society. The Vedic traditions spoke about the Trimurti, a tradition which included Brahma the creator, Shiva the destroyer, and Vishnu the maintainer—

the god Chanakya revered him most. Chanakya believed that leaders acted on behalf of Vishnu. He also believed that a great king was one who maintained order in society and led their subjects through fairness to the best of their abilities. A ruler should practice self-discipline and maintain a strict schedule in an effort to fulfill their leadership responsibilities in the best way possible. Alexander enjoyed this conversation and sought to apply Chanakya's wisdom in his duties as king.

Alexander's thirst for knowledge led him to carry other religious books on his person in addition to his prized collection of Homeric stories of the *Iliad* and *Odyssey*. A peculiar conception of god was found in the land of Palestine—a people related by culture to the larger region including Eber-Nari and the Province of Judah. This Palestinian region was fiercely contested between empires in the past. Palestine was once under the protection of the Egyptian pharaohs including the rule of the black Nubian leader Pharaoh Taharqa who warred against King Sennacherib of Assyria 300 years prior. King Sennacherib, who had defeated the Greeks, suffered border losses to Egypt and now all of these lands belonged to Alexander.

This region was once ruled by King Solomon the wise for over 600 years and the people formed a unique perspective on god. The Canaanite people of Palestine and its surrounding areas were subject to brutality, most notably under the rule of the Babylonian King Nebuchadnezzar who enslaved the Hebrews and made it illegal for them to practice their religion until Cyrus the Great freed them, including the Hebrew leader Ezra, and allowed them to return to Palestine and Judah. The history was well documented in their religious books, which Alexander had in his hands. Alexander had found it a challenge to find similarities between the Greek gods and the Hebrew god Yahweh, who was a singular god who ruled alone; the Hebrew god did not enlist other gods to help.

Alexander exclaimed he would practice tolerance during his rule, stating, "I will also follow the example of Cyrus the Great, who allowed religious freedom and let his subjects practice their cultures and the worship of their gods."

Manu spoke about his stay in Palestine, his brief stay in Egypt, and the land which the Greeks referred to as Ethiopia. Ethiopia was a land of people who possessed dark black skin like Manu and his Dravidian family members. While in Palestine and Egypt, Manu had various conversations with historians and wise men that referred to an eccentric king over a thousand years prior who altered Egyptian religion and focused on the worship of one god. This pharaoh was named Akhenaton, and he ruled alongside his queen Nefertiti and young son Tutankhamen. The priest class was important in Egyptian society and their influence was degraded by Pharaoh Akhenaton, who created his own capital of Akhenaten (or the horizon of Aten the sun disk). Akhenaton was despised by his subjects due to his insistence that everyone no matter class or position prostrate themselves in his presence. This caused many to erase Akhenaton from history upon his death—a grave insult in the Egyptian belief system. Alexander appeared uncomfortable upon listening to the fate of Akhenaton and promptly changed the direction of the conversation.

Alexander discussed the importance of the beliefs to his Egyptian subjects and that he respected and followed those beliefs and he was allowed on the Egyptian throne by the Egyptian gods. Alexander mentioned his voyage to the oracle who legitimized his rule and prophesied his future success. He called for Hephaestion, who was now talking to a one-eyed general named Antigonus, to bring a necklace that he called the Eye of Horus that represented a major Egyptian God. Horus was falcon-headed and was the son of the Goddess Isis and the god of the afterlife Osiris, who Alexander likened to Zeus' eldest brother Hades, the Greek god of the underworld. Set was the brother of Osiris who attempted to destroy Osiris and engaged in battles with his nephew Horus. Upon hearing about this god of disorder and destruction, Chanakya mentioned that Shiva in Vedic beliefs was also responsible for destruction. Anubis was wolf-headed and the son of Set and Nephthys. Anubis was the god of mummification and other rituals associated with passage from life into the world of the dead.

Hephaestion brought Alexander's Eye of Horus necklace and everyone gazed upon it. They were all curious to see this religious item from a distant land, Rishan included. Rishan could not mask his enjoyment, which caused Alexander to laugh and state that Rishan reminded him of his younger years, always searching for cultural understanding and knowledge.

This region was a challenge for Alexander to rule and he would take this time to discuss these topics with these exceptional minds seated around him. Some of the Persians in attendance, including Haxamanis, spoke about their monotheistic belief system that had been in existence for several thousands of years. It was an interesting religion known by King Porus through his relationship with the Persian Royal Achaemenid House. It was also the religion of the Persian Empire, influencing other religions in the area which included that of the Hebrews. Ahura Mazda was the Supreme Being for the Persian followers of Zoroaster— the creator and truest form of light and wisdom. The followers of Zoroaster also believed in a trinity of Ahura Mazda, Mithra the angelic judge, and Apam Napat, the creator who also existed in the Vedic tradition. Good deeds, good words, and good thoughts were important factors of the Persian belief system. Alexander admired the Persians, their state religion, and the unity it created, but he greatly respected Cyrus the Great and the other Persian rulers for practicing a policy of religious tolerance within the Persian-held territories. This was a policy that Alexander had reassured King Porus and other leaders he would also implement.

It was said that Zoroaster, at the age of thirty, received a vision while fetching water from a sacred well. The divine spirit Yazata and the manifestation of the good mind in Vohu Manah led Zoroaster to the Supreme Being Ahura Mazda, who revealed the true path for humanity. Ahura Mazda was opposed to Angra Mainyu, a lesser being of evil who led humans away from good through the use of bad spirits named daevas. It was obvious that the concepts of this belief system had influenced the Hebrews who existed under Persian rule and Alexander made the comparison. He now carried religious scriptures of the Hebrews along with the *Odyssey* and the *Iliad*. These five books represented the Law of Moses, a guide and belief that was shared by the Hebrew people. Nearly everywhere Alexander went, he had successfully captured the support of the religious classes. In Egypt he was supported by the priest class, the Persians had largely recognized him and his family, and Alexander and the House of Argos were cemented as descendants of the Olympian gods by the Greek leadership. Here in these lands around the Indus River, many of the sages had fomented revolts against Alexander and countless civilizations to the east and south were proving to be a hard fought struggle in Alexander's efforts to reach the sea. Alexander had already reached the outermost borders of the Persian Empire but it wasn't enough; he wanted to surpass Persia with his own empire, creating a Greek Dynasty to lead the largest, most powerful empire.

Chanakya was interested in Alexander's discussion of the similarities between the belief systems. Manu also agreed that the Persian Empire's state religion influenced the beliefs of the conquered people under Persian rule. Chanakya began to speak about Lord Vishnu and the avatars of the Supreme Being. These avatars came to instruct humanity or an individual who then taught others. Chanakya mentioned Lord Krishna, an important figure who was an avatar of Lord Vishnu who had existed on earth. Lord Krishna's departure from his physical form on earth marked the start of humanity's Dark Age called "Kali Yuga." This was an age of general decline in humanity. Chanakya believed that a man must still live a life focused on virtues despite living in Kali Yuga.

Manish explained that in Vaishnava Scripture, Mahavishnu existed before our world, resting in an eternal sea of only pure consciousness. The awakening of Mahavishnu created life and the Cosmic Breath of

Mahavishnu created the dance of life and destruction. Lord Brahma was born from Mahavishnu's navel. The first sages, Sanaka, Sanandana, Sanatana, and Sanat-Kumara, were created but they focused their attention on Narayana or Mahavishnu instead of worldly affairs. These four sages or Kumaras debated Lord Shiva, who took on the form of Dakshinamurthy (or great teacher). Lord Shiva instructed the Kumaras regarding the Supreme reality or Brahman by making the chin mudra sign by touching index finger to thumb, thus symbolizing the union between Brahman and Jiva and subsequently took the Kumaras as his disciples.

Shaiva scriptures and the Shvetashvatara Upanishad held that the first Brahman (or ultimate truth) was Lord Shiva. Vishnu was created from Shiva's left side or "vaamanga", however this was not a popular belief. Manish also explained that Lord Vishnu, protector of creations, slept in the middle of a vast ocean on top of a giant snake named Sheshnaga. Lord Brahma was born from the Brahma Kamal Lotus which originated from Lord Vishnu's naval while some believe Brahma was born from Shiva or one of his aspects. Om was Brahman and Om encompassed all and was described as the song of the universe.

In his loneliness, Lord Brahma split into a male and female form and created a daughter named Saraswati through his masculine essence. In his lust, Lord Brahma embraced Saraswati, bringing forth other powerful beings. Shiva destroyed the world in order to start the cycle of regeneration once again. In competition with Lord Vishnu, Lord Brahma sought to reach the top of Shiva who stood in the form of a towering Shiva Linga rising to the heavens with his roots anchored deep into the earth. Brahma flew to the heavens on top of a swan while Lord Vishnu took the form of a boar and dug into the earth to reach the base. Failing to reach the top of Shiva Linga, Lord Brahma observed a floating ketaki flower falling. Lord Brahma took the ketaki flower it in effort to trick Lord Vishnu, who had also failed to reach the base of Shiva Linga, but Lord Shiva was aware of Lord Brahma's trick. Lord Shiva punished Lord Brahma so he and the ketaki flower would be rarely worshipped. Lord

Brahma created other beings as well as humanity and it is said that one day for Lord Brahma is 4,320,000,000 years, during which the cosmos was created and destroyed and after which Brahma slept one night equaling the same as the Brahma day. With a lifetime of 100 years in Lord Brahma's lifetime, he was truly infinite. Alexander and the other Greeks found these concepts of relative time fascinating.

"And what forms did Vishnu take upon the land of men?" Alexander asked.

Chanakya stated the many forms of Vishnu the maintainer and described the creation of the first human named Manu, also the name of Manish's brother. In fact, time was cyclical with periods of creation, degradation, and destruction, with each era or Kalpa lasting 4.32 billion years—a single day in the life of Lord Brahma. The current era's first man was named Sraddhadeva Manu, King of Dravida and leader of the dark skinned inhabitants of the southern regions. Sraddhadeva Manu gave rise to the humans currently inhabiting the world and he was saved by the first incarnation of Lord Vishnu personified as a half man half fish named Matsya. Alexander was intrigued with the cycle of birth, destruction, and rebirth and the concept of time in the minds of the sages of these regions. Alexander mentioned the Greek gods who took various forms in their many interactions with mankind. "What are the avatars of Lord Vishnu?" he asked.

Chanakya mentioned the great flood where the first man (Manu) spoke to a small fish in a bowl. The fish asked to be placed in a larger tank but as it continued to grow, it asked Manu if it could be placed in the ocean. The fish grew, warning Manu to build a ship and take a male and female of each animal and many of the world's grains with him to protect. A great horn that sprouted from this large fish pulled Manu's boat to safety in the northern mountains. This fish was called Matsya and was an avatar of Lord Vishnu. Lord Matsya saved Manu, Manu's family, and the seven sages named the Saptarishi along with a multitude of life which later repopulated the earth. Manu's obedience and courage was rewarded with a female counterpart to cease his loneliness.

Manish's younger brother Manu asked Alexander if he had seen similarities in the beliefs of the Hebrew people from Palestine and Judah. Alexander replied that he had indeed noted the similarities within the story of Adam and Yahweh's instruction to Noah, the descendant of Abraham who survived by building a great boat and later repopulated the earth.

Manu added, "In fact, the Sumerians have a similar story of Gilgamesh, who ruled the city of Uruk over 2,000 years prior and met the immortal man called Utnapishtim. He was instructed by God Ea to build an ark in order to protect his wife, his family, and the animals from a disastrous flood."

Chanakya mentioned the second avatar of Lord Vishnu named Kurma appearing as half-man, half-turtle; the third was a half-man, half-boar named Varaha who defeated a demon named Hiranyaksha, resulting in the restoration of the earth. The fourth avatar of Vishnu was Narasimha, who appeared as lion-faced with lion claws. Narasimha defeated a demon called Hiranyakashipu, and was worshipped as the great protector of humanity. The fifth avatar was Vamana, who appeared as the human dwarf Brahmin and was the first avatar of humanity's second age of Treta Yuga. The sixth avatar was Parashurama or Rama who appeared with an axe during the Treta Yuga as well as the third age called Dvapara Yuga. The seventh avatar was the Great Rama King of Ayodhya and his story was written in *The Ramayana*; the eighth avatar of Vishnu was Lord Krishna, whose instruction to Arjuna in the Great War led him to victory. At the end of this war, Lord Krishna left his physical body and vanished almost 3,000 years ago, marking the last era of this time called Kali Yuga. Some also believe Gautama Buddha, who preached ahimsa (or non-violence) is the ninth avatar of Lord Vishnu. The last avatar was Kalki and he would usher in the end of time, appearing on a white horse with a blazing sword. Kalki was the harbinger of death and the bringer of the first age called Satya Yuga, where men would reach their potential and be ruled by the gods themselves. Kalki would put an end to the current age of Kali Yuga, the foulest of eras.

Alexander replied, "So the new age will be a Golden Age of mankind."

Alexander added that Zeus also flooded the earth after he was maddened by a period of warfare among mortals. In one tale, a man named Dardanus survived a flood by settling on an island called Samothrace. Another account stated that Dardanus survived a flood on an inflated skin from Samothrace to Troad near Abydos on the western regions of the former Persian Empire and then settled on Mount Ida. Dardanus' grandson Tros settled on the highlands of the same region, founding the city of Troy. Alexander remarked how he conquered the Hellespont, a site of frequent past invasions by the Persians into Greek territory. He also mentioned the similarities of the ages of humanity compared with his beliefs with the highest being the Golden Age where the Titan Cronus, father of Zeus and his brothers Poseidon and Hades, ruled mankind. The Golden Age was a time when man did not labor in an effort to feed themselves and there was an absence of warfare. Upon the defeat of the Titans led by Zeus and the Olympians, man fell to the Silver Age, where they lived to the age of 100. Due to constant war, Zeus destroyed these men and they now existed in the underworld. This led to the Bronze Age, where men were created by Zeus from the Ash Tree and lived only for warfare and strife and their tools were made out of Bronze. The Bronze Age ended in the Flood of Deucalion, leaving these men living in the recesses of Hades.

The Heroic Age, Alexander mentioned with glee, was the period where the heroes he admired and sought to surpass existed. This was the age of the bravery of Achilles and Heracles and the Trojan War, the brutality of Agamemnon, and the intelligence and perseverance of Odysseus. Men like Perseus slayed Medusa and the Argonauts, the generation of Heracles and his ten labors, after he was driven mad by Zeus' wife Hera and the generation of Oedipus and the great seven against Thebes. This was the generation of the Trojan War. Alexander idolized the demigods and the men of the Heroic Age. He believed he was surpassing them although he existed in the current age which he compared to the Kali Yuga. The current Greek age was the lowest called The Iron Age where children did not respect their parents, the social order was not respected, and men endlessly toiled and suffered. Alexander thought that surely, he was leading the greatest conquest in the history of humanity in the worst age with the only factor threatening to stop his forward movement being some of his closest friends and his own military. Alexander understood the next wars would push his army to the limit and he began to fear that the very selfishness of his own troops would threaten to topple everything he had built for Macedonia, united Greece, and for himself and his lineage.

It was starting to get late and Manish excused himself from the gathering, taking his son Rishan with him. As Rishan left, he asked Alexander if he could be allowed to take some of the texts from Palestine and other regions where Alexander now ruled. Alexander was happy to see such a young man so interested in learning and adventure, remarking, "If I had thousands of Rishans under my command I would not only rule the world of men but the world of the gods!"

Alexander gladly gathered some literature from various regions of the world and gave them to Rishan. Rajesh also left the gathering along with the Ramankrishna clan in attendance, leaving Kali Mehra, his son Karna Mehra, as well as Chanakya and the young Chandragupta in the presence of the great king Alexander.

Alexander remarked that he was impressed with Karna Mehra and Rishan Ramankrishna's stories. Alexander respected Rishan after he witnessed the young and soft spoken boy kill an experienced Greek Infantryman. However, he did not mention the battle out of respect for Manish's request to not discuss the violence in which his son Rishan was involved. Still, he believed young men like Rishan would serve valiantly in his future wars. Alexander needed to initiate peace treaties with men like King Ambhi while at the same time avoiding them after costly wars as he did with King Porus. This would be essential as Alexander moved east and believed he needed these men to offer flexibility so he would not rely on his own Greek men and most importantly, the Macedonian upper class and military leadership which he began to fear were plotting against him. Alexander drank some more wine as he asked to possibly see Rishan and Karna battle his young Spartan warriors. He was interested in observing the revered ancient martial arts of the regions south of the Indus River. Chanakya stated that he would love to see these exhibitions in the near future and there would be a call for them as everyone was interested, including the Greeks, who were in need of some relaxation and diversion.

Kali and Karna Mehra were now leaving the gathering when Chanakya excused himself to speak with King Porus along with his young student Chandragupta, who had said very little during the conversation. Chanakya was curious to learn from the new treaty between King Porus and Alexander as well as Alexander's future plans. It was wise to know that even though Dhana Nanda faced internal pressure, he still commanded a vast military. King Porus stated his desire to maintain power and that his first priority was the safety of his populace. King Porus thought perhaps if Chanakya controlled the Nanda Empire then the initial battle with Alexander would have ended differently. Both King Porus and Chanakya understood that Alexander's military was stretched thin and they also noted his supply line risked breaking several times during the Greek and Persian Wars leading up to the battle against King Porus just a month prior. King Porus explained to Chanakya his belief that initially he would defeat Alexander and improve his declining economy. The reality was that Alexander had outmaneuvered and defeated him in a costly war. Alexander's victory came at a high cost to the morale and overall fighting spirit of his military. Chanakya promised to correspond with King Porus in the future as he left with Chandragupta.

Alexander called upon his personal bodyguard and

some other generals with the intention of discussing his designs regarding the expansion of his empire. One by one, they gathered around Alexander; Aristonous, Lysimachus, Peithon, Leonnatus, Perdiccas, Ptolemy I Soter, Hephaestion, and Peucestas. Peucestas was the most recent addition to Alexander's elite, personal unit after earning the position roughly half a year earlier for distinguishing himself in battle. Peucestas also held the honorable responsibility of carrying the sacred shield that Alexander had taken from Athena's temple at Troy. He had a minor but important role at the battle of Hydaspes as one of the commanders of several triremes—impressive Greek warships with three separate levels of oars. The triremes were well known along with Egyptian battle ships in the Great Sea formerly controlled by the now conquered Persian Empire. Alexander sometimes boasted of his heavier warships, the quadriremes and quinqueremes. The conversation regarded the possible conquest of the Nanda Empire which was met with hesitancy by some of Alexander's bodyguard.

Alexander was aware that his military was growing tired but he felt that through his persuasive powers of speech and action he could carry them through what he believed would be the last few wars until he reached the sea. Coenus was also involved in the private conversation and he advised Alexander and his biggest supporter Hephaestion of the decreasing morale of the troops, who were already aware of the possible march east towards the larger kingdoms. The war against King Porus was devastating to Greek morale, which Alexander was aware of, however steadfast his resolve remained. Alexander's fierce will and self-sacrifice was a testament to his confidence in his belief in victory, but he did not acknowledge the fact that even his actions on the field of battle would hold sway in converting the negative sentiments of his men.

"We will march east," Alexander exclaimed, not wanting to listen to any more dissent.

Several months passed and Alexander began his march towards the Nanda Empire. Before he left, he scheduled some combat sports between the youth of Pauravas and Greece. One of the fights involved Rishan and a young Spartan which ended in a dominating display by Rishan. Karna Mehra also defeated his opponents but Rishan was the main subject the Greeks discussed on their way to the Nanda Empire. Alexander wished to distract his men with games and wine in hopes of raising their spirits. However, as word spread about the large army of Dhana Nanda as well as the armies of King Xandrammes, the leader of the Gangaridai Empire, the Greek army began to revolt. Alexander's Persian dress and past actions against other Greeks coupled with growing fears of facing these large armies finally led to the Greek army's refusal to march less than five miles towards a river called Vipasa (referred to as the Hyphasis River by Alexander and the Greeks). Alexander's advance was halted—a feat that an enemy was not able to accomplish had now materialized through Alexander's own men. Alexander's threats and exclamations of how close they were to the sea combined with the officers' loyalty to Alexander propelled the Greeks further but the size of Nanda's military was now common knowledge and helped to discourage Alexander's forces.

It was almost midday and the sun was at his highest point in the sky. The weather was hot and humid with light rain that would start and stop as if to tease and annoy the marching army with impending storms. It was fall of 326 B.C. and after about a month of marching east, they had reached the banks of the Hyphasis River. Some of the infantrymen began to loudly talk amongst themselves and several disturbances occurred first in the rear and later towards the front of the line where Alexander led his army on horseback. The grumbling began to increase when Alexander ordered the river crossing. Coenus asked Alexander to meet with him in private to reevaluate his plans. In an effort to spare Alexander the embarrassment of facing criticism from his lower ranks directly, Coenus appealed to Hephaestion.

Hephaestion replied to Coenus' demands, "Your king Alexander has stated his plans and he has already made an agreement with another king named Phegeus. King Phegeus will submit to Alexander before we reach the Ganges River and we need to stand with our king, and proceed with our march."

Some of the infantry heard Hephaestion and answered with cries to turn back. Some of Alexander's bodyguard remained eerily silent, including Ptolemy.

Alexander wrongly assumed that his alliance with King Phegeus would encourage his men to march forward. He spoke down to Coenus so everyone could hear. "What is it that you wish your king to do? Hephaestion dispatched several of our scouts and diplomats to secure alliances ahead of our army and this mission was successful! By the time we reach the gates of the Nanda Empire we will have increased our army. Surely you know that Dhana Nanda is a doomed ruler. Dhana Nanda is like a fruit rotting from the inside with a beautiful outer covering; don't fear his large army as they don't have the spirit to fight for their own king!"

Alexander suspected some of his generals—including Coenus—had released and exaggerated the sensitive information concerning the size of Dhana Nanda's army. One man yelled at Alexander, stating he should continue marching with his father Ammon or Zeus. Another exclaimed, "Son of Zeus! March as Achilles or conquer Dhana Nanda on your own like Heracles would have!"

Alexander turned as red as the setting sun. "You do this to your king? Have I not fought alongside you and shed my blood for you? Have I not shared the same miseries that you have had to endure? I have suffered broken bones in my body and cuts and aches and pains just like all of you!"

The men stated that the support of King Phegeus' army was not guaranteed and that Dhana Nanda's military was numerically superior. They also argued that before they did battle with Dhana Nanda they would also face various other tribes along the way.

Alexander exclaimed, "You have all benefitted from the wealth I have created for all of you. I have traveled farther than my father ever envisioned for himself before his most unfortunate assassination. We are close to our goal and yet you fail your king. Ironic that the same Asians you look down upon will fight more vigorously for our cause than my fellow Greeks and Macedonians!"

The Greeks were now in a state of heightened anger. Alexander, who had adopted Persian dress and culture, was publicly favoring the Persians and Asians to continue fighting alongside him after all the Greek and Macedonian blood that had been shed. Ptolemy advised Alexander to reexamine a different strategy but Alexander refused. Hephaestion asked Alexander to excuse himself as to not let his anger cloud his judgment. Alexander set up his private tent and said he would only come out when his army was ready to cross the Hyphasis River and advance towards the Nanda Empire.

On the second day, Alexander remained in his tent as arguments between the generals continued. Alexander was in disbelief at the audacity of his own military as he spoke to his generals, hoping to persuade them with the richness awaiting them beyond the east. He had noticed some of the fabrics worn at King Porus' court by the wealthier classes; they had come from places never before seen which existed beyond the farthest regions of the former Persian Empire. Asia was in fact much larger than they had anticipated.

Coenus began speaking for the Greek military. "My king, are you so certain of this place beyond the eastern borders of Persia? We are stretched thin and your military is tired and have suffered for almost nine years of constant wars."

Alexander responded, "Why do you question me, Coenus? I listened to Chanakya refer to this smooth fabric called cinamsuka. Apparently some of the people of the Indus have traded with these people farther east, receiving that fabric. We need to advance east to form alliances and continue to battle through even though we face numerically superior forces. We have battle-hardened men and our phalanx has proven effective in battle. We must take full advantage while we are at full strength!"

Coenus reluctantly expressed Alexander's plans to the Greek military, who hardened their hearts towards their leader even more.

Later in the afternoon, Alexander addressed his military again. "You will benefit from the spoils of war which you are ignorant of. I say this as this is the only thing that seems to interest the lot of you! I only have the clothes on my back and several pieces of jewelry although I am the Supreme Ruler of the world. Let it be known on this day that you left your king in Asia!"

Alexander retired to his quarters for the night, only allowing Hephaestion to converse with him. Hephaestion cautioned Alexander to reconsider his plans. He could cease his march, secure his border, and revisit this area in the future. Alexander informed Hephaestion that perhaps he was correct; he would conquer the Nanda Empire when Dhana Nanda faced a revolt from within. Alexander was disappointed in Coenus and the manner in which he expressed his opinions. Antigonus I Monophthalmus, who also served Alexander's father, could also be antagonistic but even Antigonus would reserve his criticisms for Alexander in private. Antigonus angered Alexander many times, including his most recent trip to the conquered Pauravas Kingdom. He had been sent back to rule his territory after he had made negative comments regarding the people of the Indus Valley, comparing them to the primates that the Greeks had encountered in the jungles. Antigonus went back to rule the territory of Phrygia and protect Alexander's supply lines—a role he had performed faithfully since 333 B.C. Alexander expressed that his anger towards Coenus was more intense than any he held for Antigonus the Cyclops, as his friends called him.

He shifted his attention towards his grievances and a new light suddenly burned in his eyes. Alexander now expressed his plans of conquering Arabia and perhaps the Romans after he returned to Babylon. The eastern push would be planned at a future date. He was disappointed and said to Hephaestion, "We could not have beaten the mighty Nanda Empire as well as the Ganderites and the Praesii with my army's fear of their mighty armies." However, Alexander had a new focus for his empire. The expansion to the eastern lands would wait until he had consolidated his empire and planned new invasions in Babylon.

On the third day, just before noon, Alexander stated that the Greeks would end their advance and return to Babylon and later Macedonia and the Greek lands. The military erupted in joy when Alexander agreed with them and they shouted their glee. Alexander agreed to compensate and reward his senior warriors and promised retirement for his longest serving military men. The men were overjoyed; they could now rest, enjoy their victories, and live a long life with their families. The celebrations began and many were drunk, loudly proclaiming the greatness of their leader. "Alexander the Great!" they shouted. "Brave Alexander!"

Alexander burned several altars to the gods in honor of his army's achievements and appointed General Nearchus admiral of his fleet. He then ordered additional ships built and placed Nearchus in charge of over 800 ships, expanding Alexander's powerful navy.

CHAPTER 10:
SATRAP PEITHON AND THE YAVANA EMPIRE
(323 B.C.)

"Among Barbarians no distinction is made between women and slaves, because there is no natural ruler among them. They are a community of slaves, male and female."
—Aristotle (*Politics*)

Following his many successes in the arts of combat, Rishan Ramankrishna's popularity increased. Rishan excelled in the ancient martial arts of his people and had amassed over fifty victories without tasting defeat—a feat only surpassed by the impressive Karna Mehra. Rishan's role towards the end of the Hydaspes battle gained him various honors in the eyes of Alexander and some of the Greeks as well as earned King Porus' respect. The quiet, reserved Rishan had shown bravery and confidence under duress when his father and his king faced dire circumstances. The subject of life and death was a serious matter for a young boy but Manish taught Rishan the necessity of protecting yourself as well as loved ones. However, brutality and the killing of innocents, the young, and the handicapped, would not be tolerated. Manish lectured Rishan on the mental strength needed in times of strife and combat. "A man who is a warrior must follow his king and respect his judgment if his king is just. He should fight bravely and valiantly if he is called for duty and he should protect himself, his family, and his homeland. A man has natural fear but he should learn how to channel that fear into self-confidence and a capable mind which is devoid of hesitancy."

With Rajesh injured and his physical abilities compromised, the young Rishan had become the next capable warrior in the Ramankrishna household.

Rishan was at his family home awaiting his dear Priyanka to join him and his family for dinner. Rishan recalled his combat with the Spartan named Andronikos, who was a year older than him, before Alexander had marched towards the Hyphasis. The Spartan was a strong athlete with a promising future in Alexander's military. It was the first time Rishan had tested his skills against a strong foreign opponent and Rishan was victorious in the match, surprising all in attendance. Karna Mehra also competed against a young Theban named Gregorios, however his contest was a lengthier test of strength and skill. Although both Karna and Rishan were victorious and were the only ones of their people to defeat the Greeks in hand to hand combat, Rishan received more recognition. For the first time, Rishan had obtained more attention than Karna Mehra. Anand and some of Rishan's friends shared in Rishan's triumph and newfound success both athletically and in various educational pursuits.

Two years ago, Alexander had led his military on a southern march following the Hydaspes River. Alexander's military fought and defeated local tribes, alerting other tribes to unite against him. Alexander had lacked reinforcements during the Hydaspes Greek revolt and now received additional soldiers including armor and weapons from Thrace. Alexander continued to march and sail with his army down the Hydaspes, rarely engaging in battle until two groups of people confronted him: the Oxydracians and the Mallians. They were able to do what Porus and Ambhi were not, which was set aside their differences and fight together against a mutual enemy. Along the way, a tribe called the Sibae with an army of 35,000 was defeated by Alexander's forces with many of the men slaughtered and the women and children enslaved. As Alexander charged with his army, the Mallians retreated deep into the jungle, drawing Alexander behind them. The Mallian leaders turned and engaged Alexander at the western bank of the Hydraotis River, but fled once again to the city of Multan where they gathered for a final showdown within one mile of the walled city. The Mallians were said to have over 50,000 troops but Alexander continued to lay siege. When the pace was too slow, Alexander grew impatient, climbing a ladder over the wall. Upon realizing that it was Alexander, the enemy descended upon him in an effort to kill the famed Macedonian. The frightened Greeks tried to scale the ladders which broke under their weight as they cried for Alexander to jump down. However, Alexander continued his fight, killing the Mallian leader with a sword to the chest while he received a major blow from a spear through the chest himself.

Rumors had spread throughout the region of Alexander's death. Soon after,there was news that Alexander survived the battle and that his bravery inspired his military to conquer the Mallians at the Multanese Citadel. Peucestas was near Alexander as well as Peithon, who had served well in leading the Greeks during the taking of the Multanese Citadel. Nearchus led the Greek fleet in the exploration of the Persian Gulf while another section of Alexander's army were ordered to march towards Carmania. Alexander was on foot, marching his way towards Persia through the Gedrosian desert. This was an area where many leaders lost large amounts of their military and perhaps Alexander wanted to surpass their legend. The decision to cross this dessert would be a major undertaking and many anticipated a negative outcome. Alexander was now being referred to as Alexander the Great by many Greeks and Persians.

Satrap Eudamus was the real power behind the throne of King Porus under the rule of Alexander the Great. Philip, appointed satrap of India by Alexander and an officer in Alexander's army, had been assassinated two years prior. Philip was the son of Machatas and brother of Harpalus, a childhood friend of Alexander. In his spare time, Alexander would ask Harpalus to send him reading material mainly from Greek writers like Aeschylus, Sophocles, and Euripides. Philip was a smart man who yearned to learn more and he and Alexander had intellectual debates on many issues regarding philosophy and humanity which helped to earn Philip the satrapy of the Indus region. Under Philip, King Porus retained a segment of his former power and there was relative peace in the region. King Porus also helped in the construction of the city of Alexandria on the Indus River.

Manish was asked to help design some of the new structures in the city—a task that helped enrich him and his family. King Porus was very proud of Manish and recommended him for future projects that Philip would demand. Manish's standing and wealth in society was at its apex but his political rivalry with Kali would soon diminish his success.

The stability in the territory decreased when Satrap Philip was assassinated by his own upper leadership, causing Alexander to appoint Eudamus and Ambhi into the role for the region. King Porus had lost considerable power and influence and to make matters worse, his old enemy King Ambhi had taken the little remaining power that he'd had and gathered his own influence with Satrap Eudamus. King Porus' brother in the east was gaining support against Eudamus, who represented Greek occupation. Manish began to retreat from an active life in politics and sought an increased involvement in architecture. Manish's sole purpose was to provide stability for his family and avoid an unstable political situation.

The other region in the northwest was ruled by Oxyartes, the father of Alexander's wife Roxana. To the southwest was the territory of a man with a muscular build who ruled with strict discipline and an iron fist named Peithon. Peithon's territory was the strongest in the region and he controlled the most influence with Alexander. His satrapy bordered the ocean, giving him important access to the sea. The Ramankrishna family still enjoyed success, however their status was not secure due to the declining standing in King Porus' court after Satrap Eudamus had taken power over two years prior. This situation was made worse by the constant arguments between Kali and Harbir at the court which indirectly involved Manish and his family. Kali was a skilled politician and would often paint the Ramankrishna clan as having the same opinions as the often outspoken Harbir. Although Manish sided with many of Harbir's viewpoints, he disagreed in the direct, irresponsible manner Harbir would express his perspectives.

This day would be one of relaxation for the family and Manish would spend time with Rishan and his female companion Priyanka at a private dinner. Priyanka's family would also visit the Ramankrisha house to converse and celebrate a possible union between Rishan and Priyanka in the future as well as other subjects regarding the current state of affairs. Priyanka's older brother Kulvir, who was excelling in his architecture studies, also would be joining both families for dinner. Kulvir was excited about the prospect of possibly working under the guidance of Manish when he completed his studies.

The Kumari family arrived at the Ramankrishna house at mid-afternoon. It was a clear and pleasant day as Lakshmi prepared vegetables and Manish cooked meats. Padmesh Kumari looked forward to getting to know Rishan and seeking an apprenticeship for his son Kulvir under Manish's expertise. The food was finally cooked as the Kumari family began to arrive and both families enjoyed having dinner together. They congratulated Rishan for joining the young leadership training in the new military as well as his continued scholastic success. Perhaps in a few years it would still be possible for Rishan to study at the prestigious school at Takshashila if political stability persisted. Rishan's main goal was to become a successful architect like his father and perhaps also increase his focus on the study of numbers. Rishan demonstrated continued intellectual growth in spiritual knowledge, languages, and nature. Rishan Manish understood Rishan's potential and Rishan could not improve unless he himself realized he had this potential. Rishan was still a work in progress but at the very least he was finally improving and the girls were beginning to take notice, which helped him form bonds despite his continued introversion and slight timidity.

During the meal, Lakshmi and Padma discussed the major spectacle of the weddings at Susa involving Alexander and his entire leadership—a topic that also interested Priya. Priya did not talk much but wanted to know the major events that many were currently discussing. Politically, the weddings were an attempt by Alexander to further solidify his empire between the Greeks and Asians. "It must have been such a pretty wedding with so many people," Priya remarked, spurring the ladies to speculate on the ceremony and what probably occurred.

Alexander had an ongoing relationship with the Persian Royal women who accompanied him on his campaigns—to the dismay of Roxana. At the weddings at Susa, Alexander finally married Stateira II and Parysatis II. Stateira II, also called Barsine, was the daughter of Darius III and Stateira I. Hephaestion married Drypetis, the sister of Alexander's wife Stateira II, solidifying the relationship of Alexander and Hephaestion. To Craterus, Alexander gave Amastrine, the daughter of Oxyartes and Darius' brother. Perdiccas married a daughter of Atropates, satrap of Media. Ptolemy and Eumenes, the Royal secretary, married the daughters of Artabazus named Artacama and Artonis respectively. Nearchus, Alexander's admiral, married the daughter of Barsine and Mentor; and Seleucus married Apama, the daughter of Spitamenes from Bactria.

Over 10,000 marriages between Greeks and Persians were officially recognized by Alexander. The ceremonies were performed in the Persian custom and Alexander gave dowries to all the couples. The spectacle was talked about mainly by the upper class and those who had leisure time to talk about such matters. For Manish, there were other more pressing matters regarding power shifts within the Greek Empire. As they finished dinner, the women conversed among themselves while the men took a walk to speak and to aid in digestion. Manish also invited Rishan; he was now old enough to begin speaking about matters pertaining to adults. As the sun was setting, the men addressed rumors about their government and politicians.

Manish was careful to remain silent on private details surrounding King Porus and the difference of opinions regarding the king, his younger brother, and elements of Greek leadership in the region. Due to his high position as King Porus' adviser, Manish had access to foreign information—including the massive purges of Greek leadership under Alexander's orders. Alexander had become unpredictable in his public—and by some accounts his private—life. King Porus' leadership was now being undermined by elements of those in his own court and Manish believed Kali Mehra was the main instrument causing internal fractions within the administration. Although he had taken a more neutral role in the foreign policy discussion, Manish was worried that Kali was now holding a major grudge against him. Harbir supported Manish but was vocal against Kali Mehra, although no one had any solid evidence to accuse Kali of ill intentions. Manish would keep the discussion at a surface level with Padmesh Kumari and his son Kulvir, mainly discussing new building projects in Pauravas and perhaps in the other Greek satrapies in the area. Kulvir was excited to work with Manish, who finally proposed that in the following year, after Kulvir completed his studies, he could work on minor projects under his guidance. Since both families would more than likely be united in the future if Rishan and Priyanka decided to get married, this was a small gift. Both parents decided that although they wished for their children to be married, the final decision would be left to Rishan and Priyanka.

The economy that had been steadily declining for several generations continued to decline under King Porus. He was able to mitigate the economic downturn, creating some work for the poor and providing increased irrigation and a general improvement in sanitation. Under Greek rule, at first the economy leveled, but it could not be improved in certain regions. Some sectors experienced great success mostly wherever there was construction. This promised to make Manish wealthier, although competition in the architecture field had steadily increased in the last several years. Many of the Greeks preferred to build the new cities in the Greek style and had brought Greek architects to build them. Manish still commanded a high level of respect and he was promised future development projects in Pauravas—much to the dismay of Greeks competing for the opportunities.

Rajesh had recovered but had a limp, which limited his role in combat. Perhaps he would excel in another position within the military, possibly as a strategist or an adviser. Manish understood the importance of hard work and he wanted his son to succeed, especially now that Rajesh had the additional responsibilities of being a husband. For these reasons and the growing Ramankrishna household, Manish decided it was best to remain neutral on political issues as they became more layered and polarizing.

Wealth was being created in certain sectors of society and the Greek rulers were in control of who had access to the major streams of wealth. This created greater competition and political maneuverings and although Manish was astute regarding architecture, he was still outmatched by people such as Kali Mehra. Padmesh Kumari was slightly aware of the increasing turmoil but he did not know the extent of the situation. Padmesh's main concern was a great future for his son Kulvir and a possible union between Priyanka and Rishan. The sun had slipped below the horizon as the men headed back to the Ramankrishna house.

The Kumari family readied to leave before nightfall and t he guests departed after an enjoyable evening of dinner and conversation. Rishan and Priyanka said their goodbyes and planned to meet later in the week. Rishan was now getting ready to complete his military training and was close to starting his duties as a young military leader. Rishan also had goals of attending the advanced school at Takshashila to study disciplines including architecture like his father. After the Kumari family left, Manish took the opportunity to speak honestly to his son Rishan about the current political situation in the region as well as his progress as a young leader. Manish had spoken to King Porus about the future of the region and his hopes for Rishan in his new career. He wanted to see what direction his son Rishan wanted to take, informing Rishan of King Porus' wish to have a private meeting with him to discuss these very same issues.

Rishan expressed his goals of attending school at Takshashila perhaps during or after his primary obligation to the military. Manish supported his son but warned Rishan that the thin veneer of peace that currently existed was being threatened by internal and external forces. He advised Rishan that if he continued his service in the military he should focus only on his role as a leader and stay away from political matters altogether. Peithon, the satrap of the territory bordering to the west, was gaining power and influence while Eudamus, the current satrap of King Porus' territory, was growing envious of Peithon. There was an element of competition for power and wealth among the Greek leadership, and with Alexander away in Persia they began to exercise more control over their respective dominions. Manish expressed his fear of Rishan's involvement in potential wars over resources and the way in which they would be divided among the Greeks. Manish also feared the continued erosion of King Porus' powers. Ironically, King Porus had more influence when Alexander was in the Punjab, but now that Alexander was away, King Porus found himself in more danger. The Satrap Eudamus seemed to favor King Ambhi over King Porus—a delicate balance that Alexander had navigated comparatively better.

A few days later, Rishan was summoned to meet with King Porus personally; it was the first time Rishan had a private meeting with the king. King Porus admired the Ramankrishna family, especially the young Rishan, who showed a lot of potential. Secretly, King Porus thought Rishan's talents would be misused by the Greek governorship and he felt growing anger towards the Greek satraps. His kingdom and his resources were not fully under his control and Greek leaders were now debating over resources that did not belong to them. At least the Persians left the affairs of his kingdom under his control; the Greeks were positioning themselves over who would control these regions. King Ambhi seemed happy to go along with whatever the Greek leadership wanted and perhaps this would enable him to increase his power and punish his rival King Porus. King Porus expressed some of his thoughts to Rishan, advising him to be careful, for although he was not involved in politics, his father Manish was being targeted by certain families who were aligning themselves with the Greeks. Rishan should listen to his father's instructions and remain neutral regarding politics. Perhaps with time, the situation would favor King Porus and the Ramankrishna family. He told Rishan to remain calm and focused and to keep the conversation private, but his advice did little to mitigate the fear welling within Rishan.

As Rishan left the Royal Palace, King Porus thought that perhaps his younger brother was right in his growing campaign against the Greeks. Perhaps a long term strategy would fail him but the short term aggressive policy that his brother Porus Balarama and his son Parvateshwara were pursuing would be the best policy. In fact, the nephew of King Porus, Prince Parvateshwara, was now his father's most influential advocate for cutting ties with the Greeks and King Porus, naming themselves the new rulers of the region. Perhaps the powerful Nanda Empire to the east would play a major factor in these growing disputes, but how could King Porus or his brother form an alliance with the unfit King Dhana Nanda? Communications had now ceased and King Porus could not even reach his primary adviser—the only man in the Nanda Royal Court who King Porus still trusted and respected. It was an uncertain time in the region as King Porus sought to regain some of his eroding powers and protect those whose loyalties to him remained firm and unwavering.

Alexander had purged a large segment of his top

leadership in the last several years. The killings were committed as a warning to anyone who attempted to undermine him. Alexander had faced recent rebellions among the Greek and Macedonian veterans in his military and had become skilled at pitting the Persians and Greeks against each other to push an overall agenda that he had already planned. /his mother Olympias was extremely skilled at political maneuvering and his father Philip II had also shown this political intelligence in his ability to build and rally his army. Alexander promised to send his Silver Shields—his war-hardened and most experienced men— back to Macedonia and various Greek lands. However, some viewed this as Alexander's attempt to favor his new Persian and Asian military members. Alexander offered to pay his military and clear the debts of many of its members in an effort to ease the tensions—specifically with his fellow Macedonians. He then made sure to emphasize the fact that his father had built Macedonia from a barbarian location north of the Greek city-states into a military power. Alexander spoke about how the Macedonians could not afford the luxury of extracting their own mineral resources or how they lacked adequate defenses against the Illyrians, Triballians, and neighboring Thracians as they were simple people who walked their flock wearing sheepskins. He exclaimed, "Oh how Macedonians used to shudder in fear at the sight of the Thracians and shook in terror at the thought of the Athenians."

Alexander made sure they understood that he was the one who crossed the Hellespont where Xerxes had previously crossed to terrorize the Spartans and other Greeks hundreds of years prior. Alexander stated how the wealth of Egypt and Cyrene and his additional acquirement of the territories of Coele-Syria, Palestine, Mesopotamia, Babylonia, Bactria, Elam, and Lydia brought the Greeks great wealth and resources. The treasures of Persia, the riches of Egypt and the Indus regions, and control of the major sea and land routes connecting east and west, were now under Alexander and Greek control.

Alexander finally said, "You are satraps, you are

generals, and you are captains. What do I have left from all of our labors? I only have this purple cloak and a diadem stating my position as your king."

Alexander appointed Persians and Asians to different leadership positions, causing infighting between the Greeks. Greeks began to accuse other Greeks to take the blame for their previous discord with Alexander while asking for forgiveness. Alexander had now won his military and planned to unify Greeks, Persians, and Asians. Large celebrations followed with thousands of guests. In one celebration, Alexander was encouraged to view a dancing contest in which Bagoas, the Persian young man from Darius' court, was participating. Bagoas had won the contest and upon seeing the joy on Alexander's face, the Greeks encouraged their king to kiss him. Usually one to never show public displays of love, Alexander finally agreed and kissed Bagoas, sending all in attendance into a joyous uproar. These events would be the last moments of happiness in Alexander's life.

Alexander was now suffering through the sudden death of his closest friend Hephaestion, whereupon he had taken to his bed for several days in a severely depressed state. Alexander did not remove himself from his seclusion even to relieve himself, lying in his own bodily waste. Food and water were brought to him reluctantly by personal servants who had to cease their breathing in order to not inhale the foulness. This was a tragic situation; Alexander had always taken special care to address his own personal hygiene. Also adding to Alexander's mental anguish was the growing illness of the sage Kalanos, who had become sick in Persia. Kalanos had lost his ability to walk and did not want to live without control of his body despite Alexander's attempts to dissuade him. After convincing the general Ptolemy to build a pyre, Kalanos gave away all of his material possessions bestowed upon him by Alexander to other Greeks, including one of his pupils, Lysimachus.

Alexander asked Kalanos to reconsider his suicide and Kalanos weakly turned to Alexander, stating, "I will see you again, Alexander, in Babylon."

Nearchus and Chares of Mytilene, among others, witnessed Kalanos lay still as fire consumed his body until he fell over dead. Alexander wondered in amazement who was this Siddhartha Gautama the Buddha, whose followers simply by mental discipline could sit still as a fire consumed their bodies until death? He was curious about Kalanos' last words due to the fact that Kalanos was ignorant to the fact that Alexander would return to Babylon. Kalanos' words would prove to be prophetic.

CHAPTER 11:
DEATH AT THE PALACE OF NEBUCHADNEZZAR II (321 B.C.)

"Who, my friend, can ascend to the heavens? [Only] the gods can dwell forever with Shamash. As for human beings, their days are numbered, and whatever they keep trying to achieve is but wind! Now you are afraid of death—what has become of your bold strength? I will go in front of you, and your mouth can cry out: Go on closer, do not be afraid! Should I fall, I will have established my fame. [They will say:] It was Gilgamesh who locked in battle with Humbaba the Terrible!"
—The Epic of Gilgamesh, 2:2

The news of Alexander's death had become known two years ago, but had only become public knowledge last year. There was an effort to control the information of the conquerors' death due to restrictions of various Greek generals. After reaching Babylon in July of 323 B.C., Alexander held a vast festival with food, dancing, and copious amounts of drinking. He remained grief-stricken over the death of Hephaestion and had become less disciplined in his wine consumption, at times drinking from sunrise to sunset. Alexander had many enemies—including family members of men he previously executed and most famously, his childhood teacher Aristotle. Aristotle had previously kept his criticisms private but was now publicly expressing his discontent over the killing of his great nephew at the hands of Alexander and the recent mass executions under his orders.

Alexander developed a close relationship with Medius while discussing his future plans to conquer Arabia and possibly the Romans. He hoped to build more Alexandrias and was debating whether to build a new capital for his new empire. The most important instrument in future domination of the Punjab and southern regions of that land was not only a client-king, but a man supporting Alexander from among their own Punjabi people—a man to be respected or feared from an influential family. Chanakya was strong and intelligent but he operated outside of Alexander's influence and was potentially an enemy. Seleucus mentioned several families, including the Mehras, who could support Alexander's occupation of the Indus Valley. Alexander stated he would hold a discussion at a later date after the celebrations, where he and his friends drank until sunrise before Alexander became ill with a high fever, limiting the Macedonian leader to his bed. Although he continued having high fevers, Alexander would attend religious events such as ritual sacrifices and festivities where he would depict himself as Achilles or Heracles wearing a lion head and consuming large amounts of wine. Alexander subsequently fell gravely ill and by the fourth day he was unable to get out of bed even for brief occasions.

On the sixth day, Alexander's condition rendered him unable to move. Worry began to cloud his bodyguards' minds as each began to ponder who would lead his empire. Alexander's half-brother, Arrhidaeus, was ill prepared and Alexander understood he would be used as a pawn by political rivals in Macedonia and Greece. Alexander kept Arrhidaeus with him throughout his campaigns in order to avoid others manipulating him. Queen Roxana was currently pregnant, so Alexander asked Peridiccas to safeguard his child's succession to the throne if he was born a son. Alexander did not mention another son he supposedly had fathered and his generals did not dare bring the boy named Heracles to his attention. On the ninth day,

Alexander could barely speak as his generals began to ask him who would lead his empire. The tension was thick and manifested itself in verbal arguments as well as physical altercations.

On the tenth day, Alexander struggled to speak . "I want the strongest of my family to rule and continue our dynasty." However, this statement was heard only by Peridiccas and it would be the last Alexander made, spending most of the day mute and motionless until he died later that evening. Alexander's half-brother, now named Philip III Arrhidaeus, was named king. Alexander's son, Alexander IV, born several months after Alexander the Great's death, would be allowed to rule after he became an adult under the orders of the powerful leader Regent Peridiccas.

In the Punjab, the situation had become very unstable the last two years and the rule of the unfit Philip III Arrhidaeus created a power struggle. Now many of the Greek satraps and generals were forming alliances, reluctantly sweeping the Ramankrishna family into the fold. It all began slowly, starting when King Porus had provided Manish several potential sanitation and building projects in the region. Feeling his influence beginning to decline with King Porus and now seeing true power being held by the Greek satraps in the region, Kali Mehra began to privately speak with some of the Greek leadership. Some of the Greek architects were envious of Manish's skills which placed doubt in their beliefs of their own superiority. Manish secured some building projects in the city of Alexandria on the Indus and decided it was a great opportunity for the young Kulvir Kumari to start his apprenticeship as well as his son Rishan to gain some experience by observing planning, design, and construction. Manish began to work on construction projects and King Porus gave him a more limited role in his court. This was a conscious decision made by Manish; tensions were rising between different political factions and he chose to remain neutral. King Porus would rarely ask Manish for advice on foreign affairs, limiting him to mostly domestic policies.

King Porus' opinion of Manish was better than the opinion he privately held of Kali Mehra. Kali continued to hold a high position under King Porus and now his position was rising among Geek leadership outside of the territories. King Porus had advised his ministers to not involve themselves with the growing tensions between the Greeks—advice that Kali would frequently disobey. The tension among the ministers of King Porus festering among the minds of the calculating and disgruntled now began to explode into the open. Kali Mehra would spread rumors of the association between Manish and Chanakya. Kali would also express news concerning the turmoil in the Nanda Empire. Observing the tension mounting, King Porus held a meeting to discuss the internal turmoil in his court and kingdom. During the meeting, Kali accused Manish of increasing wages in the city of Alexandria on the Indus, which made it harder on other projects in the new Alexandrian city. Manish stated that he was providing work and good pay for the working poor people and their families who had suffered most during the previous war.

The always outspoken Harbir said, "You accuse Manish of purposefully creating an unfavorable market for the Yavana-Greek foreigners, however while doing so you neglect the fact that Manish is creating work for our own poor of all castes who are willing to work. This not only serves our poor but also uplifts the morale of our people and gives King Porus a more positive standing!" Some in attendance agreed with Harbir.

Kali responded, "This is more than just our people. This is about working together in a new world paradigm. We now exist in a community of our people along with Persians, Asians, Macedonians, and Greeks. It serves us well to work with them and this is what my family is doing along with my two sons Randeep and Karna."

Harbir responded, "The primary duties of your sons are to develop leadership skills to lead the military under King Porus; it is not to get involved in foreign politics and business as you are doing, Kali. You are more concerned about building projects at the Alexandrian city of the Indus. You seem to speak more in favor of Satrap Peithon who has his own Alexandria by the sea. Peithon should concern himself with his own Alexandrian city. You should inform him of this on your next trip to Peithon's capital at Patala!"

Harbir angrily continued, "Manish is a great man and has a great family. His son serves the military just as well as any son of Kali Mehra and his youngest son Rishan fought against Alexander as a twelve year old boy! Rajesh and Rishan are great men—just like their father—and perform their duties as warriors very well. Rajesh is the husband of my daughter and he has been a great man who does not involve himself in political affairs. Kali Mehra, you have involved yourself in foreign affairs far exceeding your area of responsibility. This includes your involvement in certain businesses and political affairs dating from the period when the Achaemenid Dynasty still controlled the Persian Empire. Before Alexander began his war, you had business and political interests outside of Pauravas!"

Kali Mehra was annoyed but did his best to mask his anger and laughed. "What evidence do you have? You want to diminish my status in the eyes of our King Porus by bearing false witness in the presence of the ministers. I assume this is your strategy along with Manish and perhaps Chanakya! Careful, my king, Chanakya will seek to influence even your own brother and his son."

"   " This caused King Porus to interrupt. "My family is of no concern to you. I alone will deal with my family affairs. As for Manish, he is only concentrating on providing jobs for those who are willing to work. This is not a political matter, Kali."

Everyone understood that it had *become* a political matter and the thin veil of peace would soon be shattered in the region. King Porus' younger brother had announced that he was the true king, the Nanda Kingdom had been under turmoil in the previous year, and now information was known among the populace that Dhana Nanda had been overthrown by conspirators in his own court.

Dhana Nanda's current location was unknown but

it had become public knowledge that the former Nanda Kingdom was predominantly now in favor of Chanakya and his adopted son Chandragupta Maurya. Dhana Nanda's adviser, Amatya Shaktar, was previously imprisoned and subsequently released by Chanakya, although he was in a weakened state. Shaktar, who was a close friend of Chanakya's father, would help solidify the people in support of Chandragupta and offer important intelligence against the remaining resistance. Shaktar would succumb to illness just two years later and Chandragupta would protect his widow Bhamini.

Chanakya's alliances were being formed and the self-proclaimed King Porus Balarama and his son Parvateshwara were feared to be negotiating with the new Mauryan Kingdom. Dhana Nanda was not respected by his own people; he was corrupt and did not serve his kingdom well, he was preoccupied with his own life of greed and corruption, and he was not a major determining factor in the Hydaspes War. However, his military was so large that it deterred Alexander's men from marching forward and now the highly capable, dangerous Chanakya and Chandragupta had become the rulers of this kingdom and its mighty military, sending a shockwave of fear among the Greeks.

Kali Mehra and his sons Randeep and Karna used this fear to their advantage, portraying the Ramankrishna family in a negative light and severing potential construction projects from Manish. Many of the Greeks in the region felt disenfranchised and were suffering without jobs and degrading levels of poverty almost equivalent to the lower castes of the Hindu people of the Punjab regions. This infuriated many of the Greeks, who viewed these Indus people and their exotic Hindu religion as inferior, and their anger was directed at certain wealthy native people like Manish. In an effort to mitigate rising tensions, King Porus advised Manish to expand the numbers of Greek employees in his building projects, which Manish gladly followed. Manish's efforts were to no avail; King Porus could not protect him from the combined efforts of the

Greek satraps Eudamus and Peithon and his own ministers working against him—including Kali Mehra, who King Porus viewed with growing suspicion.

With the Partition of Triparadisus, Satrap Peithon further consolidated his power and authority in the region beyond his borders. This treaty gave Peithon more powers than the previous Partition of Babylon in 323 B.C. Restrictions were placed on Manish and his construction projects. Rajesh and Rishan's positions in the military were now also in question as Randeep and Karna Mehra grew in power. The situation became worse one morning within the border city of Alexandria on the Indus at Manish's construction site. Some disgruntled Greeks felt they were not compensated fairly and should have been treated above some of the native workers. Rishan and Kulvir were present with Manish when the fighting occurred. Manish desperately tried to calm some of the Greeks violently harassing natives when a Greek man suddenly landed a blow upon Manish's face. Rishan was now a tall, strong physical specimen with combat knowledge, which he enthusiastically unleashed on the aggressive Greeks. He managed to knock the offensive Greek on his back while others charged at him. Rishan continued to fight them off while Kulvir and Manish joined him. Gaining courage from Rishan Ramankrishna, many of the lower caste natives joined in the brawl.

A few of the Greeks picked up their weapons and lunged at Rishan, who himself had a sword. A sword fight ensued between Rishan and three of the Greeks, which ended in Rishan injuring the them and almost severing the left hand of the main offender before Greek military members were alerted to the altercation and quickly suppressed it. Rishan suffered minor injuries but inflicted major ones on four men. The Punjabi natives yelled their support of Rishan as he was taken away along with his father and Kulvir while work was suspended for the day. Rishan did not recognize some of the Greeks and Manish suspected they had crossed the border from the satrapy pertaining to Peithon.

Peithon had gained power and legitimacy after his successful defeat of a rebellion led by King Musicanus (or Mûshika) of the Indus just two years prior. Peithon felt this latest disturbance across the border was another potential rebellion he had to suppress and thus he contacted King Porus and Eudamus. Eudamus advised King Porus to hold Rishan as a prisoner for questioning while they gathered evidence as to what happened the previous day. King Porus refused, saying that all witnesses stated that the riot had been initiated by the Greeks at the construction site. After a week of pressure and risking internal revolt, Eudamus ordered the Macedonian military to arrest Rishan.

Rishan's position as a young leader was suspended pending the outcome of the investigation and Manish's construction project continued for a brief period before it was transferred to Greek architects. Many of the native Punjabi workers lost their jobs and they were transferred to Greek workers, some of whom were less qualified than the Punjabi men they replaced. King Porus tried to diffuse the situation but growing tensions among his ministers and between him and the Greek leadership eventually led to Rishan being held for a prolonged period of time without a trial. King Porus wished to hold a trial in the customs of the Punjabi people but the incident involved Greeks and natives as well as workers from Peithon's territory, which complicated the issue. King Porus was aware of Peithon and Eudamus' growing power and believed that Ambhi was actively undermining him; perhaps Porus' younger brother was right. The situation within the Greek Empire was troubling and King Porus understood it might fracture in the future, however he had limited knowledge of the internal politics of the Greek Empire and many of his spies had been captured or murdered. This blinded King Porus in the areas of foreign affairs and limited his ability to make informed decisions about the future of his kingdom.

Rishan was now being held by troops loyal to the Greeks and Satrap Eudamus. Manish appealed to Eudamus for Rishan's release to no avail; the injury Rishan inflicted on one of the Greeks was severe. The Greek man had now lost his hand and wanted justice and other Greeks asked for Rishan's punishment despite the eyewitnesses stating that the Greeks were the aggressors. Others went to see Rishan, including his mother Lakshmi and his sister Priya, who were overcome with grief. Lakshmi pleaded with the Greeks to let her son go—he was a man of peace and education—but her pleading was ignored and they were told to leave. Eudamus finally ceased all communication between Rishan and his family and friends and intimidated Rishan to publicly state a lie about the events that had transpired at his father's construction site. When he repeatedly refused to comply, Karna Mehra came to see him.

Initially Rishan was happy to see a member of his military. Rishan pleaded with Karna to speak with King Porus and the Greeks about what transpired but Rishan understood that the Greeks did not view him favorably. In physical competition, Rishan had continued to fight for sport, frequently displaying the very best of the martial arts of his people by besting other Greeks—which also soured his relationship with the Greek occupiers.

Karna replied, "Your family has committed a grave mistake, Rishan. Your father remained silent while your brother's father-in-law publicly slandered my family about our business practices and alleged political connections without any evidence. Is this how your family conducts affairs? You are Dravidians from the southern regions who pretend to be equals to Punjabi Aryans like us! And you, Rishan. You'd rather socialize with lower caste people like your friend Anand Agrawal and your family allows that disgrace to occur within your own home. I question your position as a warrior in our caste and question your family—especially Harbir, who may not be your blood but has infected your family with his ideas and rhetoric. Your family is very fortunate you are under the good graces of our King Porus because Eudamus and Peithon want your execution. Thank me and remember my name, for I have asked my father to speak to Eudamus about sparing your life. The Greeks will be appeased if your father gives Eudamus a large amount of gold pieces. Your position in the military will be suspended and your leadership status will be stripped upon my suggestion. If you wish to keep your position you must convince Harbir to speak with us to reach an understanding about his misinformation."

Rishan was angered at the actions of this man he had believed was his friend. "Karna, you speak to Eudamus and Peithon but you should speak directly with King Porus. Where is my trial? What about the witnesses on that day? Do you simply ignore them? We are one people. Why do you speak to me in such a way?"

Karna Mehra snapped, "You and your kind start trouble when the Greeks have their own matters to attend. One day we will have peace in these lands but you along with those who think like you will ravage that peace if we don't put an end to you. For hundreds of years, these lands were subject to wars among rival kings that claimed the lives of our own people. If we stabilize these regions, we can have peace as long as the Greeks can organize what is left of Alexander's Empire. You should be very thankful, Rishan. You should be relieved to know that you will only receive a beating—the same beating that your father should have given you—and at least you will still have your life!"

With that, Karna Mehra walked away. Rishan had known that Karna had been growing distant, but he was surprised to see him suddenly turn on him and his family. Macedonian guards routinely greeted Rishan with severe beatings daily for roughly two weeks before they finally stopped and began to mentally torture him. For about a month, Rishan was held with little food until his wounds were mostly healed before he was escorted to the Ramankrishna household. Rishan was warned not to speak of these events or they would threaten the lives of Rajesh and Kulvir. King Porus was informed that Rishan was set free but he remained ignorant of the beating Rishan received at the hands of the Macedonians.

The Ramankrishna family was saddened regarding some of the wounds that Rishan received but little did they know that Rishan's wounds had previously been far greater in number. Rishan was gripped with fear and decided not to inform his father about what had occurred. It was a fear that he only remembered facing on the side of the Hydaspes River when he decided to fight for his father and King Porus' lives. For several weeks, Rishan rarely spoke of the incident, deciding to turn his attentions to the welfare of his father and brother's respective careers. Rishan did not want to endanger the success of his family for the events that had occurred that day at the construction site.

Rajesh had arrived to the Ramankrishna house to see his younger brother full of anger and questions. Rajesh's questions could not be answered, and the family began to think of ways to clear Rishan's name until one rainy night Harbir arrived.

Harbir informed the family that there had been a speedy trial in Rishan's absence. To appease the growing anger among the eye witnesses who supported Rishan, it was decided that Rishan would receive no further punishment and a payment would be made by Manish to the Greek victims— it was a large payment which amounted to roughly twenty percent of the Ramankrishna's combined wealth. Rishan was suspended from his position in the military and it would be decided if he would keep his leadership role while Rajesh's standing in the military was kept secure. This was an unfair judgment but it also avoided further rebellion for Eudamus. Harbir stated that Alexander's half-brother, Philip III Arrhidaeus, was not able to exert control over the Greek Empire and could not even manage his own household with his wife and mother dictating policy. Philip III Arrhidaeus was a mentally unfit man who never received a political or military leadership position and as the leader of the Greeks, Asians, and Egyptians, he could not truly employ his new powers. Philip III was not respected and the Greek generals were now fighting a civil war as they all regarded themselves the rightful heirs to Alexander's Empire, each claiming to be the true Diadochi.

Manish had been denied the information and King Porus had most likely also been kept in the dark. The initial clash began when Ptolemy, now the satrap of Egypt, stole Alexander's body and brought it to Egypt, where he placed it in Alexandria and infuriated the other Greek leaders.

Manish asked, "And how did you learn of all this information and what should we do with this knowledge? This will prove to be dangerous. Think carefully, Harbir!"

Harbir replied, "Manish, you have been careful with your family and although I don't have my wife and young children anymore, I once did and I understand. You and your son Rajesh now are responsible for my daughter Divya and I respect you for it but if you will not fight you should take your family and my daughter to a safer region because this situation might get worse. I will stay behind and provide a cover for your family as you flee. I suspect King Porus is also unaware of the vast wars and the planning going on among the Greeks in this region— including Peithon and Eudamus and some of our fellow ministers. I also suspect the Mehra family to be working with Eudamus and Peithon and I have found some documents which may prove my theory as fact!" Harbir then went on to explain some previous business dealings regarding the Mehra family without the knowledge of King Porus.

When Manish asked for Harbir to provide this evidence, he placed a few documents on a table and indeed it showed a correspondence between Kali Mehra, Eudamus, and particularly Peithon. These letters displayed evidence of business collaborations between Eudamus, Peithon, and the Mehra family. There were also records of possible positions in the Greek leadership for Kali's sons Randeep and Karna outside of the direct control of King Porus. There were other documents that Harbir could not gather because of his fear of Eudamus' suspicion. Eudamus was also envious of Peithon's growing influence and power in the region; it was causing a hidden power struggle between the satraps. Manish demanded Harbir to hide the documents and not make them public unless Kali Mehra indeed sought more power—a plan which Harbir reluctantly agreed with at least for the time being.

Manish then spoke with his family in order to decide what they should do in case war spilled into the region. Two possibilities arose. One choice was to move south with Manish's parents or east into the neutral territory of King Porus' younger brother Porus Balarama. The tough rhetoric of King Balarama against the Greek occupiers had recently mellowed, giving way to the more neutral rhetoric of his son Parvateshwara. The self-proclaimed Prince Parvateshwara was now leading the day to day operations of his territory and his relationship with the new king, Chandragupta Maurya, was neutral, making it a safe place for the Ramankrishna family to reside. Manish also believed Eudamus and his agents would reach the family if they were to flee south and it would also endanger Manish's parents. At least if they fled to the east they would be able to flee into the safety of the empire of Chandragupta Maurya under the protection of Chanakya. Rishan and the other family members agreed, including Rajesh, who promised to take his new bride Divya with him to safety.

Rishan stated, "Harbir, let's not have further meetings in the future as we are not sure if we have spies after us."

With that, Harbir left and the family quietly discussed further preparations and when they could possibly carry out their plans. Manish decided that his brother Manu would help protect and lead the family to the east while Manish and his sons stay behind so as not to arouse suspicion. Manish and his sons would then leave at a later period if the situation became serious.

Manish's plans for his family would begin to prove necessary as the Ramankrishna family was facing rising isolation from the upper classes. The Kumari family was also not associating with the Ramankrishna family, which resulted in a rapidly increasing strain in Rishan and Priyanka's relationship. The woman Rishan had grown to love was now distancing herself from him, causing deep pain. Rishan now felt as he did when he was the young boy isolated and unloved by his peers. Everything Rishan had accomplished academically and athletically seemed unimportant to Priyanka. His athletics were a matter of pride for him because unlike academics, athletics was something Rishan put a lot of work and sacrifice into. Several times, Rishan tried to reason with Priyanka, promising a future where both could grow together as husband and wife as planned, but to no avail. Rishan's future was not guaranteed, as he rapidly lost control of his own destiny. Rishan realized his future was now in the control the Greeks and the Mehra family.

King Porus was growing older now and his correspondence with his younger brother Porus Balarama had slowed. King Porus had to continue correspondence with his nephew Parvateshwara, who now carried most of the responsibilities previously held by his father. King Porus still advocated a long term strategy to strengthen his kingdom and eagerly awaited the strategy Chandragupta Maurya would choose, however Chandragupta and Chanakya were still putting down pockets of rebellions mostly made up of the few who benefited from the widespread corruption of Dhana Nanda. King Porus advised his nephew to be aware of the foreign Greek Yona people and their spies who were actively seeking to see if Parvateshwara wanted an alliance with Chandragupta as his father once had. Peithon was the most powerful Greek leader in the region but Eudamus was more unpredictable due to his poor self-esteem and envy of Peithon. King Porus felt he could be patient for only so long; he had to devise a strategy to reclaim his power and possibly kill King Ambhi, who he suspected of undermining his authority.

The Ramankrishna family was facing increasing trouble and possible surveillance by Punjabi and Macedonian scouts. Some families close to the Ramankrishna family chose to minimize or completely stop communications with the Ramankrishnas with the exception of the Agrawal family. The Ramankrishna and Agrawal family had grown very close as they watched their sons' friendship grow. Anand had become Rishan's best friend and the Ramankrishna family aided in Anand Agrawal's education, which had helped him learn basic architecture. The Agrawal family publicly supported the Ramankrishnas despite Manish advising them to disassociate themselves from the toxic political environment enveloping the land.

CHAPTER 12:
FALL OF THE HOUSE OF RAMANKRISHNA AND THE SECOND WAR OF THE DIADOCHI (320 B.C.)

"The strong do what they have to do and the weak accept what they have to accept."
—Thucydides

Rishan was frustrated with his father's perspective. Rishan also faced internal turmoil over the failure of his relationship with Priyanka and uncertainty of his future. Rishan felt he had worked hard his entire life both academically and athletically and now others who he felt didn't exert the same effort now had access to prosperity. The main contributor to Rishan's condition was Karna Mehra, who Rishan despised. Rishan's mental anguish now manifested itself in the enjoyment of wine and substances that removed him from reality. Manish was increasingly frustrated with Rishan and would occasionally suffer through his various states of drunkenness—an act that was outside of Rishan's personality.

Rishan's growing rebelliousness against authority and sometimes Manish began to create a rift between father and son. Manish remained patient with his youngest son because he understood his pain under their stressful situation. A one on one talk with Rishan was in order whenever he had time. The Ramankrishna family were beginning to gather their things for a possible move when they were interrupted by the unexpected arrival of Kulvir Kumari, sobbing and upset.

Manish was surprised. "Why do you appear so distressed, Kulvir?"

Kulvir replied, "I apologize for the actions of my family and I feel saddened for the conditions your family now find yourselves in. I also apologize for my sister Priyanka's actions towards your son Rishan. I am ashamed to say that my sister is now romantically involved with a cousin of Karna Mehra called Kanchanpreet Mehra, who is involved in the construction projects at Alexandria on the Indus. Kanchanpreet was also involved in projects in the coastal city under the rule of Peithon named Alexandria as well."

Manish now had some evidence of a possible conspiracy between Eudamus, Peithon, and the Mehra family. Manish turned to the young Kulvir, calmly responding, "I thank you for your honesty and I understand your family's fear. I believe it's safe to assume you were offered new opportunities with the Mehra family if you disassociated from us. You are a good young man Kulvir, but you must understand the danger you are under if you disobey your family. Perhaps in the future we will meet again under different circumstances but until then leave my house and watch your safety. I would also advise your sister to be careful of the Mehra family; they have no friends. May Lord Krishna enlighten you and keep you safe, Kulvir." With no other choice, Kulvir left the Ramankrishna home. Rajesh, who had been listening to the conversation, was angered with his father as he exclaimed, "Perhaps Kulvir is here to seek information for the Mehra Family and the Macedonians."

Manish looked at his worried son and replied, "You cannot stop the flood once the dam has broken." Manish would explain what he had learned and advise Rishan on how he should handle the negative information.

Rishan continued to face punishment and suspension from his military position. His silence began to give way to open questioning of Karna Mehra and his family. Rishan also continued to seek information from Harbir, who detailed the fracturing of the Greek Empire and Alexander's half-brother ruling as a puppet. Many of the major leaders positioning themselves to succeed Alexander were the same generals Rishan had met only a few years prior. Peridiccas the Chiliarch was known to command at least 1,000 men previously and had become the strongest man in the Greek Empire, acting as regent for Alexander's mentally unfit half-brother. Peridiccas carried Alexander's ring and sought to solidify his control by marrying Alexander's sister Cleopatra. Many of the generals and satraps felt the possible transfer of power to Alexander's two year old son was in jeopardy and used this to rebel. Secretly many of the generals wanted power for themselves and one by one, they rose and united against Peridiccas, including Craterus, Antipater, Antigonus, and Ptolemy.

Eumenes was dispatched to combat the rebellion but it did not matter; Peridiccas was murdered by his own generals Antigenes, Seleucus, and others during an attempted invasion into Egypt. Ptolemy made an agreement with the murderers of Peridiccas and through different agreements the conspirators gained control of various territories— Babylon was given to Seleucus. The new regent was now Antipater and the one-eyed General Antigonus had the largest army in the region. Harbir explained that battles were still currently being fought but that there was a general peace in the empire. They believed it would not last long.

Rishan also learned about the murders of Alexander's Persian wives Stateira II and Parysatis II, possibly by Roxana and Alexander's mother Olympias. It had become a huge scandal yet information was closely guarded to maintain the façade of control. Eudamus had some trouble maintaining secrecy and did not keep the high level of order that Peithon had, as evidenced by Harbir's apparent access to this sensitive information. Rumors of threats against the Ramankrishnas were spreading and King Porus sought to protect the family that had served him and his kingdom so well. King Porus would summon Manish and his son Rishan to the Royal Palace for a private meeting.

Rishan and his family were under increasing scrutiny and the Macedonians and Mehras seemed to have eyes and ears everywhere. Karna Mehra was now growing in power within the military, getting closer to the influence that his older brother Randeep had and now surpassing the position of the respected Rajesh Ramankrishna who had continued to suffer from his leg injuries. Karna was now requesting to hold Rishan for questioning once again and this was one of the reasons King Porus wanted a meeting. King Porus was happy to see Manish and Rishan and inquired about any developments regarding the incident at the construction site. King Porus also admitted to growing discord between the Greek leadership as well as his own conflicts with the Greeks. King Porus advised Manish that he should be careful of the Greek people who had grown frustrated and were easily manipulated by leaders like Peithon to redirect their anger towards the native people of Pauravas and the surrounding territories. He stated he would reprimand Kali Mehra and his sons if they actively continued to motivate negative behavior towards the Ramankrishna family.

Manish informed King Porus of his plan to begin relocating his family east to the territory of his nephew Parvateshwara. King Porus agreed that Manish's idea was a good one since Parvateshwara distanced himself from his father's openly antagonistic position against the Greeks. However, King Porus warned that he had little communication with his nephew and did not know what political stance his nephew would possibly take given the growing power of Chandragupta Maurya, who was now legitimizing his rule of the Magadha Empire.

King Porus then stated, "I will protect your family from further persecution, however I am not certain about the political alliances my nephews will create—especially my grand-nephew Malayaketu. Malayaketu makes many unwise decisions and his behavior is dangerous, especially in the political instability that rules today's world."

After this meeting, Manish began the preparations for Lakshmi and their daughter Priya's departure under the care of his brother Manu. Within days, Lakshmi and Priya left along with Manu away from Greek rule. Manu secured most of the Ramankrishna family's silver and copper currency, including golden jewelry which Lakshmi mostly wore. Other materials including the Ramankrishna family's documents and important correspondence were also gathered as Manu escorted the family east. Lakshmi, Priya, and Rishan exchanged tearful goodbyes and Rishan promised his mother they would soon be reunited.

A few days later, Rishan was to be escorted to meet Karna Mehra and Eudamus for questioning. Manish decided that now was a good time to speak with his son, preparing him for a potential negative situation.

Manish advised Rishan to release the anger he had inside, especially relating to matters that were trivial—issues such as Priyanka and her family deciding that Rishan would not be a good choice for a husband.

Rishan responded, "Father, anger and focus is what helped make me a better athlete and student. I was angered and wanted to fulfill my duties as a born warrior to the best of my abilities. Anger helped me focus and succeed and has helped me excel."

Manish responded, "Yes, my son, you had focused anger and motivation to learn through error and improve in combat and other athletic pursuits just as you have in your studies. However, there are situations in life where focused attention will not change the outcome. For example, the woman you care for has already decided she does not wish you to be her husband—a decision she most likely reached with the influence of her family. You can't make her change her mind so it is best to forget her. In the affairs of choosing a woman, you must make sure that just as you fight for her she is equally fighting for you. Speak with Karna Mehra in honesty and if he choses to punish you further you should join Lakshmi and Priya east outside of the Greek Empire so you may begin your life again. Always use your intelligence Rishan before you use force.

If you have no other method to excuse yourself from a violent altercation, make sure you attack with your full might and experience because no one will protect you more than yourself." Manish also chose to reveal that Rajesh's wife Divya had begun to show the initial stages of childbirth—a fact that was later confirmed by Harbir. The Ramankrishna family now had additional incentive to leave Pauravas.

The day eventually arrived when Rishan met Eudamus and Karna Mehra. Eudamus was a strong man who was capable at leading men in war, however he was insecure as an administrator. These insecurities were thinly concealed under a veil of false bravado and political savvy. In reality, Eudamus feared an insurrection by both Greeks and or native Punjabis—an insurrection that even the more capable Peithon had difficulty suppressing. Eudamus incorrectly labeled Rishan as a possible rebel leader, most likely believing the lies of the Mehra family. This also strained his relationship with King Porus, who he believed was helping the Ramankrishnas to the detriment of his own kingdom and Eudamus' legitimacy as a governor. Eudamus did not know what action to take and entrusted Karna with extracting the important information from Rishan.

Karna exclaimed, "What is your affiliation with Chanakya and the usurper Chandragupta Maurya?" "Who are Chandragupta's allies and what are your opinions of him?" These questions did not result in any satisfactory answer, as Rishan was ignorant to the intricacies involving the overthrow of Dhana Nanda and the current situation of Magadha. Rishan was also unaware of the location of the deposed Dhana Nanda.

Karna requested that Rishan be beaten by Macedonian security, causing Rishan to state, "Does King Porus have knowledge of what you are doing now? Why must I get beaten once again even though my family has paid a large price for actions they were not guilty of? King Porus should understand the level of disrespect you and your family now have for him, undermining him by affiliating yourselves with the Greeks. You are a great fighting champion, but so am I, and I have beaten every man placed in front of me no matter if they are Persian, Asian, or Punjabi. I have also gladly beaten all fighters from Macedonia or Greece, including Thebans, Athenians, and Spartans. It has mattered little to me. I have no fear. They can place an Olympiad champion in front of me and I will not be impressed."

Karna Mehra grew agitated at the fact that Rishan had openly challenged him to a fight—something very few ever dared.

Karna hid his feelings under a false laugh. "You believe you will beat me in a fighting match? You are clouded by your anger and your jealousy that the beautiful Priyanka has accepted my cousin Kanchanpreet's advances. Your family is of Dravidian and southern origins and has only risen to the upper level of society because King Porus has mistakenly believed your father to be more valuable than he really is. I would personally love to best you in a physical contest and I would like it to be a public affair. I want to erase any reputation you have of being a great champion. If I win I suggest you remove yourself from the military before you suffer any more embarrassment."

Rishan responded, "I don't fight for the affections of a woman who is no longer willing to fight for me—that is the endeavor of a foolish man. Priyanka's behavior is not of a woman I would call a wife but it is enough for someone from the Mehra family. I also would like to suggest that upon my victory perhaps you should resign your Greek influenced position and leave my family alone."

Karna laughed, dismissing Rishan. "If you win just be happy I don't punish you further."

Rishan was released and free to go home, eager to finally get revenge on his false friend and new adversary.

As the days passed, tensions began to build as word spread of the fight between the two great champions. Manish initially did not want his son to participate in combat against Karna Mehra because he viewed it as a situation where Rishan would not receive a positive outcome. Once the night of the match was cemented, he encouraged his son to defeat Karna just as he had defeated over 100 of his previous opponents.

Eudamus viewed Rishan and the Ramankrishna family as a potential spark against the legitimacy of his rule, so he encouraged Karna to not only defeat Rishan but to publicly humiliate him.

Peithon was influenced by the rise of Chandragupta and recent rebellions by Greeks and Punjabi natives also became interested in the contest as a method to unite Greeks and turn their frustrations on the Punjabi natives. Peithon believed Eudamus would eventually fail to hold the eastern borders of the Greek Empire and would also have difficulty suppressing rebellions. Peithon and Eudamus agreed to have the match at a border town between their areas of responsibility: the city of Alexandria on the Indus. It was the city where the case was made against Rishan's family and the location that sparked further anger within the native community against the Greeks.

News of the fight spread among the people and because of their internal frustrations, many supporters were ignited by their views on the social, economic, and political landscapes favoring one champion over the other. Many of the Greeks, Macedonians, upper caste, and wealthy native Punjabis chose Karna Mehra while many lower caste Punjabis and Dravidian people favored Rishan Ramankrishna. Haxamanis remained one of Rishan's most vocal Persian supporters, which placed him at odds with the Mehra family and other Persians who wanted to further solidify their relationship with the Greeks.

Men filled the combat area specifically built for this contest and most of the women in attendance were Greek. Other combatants were asked to fight or chose to participate to create a larger event for the public who demanded more. The akhara was a fighting pit mixed with clay, dirt, water, and oils, creating a desired level of consistency in the mud. Rishan began to feel nervous as the other combatants fought, causing excited cheers from the crowd. Rishan's father was in attendance as well as his brother Rajesh, and he wondered who else would come to see him fight. Rishan prayed to Hanuman, the monkey headed God, to guide him. The crowd began to shout as Rishan and Karna entered the circular pit.

Extra water and some yellowish butter called ghee were sprinkled into the clay and dirt as Rishan stretched. It would be a technical fight and no bone breaking would be allowed—much to the dismay of Rishan, who wished to break every bone in Karna's body. The anxiety within Rishan had manifested in laborious breathing as he tried to relax. Both men wore only some clothing covering their waist area, leaving their chests and legs exposed.

Karna yelled at Rishan that he would lose and would not win Priyanka. Rishan yelled back, repeating that he did not fight for a woman who did not also fight for him. Rishan viewed this contest as an opportunity to win back his honor and that of his family, not the affections of a woman who did not care for him.

The fighters were signaled to begin, and they circled each other slowly. At once, Rishan saw an opening and struck Karna with a hard right hook to the temple, which he promptly followed by a stomach blow with his left hand as the largely Greek crowd remained silent. Manish, Rajesh, and Anand stood and watched in awe as Rishan continued to hurt Karna as he stumbled backwards.

Karna was in unfamiliar territory; he was now on the defensive, acknowledging that he had made a mistake in underestimating Rishan. Karna managed to land a good strike to Rishan's midsection, Rishan subsequently chose to tackle him to the ground.

Karna held onto Rishan's waist as he scrambled to get up, the Greek crowd roaring with satisfaction. Rishan was overtaken by Karna's strength; he now found himself on his stomach, swinging and blindly hoping to connect a blow. Rishan finally landed an elbow to the top of Karna's head, sending him backwards and allowing Rishan to stand. Rishan rushed forward, landing a few more hits to Karna's head and body as he tried to block. Rishan wanted to showcase his knowledge of kalaripayattu martial arts just as he had shown his superiority in Greek martial arts by defeating his previous Greek opponents. Rishan continued to land powerful strikes, causing Karna to yell in anger and lose his discipline. This enabled Rishan to draw first blood.

Karna dodged some strikes, trying to keep his distance and allowing Rishan to momentarily notice his father, brother, and the Anand family encouraging him among the spectators. Once again, Karna tried to push Rishan to the ground but Rishan continued to dodge his attacks, blocking with his feet and eliciting a gasp of surprise from the crowd. Rishan continued to demonstrate his superior speed and technical abilities as Karna desperately tried to catch his elusive opponent. For the first time, Karna Mehra was clearly outmatched and faced a potential embarrassing defeat.

During a brief intermission, one of the Greeks asked Karna if he wished to use weapons but Karna rejected the idea, claiming he would eventually beat Rishan with his bare hands. When the fight resumed, Karna was able to land some powerful strikes upon Rishan, creating deafening shouts of glee from the Greek crowd. Finally, Karna managed to grapple Rishan to the ground although he didn't fare any better this time.Rishan A desperate Karna grabbed a fistful of dirt and clay and mixed it with an oily substance between his hands. Sensing victory, Rishan attempted to land a final devastating blow and missed, sending Rishan face first into the mud. Karna spread the mud across Rishan's face, decreasing his ability to breathe. Karna then began to land hard blows to the back of Rishan's head. The Greek crowd roared as Rishan found himself in a strange place—as the same eight year old boy who would have fled in fear. It would be the first time Rishan lost since he began fighting in official combat. Blood streamed from Rishan's face as his father and Anand shouted for the contest to stop. Finally, Rishan's teacher Akas stepped between the fighters, pushing Karna to the ground.

Shouts of disapproval were directed at Karna Mehra when some spectators noticed the mud on Rishan's face, sparking arguments between the Greek and Punjabi spectators. Peithon, in attendance with Eudamus, dispatched Greek soldiers to calm the crowd as both combatants left the circular arena.

Karna exclaimed his victory, to which Rishan responded, "You fought dishonorably, and everyone knows!"

An angered Karna Mehra stated that Rishan would be stripped of his position and forced out of the duties of his caste. Karna was declared the winner but his bruises were far greater than Rishan's.

As the days passed, rumors and threats spread and the idea of Rishan leaving became more legitimate in Manish's mind. Perhaps it was time for his son to leave while Manish and Rajesh spoke with King Porus to reach an agreement to mitigate the growing tensions.

Rishan had met with Harbir, who had given Rishan some documents without Manish's knowledge. It detailed some political scheming within the Greek leadership— mostly Eudamus—and some documents hinted at collaboration with Satrap Peithon. Manish would speak to Harbir about the best strategy to use against Kali if he continued to foment trouble among King Porus' advisers.

Manish prepared a horse for Rishan and gave him gold jewelry and coins. He advised his son to stay just beyond the borders and possibly seek shelter among some family members outside of Greek territory. Manish told him that if the situation worsened, he should leave south to his grandparents' home. As Rajesh and Manish prepared to have a meeting with King Porus, Rishan returned to the Ramankrishna home for what he believed would be the last time and Rishan gathered a sword, shield, and small dagger from his teacher Akas. The sun was beginning to set as Rishan gathered his clothing and weapons and prepared his horse to leave. Rishan's heart suddenly began to beat faster when he heard someone nearby.

As the steps grew louder, Rishan hid in some trees behind the stable. Men were whispering as they paced around the Ramankrishna home.

"I only wish to kill Rishan. That will greatly intimidate his family," one voice said.

Another man stated, "Why did I get involved in the affairs of animals? Now I suffer the loss of my hand all because of their plotting and politics!"

Finally, both men came into view: two Greeks, one with a severed left hand. Rishan wanted to flee but fearing for the safety of his family made him hesitate, alerting the men to his presence.

Rishan "It is him!" one of the men shouted. "That is the son of a dog that cut off my hand!"

Already having an idea as to who the handless man was, Rishan asked the men for their identities. The handless man responded, "Yes, it is you, the educated animal who has learned Greek and the man who severed my hand. My name is Arkadios and my friend is a warrior from Thebes. Before you draw your last breath tonight, my name will be the last you remember. I seek justice and not your father's money. How insulting to accept money from people who are below me." Arkadios approached Rishan with a sword in his right hand but remained shieldless and defenseless, relying on his partner to flank Rishan.

Arkadios faked a step forward as his partner rushed towards Rishan's right side, Rishan lunging with his sword and causing Rishan to leap backwards and counter with an attack of his own. The power of Rishan's strike sent the Theban backwards as he continued forward, striking with all his might with his sword glancing of the Theban's shield but cutting the man's right thigh. Using his sword, he turned and kicked Arkadios in the groin, sending him to the ground writhing in pain. The Theban took the opportunity to remove the sword from Rishan's hands. The Theban continued to land hard punches upon Rishan's head as Rishan reached for his shield, striking a hard blow to his opponent's head. Rishan reached for his urumi coiled and tucked into his belt as the two men rushed forward. Extending five long flat strips of metal, each about five feet in length, Rishan spun them and whipped them forward. He struck both men in the head and torso. The Theban received most of the damage and became incapacitated, allowing Rishan to grab his sword and cut off Arkadios' left arm clean above the elbow.

As Arkadios screamed, Rishan screamed, "Now an arm to go with the hand you lost!"

Arkadios sobbed, "This is the price I pay for dealing with you animals in the name of Peithon. Damn all of you to the darkest recesses of Tartarus!"

Rishan asked Arkadios about his collaboration with Peithon and Eudamus but Arkadios only responded with cursing. As Rishan raised his sword, the Theban cried out for mercy, causing Arkadios to yell, "Silence, coward! This animal does not wish to spare us; he knows we will come back to kill him and his family. Whatever choice this animal makes, his fate has been sealed and his days and nights are numbered."

Before Arkadios could add another sentence, Rishan drove his sword through his chest and he choked on his own blood.

The Theban pleaded for his life, saying he would act as a witness against Arkadios. "Think about it, Rishan. My name is Myron. I can help clear your name and prove the innocence of your family. You cannot kill me, for the evidence will die along with my body."

Rishan raised his sword. "Your cadavers will lay at the bottom of the river for the beasts of the water to feast on." Rishan then violently struck Myron the Theban, which resulted in his death.

After cleaning the area, Rishan gathered the bodies and placed them in his chariot, tying them in place. Rishan took two horses instead of one as he initially planned and began to ride south, slowly at first and then as fast as he could. Rishan found the nearest river and dumped the bodies, fastening boulders to them tightly with rope. After cleaning his body at another location five more miles to the south, his heart rate finally began to decrease and he decided he would ride towards his grandparents' home. Darkness began to envelop the world as Rishan raced towards the border of the Assaka Kingdom.

Rishan's thoughts swirled in his mind as if they were locked in a life and death struggle with each other.

How deep was the connection between Arkadios, Peithon, and the Mehra family? What were the Mehras hiding? Rishan also thought of the safety of his father, brother, and Harbir back in Pauravas. Finally, a smile broke the saddened expression on Rishan's face as he pondered becoming an uncle upon the birth of Rajesh and Divya's child. Thoughts of the new child and reuniting with his family someday warmed his heart and he attempted to maintain these positive thoughts as he rode through the night.

CHAPTER 13:
THE JAIN SAGE OF THE DANDAKA FOREST
(318 B.C.)

"Truth is one, but the wise men know it as many; God is one, but we can approach Him in many ways."
—*The Rig Veda*

Rishan was exhausted and troubled by the idea of possible pursuers. The journey had been long and dreadful but he had managed to reach the Assaka Empire and the home of his grandparents roughly six months ago. Rishan was plagued with thoughts of probable events back in the Greek occupied Pauravas territory and often pondered the fate of his family and friends. Did his father, brother, and Harbir make it east and join Manu and the Ramankrishna women? Rishan worried about the possible actions taken by the Greeks on behalf of the men he had killed in self-defense. Rishan understood the Greek satraps Eudamus and Peithon might have known the Ramankrishna family was missing. Most likely Eudamus and Peithon had sent Greek agents to disrupt his father's construction site and they probably also sent agents once again to the Ramankrishna residence that fateful evening.

When he had arrived to his grandparents' home, he was welcomed with surprise and joy. The little Rishan had grown over six feet in height and displayed great strength and intelligence. He was a sight to behold. Rishan tried to mask the fear ready to spring from within him, but he waited a few days before fully divulging the reasons for his sudden arrival. Over a warm meal prepared by Seeta, Rishan explained the situation. Rishan spoke calmly and stated that the Ramankrishna women had relocated to a safer region and that the Ramankrishna men would soon follow. Rishan took special care not to mention the fight that led him to killing the two Greeks the night he fled or the political turmoil and the high level of threats the Ramankrishna family faced. Rishan also took time to explain the civil war enveloping the Greek Empire after the death of Alexander over five years ago. Rishan stated that Alexander's half-brother Philip III held all the titles Alexander the Great once had, including King of Persia, King of Asia, the Punjab region, and Pharaoh of Egypt. Rishan explained that although Philip III held all these titles he could not manage his own household and that even the powerful regent could not control the different successors maneuvering to gain greater control of their territories. Rishan feared this violence would soon spread into the Punjab and perhaps Peithon would call himself leader of the region and destroy all his enemies—possibly the Ramankrishna family among them.

Mahesh was alarmed and inquired about the thoughts of his son Manish and King Porus regarding this turmoil. Rishan explained the new role of the great King Porus under the Greeks. King Porus was as now a client king with minor administrative duties and he had failed to stop the Mehra family from publicly humiliating the Ramankrishnas. King Porus was locked in a tough political battle with King Ambhi and the Greek satraps, which gradually isolated him from foreign affairs.

Rishan had a feeling that the situation had worsened in Pauravas and spies were possibly following him. Rishan had noticed men acting suspiciously within the Assaka territory and he was unsure whether they originated from Greek controlled Pauravas or from the Royal House of Assaka. Rishan had basic knowledge of the history of the

Assaka Kingdom and he questioned his grandparents about the political stability here. Mahesh explained that the Assaka Empire had been founded by a Royal sage named Ashmaka. They referred to the territory as the Ashmaka Empire and the Royal Family traced their roots to the Ikshvaku Dynasty.

Rishan recognized the Ikshvaku Dynasty as the Solar Dynasty mentioned in the words of the *Ramayana*, *Mahabharata*, *Harivamsa*, and the *Puranas*. Rishan also remembered that Anupa Jhingan had mentioned this dynasty. It was the first time Rishan had remembered Anupa and the depth of spiritual knowledge she possessed. Anupa was an oasis for Rishan in times of despair and a relationship Rishan truly needed in order to replenish the peace within his mind.

Brahmadatta was an ancient king of this region and King Aruna claimed to be related to him. With the help of his minister Nandisena, King Aruna of Assaka was able to secure a victory over the king of Kalinga. This was a historical victory that was a matter of pride for the current King Aruman of Assaka, who claimed to be a descendant of King Aruna. The current king had grown weak and he feared war with the Kalinga Empire, which had grown very powerful and remained unconquered throughout many generations.

Rishan was concerned with the stability of Assaka and he feared the kingdom might fall victim to civil war. Rishan encouraged his grandparents to leave back north to Pauravas with him but he realized they were now growing old. Mahesh was declining in health and the stressful trip might cause his death. Rishan believed his prolonged stay would encourage spies of the Royal Family of Assaka to investigate his grandparents and would place them in greater danger.

As if Mahesh was reading Rishan's mind, he stated, "My grandson, you are not at fault and you have been brave. They will not inflict harm on you or us, and if they are as politically astute as you say they are, they would not dare travel here. Would these Yavana Greeks risk infiltrating so deep into a land and culture they do not understand? A land with people and languages exotic to them, where they would confront the different tribal forces in battles with which they cannot afford to engage? You are an intelligent man. Do what is best for you first and your family will respect you for it."

Rishan explained that it was individual infiltrators and the influence of Greek leadership that made him nervous. Rishan replied, "It is wealth, grandfather; their wealth is power. It makes others carry out their evil wishes."

Seeta cried that perhaps this would be the last time they would see their grandson but Mahesh consoled her. "There comes a time when a man has to choose his own path. It is the choice we are given by Lord Krishna. Let us rejoice that at this moment and this time our grandson is smart, healthy, and strong. Our world will change and we are not sure which power will win, but the Greeks will taste defeat and I encourage Rishan and our family to find the best path to this. I hope I live to see the day when our grandchild is victorious and our family name is restored. Stay safe Rishan, and hopefully we will meet again during better circumstances."

With that, Rishan left the Assaka Kingdom with his chariot and two horses. He headed northeast towards the Dandaka Forest with plans to follow the boundary towards the territory of King Porus' nephew Parvateshwara.

Rishan entered deeper into the Dandaka Forest in an effort to remove himself from the view of potential spies or roving bands of criminals. The travel proved difficult; Rishan had to actively avoid potential Greek agents. Rishan believed the little protection offered by King Porus would soon deteriorate, leaving him and his family in the utmost danger. King Porus had lost a younger brother Akar and his two sons who had been in line to become king when his wife died shortly after the Hydaspes war. King Porus' other wife had not bore him a son, leaving an unrecognized son left to take the Pauravas throne. Rishan understood that the loss of the major members of Porus' family would make King Porus' dynasty an easier target—a thought that made

Rishan shudder as he tried to set up a shelter to sleep for the night.

Rishan heard tales of the Dandaka Forest. It was the journey of Lord Rama's life, the seventh incarnation of Lord Vishnu, through this very forest that intrigued Rishan and many others who had been educated on the story. The *Ramayana* was a lesson in the proper way to handle various relationships including the dynamics between characters like the ideal father, the ideal wife, the ideal servant, the ideal brother, and the ideal king. Rishan was interested in having a wife like Sita, the avatar of Lakshmi and ideal wife of Lord Rama. Rishan's reading of Homer's story of the *Odyssey* led him to compare Sita to Penelope, the wife of Odysseus who waited faithfully for her husband despite the countless hardships she endured and the suitors who asked for her hand. Rishan believed these were ideals seldom met by many in society.

Rishan's hair had grown long and unkempt and his beard had also grown rather large. He had become as the hairy beasts he actively avoided living within the immense wilderness. Rishan had miscalculated the size of the Dandaka Forest and was now running out of food and suffered from bouts of thirst. Whenever he did manage to eat, the food would cause pain in his stomach and would rapidly exit his body, further weakening him. As the days went by, Rishan began to lose his once impressive muscles and lose weight. The days stretched with no structure and the nights filled Rishan with fear as he imagined large beasts roaming around waiting for a moment to strike. Sometimes Rishan would violently wake from frightful dreams where superhuman Asura beings attempted to consume him. These Asuras were led by Lord Varuna, who maintained the night sky, the oceans, and the souls of the dead. Rishan wished the good Deva gods would protect him. His fear of these Asuras originated from readings of the *Ramayana,* where the forest was occupied by many of these Asuras as well as Rakshasas. The Dandaka Forest was often called the Rakshasa Forest, as many believed these spirits to reside here. Rishan's hungry, tired mind

Rishan would mistake the swirling wind and the whipping of tree branches for Rakshasa spirits. Rishan needed to find the closest community and hoped to receive aid. Otherwise, he would perish alone in this dark unknown forest.

Rishan continued to weaken and could not keep food in his stomach, vomiting frequently and suffering from severe headaches. Both horses continued to graze but were curiously anxious. Rishan tied both horses to two trees as the sun set and darkness enveloped the land. In the morning, Rishan would force his way to the river to cleanse his body and try to eat once again to see if his sickness would begin to decline. Rishan willed himself to find a way north to his family and see his brother Rajesh's newborn child. Rishan wanted to experience being an uncle and there was so much left for him to do in life. Rishan constantly reminded himself that he would not perish in this forest.

Rishan took a deep breath and closed his eyes, trying to rest and gather strength. The bugs that bothered Rishan's peace of mind were now not as bothersome due to his overpowering fatigue. There were people who lived in this forest, away from kingdoms and rules of law set by man. Perhaps they were peaceful or perhaps they were of a violent nature. Rishan remained vigilant but fell victim to his sickness and exhaustion as he succumbed to a deep sleep. Rishan promised himself that if he did wake up he would seek to cleanse his body and find the nearest community to relieve himself from his ailments and uncleanliness.

As the sun rose, a ray of light peaked through the overhead branches and shined on Rishan's chest and head. As the sun continued its climb, it heated Rishan until he began to wake. Thinking he heard footsteps and still drowsy, Rishan glanced around. The footsteps slowly continued, partially masked by the howling winds as Rishan fell in and out of sleep. Startled by a snapped branch and a shadow cast upon him, Rishan noticed a figure. Mustering all his remaining strength, he reached for his sword.

Rishan managed to place his left foot flat on the

earth as he attempted to stand and lunge at the stranger before he was met by a fierce front kick to his face, knocking him to the ground. As Rishan attempted to get up, the stranger swept his foot upward, knocking Rishan out with his back on the ground and blood pouring from his nose and mouth. Rishan saw the man approach as everything went dark.

Rishan awoke later that afternoon severely hurt and weakened. He was near a fire with the welcoming smell of food in the air. At first experiencing panic, Rishan soon felt relieved when he saw a calm dark-skinned man sitting by the fire. Rishan was given some meat; it had been about a week since he'd had any.

Rishan asked, "Who are you and what is your purpose with me?"

The older man responded, "I am a man of learning and a seeker of truth. That is all you need to know now. Your primary concern is for the improvement of your health and perhaps later I will quench your curiosity. You are safe now. If I wanted your life I would have taken it before you opened your eyes."

Rishan rested after he ate and later washed in a small river nearby. After Rishan filled his belly and cleansed his body, the older man asked him to sit and converse with him. The man stated his name was simply Saket and he once lived in the well-known kingdom of Kalinga further east. Rishan told him his name and Saket asked where he came from due to the fact that Rishan spoke the local language with an accent.

Saket rubbed oils upon Rishan's head and massaged his temples and back, relieving his pain. Saket then helped Rishan induce vomiting by giving him madya, an alcoholic drink mixed with herbs, to purge his system. Afterwards, Saket prepared fruits and some ghee, a clear butter, to alleviate Rishan's digestion. The rich nutty aroma of the ghee made Rishan feel better not only physically but mentally; it helped bring back his fire and determination.

After several days, Saket offered Rishan Bhang, an

ancient medicine which grew wild and tall without human care. It relieved Rishan of the little pain remaining and helped him restore his overall appetite and mood. It also eased the relationship between the two men. Rishan thanked Saket for his help and began explaining the reasons he found himself in the Dandaka Forest in the state that Saket had discovered him.

Rishan was surprised to know that Saket had some knowledge of foreign affairs and had general knowledge of the Greek wars in the Punjab region. Saket was ignorant of much deeper conflicts occurring between the Greek leaders and the current fracturing of Alexander's Greek Empire, but appeared to be more informed than many of the people in Pauravas who were at the center of these events. Rishan was surprised that Saket, a man who had spent most of the time naked in this dark forest, was knowledgeable about many of the events far away from where he lived. Rishan was also curious to learn about Saket and his family.

Saket was saddened by Rishan's story and felt he needed to put the young man at ease by sharing who he was. He said the Greeks would find it hard to advance south and would not match the strength of Chandragupta, who led the overthrow of Dhana Nanda. Rishan was anxious to know further details on the situation with Chandragupta Maurya because the Greeks had almost effectively censored information regarding foreign affairs in their respective satrapies, and particularly denied the Ramankrishna family access to sensitive information.

Saket explained that his family was well respected in the Kalinga Kingdom where he was born. The Kalinga Kingdom had a relationship with Dhana Nanda, but it ended after Chandragupta Maurya gained power along with Chanakya, who orchestrated the entire revolution. As far as Saket knew, Chandragupta had not established a specific agreement with Kalinga and they remained independent and strong for many centuries.

Saket stated, "My mother was a doctor named Suta, from whom I learned the art of healing that I have applied on you. My father was named Ronak and he traveled by land and mostly sea. My father was an intelligent man who imparted me with knowledge of lands far from our home in Kalinga. My father visited the southernmost kingdoms of the Cholas, Cheras, and Pandyas. He also visited the land surrounded by water connected by small island bridges—a land with a city named Anuradhapura. My father also sailed to faraway lands in the east and met people with cultures that were very different from ours. These lands contain ancient people with their own writing and languages vastly different from ours."

Saket informed Rishan of his Jain beliefs and how his search for purpose in his life led him to a stricter form of Jainism. Kalinga had a large Jain population which included Saket's family and Saket, who had left Kalinga to go into the forest in an effort to attain enlightenment and Jina during the last years of his life to liberate his soul. Rishan was aware of the Jain faith but sought a more thorough understanding. Saket explained the three sages who lived over 100 years before. Gautama Siddhartha the Buddha was the prince of Kapilavastu, Makkhali Gosala began the Ajivika philosophy, and Mahariva delivered the message of Jainism. However, Mahariva was the most recent sage with one of the original teachers named Parshva existing over 500 years prior. Saket now lived for the purposes of conquering himself and for the pursuit of nonviolence in an effort to stop samsara, the cycle of death and rebirth. Ahimsa was of vital importance in Saket's beliefs—the pursuit of non-violence that was part of all aspects of his life.

Rishan laughed and said, "You were very quick to strike me during our first meeting!"

Saket smiled and replied, "It was not my intention, but only for the purposes of self-defense and for the preservation of both your life and mine, Rishan."

The men shared a much-needed laugh as the conversation continued.

Saket said, "I took five major vows: non-violence, honesty, no stealing, chastity, and non-attachment. It is also important to realize that non-violence, non-possessiveness, and non-absolutism is fundamental to achieving a good life. When you have no greed, it has no power over you. You also must conquer your hatred which fuels violence and realize that your truth is different from another person's. You see, my perspective is different from yours and your perspective is different from mine. We must acknowledge and embrace these views to reach a greater understanding. You must understand or attempt to comprehend your enemy's viewpoints as well, Rishan. For example, the friend who betrayed you named Karna Mehra. Why would a family of high standing like the Mehras hate, fear, or envy your family? What benefits do they seek in allying themselves with the Greeks and how do they view the emergence of Chandragupta Maurya? These are all questions you must ponder Rishan."

In previous months, Rishan's thoughts had only related to his personal survival, however he had resumed wondering about many possibilities regarding the Mehra family as well as the safety of his own. Rishan informed Saket that indeed he had thought of various scenarios regarding the Mehra family's involvement in Greek leadership. Rishan also told Saket that he was attempting the journey northeast away from direct Greek influence.

Saket replied, "What is driving you, Rishan? Is it vengeance, love for your family, a potential position of power?"

Rishan stated that his only need was to reclaim his family's honor and true justice. Rishan hesitated to detail the events that occurred the night he fled his family's estate and the two Greeks he had slain, although he had every reason to protect his life and the safety of his family. These thoughts haunted Rishan but he understood that he had to remain strong and was comforted in his knowledge that war was part of the world of man. War was known to the gods, for they were the ones who created humanity. Lord Krishna himself had advised Arjuna in the tactics of war on the battlefield and was celebrated by the people of these lands.

In his conversations with Saket, Rishan also looked deep into himself and grappled with his own flaws. Was he envious of the fact that Priyanka now welcomed the affections of Karna's cousin, Kanchanpreet Mehra? Rishan felt intense betrayal and anger but conversations with his father had tempered his emotions and gave him perspective. However, he continued to feel the lingering feelings of sadness relating to that unfortunate event. When Rishan explained this to Saket, Saket stated that it was the way of the world of men, women, and their relationships.

Saket explained, "You cannot make a woman love you, Rishan. Everyone has choices to make and we all live with the consequences of those choices. You have to respect her decision and let her live with her choice. You should move on and find a woman who is a better match for you."

In a land of arranged marriages, people of wealth and power had the flexibility to choose romance as a deciding factor. Saket advocated that even within this class, the family still deserved a right to choose the best partner for their children with the final decision resting on the people to be wed. The wedded couple ultimately had to live with their decision and raise a family.

Living in the Dandaka Forest—which was mentioned in various texts including the *Ramayana*—encouraged Saket and Rishan to speak about the tales of Rama's journey. Rishan understood that the Dandaka Forest was where Prince Rama, one of the three sons of King Dasharatha of Ayodhya, was exiled along with his wife Sita. King Dasharatha had three wives; Kausalya, Kaikeyi, and Sumitra. After being childless for a prolonged time, King Dasharatha performed a sacrifice and was instructed by Rishyasringa to feed his wives rice so they could give birth. Rama was the eldest son of King Dasharatha and his Chief Queen Kausalya, Kaikeyi gave birth to Bharata, and Sumitra gave birth to Lakshmana and Shatrughna. The sons were endowed with attributes associated with the Supreme Lord Vishnu, who had chosen to be born as a mortal in order to combat the demon Ravana. The boys were taught warfare and scripture, and by the age of sixteen the sage Vishvamitra arrived at the court of King Dasharatha to seek help in combating the demons. Rama was chosen and his half-brother Lakshmana followed him in his adventures.

King Janaka of Mithila had a female daughter named Sita who became the most sought-after beauty in the land. The king held a swayamvara which included a contest. King Janaka was in possession of a heavy bow that was presented by Lord Shiva the destroyer; whoever could wield this bow would marry his daughter. Rama was able to wield the bow and subsequently married Sita. The rest of King Dasharatha's sons married the rest of King Janaka's daughters; Lakshmana to Urmila, Bharata to Mandavi, and Shatrughna to Shrutakirti. The weddings were celebrated at Mithila and afterwards the marriage party returned to Ayodhya. Rishan stated that he had lost his love Priyanka without a contest, although Karna tried to incite his anger by mentioning Priyanka's betrayal. However, Priyanka never belonged to Rishan so he in fact had not lost anything.

With the help of his father and the guidance of his uncle and older brother, Rishan had learned to respect others who respected him. One of the most important lessons Rishan's father had imparted on him was respect for self. A person could not expect respect to be given without self-respect.

Rama's journey weighed heavily on Rishan's mind as he conversed with Saket. Saket stated that everyone had a journey filled with hardships with the purpose of teaching how to overcome. "Things are never as they appear. Birth and death occurs and repeats again. The events of today are echoes from the past, Rishan. For example, look at the tales of Rama and his travels with his brother Lakshmana. Some of the women in human form that Rama encountered were demons and Rama himself was initially unaware that he was the human incarnation of Lord Vishnu on earth. The love story of Rama and Sita is celebrated in all these lands and both share their love in their godly forms of Lord Vishnu and Lakshmi as well as in their worldly manifestations."

Rishan agreed that things in life were not as they appeared and he was reminded of the Goddess Lakshmi and her guidance. Lakshmi's four hands signified dharma or the right way to live, desire or Kama, Artha or purpose, and Moksha, the release and freedom of the soul. Rishan focused on his goals and purpose to continue to regain his health and protect his loved ones.

Rishan thought of the heavy bow carried by many men and the surprise when Rama was able to fire this bow. Saket and Rishan discussed the many hardships in life that first needed to be overcome by self-confidence even when everyone doubted you. Doubt was the first enemy when one attempted an arduous task; it caused failure before they even began. Sita was happy that Rama was the man who successfully handled Lord Shiva's bow, which helped create the celebrated love between Rama and Sita. Rama was chosen to succeed his father Dasharatha as king when the moon and the Pushya star aligned. The study of the stars and planets was of utmost importance in determining special occasions such as the crowing of Prince Rama as king. The crowning of Rama was interrupted by his father's other wife Kaikeyi, who was encouraged by her malicious hunchbacked maidservant Manthara to pass the kingship to her own son Bharata. Owing two favors to his wife, Dasharatha complied and sent Rama into exile for a period of fourteen years. Rama's father died soon after from grief.

Bharata uncovered his mother's schemes and offered Rama the throne but Rama refused, promising to carry out his missions defeating evil. Bharata asked for Rama's paduka footwear to keep while he ruled as Rama's regent until his return. Rama's half-brother Lakshmana and Rama's wife Sita were approached by a female Rakshasi (demon) by the name of Surpanakha, who in her attempt to seduce Rama and Bharata, became envious of the lovely Sita and attempted to kill her. Bharata cut off the demon's nose and ears. The demon Surpanakha's brother was King Ravana of the island kingdom of Lanka southeast of the mainland. King Ravana kidnapped Sita with the aid of another demon named Maricha, who arrived in the form of a beautiful deer which attracted Sita and led her to her capture and arrival at Lanka. A vulture named Jatayu heroically tried to rescue Sita but was defeated by Ravana, maintaining Sita's captivity at Lanka. Rama and his half-brother Lakshmana joined forces with a heroic monkey by the name of Hanuman as they attempted to rescue Sita.

As Rishan and Saket spoke of Rama's journey, Rishan also spoke about the story of Adam and Eve from the people of the Palestinian lands where his uncle Manu had visited. Rishan and Saket enjoyed their conversation and the stories encouraged Rishan to continue his journey despite his many setbacks and enemies. Rishan informed Saket of Eve's seduction by a demon in the form of a serpent which led her to misfortune just as Sita was led to misfortune by Maricha the Rakshasa in the form of a beautiful deer. Rishan enjoyed conversing with Saket as it filled his heart with hope and positivity. Rishan also enjoyed speaking about the similarities in beliefs shared with people of various cultures.

Saket stated, "What an interesting comparison. Their gods must be the same as ours!"

Rishan replied, "The Hebrew people have apparently rejected their other gods and now worship a single supreme god named Elohim."

The Jain sage was intrigued by these monotheistic people. It was interesting for him to learn how these people of Palestine now worshipped their sole god when they previously worshipped a multitude of deities. There were different religious movements within this land where the importance was focused on the release of the soul from the constant cycle of birth and death called samsara—movements which now focused on various perspectives in the way men lived.

These were the ancient forests of the Varna army of forest dwellers and monkey people. The banished King Sugriva of the kingdom of Kishkindha made a pledge with Rama to aid him in the rescue of his wife from the clutches of King Ravana. The vulture Sampati, the elder brother of Jatayu who tried to rescue Sati, informed Rama that Sita was being held in captivity at Lanka. Major battles commenced between Rama and the Varna monkey army as well as the armies of King Ravana. In two of these battles,

Prince Indrajit, the son of King Ravana, twice defeated Lakshmana. Indrajit was the only warrior to hold the three powerful weapons of the Trimurti which were the Brahmanda astra, Narayanastra, and Pashupatastra. These weapons were held by Brahma, Vishnu, and Shiva. Brahmas Astra was a weapon manifesting in all five heads of Lord Brahma with the power to destroy the fourteen realms of the Universe. The personal weapon of Lord Vishnu was the Narayanastra which fired a powerful tirade of millions of deadly missiles simultaneously. The last weapon was Shiva's; the Pashupatastra with the ability to destroy all creation and all beings. Despite Indrajit's abilities, Rama's younger brother defeated Indrajit by interrupting his yajna (or ritual sacrifice). Hanuman killed many of Ravana's warriors and destroyed many of the trees and buildings before he was brought before King Ravana. The monkeys Nala and Nila created the Rama Setu Bridge which connected the mainland to Lanka. After a final battle, Rama defeated King Ravana and restored Vibhishana as king of Lanka.

Rama and Sita were then restored as king and queen, however although Rama had tested Sita's purity, he still gave in to public opinions about Sita and banished her to the forest where she gave birth to two twin boys named Lava and Kusha. Mother Earth took Sita and a grief-stricken Rama finally returned to his celestial body of Lord Vishnu. This was the purpose of Lord Vishnu: to return to the earth as a physical being to kill the demon King Ravana.

Rishan and Saket discussed the many perspectives of the *Ramayana* and its importance as a teaching tool in the way kings should rule; how to run a kingdom, and the affairs of love. The men spoke of the negative aspects of the tale between Rama and Sita. Rama deeply loved Sita but still fell victim to public opinion. Even as a king, the power of rumors and the people swayed his decisions.

Saket asked, "And does your enemy Karna hold sway with the people or do the people control him? What is the opinion of this man?"

Rishan replied, "Does it matter? I believe Karna

Mehra allied himself with the Greek governors and now holds an important position in the military."

Saket said, "Karna is gripped with fear and his power seems hollow. Why would such a powerful man secure in his position seek a single man who has no power? The *Ramayana* has different perspectives. In our Jain faith we have different views on the characters and enjoy certain qualities each possesses. This includes negatives aspects of people. It is a lesson for young children on the right way to live, but it is also a lesson for adults. The same story changes in the mind of a person as time goes by. You thought differently as a small boy as compared to now and as an old man your perspectives will change once again. You are a smart young man, Rishan. I would implore you to stay with me and learn from my Jain beliefs. You can remain with me and the other Jains here in the forest, but I understand your family could be in danger and your story is yet to be completed."

Rishan thanked Saket for helping him in his recovery but reminded him that he had an important mission. The danger Rishan was in could possibly put Saket in danger as well and he wanted to protect his savior. There was one curious question brewing in Saket's mind. If Rishan had made the trip south with little hardship, what caused his return trip north to be filled with so much hardship in such a short period? Rishan admitted the mental stress regarding the safety of his parents coupled with the knowledge of others in pursuit created his stress and sickness. During his escape from who he believed to be bandits, he lost some of his food, causing him to go hungry and delirious. Rishan's hunger had been so great he thought of even killing a cow for food. The theft and slaughter of a villager's cow remained only a thought and not pursued due to the fact that Rishan did not have energy to flee if he was caught.

Saket smiled. "Wise choice, Rishan. I hope you are able to maintain the ability of reason even during times of great stress."

Rishan thanked Saket for his help and promised to search for him in the future.

After almost a month in the forest with Saket, it was time for Rishan to take his horses and continue his journey northeast. It was early morning and the sun began to rise when Rishan made his way to a nearby stream to quench his horses' thirst. Rishan was still battling his own mental anguish regarding the loss of his love and the loss of his family's position in society. The Ramankrishna name had been uplifted through the hard work of Rishan's grandfather and father but it had been seemingly lost in a just a few short years. The Ramankrishnas generations of hard work and sacrifice had gone to waste over the political games of the Mehra family—a family who had grown in power in recent years.

As Rishan thought of his troubles, he heard a noise in the distance originating from Saket's camp. As Rishan walked towards Saket, he spotted a great multitude of men arguing and questioning him.

Saket replied, "I do not know Rishan or his whereabouts. Under whose authority do you make such demands?"

One of the men proudly declared, "Under the authority of Karna Mehra and his elder brother Randeep Mehra of the reorganized kingdom of Pauravas. We are here to apprehend Rishan Ramankrishna for crimes committed in Pauravas."

A scuffle ensued and Rishan attempted to save Saket's life, but before he could a Punjabi man stuck a sword through his chest. Full of fear, anger, and confusion, Rishan mounted his horse, leaving his other horse and chariot behind as he desperately fled northeast with the goal of escaping his pursuers and the Dandaka Forest.

One of the men—possibly a Greek—spotted him from far away, alerting the others as Rishan tried to expand the distance between them.

Rishan rode east as fast as his horse could carry him with his thoughts racing. His heart felt as if it would jump out of his chest and worry filled his mind. He believed he would not be given a trial but murdered like a wild beast in the forest. These men could possibly murder Rishan and discard him like garbage never to be found again just as Rishan had disposed of his would-be murderers. As far as Rishan understood, no one witnessed what had occurred the night Rishan fled Pauravas. However, Rishan remained unsure. Even if they did not have proof, Karna Mehra and the Greek leadership could spin whatever lie they wished—as evidenced by the prior lies they stated as truth and the misinformation they had previously spread. There would be no justice if Rishan were to be killed away from civilization—or worse, under the power of his enemies who would bend truth to fit their own reality..

Rishan rode night and day as fast as his horse could go, only stopping to fish at the local bodies of water and feed and provide water for his horse. Rishan only rested for a few hours during the night, eventually leading him towards the northeastern borders of the Dandaka Forest. Tired and desperate for food and rest, Rishan encountered what seemed to be a small village with a group of people milling about. Rishan stopped his horse out of sight in a wooded area as he spotted a beautiful woman with skin the color of a starless night and piercing brown eyes. Perhaps luck would begin to change for Rishan Ramankrishna.

CHAPTER 14:
THE HORRIFIC ACCOUNT OF BRAMILAN THE BUTCHER (317 B.C.)

"To retaliate against him, who has earlier inflicted harm, is no sin."
—The Ramayana

Rishan beckoned to the beautiful woman for food and water. The woman looked beaten and tired but her beauty shone through and the fire in her eyes refused to be extinguished.

The woman asked, "Who are you and what is your business here? We are people forgotten by our families and the law and power resides with one man who decides whether we live or we die. I can help you but you must leave unless you wish to try to free us." Rishan revealed his identity and asked for the woman's name. She replied, "My name is Ratnavali."

Rishan had many questions for Ratnavali and the other people who seemed to live an existence of fear and desperation. Rishan"What has occurred that enabled this miserable life you share with others here?"

Ratnavali replied, "We belong to lower castes here. We were given away by families that were heavily indebted while others are here working to pay off their own debts."

Rishan's father had spoken of this. Unlike the

members of the warrior caste and Brahmin scholar/priest caste who ignored or were ignorant of the issues regarding the poor, Manish taught his children about the disadvantages of others within their society. Manish also taught his children to be thankful for the opportunities afforded to them by the combined efforts of prior generations of their family which opened opportunities for him and his children. These lessons resounded greatly with Rishan and his siblings and helped them shape their views of the world. However, in life there were priorities and Rishan had also learned that selfishness could be essential—especially when matters of life and death were involved. Rishan felt he should refocus his efforts to avoid the madman who was the cause of the pain and suffering he was witnessing, but he felt sympathy for Ratnavali and the children held captive.

When he questioned Ratnavali regarding the name of such a horrible man, she described him. "His name is Bramilan and he is called the butcher. Bramilan is a man who centers his life around greed and power and he finds pleasure in the suffering of others."

Rishan tried to gather as much information regarding Bramilan and thought about taking his weapons for himself. As Rishan hid, he was able to identify Bramilan with the aid of Ratnavali's description. Bramilan was a large man with dark hair, dark brown skin, and a permanent scowl. He would only smile whenever he inflicted pain on his victims, beating them or violating the women and girls. Rishan thought the only difference between a man like Bramilan and Karna Mehra was that Bramilan did not bother to hide his sadism. On the other hand, Karna was an expert at shielding his true nature, secretly imposing long term anguish. Rishan wanted to leave these people to their fates but as he observed the situation, his purpose and strategy began to sway. Rishan appreciated the food and water Ratnavali had given him despite the possibility that she would be severely punished for it. Ratnavali also informed Rishan of her young son named Atallan, an innocent victim of the physical embodiment of evil that was Bramilan.

Rishan noticed that these perpetual servants were

forced into farm working, tool making, weaving, and most importantly, the manufacturing of metals for weaponry.

Rishan observed the numerical superiority of the dasa servants as opposed to Bramilan's security. The village was larger than what he initially thought; several hundred miserable people subjected to abuse under Bramilan and roughly fifty of his well-armed men. Rishan had to think of a plan and act upon it quickly. Perhaps he could free these people from the brutality and seek protection under a greater numerical force against those who sought to capture and kill him. Rishan shared his ideas with Ratnavali. Initially, Rishan only thought of helping Ratnavali and her son Atallan, but the mother and child would slow him down. Liberating a large group of people and obtaining control of the weapons manufacturing would provide an adequate defense against his pursuers. Helping Ratnavali and many of the perpetual servants could enable Rishan to secure safety in numbers and could benefit not only Rishan, but the servants who sought similar goals of freedom and security. Ratnavali was skeptical at first, warning Rishan that his attempts could lead to his early demise. Rishan understood that Bramilan was not only feared but hated. Rishan understood that if the people could overcome their fear they could easily emancipate themselves.

Rishan's experience was shared with many in the kingdom who spoke against or fell out of favor with the Greeks and those politically allied with them. People who fled the Punjab sometimes followed the same path south that Rishan had taken. Rishan was also informed that the violence had increased in the Punjab and that many more people had fled south; perhaps Rishan could ask for their assistance in his attempt at liberating the dasas. Rishan asked the man to inform anyone who had fled Pauravas like him to travel east of the Dandaka Forest and meet him at a location south of Kalinga. Rishan also instructed the man to warn the others of Bramilan the Butcher.

Rishan, Ratnavali, and a few others discussed different plans to take control of the iron smelting center and the armory filled with the weaponry needed for the attack. It had to be a surprise attack and the top leadership needed to be killed or captured. Finally, a plan of action was created to organize the people for the attack and to possibly join others who had fled Pauravas. As the plan was shared among the most trusted dasas, Rishan was made aware that others from Pauravas were near or within the forest and knew his location. Rishan's constant depressive bouts seemed to be relieved at the thought of being accompanied by others from home who found themselves in the same situation as him. Rishan smiled as he drank some bhang he had saved for the purposes of relaxation and deep thinking.

After a few weeks had passed, the conspirators agreed to overtake Bramilan and his guards and they were prepared to strike on Rishan's command. Rishan had meticulously noted the schedule of the guards working under Bramilan and at various times had walked around the compound. Rishan observed the workers at the factory smelting steel weapons of the finest quality and realized this was an operation generating lots of wealth for Bramilan. Rishan pondered who was purchasing these weapons and who allowed Bramilan to operate outside of the law. Rishan heard footsteps behind him and as he turned, he witnessed Bramilan aiming the edge of his sword at his neck, ready to strike. Rishan pulled out his own sword but as he attempted to attack, he was struck from behind by guards and disarmed. Rishan's weapons and horse were taken from him and he was thrown into a holding room with several other men. To Rishan's surprise, some of these men were also from Pauravas. Many had significant injuries and bruises on their bodies—a sign of daily beatings.

Rishan spoke with the men who had some details regarding the kingdom of Pauravas. There had been a change in the entire political and social dynamics of the Punjabi region which drastically increased the danger faced by Rishan and the Ramankrishna family. The men stated that King Porus was murdered a few months past and that several men were suspected to include Manish Ramankrishna. The men also stated that the Greeks had increased their control of Pauravas and the surrounding territories under the governorships of the Macedonians, Eudamus, and Peithon. The wars within the Greek Hellenistic Empire were set to begin, once again leaving the hated King Ambhi—now known as Taxiles—as a puppet king in the region. Rishan required more detailed information and asked the whereabouts of close friends. He was surprised to find that Anand Agrawal had accompanied one of the men now captive with Rishan; there was a strong possibility that Anand was close by and aware of his current location. Rishan had renewed hope that he would soon reunite with his friend if he could find a solution to his current problem.

Screaming and beatings were heard throughout the night, causing Rishan to go without sleep. Before the sun rose, he was dragged and beaten by guards and brought before Bramilan for questioning. Bramilan was a large man—almost as tall as Rishan but twice as big. Bramilan stated, "I am aware of the presence of men fleeing from the north here into the Dandaka Forest and surrounding areas." Bramilan continued after a brief pause, "My men captured and forced the truth from some of them about events occurring in the north. I have also been notified about a reward to be given for your capture and return to these authorities from whom you flee. My scouts have also informed me of your collaboration with Ratnavali and a possible revolt against me. What about debts owed to me? Are agreements not to be honored anymore?"

Rishan responded, "From what I have gathered from Ratnavali and from simple observation is that the men under your employment as well as you operate outside the law. You answer to no one but yourself and you abuse your servants sometimes to the point of death. You abuse your female servants, which is against the laws regarding the treatment of the dasas. Under the laws of various kingdoms, you would forfeit the labors of your servants and forfeit any money still owed to you."

Bramilan grew angry and struck Rishan as hard as he could across the face, drawing blood from Rishan's nose and lip. Bramilan shouted, "Who are you to tell me how I should conduct my affairs? I answer to no one! The only importance here is the production of weaponry and the money that it generates. You come here to disrupt my business and seize my workers who have yet to complete their service. You are a lawbreaker in Pauravas and now you wish to dictate the law to me? What standing do you have? What other crimes have you committed? I would have executed you if your life was not worth money. I will beat your companions and make an example out of some of these men and the dasas who wished to destroy my business. I will punish your friend Ratnavali as well. She is a woman of low caste—too dirty for me. Perhaps I will give her to my men."

Rishan erupted in anger and was beaten down and placed back into a holding room. Bramilan could be heard yelling at one of the guards followed by laughter as Bramilan and the others left Rishan alone, anxiously anticipating in the potential horrors awaiting the captives.

When the sun was at its highest point in the sky, Bramilan escorted Rishan and the other captives outside to witness a grim showcase of torture. Bramilan and his guards had beaten a man unconscious and stripped him naked. They had carried the man outside in the hot sun, burying him in the dirt up to his neck and making sure to keep the dirt loose from his stomach up and covered him in milk, honey, and sugarcane juice. They continued to beat him and only granted him reprieve so he would awaken to witness a swarm of ants already in the process of biting his flesh and entering his mouth. The man screamed and desperately tried to close his mouth that had been propped open with a wooden stick. People who tried to turn away from the grisly sight were beaten mercilessly by guards while Bramilan displayed a rare smile which turned into a chilling laugh. Bramilan then instructed his guards to bring Rishan to the front of his audience in an effort to make an example of him.

Bramilan exclaimed, "This is your leader Rishan Ramankrishna, an outlaw fleeing from justice in the Punjab to the north. You follow this lawbreaker who encourages you to break your agreements and debts still owed to me. This man also has the audacity to presume to speak to me about justice and law. I will torture this conspirator as I would torture any man or woman who harbors this hatred of me. I will return Rishan Ramankrisha to those who pursue him so that he may face justice and I will find the others who are currently heading towards our location. My laws are just and I only ask that you continue your duties until you fulfill your respective agreements. Only then will you be free to leave."

The crowd watched in horror as the man struggled to breathe as a swarm of ants entered his mouth, nose, eyes, and ears. Bramilan turned to Rishan and asked him if he had any more gold. Bramilan whispered, "I know you have more wealth hidden away somewhere in the forests. I was informed of your family's wealth. I cannot kill you, as I will get a sizeable reward for my troubles from these foreign Greek people. If you inform me of where the rest of your gold is and of your other friends still in hiding, I vow that I will not torture you."

The man ceased his struggle as he went into shock and the ants continued to eat him alive. Rishan turned to those watching in horror. "If I broke any laws please understand that they were unjust laws—just as the laws based on Bramilan's immoral disposition. They are twisting the truth to make their own truths just as Bramilan makes his own truth as he tortures or kills his victims!"

Bramilan struck Rishan and his guards beat him down as they brought Ratnavali and her son forward. Bramilan threatened to violate Ratnavali and give her to his guards so they could do as they please. Suddenly, a large group of Punjabi men and some Greeks arrived before Bramilan. Many of the Greeks were young, strong, with determination in their eyes. They arrived on their horses and chariots while carrying swords and shields. The men appeared to have received intelligence that Rishan and other dissidents had escaped south and that Rishan was under Bramilan's custody. The leader of the group named

Gurjas, a man unknown to Rishan, walked towards Bramilan to initiate the transaction that would transfer the prisoner Rishan to his pursuers. Gurjas could speak the local tongue and was best able to communicate with Bramilan.

Gurjas confidently stated, "I have come as a representative of Satrap Eudamus and King Ambhi Taxiles. I have come for the purpose of apprehending the lawbreaker Rishan Ramankrisha for questioning by the high leadership—specifically Karna Mehra and the Mehra family. Crimes which include slander against the Mehra family and the questioning of Rishan Ramankrisha regarding the whereabouts of his father Manish Ramankrisha, a criminal guilty of the assassination of King Porus early this year."

Rishan denied the allegations, shouting, "Liar!" at the top of his lungs. Others who had fled Pauravas were highly skeptical while the dasas serving Bramilan tried to decipher what the truth was.

Rishan responded, "My father did not harbor any hatred for King Porus and he has served him well. Assassination plots and political maneuvering are used by the Mehra family, not ours. You have committed an injustice towards my father just as you committed one towards me!"

Angered at Rishan's defiance, Gurjas approached him and quietly stated, "What about those two Greek men who have now gone missing? Do you have any information on their whereabouts?"

Rishan replied, "How do you know I am guilty of any foul play, or did you already have prior knowledge of where these men might be in the first place?"

Gurjas smiled. "You think you are smart Rishan just like your father, yet you and your father never learned their place in society and this is why your family finds itself in the situation it does now."

Gurjas attempted to strike Rishan, causing Bramilan to intercede. "First you will give me what you owe me for this transaction. I have gone through much trouble in keeping this criminal in my location of business. Rishan tried to cause harm to me and my men by causing a riot and encouraged my dasas to fail in their agreements to pay what they owed through labor."

One of the Greek leaders named Diokles stated to his Greek soldiers, "We are here deep in the land of savages led by animals and waiting on animals to fulfill their negotiation!"

Through his years of studying, Rishan understood and spoke Greek nearly fluently and translated what Diokles had said for everyone to hear.

Slightly embarrassed, Gurjas said, "I will not be forced to negotiate with a savage warlord. I will give you what was promised after you hand over Rishan Ramankrisha and the others who have fled Pauravas!"

An angered Bramilan drew his sword and Rishan took his opportunity to kick him in the back, causing Bramilan to fall forward and strike Gurjas in the process. A fight that began between Bramilan and Gurjas quickly became a wider fight between the forces of Bramilan and those under the orders of Eudamus and Karna Mehra.

Rishan ran to Ratnavali, who untied him as they signaled the dasas to enter and surround the major armory at Bramilan's compound. Rishan rushed to take his sword and ordered the other men and women servants to pick up a weapon and fight for their freedom.

In the mayhem and confusion, Rishan and the servants attacked Bramilan and his men, who were already outnumbered by the Greeks and Punjabis. Bramilan had managed to overpower Gurjas and took his horse as he attempted to kill Rishan as he fled from the battle. The dasas turned on the Greeks and Punjabis when Bramilan's forces were on the verge of defeat—a tactic dictated by Rishan which eventually was successful. Rishan took a horse and rode into the forest to pick up some of his own weapons with Bramilan in close pursuit. Just as Rishan gathered the rest of his weapons, Bramilan attacked Rishan from behind, knocking Rishan to the ground. Rishan had trouble defending himself, but as the fight progressed Bramilan's anger gave way to fatigue and mistakes. Rishan's skills in the art of combat were clearly displayed as he connected strikes against Bramilan with his sword.

Bramilan cried out, "You have taken everything from me while you pretend to be better than I am, but you are simply a criminal! By Lord Shiva you will never live to see the sunrise again!"

Rishan responded, "I am only recognized as a criminal by those who unjustly judge me! Injustice prevails when the judges are unjust! And you have tortured your servants and only the gods have seen your true violations. You have planted seeds of fear into the heads of your servants that have now sprouted into retribution. Now you will see the face of Lord Shiva!" Rishan came down with all his strength upon his neck and shoulder and left Bramilan to die in the forest. The man who had caused so much fear, pain, and suffering was now simply a ghastly memory.

After a few hours of fighting, a little over one hundred Punjabi and Greek military remained, chasing away less than twenty of Bramilan's men. Rishan now had over 200 former servants who had fought during the clash and were ordered to join him in the forest nearby. After taking most of the steel weapons and initially fighting both the northern Punjabi forces and Bramilan's, they had wisely taken shelter. Although Rishan had superior numbers, these former servants were not trained in the art of organized combat. Rishan grew anxious as he realized Gurjas and Diokles had survived the initial clash and would soon resume their pursuit. A man reached the group, stating he was part of some men who had also left the military of Pauravas and had witnessed the battle from miles away. Rishan recognized some of the men in this party from his time in the Pauravas military and was surprised to learn that his closest friend Anand Agrawal had also escaped with them. Rishan at once felt a rush of hope and purpose as he believed an opportunity of redemption would soon crystallize against Bramilan and the Greeks, with the aid of Anand and the other rebels. Rishan relayed a message explaining the reasons for the battle against Bramilan and informed Anand and the others of his current location. Rishan celebrated victory over the first battle which resulted in the resounding defeat of Bramilan's men with his friends; Rishan understood he had to create a strategy for the upcoming second battle.

Rishan gathered the men with military experience to lead the mass of dasas in preparation for a potential battle with the victorious Greek-backed Punjabis.

Another group of men numbering close to twenty included Anand Agrawal. Rishan was overjoyed to see his old friend and he inquired about the specific details regarding the death of Porus and his father's involvement.

Anand said, "Rishan, I am happy to see you but I fear that your family will face the tragedy that has fallen upon mine." Intrigued, he questioned Anand about what had happened, to which Anand replied between tears, "My entire family was murdered by Karna Mehra and his agents. Harbir, your brother's father-in-law, was also murdered and King Porus was assassinated. Karna publicly placed the blame on your father, who managed to flee east to join the rest of your family. A few Persian advisers were also murdered including Haxamanis, who had spoken with your father about possibly leaving Pauravas. I turned down your father's invitation to join him in the east and I informed him that I would flee south with others who had managed to escape the purge. Your father then instructed me to join you."

Rishan was relieved that his family could possibly still be alive Rishan and then inquired about the political scene in the kingdom pertaining to King Porus Balarama.

Anand replied, "After King Porus' brother King Porus Balarama died, his son Parvateshwara became king. King Parvateshwara infuriated the Greek leadership after he sought formal relations with the new ruler Chandragupta Maurya. However, his reign was short. King Parvateshwara mysteriously continued to grow ill soon after you fled. Seeing his own health decline, King Parvateshwara named his young son Malayaketu as king last year. At the time of King Porus' death, King Parvateshwara was himself near death and King Malayaketu had taken over all affairs of his kingdom. We assume that Parvateshwara has died at this time and King Malayaketu has reversed nearly all of his father's policies."

King Malayaketu was now in the middle of two great powers of the Greek Hellenistic world to the west and the growing power of Chandragupta Maurya to the east. Rishan understood that if King Malayaketu allied with the Macedonian and Greek power structure under the protection of King Malayaketu, his family would soon be in imminent danger.

Rishan exclaimed, "Anand, Karna and his agents have been behind all our problems. We will avenge the murders and we will clear my father's name, but first we must defend ourselves from our pursuers!"

Anand instructed the women with children to hide further within the forest while he and the former military members devised a strategy to defeat the combined Greek and Punjabi forces. Rishan took about 100 of his men who were experienced in battle and equipped them with swords and arrows. Rishan's archers climbed trees and hid behind rocks and brush awaiting their pursuers. The remaining 100 men were left towards the rear, ready to ambush in case the first encounter failed.

The sun began to set as the pursuers approached the forest with Diokles in the front, taunting Rishan in his native Greek tongue. "We will kill you in the jungle like the animal that you are! Rishan Hand yourself over so you may face your crimes as a man and die with dignity!"

Gurjas and his men entered the forest and after walking for a few hours, his men grew complacent as they believed Rishan's mostly dasa men were unruly and had simply fled in fear. Gurjas then broke his formation and the famed Greek battle formation now became a glorified search party. Even the Greek phalanx split under Diokles' orders; they had little respect regarding the intelligence and leadership of Rishan Ramankrishna. This proved disastrous as Rishan signaled his men, hidden in the tree tops, to launch a hail of arrows. Gurjas retreated as many of his men were cut down. Rishan remained at a hidden location wishing to draw Diokles and his Greeks towards him.

Gurjas took cover behind a tree as his men were showered with a wave of arrows. A second wave descended upon the Greek men, striking many of them before they directed their shields upward. A third wave of arrows now originating from ground level began piercing through the Greeks as they attempted to cut down the Rishan-led Dravidian fighters out of the trees. Gurjas identified Rishan's position and waited for an opening, taking ten fighters with him as soon as he found a break in the fight. As Gurjas advanced, he was met by Rishan's fighters and a bloody clash ensued. Anand recognized Gurjas as one of the military men who had accompanied Karna in the murder of his family, causing a violent confrontation between the two men. Diokles and the Greek men now pursued Rishan deeper into the forest.

Gurjas' men clashed with Rishan's and the battle raged on with Gurjas' men advancing until they were suddenly halted when additional men crashed upon the Greek-led Punjabis, killing most of those who began to retreat. Gurjas cried out, ordering his men to come back to formation as he battled Anand. Anand cut down the men surrounding him, leaving Gurjas isolated as he growled, "You and that monster Karna Mehra murdered my father Abichal Agrawal and my mother Anahat Agrawal and now your blood will pay for your sins!"

Anand proved to be stronger than Gurjas as he continued to strike down on his shield, causing him to fall and cry out for mercy. Gurjas screamed, "It was Karna who killed your family and he made me join in his foul deeds. My purpose was only to apprehend you so you could dispute your claim in court!"

Anand replied, "A corrupt Macedonian court is not a place of justice for people like me. Where was the justice for Rishan and Manish? The only justice that is fair is the justice I will give now!" Anand brought down his sword multiple times, hacking Gurjas' chest and leaving him to die in the dirt. He then motioned for the rest of the men in the trees to move forward and close in on the Greeks. In an effort to reach Rishan's rear location, a few Greeks mistakenly reached the women and children. Ratnavali and others defended the women and children at the rear.

Diokles and the Greeks located Rishan's position and were now in pursuit as he led them deeper into the forest. Rishan wished to engage Diokles in combat but he was outnumbered and separated from the rest of his men. Rishan thought of retreating towards the main battle where he hoped to engage Diokles. As Rishan hid, he noticed a group of lions walking through looking for food and water. A female drank at a nearby creek while a male with a large belly fold swaying in the wind spotted Rishan. Rishan backed away just as Diokles and some other Greeks also found themselves paralyzed with fear when they noticed the lions. The male gave a majestic low growl, warning the men interfering with his attempt to mate with the female. The cornered Rishan, bloodied and bruised from his previous captivity and battle, took the opportunity to flee and join the rest of his men, which drew the male's attention just before it gave chase. Rishan turned towards Diokles and his men hoping to take the lion's focus away from him and possibly cause it to turn and maul the Greeks.

Rishan drew his sword as the charging lion made him lose his footing. Rishan struck the beast, drawing blood as he lay on the ground. Diokles took the opportunity to attack Rishan while he was disabled. The lion swiped at Diokles, injuring him and knocking his sword away as the rest of the Greeks fell upon the jungle cat. The lion mauled several of the Greeks, creating the opportunity for Rishan to flee with Diokles in pursuit. With Diokles now isolated, Rishan turned and kicked him backwards as he unsheathed his sword. Diokles and Rishan were now locked in a sword battle that quickly saw Diokles outmatched. The brawny man managed to hit Rishan's lower jaw with his shield but as he went to strike, the swift Rishan was able to evade Diokles' attack and sneak below Diokles while landing a slicing blow to his right leg. After taking Diokles' legs from under him, Diokles yelled, "You will soon face justice and death at the hands of the Greek army!"

Rishan replied, "You Greeks will face punishment for violating our people. You are guilty of carrying out unjust orders!" Rishan quickly defeated Diokles, thrusting his sword deep into his heart and leaving him gasping for air and Diokles attempted to reach towards Rishan in vain as he felt the embrace of death.

The remaining Greeks were now being defeated by the Dravidian dasas led by Rishan. The embarrassment of tasting defeat at the hands of the Dravidians that led the Greeks to fight harder was the same embarrassment they shared along with fear as they ran for their lives. The fear surpassed their shame as Rishan ordered his archers to rain arrows on the fleeing Greek soldiers. Many were killed, leaving less than twenty scared Greeks and Punjabis. Anand, Rishan, and the dasas took the horses left by the defeated Greeks to chase down the few who managed to reach the open field, cutting most of them down and capturing one young Greek named Pylas. Five men managed to escape to the north, where they informed King Ambhi and the Greek leadership about their stunning loss at the hands of Rishan Ramankrishna, Anand Agrawal, and a multitude of Dravidian servants.

News of the defeat circulated in the satrapies of Eudamus and Peithon and the surrounding territories. The Punjabi people grew bolder with tales of Chandragupta Maurya, his new empire, and the disgraced Dravidian hero Rishan Ramankrishna. Trying to avoid further embarrassment, one of the Greek survivors embellished the description of the battle. According to him, Rishan was a wild man with his matted hair made into locks and a ferocious expression. Rishan had stripes and markings on his face like a lion and had seemingly physically coerced another lion to turn his attention from him towards the Greek soldiers. They called him the Dravidian Lion and the name and Rishan's views promulgated quickly.

The tongue traveled faster than feet and news of the death of warlord Bramilan spread among the surrounding kingdoms. This would bring both trouble and aid to Rishan and his men. Bramilan held a powerful, influential business in the making of steel and Rishan asked the dasas about the various buyers. Some ministers traveled to Rishan Ramankrishna's camp to gather information for their respective kings regarding the battle and Rishan's intentions. Various ministers traveled from the nearby Kalinga Kingdom and the south. A minister representing the young embattled ruler King Aruman of the Assaka Kingdom particularly interested Rishan—his grandparents were currently residing within the Assaka Kingdom's northern border.

Rishan established a camp and took control of the steel making equipment. The dasas worked tirelessly cultivating wood and creating steel as they constructed armor, weaponry, and chariots. Rishan also designated the trained military men to teach the former servants in the art of combat. A few women who had proven themselves in combat, including Ratnavali, also desired to learn. Rishan was confident that his group of men and women would be prepared for battle. Rishan welcomed some of the women into his small military unit as he sat with Anand and some others to devise further strategies in their march towards the north.

CHAPTER 15:
MALAYAKETU'S WAR (316 B.C.)
"Truth cannot be suppressed and always is the ultimate victor."
—The Yajur Veda

Rishan and Anand led a small band of warriors north for several months, pausing only for rest, food, and training. Many of the women and children who had been previously locked in perpetual servitude were now able to exercise their freedom. Rishan allowed them to leave the group and filter into the surrounding kingdoms. Many former servants were accepted into the Kalinga Kingdom after some of the Kalinga ministers agreed to certain terms with Rishan. Rishan and Anand had stopped the northern march one night to discuss their previous conversations with ministers from the southern and eastern kingdoms several months before. As the men drank wine, ate, and danced, Rishan smiled as he remembered the look of lifelessness and fear of many of these people just months ago. Many of the men and women chose to continue northward with Rishan in appreciation for their newfound freedom and some young men marched northward in search of adventure and a chance at a new life.

The ministers who had appeared most interested in speaking with Rishan were Manoj, a slender, strong, and confident man who proudly represented the kingdom of Kalinga and ministers led by Ashva, representing King

Aruman of Assaka. Kalinga was now free after the overthrow of the Dhana Dynasty and wished to remain independent despite the growing power of the new Emperor Chandragupta Maurya. King Kharasala of Kalinga was the head of his government, however officials were chosen by the people to carry out the policy that they wanted. There was a higher level of representation for the common people of Kalinga which manifested in wider policy changes corresponding to the majority opinion.

There were obvious tensions between Manoj and Ashva due to the fact that the Kalinga and the Assaka Kingdoms had historical rivalries. In their records, the Assaka Kingdom had long celebrated a king named Aruna that with the help of his minister Nandisena, recorded a victory over the king of Kalinga. Rishan did not want needless fighting between the ministers; it would arouse military action upon him and his men before their march even started. Manoj spoke with Rishan regarding the motivations and destination of his march. Rishan informed him of his ordeal in Pauravas as well as the war with the advancing Alexander the Great and the Macedonian-led Greeks. Manoj was well educated as to the man they referred to as Sikander and his wars which toppled the Persian Empire. The Nanda Empire had been far too strong for Alexander to conquer, causing his Greek troops to rebel and now Chandragupta Maurya ruled this empire. Dhana Nanda suffered a revolt by his people and some of his ministers joined Chandragupta Maurya. Dhana Nanda was now rumored to have been assassinated while in exile.

Manoj and King Kharasala were concerned with Chandragupta's motivations—particularly if he would seek to rule Kalinga as Dhana Nanda once had. King Kharasala was the crowned prince and a client king under the reign of the now deposed King Dhana Nanda. In the power shift from Dhana Nanda to Chandragupta Maurya, King Kharasala declared independence for the kingdom of Kalinga, further strengthening his army and legendary navy.

Rishan stated, "I am not sure what Chandragupta's motivations are. I only seek to go to the Punjab to defend my family from the young King Malayaketu."

Manoj replied, "And with whom does King Malayaketu ally himself: the Greeks or Chandragupta Maurya? In your fight against the Greeks and Malayaketu you will also further strengthen Chandragupta Maurya, who may soon seek to conquer Kalinga. I also wish to ask,Rishan how are you so sure about the state of the Greek territories while being so far from the Punjab?"

Rishan pondered the possibilities. "I am a simple, good, and honest man, but I am not a god. I cannot see events that have not yet occurred. What I know for certain is that the Greek occupation of our lands will not benefit any of us nor the Punjabi families that are allied with the Greek rulers—including the Mehra family. Families like the Mehras only seek to take from their own people to provide wealth for the Greeks and themselves. The Kalinga are a strong and smart people with a large, formidable military and powerful navy. Chandragupta Maurya is far too concerned with his battles in the Punjab against the former territories of Alexander the Great to focus on a worthy opponent such as the Kalinga army. What I know for certain is my growing respect for your people and the Jain faith. When I was dying of disease, hunger, and thirst in the Dandaka Forest, a great Jain sage by the name of Saket helped me survive. Saket said his family was of great standing in Kalinga and this man was shown no mercy and killed by the same Greeks and Punjabis who sought to capture me. I have also avenged the death of Saket and will seek further revenge for the people who I now lead who have suffered great injustices. As for the state of Greek affairs, we have captured a Greek soldier named Pylas and we will gain intelligence from him."

Manoj respected Rishan's honesty and his mission, but he warned Rishan that he should never turn his army against the Kalinga should he ally himself with Chandragupta Maurya. Manoj had welcomed some of the women and children into Kalinga and he wished Rishan well in his future endeavors. Ashva invited Rishan and the rest of the men to Potali, the capital of the Assaka

Kingdom, for an audience with King Aruman who was eager to meet them. Rishan deeply thought about meeting King Aruman and reuniting with his grandparents, however Rishan desired to march north and rescue his family from the potential danger they might face. Ashva asked Rishan if he had any relatives within the Assaka Kingdom due to the fact that Rishan had previously entered its border. Rishan stated that his ancestors had lived there but did not provide specific information regarding his family; he did not fully understand Ashva and King Aruman's intentions and he did not want to make the whereabouts of his grandparents publicly known. Rishan explained the urgency of his march, stating he would possibly meet the king in the future.

Ashva stated, "Rishan, if you have family or acquaintances within our kingdom of Assaka it will benefit them just as our new friendship benefits us. This man Bramilan was becoming a problem in this region and the abuse of his servants and the placing of his laborers into perpetual servitude is widely known. Bramilan's growing wealth, unfair business practices, and political donations were beginning to purchase influence in the surrounding kingdoms that gained him numerous allies as well as numerous enemies. On behalf of King Aruman, we wish you well on your journey and in battle. Perhaps in the future you can have an audience with King Aruman. We can all help each other in the future through new political alliances."

Ashva gave gifts of horses and gold to Rishan and his men in an effort to possibly forge a new alliance.

Rishan gathered the armor and steel weaponry as well as Bramilan's large personal wealth and purchased clothing, horses, chariots, and other necessities needed for a growing group of fighting men and women. Rishan also released the servants from debt and gave each a share of the wealth. Rishan, Anand, and Ratnavali discussed previous meetings with the ministers as well as the potentially violent encounter with King Malayaketu's forces. News of Rishan's advance to the north soon reached King Malayaketu and the possibility of a battle was becoming close to a reality—Rishan was now reaching the southern borders of the Punjab. Rishan and Anand discussed the possibilities of recruiting additional men from Kalinga or Assaka.

Anand replied, "Kalinga would rather not aid us directly with additional warriors, as they do not wish to give Chandragupta Maurya reason to attack. King Aruman of Assaka wishes to benefit only himself. He and his minster Manoj are ignorant of your true motivations and potential alliances so they would rather pursue a conservative approach in their relations with you. It was wise of you to not provide specific information of your family in Assaka; it could be used against you."

Ratnavali added, "Rishan, your quick defeat of such a powerful man as Bramilan caught the attention of important officials. They fear Chandragupta Maurya and his growing power and they wished to know your relationship with him."

Rishan understood that as he gained financial power and support, he would be drawn into the world of politics whether it was by his choosing or not.

The men continued to drink wine into the night with everyone retreating to private conversations. Rishan took a moment to walk alone to ponder his current situation and his potential actions until he reached the Punjab when Ratnavali suddenly interrupted him. Rishan was pleasantly surprised to be in the company of a woman he had grown close to in the last few months. There were many thoughts deeply hidden inside his mind and he found freedom in his conversations with Ratnavali. With a few tears escaping his eyes, Rishan was able to discuss in detail which had pained and plagued him for many years. Rishan had failed in some aspects of his personal life and believed Rishan abandoned his family and had failed to protect them. Perhaps his father should have fought Kali Mehra from the very start of Kali's antagonism as Harbir had.

Ratnavali consoled Rishan, calmly saying, "Men often carry the weight of burdens not meant for them to carry. You are a man who understands the troubles that others have because you share the same struggles. You speak to men and women as equals regardless of caste and wealth; your word is respected, pure, and weighted with intelligence. You have wisdom far beyond your years, as if you have taken a life full of knowledge from your previous life and now enjoy one with combined wisdom and perspectives. When you speak others listen as if they have known you all their lives. You have to believe in yourself Rishan as fiercely and easily as others believe in you."

Ratnavali consoled Rishan and helped relieve his anxiety and stress with a gentle kiss. Rishan admired Ratnavali's warrior spirit and femininity—an interesting combination indeed. Her hair was long, black, and flowed in the wind. Ratnavali's dark brown skin blended into the night and felt like the smoothest of fabric. Ratnavali was pleasant to converse with and pleasing to the eye. Rishan deeply enjoyed her company.

"Shall we get comfortable and enjoy this night together?" Ratnavali whispered. "For tomorrow is not always promised in this turbulent land."

As the wine flowed, Rishan let go of his inhibitions, embraced Ratnavali, and they both enjoyed the night for themselves. In only a few days they would approach King Malayaketu's southern border.

With Chanakya's help, King Chandragupta Maurya continued to consolidate his power within his kingdom. Dhana Nanda and the Nanda Dynasty had been plagued by widespread rumors of their lower caste origins. Dhana Nanda's grandfather married two women and one was the daughter of a barber, which was not accepted by the orthodox Brahmin and Kshatriya castes. The powerful families belonging to the priest, teacher, and the warrior castes suspected the Nandas of originating from the lower servant Shudra caste. The people of the lower standings of farmers, merchants, and traders of the Vaishya caste and those of the servant Shudra caste also revolted against the Nandas for their high taxation rates. Dhana Nanda converted to Buddhism shortly after his exile in an attempt to change his public persona and alter the negative attitudes towards his family's rule. Dhana Nanda's new Buddhist leanings did little to stem the damage he had inflicted during his rule and Chanakya encouraged this widespread anger. Dhana Nanda tried to live as a Buddhist speaking against his former life of greed and luxury, but encouraged by the words of Chanakya, Dhana Nanda's enemies assassinated him.

Chandragupta Maurya had eliminated most of his rivals, including all of the potential threats within the House of Nanda and subsequently inherited Dhana Nanda's vast army. Chandragupta now was in command of an over 200,000-man infantry with a cavalry approaching 60,000, 8,000 war chariots, and over 6,000 war elephants. Chandragupta Maurya was now increasing his infantry and cavalry while promising to repeal many of Dhana Nanda's disastrous tax policies. Chanakya was his chief adviser and a renowned economist who instructed Chandragupta on a revised economic plan that would give tax relief to the disadvantaged.

Under Chanakya's advice, Chandragupta actively expanded west to reclaim the territories held by the Macedonians and Greeks. King Porus and his younger brother King Porus Balarama were now dead, which left a power vacuum. Chanakya's spies also informed him that King Parvateshwara had succumbed to poison. The poison had been administered multiple times and had rapidly degraded Parvateshwara's health, leaving the young Malayaketu to be named king by his father as he neared death. Parvateshwara's demise was not public knowledge and neither were the circumstances. King Malayaketu continued to work feverishly to find the men responsible for his father's death while initiating new political alliances in an effort to legitimize and expand his power.

Only a few ministers of the Nanda Dynasty remained after the ascension of Chandragupta as king. Minister Sakatala proved to be the most supportive of Chandragupta Maurya as king after the death of Shaktar roughly three years prior. Chanakya had entrusted Sakatala with a position of leadership in the new military and had developed a positive relationship with Chanakya but was believed to have been killed by a female assassin under the orders of Rakshasa, a former minister who had been under the orders of the now deceased Dhana Nanda. Rakshasa was a powerful, intelligent man with designs to topple Chandragupta Maurya and Chanakya. The last few years proved to be a large political battle between Rakshasa, Chanakya, and their numerous agents. Rakshasa allied himself with King Malayaketu in order to use his army against the Mauryan Kingdom and advised King Malayaketu to create a stronger alliance with King Ambhi and the Greek leadership. Hoping to legitimize his position, King Malayaketu trusted Rakshasa and proclaimed him as a top adviser. The ongoing Greek Wars of Succession and Chanakya's agents would soon create fissures within the Greek sphere of influence in the Punjab.

King Malayaketu's expanding power had stalled due to further instability in the Greek Empire after the Macedonian King Philip III Arrhidaeus and his wife were assassinated under the orders of Olympias the previous year. The second war of the Diadochi had continued for over three years and the only heir to Alexander's throne was his baby son Alexander IV, who was now under the protection of Cassander (while his mother Roxana was also under his control),whoruled Macedon and assassinated Alexander the Great's mother. Cassander also had defeated his main rival Polyperchon and forced him to flee in an effort to possibly seek allegiance with Antigonus. Cassander had solidified his power in Macedon. The Greek wars continued in Asia where Antigonus had gained considerable power and now the governors Eudamus and Peithon were joining the battle against Antigonus, leaving King Ambhi Takshashila in control of the Punjab.

The alliance between King Malayaketu and Rakshasa which had become a risk to Chandragupta Maurya and Chanakya was now threatened due to the weakened backing of Eudamus and Peithon. For several months, Chanakya had pondered and discussed various strategies to break king Malayaketu's growing support from within. Chanakya's spies provided valuable information about Malayaketu's alliances with the Greek foreigners to the west. Chanakya had informed Chandragupta of King Malayaketu's attempted alliance with King Ambhi and the satraps Peithon and Eudamus as well as the weakening of the Greek presence in the Punjab. Chanakya also began to activate his agents in a plot to weaken King Malayaketu's power structure before marching Chandragupta's army to face King Malayaketu. The time to initiate the plot was now, while the Greeks were involved in their Wars of Succession.

Agents working for Chanakya swiftly began to work against Rakshasa, whose blind hatred of Chanakya made him increasingly unaware of the plots unfolding within King Malayaketu's palace. As King Malayaketu's power base weakened, Rakshasa's desperation grew and he increased the amounts of assassination attempts on King Chandragupta Maurya. Many of these were intersected by Chanakya and Chandragupta's guards. Rakshasa expected similar attempts on his life and King Malayaketu's, but no such thing had occurred. Operatives under the direction of Chanakya were instructed to gradually relay several messages to King Malayaketu concerning a false rift between Chandragupta and Chanakya and Chanakya's dismissal as chief adviser. As the weeks continued to pass, agents relayed messages to King Malayaketu about supposed secret messages between King Chandragupta Maurya and Rakshasa. King Malayaketu also received false intelligence about a potential alliance between Rakshasa and Chandragupta Maurya. King Malayaketu also acquired false information that his major alliances might potentially work against him, causing the young king to grow desperate and foolish.

Chandragupta Maurya removed Chanakya from the Royal Court in a ploy to further sow discord among King Malayaketu and Rakshasa. As the weeks passed and war was imminent, Rakshasa began to worry about losing to the powerful Mauryan military. Rakshasa secretly sent word to Chandragupta Maurya about a possible alliance as his relationship continued to weaken with King Malayaketu. The paranoid King Malayaketu began executing numerous ministers and military leaders he believed to be involved in a conspiracy to remove him from power and rumors spread that Rakshasa would soon face execution as well, which prompted him to prepare his escape to Chandragupta Maurya's court. Peithon and Eudamus were now traveling west to face the powerful Antigonus, drawing away much of King Malayaketu's Greek support. King Malayaketu's alliances were weakening and his attention was diverted from Rishan, who was now marching towards his kingdom to rescue his family.

The Ramankrishna family, who previously lived under relatively peaceful conditions, were now confined to the Royal Palace of King Malayaketu. King Ambhi repeatedly requested the family be escorted and placed under his supervision, but the potential wars caused by the advancing Mauryan forces put a stop to this plan. Out of desperation, King Ambhi sent Randeep Mehra along with thousands of Greek and Punjabi troops to aid King Malayaketu and to capture the Ramankrishna family. Karna Mehra had been elevated to a high leadership position and was traveling with King Eudamus to participate in the Greek Wars of Succession, leaving his older brother Randeep Mehra more than willing to prove himself.

Chanakya's plot was successful; Rakshasa had fled King Malayaketu's court with the aid of Chanakya's conspirators. King Malayaketu was denied the capture of Rakshasa for questioning, causing the king's mind to dance with ideas that his various battle strategies would find their way to Chandragupta. King Malayaketu mobilized his army ahead of Randeep Mehra's arrival and began to march them east to confront Chandragupta's forces. He also sent scouts north and a smaller force of a few thousand men southeast in case Chandragupta's army arrived at different locations. King Malayaketu could not wait for reinforcements—his scouts had informed him that Chandragupta was already on the march.

Rishan Ramankrishna continued north where his small military had now increased to over 500 men and over fifty women all ready for battle. On his way, he gathered valuable intelligence from his young Greek hostage Pylas. Pylas had been intimidated with death by the angry men led by Rishan but was only beaten under Rishan's strict orders. With the threats swirling through his young, frightened mind, Pylas imparted sensitive Greek information regarding the Diadochi wars and political realities in the Punjab. Pylas informed Rishan that King Malayaketu's Greek support would be weakened as long as Eudamus and Peithon had marched west against the growing power of Antigonus The One-Eyed. Rishan also learned of the power shifts, the death of King Philip III, and the wars drawing Eudamus and Peithon and their respective military forces away from their respective satrapies.

Rishan asked, "What about Eumenes and his Silver Shields? Will they be victorious?"

Pylas responded, "The Silver Shields are respected war veterans and served valiantly under the leadership of Alexander the Great. The reality is that the Silver Shields are now men over the age of sixty and they are facing a young, hungry military under a very capable regional leader in Antigonus."

Rishan remembered Antigonus as a child during the dinner party with Alexander, his generals, his father, Chandragupta Maurya, and Chanakya. Now, ironically, they would cross paths as adults.

Pylas informed Rishan of the continuing Greek wars and that his family was relatively safe. Through his prisoner, Rishan learned that his father was rumored to be with the rest of his immediate family, which helped confirm the other information identifying Manish's location in Malayaketu's kingdom. Karna had encouraged King Ambhi and Satrap Eudamus to capture Rishan and bring him to justice. King Malayaketu was also actively reaching out to King Ambhi and the Mehra family for military support in exchange for Rishan's family. The continuing Greek Wars of Succession had delayed that plan, giving Rishan an opportunity to reach his family before they were captured.

Armed with this knowledge, Rishan led his men north, where he met with a segment of King Malayaketu's army, who were unaware that Rishan had made his way into King Malayaketu's southern border. Rishan, Anand, and Ratnavali planned to ambush King Malayaketu's men as they prepared to rest for the night. Rishan and Anand agreed that a full attack should be carried out while the enemy forces were spread thin and Randeep Mehra and the additional Greek troops were still in transit. Just as the sun was setting, Rishan charged, catching King Malayaketu's army by surprise.

Rishan arranged his archers on his left flank, raining arrows on Greeks deep within their own lines as he rode at the lead of his cavalry. Anand charged on foot, taking command of Rishan's right flank as the confused Greeks and Punjabis ran away from the arrows already falling at the center of their camp. The Greeks screamed while Anand encouraged his men to continue their fight and forward momentum. The arrows endlessly showered down, killing Greeks and Punjabis who were unable to react fast enough. Rishan understood that he had to engage the far superior Greeks in a surprise attack before they could utilize their legendary phalanx formations. Hundreds of Greeks and Punjabis were killed by Rishan and his Dravidian army before they could establish a counterattack. Rishan continued to push his men forward as Ratnavali waited in the rear with 100 fighters. The Greeks pushed forward while Rishan's men met them in a violent clash.

Malayaketu's forces suffered massive initial losses but were able to strike back. They lost a majority of their men and faced a less professional but more numerous fighting force. Rishan and Anand encouraged their combatants to continue to press forward with no fear but the more experienced Greeks eventually broke Rishan's right flank, causing Anand to call a tactical retreat towards the reserve forces led by Ratnavali. Rishan then gave the order for his archers to unleash several rounds of arrows, killing and impeding their forward motion. Ratnavali ordered her troops to advance in order to cut down the remaining Greeks trying to reach the last of Rishan's forces. Rishan led the center line where Malayaketu's main forces were. Rishan desperately called for his archers to put down their bows and pick up their swords to help and Rishan found himself in the middle of the conflict as darkness enveloped the battlefield. Rishan ferociously cut several Greeks down with his sword; his bravery and skill in battle encouraged others to bravely engage the Greeks as the night progressed.

Anand's tactical retreat left the pursuing Greek and Punjabis' right flank open to a side attack by Ratnavali's forces, causing devastating losses. Ratnavali fought valiantly and managed to push towards the injured Greeks behind Rishan's line who threatened to attack Rishan. Anand remained with the reserve units in the rear while Ratnavali joined the fight with Rishan, killing the remainder of Malayaketu's forces who had begun to lose their fighting spirit. As morning arrived, the rest of Malayaketu's forces retreated after a surprise defeat.

The Greeks who fled were able to relate their story to a shocked King Malayaketu, who could only order a few reserve units to guard his capital as he marched to join his forces east to meet Chandragupta Maurya in battle. The path towards King Malayaketu's Palace was seemingly unprotected as Rishan cautiously marched towards the capital.

Rishan Ramankrishna understood that he had to make strategic decisions quickly and without error as the information regarding his surprise victory would spread to his enemies before the end of the night. Only a little over 200 men and women along with some children that had remained in the rear survived. As everyone celebrated, reality set in and created anxiety within Rishan as he angrily called for his Greek captive Pylas.

Taking Pylas to a secluded location with sword in hand, Rishan asked, "Where are the forces backing King Malayaketu? Will your information lead us into a trap?"

Pylas replied, "I am only aware of Eudamus and Peithon's previous plan to join the Greek Wars of Succession in the west. They face a greater threat from the other Greek leaders to the west—particularly Antigonus. I am ignorant of the location of the Mehra family. Perhaps some have joined the war to the west or perhaps they are with King Malayaketu. Why would I lie to you? My very life depends on your success on the battlefield. To be honest, my own Greek people probably view me as a traitor."

Rishan had no scouts to relay sensitive information regarding King Malayaketu's battle strategies and he became skeptical that Chandragupta would send him aid.

Anand was also skeptical of potential support from Chandragupta Maurya. The only help had come from the Assaka Kingdom and the Kalinga Kingdom, the latter being minimal with conditions that Chandragupta would not mount a future attack on Kalinga.

Anand stated, "Although we defeated a force more than double our size, I doubt we can take Malayaketu's capital with so few numbers. We need to send a scout towards Chandragupta's army to see if he will help us. Surely he will want us to open a new front in the war. I have heard rumors that Chanakya is your father Manish's cousin. Surely he will support you and your family's efforts."

Rishan was slightly relieved. "Perhaps you are correct. We will send one of our men to deliver this message and we need to gather support from the people opposed to King Malayaketu's reign. There will be many people choosing sides and I suspect many Punjabis will choose ours."

There was considerable risk in a march northward towards Malayaketu's palace and Rishan could not openly share the same doubt within some in his army. Any hesitation would risk open dissent and halt Rishan's momentum towards his primary goal.

Ratnavali offered her support. She was grateful that Rishan had freed her from perpetual servitude and told him that many of the other dasas also supported Rishan for delivering them from the bondage of Bramilan the Butcher.

However, Ratnavali had other concerns.Rishan "Rishan, your main focus is to free your family from King Malayaketu and the Greeks, but what about the rest of the men you lead?" she asked. "What incentives can you give these men and women who fight for you?"

Rishan replied, "I have helped give them their freedom and I can help them in creating a new life for themselves and their families. The young men can have new beginnings so they can work and cultivate a life; create new families free from the clutches of the Greek invaders and their corrupt Punjabi kings who follow their will. Perhaps we can all carve out a better life for ourselves under the command of a native leader like Chandragupta Maurya."

Anand, who was listening to Ratnavali and Rishan, added, "Perhaps you will live well, Rishan. You are in the warrior caste and although your family was disgraced by the Mehras, if you restore your family's honor you will regain the status your caste affords you. Perhaps even under Chandragupta Maurya the lower castes will remain in the same life of hardship they have always experienced."

Ratnavali and Anand had raised important issues and Rishan would find out soon what he could gain for the people he led as well as his family.

After a few days, Rishan's messenger returned, stating that the war had already begun between the forces of Chandragupta Maurya and King Malayaketu. Initial reports were positive with King Malayaketu's forces receiving massive losses. No large military remained to resist Rishan in his march with the exception of the Greeks—and Randeep Mehra, who was possibly arriving with them. The region was on the verge of chaos with men and women in the street in open opposition to King Malayaketu's rule. This gave Rishan an opportunity to attack.

Rishan ordered his small band of combatants northward through the outskirts under King Malayaketu's control. Surprisingly, Rishan and his Dravidians received a large amount of support, gathering many young men who wished to join in the fight and swelling their numbers. As his heroism in combat filtered into the minds of the adults and the imaginations of the youth, Rishan's popularity abounded. The people spoke of how Rishan's small force was able to hand a resounding defeat to King Malayaketu's southern defenses as they came out in support of Rishan Ramankrishna.

Chanakya informed Chandragupta Maurya regarding reports of Rishan's advance in the west. This was a surprising victory, encouraging Chandragupta Maurya to send 5,000 men away from the battlefield and toward King Malayaketu's capital to aid Rishan in holding the city. Chanakya had doubts regarding Rishan; he was a young former military leader with little experience and leading former Dravidian servants from lower non-warrior castes. However, Chanakya regained confidence in Rishan upon hearing of his stunning victory just days prior. Chanakya had emphasized creating a military largely made of warrior caste men for Chandragupta Maurya but was pleasantly surprised when Rishan was able to defeat a professional Greek and Punjabi force that more than doubled Rishan's forces. Chanakya was emboldened, sending additional men to support Rishan in his attempt to capture the capital as Chandragupta's forces began to defeat King Malayaketu's army after they had crossed the Hyphasis River. Chandragupta's elephants on his right flank crushed into Malayaketu's army, forcing them to flee towards the center. Chandragupta positioned one of his chief commanders Sakatala on his left flank.

The clash was violent as Chandragupta's elephants trampled over King Malayaketu's forces, causing fear and disorder to spread. The elephants broke through the Greek Phalanx and left the Greeks without protection. The Mauryan forces fought well, hungry to showcase their might against the Greek foreigners. Chandragupta had spoken frequently with his military leadership regarding Alexander the Great, and many of the older combatants relished the fact that they had the opportunity to fight the Greeks now—an opportunity they had missed under Dhana Nanda's leadership. Chandragupta's military observed as the Greeks occupied the Punjab lands to the west and they believed that Alexander could have been defeated when facing a unified military. Chandragupta and Chanakya understood the anger and potential of their military who wished to realize their dreams of fighting the Greeks and Chanakya purposefully encouraged his own troops, mentioning the legend that was Alexander and his glorious warriors. The Mauryan forces wanted to fight the legendary Greek soldiers like the Silver Shields they had frequently heard about. The anger and dislike for the Greeks found within the hearts of Chandragupta's military manifested in massive losses for King Malayaketu.

Sakatala led his cavalry into a violent clash, defeating the remaining chief loyal to King Malayaketu and his military. Sakatala now ordered his men to crash into the center in a combined effort with Chandragupta, resulting in devastating losses to the enemy. Commander Subandhu remained in a defensive position under the orders of Chandragupta Maurya, directing his archers in position to fire upon the now fleeing troops. King Malayaketu ordered a retreat, scampering along with his troops in fear of being captured and with the goal of regrouping with Randeep Mehra and the Greek reinforcements in the west. Chandragupta ordered his military to chase and capture the remaining troops and King Malayaketu.

Rishan reached the capital with little opposition while hundreds of young men joined his small army. A large number of Malayaketu's forces had fled as word of his defeat spread in the Punjab. King Malayaketu's palace was east of King Porus' palace, but recently he had also ruled from his great-uncle King Porus' palace as well. King Malayaketu was handed more power and it had spread into King Porus' former territory of Pauravas by the satrap Eudamus. However, he was not seen as a legitimate ruler by the populace. Open rebellion spilled into the streets while support of the advancing Ramankrishna army grew. Rishan quickly engaged the palace troops, leaving Anand and Ratnavali to lead the fight against King Malayaketu's forces while he searched the rear of the palace grounds for his family along with fifty other men. The Palace Guard desperately attempted to defend their leader, however they were quickly outmatched by Rishan and his soldiers. Anand and Ratnavali quickly overwhelmed the Palace Guard who refused to retreat as the battle continued. Punjabis who were disenfranchised by Greek occupation and angry with King Malayaketu—and other leaders they regarded as Greek puppets—joined Anand and Ratnavali in the liberation of their city. Rishan and his men fought some Greek soldiers guarding a room at the back of the palace where Rishan found his family, including his father. To Rishan's surprise, the entire Ramankrishna clan was found safe and alive, among them his older brother Rajesh and his newborn baby boy Raahi Ramankrishna. Rishan was overcome with happiness as he finally reached his primary goal of saving his family. It had been the only thing that kept him alive through his struggles with thirst and hunger. However, Rishan's reunion would be short-lived; there were battles remaining to be fought. Rishan called on Anand and some of his men to secure his family away from the palace as he awaited Chandragupta and his forces.

The next morning, over 5,000 of Chandragupta's men were finally within a few miles of King Malayaketu's palace to defeat the remnants of his army—to the excitement of the Punjabi people. King Malayaketu was now a king only by name. With the Ramankrishna family safe, Rishan ordered his troops to fight and defend the palace.

King Malayaketu and his retreating forces faced a fierce unruly mob who viewed him as a usurper, making Malayaketu's attempt to reclaim the city difficult. Seizing this opportunity, Rishan ordered his men to attack the remainder of King Malayaketu's army, which separated King Malayaketu from his personal bodyguard. Rishan's men began to defeat the remainder of King Malayaketu's forces until the last of them surrendered the capital and renounced their king. On horseback, King Malayaketu desperately tried to reach his palace only to find Rishan Ramankrishna there.

The king leaped from his horse.Rishan. "You, your

father, and Chandragupta Maurya slowly poisoned my father Parvateshwara. Was this the plan of Chanakya and Rakshasa? Manish killed King Porus and you and your agents conspired against my father. Where is that traitor Rakshasa who helped poison my father?"

Rishan was unaware of the extensive plots designed by Chanakya meant to fool King Malayaketu. Rishan denied any involvement or knowledge in the poisoning of the former king and waited for Chanakya to clarify any remaining questions.

Rishan now had temporary control of the palace and the capital; he felt it was safe to ask his family to join him in conversation with King Malayaketu. Rishan "My father Manish Ramankrishna served your great-uncle King Porus to the best of his abilities. Our family served and fought against Alexander at the Hydaspes along with King Porus and your grandfather, King Porus Balarama. Your father Parvateshwara also favored our family and respected Chandragupta Maurya. Our potential alliance threatened the Mehra family, King Ambhi, and the Greek rulers—specifically the satraps Peithon and Eudamus."

Manish Ramankrishna stated, "This will be the last time I address you as king. Your reign is at an end. I never betrayed and killed King Porus or your father. King Porus was probably killed by Karna Mehra under the direction of King Ambhi and Satrap Eudamus. The Greeks wanted to eliminate your great-uncle, grandfather, and father and they supported you—a king they could easily manipulate. Rakshasa is an opportunist who sought to elevate himself rather than serve his king. Rakshasa was a minister under Dhana Nanda that sought an alliance with you then he fled to Chandragupta. If it offers you solace, I suspect my cousin Chanakya will soon execute Rakshasa after he has exceeded his usefulness."

Rishan was surprised to discover, now after the capture of King Malayaketu, that his father and Chanakya were indeed cousins.

King Malayaketu asked, "Why should I believe you, Manish?"

Manish replied, "I have no reason to be dishonest. You have been deposed; I do not fear you. We could have you executed as many of your former subjects would wish. We will not execute you, but because you treated us well under the circumstances while we were incarcerated under your protection, we will await Chandragupta's decision regarding your fate. I only wish to clear the Ramankrishna name to the public and bring justice to those who wished to harm my family like the Greeks and the Mehra family."

Malayaketu was directed to retrieve some documents within his palace in order to reveal information regarding the Mehra family and their business dealings as well as designs against King Porus. Rajesh and some other men also combed through the former king's private documents in order to reveal evidence against the Mehra family, King Ambhi, and Eudamus. Rishan questioned his father about Chanakya and his relationship with the Ramankrishna family.

Manish revealed the truth. "Yes, my son. It is true. Chanakya is a cousin of mine from my father's side of the family. He is the child of my father Mahesh's older sister Chandanii and his father was a teacher named Chanak. Chanakya is from southern origins like us but he moved to the Punjab as a young child, where he later attended the university in Takshashila. My aunt Chandanii passed away when I was still a boy and we did not know her very well. It was unwise for me to reveal Chanakya as being of our bloodline. I feared it would be used politically by the Mehra family against us. The Greeks feared Chanakya and Chandragupta's rise and any alliances with Chanakya. Exposing that Chanakya was my cousin would have been exploited by Kali Mehra and his family. However, all the other allegations against us made by Kali Mehra and his son are false. It was a political lie in order to blame us for the assassination of King Porus in hopes of gaining favor with the people they wished to rule. However, the balance of power is now shifting towards us and against them. You must help Chandragupta and Chanakya in holding this city and their push towards the north against Randeep Mehra and King Ambhi."

Documents linking the Mehra's family business dealings outside of Pauravas were recovered—many of which were written in secrecy without King Porus' knowledge. Rishan placed these documents verifying Harbir's previous statements against the Mehra family into his father's hands to be transferred over to Chanakya for Chandragupta's review. Rishan then ordered his men into battle formations against the approaching Randeep Mehra and the Greeks who sought to recapture Pauravas and the surrounding territory.

With less than 300 men, Rishan would rely on the incoming Mauryan forces as well as the population of Pauravas and the surrounding areas to help hold both King Malayaketu's city and King Porus' old palace. Hoping to gain ten miles before meeting Randeep Mehra, Rishan ordered his men on a quick march west. Rishan's older brother Rajesh took a sword and joined the march—he had a personal grudge with Randeep.

Anand joined Rajesh, saying, "Randeep and Karna Mehra were responsible for my family's death and I wish to deliver justice with my sword."

Rajesh teamed up with his brother Rishan along with Anand and Ratnavali as they took their army northwest, marching into the center of Pauravas towards the palace of King Porus where they set archers ready to attack the incoming Greeks.

Pylas was unsure of the status of the Greek leadership as he informed Rishan, "If it so happens that Eudamus is at the head of this Greek army, we may need more reinforcements. However, if it so happens that Eudamus and Peithon have indeed followed Eumenes into battle against Antigonus, then you can more easily defeat an army led by King Ambhi Taxiles and Randeep Mehra."

Rishan nodded."I agree, Pylas. However, it does not matter who is leading the Greeks. The only thing that matters is our victory, or else we will meet death in battle. We will not make it easy for them."

The day was coming to an end as Randeep Mehra

appeared leading a combined army of Greeks and Punjabi combatants towards King Porus' palace. Rishan ordered his archers to fire upon Randeep Mehra's army, causing numerous causalities. Arrows continued to rain down on the incoming Greek and Punjabi forces and Randeep Mehra ordered his left flank to take cover and outflank Rishan's forces, causing the archers to pick up their swords and engage in combat. At the center line, Rishan led his troops into a clash with Randeep's remaining forces. It was violent, the setting sun in front of Rishan's combatants blinding them. In the distance, Rajesh identified Randeep Mehra who was urging his troops to crush Rishan's small army. Randeep ordered his army to kill all enemy combatants and spare no hostages except the Ramankrishna family. Randeep ordered the capture of the Ramankrishna family to locate the documents that had been seized. The numerically superior, professional army of Randeep Mehra forced Rishan and his men into a temporary retreat. Rishan sent a scout eastward towards the advancing Mauryan forces to urgently inform General Sakatala that they were in need of reinforcements.

Rishan screamed, "Let us turn and fight them! Let them stare into our eyes and dare to kill us rather than letting them kill us with our backs turned like wild animals!"

Anand and Rishan were pinned, fighting as hard as they could as they continued their offensive. Fearing death, Anand attempted to reach Randeep. In the darkness of night, General Sakatala finally arrived leading an army of over 5,000 Mauryan troops with additional reinforcements on the way. Encouraged by the sight of Rishan, his dark skin glistening with sweat and blood and his long hair in locks swaying in the wind, the Punjabi population joined Rishan in repelling the Greeks from Pauravas. Randeep tried to burn down King Porus' palace, but was stopped by Anand and Rajesh, who had managed to chase down the disgraced leader.

Rajesh was able to knock Randeep down as Randeep shouted, "You are weak and never deserved a woman like Divya! Soon you and the rest of the Ramankrishna family will perish just as your father-in-law Harbir did!"

Randeep was able to strike Anand as he got on his horse and barely managed to escape into the night. Rajesh exclaimed, "We know the truth about the assassination of King Porus and your lies. We have the evidence! Your family, King Ambhi, and the rest of the Greeks are no longer safe and your corrupt reign along with your lies and love of wealth will all come to an end!"

Rishan had just over fifty of his original Dravidian combatants remaining. These former servants had fought long and hard and they had become fiercely loyal to Anand, Ratnavali, and Rishan. The battle continued for a few more hours but many of the Punjabis loyal to the Mehra family and King Ambhi had surrendered while a significant amount of Greeks decided not to continue fighting for Randeep, who they secretly viewed as unfit to lead them. Sakatala secured Pauravas as Chanakya entered along with Chandragupta and the massive Mauryan army. The people erupted in celebration and praised Rishan Ramankrishna as well as Chandragupta Maurya. When morning came, Malayaketu was officially dethroned and forced to submit to King Chandragupta Maurya.

King Porus' palace was saved from destruction and searched by Rishan. Various Greek leaders were apprehended and sensitive information implicating Eudamus, King Ambhi, and the Mehra family in the assassination of King Porus and the plot against the Ramankrishna family were publicly revealed to the people of Pauravas and the Punjabi region. The murder of Rishan's teachers including Guru Rampal and his martial arts instructor Akas were also revealed, as the Mehra family attempted to destroy all evidence connecting them to their political betrayals of the Punjabi people. Public support for Chandragupta Maurya grew and his legitimacy as ruler was solidified while support increased for continued war against King Ambhi in the north. Rishan urged Chanakya to pursue Randeep Mehra and the Greeks.

Chanakya advocated the need for patience, stating, "King Ambhi and the Mehra family have nowhere else to run. My spies have informed me that Eudamus and Peithon are facing defeat at the hands of Antigonus in the Greek wars. It is also possible that Eudamus and Peithon will not survive their wars and King Ambhi and the Mehra family have lost a majority of their Greek support. I have also obtained information that Karna Mehra is possibly participating in the Greek Wars of Succession and may not survive." Chanakya instructed Rishan. "A leader must control his emotions and patiently study his rival's personality and weaknesses—both personal and within his administration. I remember once noticing a young boy who had burned himself while eating hot bread. His mother scolded him and taught him to eat the edges first. This was my tactic with Malayaketu in creating division within his leadership and attacking his surrounding territories first. Malayaketu helped destroy his own regional alliances as well as assassinated important members of his own administration. Rishan, you were a pleasant surprise. You helped weaken Malayaketu's defenses further when you attacked Malayaketu's southern border. We will use the same strategy we used against Malayaketu on King Ambhi and the Mehra family. Patience, my cousin. We will be victorious very soon."

CHAPTER 16:
THE MAURYAN EMPIRE AND THE FALL OF KING AMBHI (314 B.C.)

"Methods and techniques of governance can be learned from the texts but the wisdom of the aged and experienced provides accurate practical knowledge when the theory and practice come together. It is called Wisdom."
—Chanakya (*The Arthashastra*)

Chandragupta Maurya had grown in power and through combat, had pushed most of the Greeks out of the Punjab regions of the north. The Indus people and the southern kingdoms had been ruled by numerous kings which warred against each other for many generations. They referred to their homeland as Bharat; the Persians who had controlled the Indus Punjabi regions referred to this land as Hindustan and the Greek foreigners referred to it as India. For the first time, the people began to recognize Chandragupta Maurya as the supreme Samrat leader.

Rishan's successes swelled in various battles throughout northern India and his name was known across the land. Rishan spoke with Chandragupta Maurya and Chanakya regarding his status under Chandragupta's rule. Chanakya realized that although Rishan led a small army, he had the potential to attract recruits through his name alone. Large amounts of people—particularly those belonging to the poor lower castes—supported Rishan Ramankrishna. This appeal was particularly striking due to the fact that the Ramankrishna family belonged to the warrior caste and were partially accepted into high society. The shame and loss of financial security they had been subjected to by the Mehra family and the Greeks, as well as the subsequent rise in status and power through Rishan's determination and bravery, earned him the support of the lower castes that could now relate to him. Many powerful ministers in Pauravas of a higher caste respected Manish for his hard work and honesty during his service to King Porus, while some sided with Kali Mehra against him. The Punjabis against Manish Ramankrishna now were in an awkward position under the new leadership of Chandragupta Maurya.

Manish urged Chanakya to reveal information relating to the Mehras and their external businesses as well as alliances they had formed without King Porus' knowledge. Manish also spoke to Rishan regarding the disappearance of the two Greeks he had murdered and the need for his son Rishan to expose the truth of the disappeared men. The Mehra family had accused Rishan of murdering them but questions arose among the people as to why the Greek men were at the Ramankrishna residence in the first place. There were also rumors that the fight at Manish's construction site within the city of Alexandria on the Indus and the Greek men who disappeared were one in the same. The documents were reviewed by Chanakya and Mehra's former political allies and they revealed business dealings with various families allied with King Ambhi. Some families had ministers working for King Ambhi and called the Mehra family's loyalty to King Porus into question. The powerful families of the Kamboja tribe also were exposed in having business connections with the Mehras. The documents detailed covert conversations between Kali Mehra and various family members belonging to the Kamboja Clan involving sensitive Pauravas government information pertaining to possible conflicts between King Porus and King Ambhi. Some of this information pointed to the fact that perhaps Mehra family members residing in the northern regions of King Ambhi's territory of Gandhara could have political connections within the city of Takshashila and King Ambhi.

Regarding the possible alliance between the Kambojas and the Mehras, Manish remarked to both Chanakya and his son Rishan, "They are of a powerful warrior caste and are Aryans like the Mehra family. These Kamboja men seem to be not only powerful, but wealthy. However, that is where the similarities between them seem to end. These documents are old and a rift could have formed with the possibility of war between King Porus and King Ambhi and the arrival of Alexander. I remember Kali Mehra strongly advised war against King Ambhi and opposed my idea of recruiting King Ambhi into an alliance with King Porus. It seemed as if Kali wanted to keep peace, wanted to give Pauravas over to Alexander, and desired to have King Porus become a client king while avoiding a declaration of war."

Chanakya replied, "I know the Kamboja clan. They are a prideful people and expert horse riders. Their horses are the envy of all military leaders and their skill in combat is feared and respected. They view kings and rule differently than we do but they will respect other cultures as long as they are also respected. I have gathered some information with the help of my informants and I believe the families of the Kamboja clan never fully trusted the Mehra family. The Kambojas were also very careful in their correspondence with the Mehras—they did not reveal their individual names in any of the documents. We only understand they are Kamboja people and most likely a conflict formed between the Mehra and Kamboja clans during the Kamboja wars against Alexander."

Chandragupta listened carefully to the information before he stated his opinion to Rishan's father. "Manish, I remember you when I was a small boy and always admired your wisdom. I have always viewed you as an uncle and your wife Lakshmi as my aunt. I view your sons as brothers and your youngest daughter as a younger sister. Your cousin Chanakya has taken care of me and taught me how to be a good king, instructed me in the art of war, and advised me on how to run a government and economy. The events that unfolded have not been good for you and your family, but if you wish, we can release this information to the public. The people understood that the Greek trials regarding you and your son Rishan were a public display of corruption and injustice." Chandragupta paused and approach Manish as he continued. "These documents will prove the betrayal of the Mehra family, who chose to ally themselves with factions which were interested in seeing King Porus removed from power. Rishan's friend Anand Agrawal identified Randeep and Karna at the scene of his family's murder. There is reason to believe Eudamus sent the Mehra brothers with the approval of King Ambhi to assassinate King Porus and then blame you for the crimes they committed. The other mysterious murders were committed by the Mehra brothers and their Greek and Punjabi co-conspirators. Most of these victims were of lower caste and of poor origins. We need to reveal the Mehra family's conspiracy and find a way to gather further evidence that Eudamus and the Mehras assassinated King Porus."

In their defense, many of the Punjabis who supported the Mehra family admitted they had been fooled into believing the statements made by the Greek courts accusing Manish of King Porus' assassination as well as the accusations of Rishan Ramankrishna and his possible involvement in the disappearances of the two Greeks. Chandragupta revealed the documents that pertained to the Mehra family's secret alliances outside of Pauravas and possible involvement in the assassination of King Porus through writings by Satrap Eudamus and Peithon. There was also fear among the Greeks that the now deceased King Parvateshwara would seek an alliance with Chandragupta Maurya and various agents were sent to poison him, leaving his son—the now disgraced and deposed King Malayaketu—to be manipulated.

Trials were held, resulting in many of the conspirators directly named in the documents executed and some imprisoned. The lucky ones were exiled or left to live in shame like Malayaketu, who would await a decision by Chandragupta regarding his fate. Chanakya did not wish to execute a remaining blood relative of King Porus—he was a legendary figure in Pauravas. Politically, Chanakya sought to distance King Porus' grandnephew from the good and noble acts of his ancestors and pondered exile for Malayaketu.

Although Chanakya disagreed with some of the actions Rishan had undertaken in his battle strategies and the predominantly lower caste combatants in Rishan's army, he also understood that Rishan could unite people across class and caste lines under the rule of Chandragupta. Anand Agrawal, who often spoke to Rishan about a future without caste distinctions, caused anxiety within Chanakya, who viewed caste distinctions as necessary for the function of government and a defining factor in a new, united India. Anand agreed that under Chandragupta, lower caste people would fare much better than previous rulers but he sought to abolish the practice altogether and had convinced Rishan on many of his ideas. These views were shared by the Ramankrishna family but were not spoken about publicly. Anand and Chanakya would have several agreements on the uplifting of lower caste people under Chandragupta's reign. However, Chanakya felt that a complete abolishment of this ancient caste system would only help to foment unrest among the people along caste lines, which could hinder unification. Chanakya promised Rishan, Anand, and Ratnavali that he would welcome this discussion only after the defeat of King Ambhi and the remaining Mehra family.

Rishan's nephew, Raahi Ramankrishna, was now a healthy large three-year-old boy. Rishan was overjoyed that his family had survived the political assassinations and Rishan was also enjoying his success as a military leader along with the attention it had garnered him—mostly from the poor and many of the beautiful young women throughout the land. Rishan's popularity now extended beyond the Punjab and had attracted Indus Valley women as well as Greek, Persian, and Bactrian women. Other men were amazed regarding the numerous Punjabi and foreign

Greek and Persian women interested in Rishan. His popularity, power, and his family's redemption also created jealousy among the young men of some of the established wealthy Punjabi families that always viewed the Ramankrishnas as outsiders. Rishan secretly enjoyed his success but refused to embarrass his former adversaries, choosing to continue to establish his family name through continued victories in battle while building his family's finances once again. Anand advised Rishan to take advantage of his new position and influence King Chandragupta to widen his punishment of suspected families possibly aiding the Mehra family. As Chanakya advised, Rishan and Manish chose to take a more patient approach and address these concerns after forcing King Ambhi to abdicate his throne.

Rishan was now approached by beautiful ladies everywhere he went, often causing jealousy among his closest female admirers—including Ratnavali. Unlike the other women, Ratnavali understood that she alone stood in a special part of Rishan's mind; only with her did Rishan reveal his deepest thoughts without fear of being manipulated. Rishan knew that if he was to pursue a life of power within the Mauryan Army that Ratnavali would not be a suitable wife because she was widowed with a son and she belonged to a lower caste. Rishan weighed the option of living a life outside of politics and the military alongside Ratnavali and her son and expressed these thoughts with her. The primary wish Ratnavali had voiced was for her son to be taken into Rishan's care and that he would have access to a great education and a career as long as his skills and talents qualified him. Rishan often viewed Ratnavali's son as his best friend and although he could not promise Ratnavali marriage, he loved and respected her enough to guarantee that he would take her son Atallan as his own.

Rishan sought to uncover the Greek and Mehra family conspiracy against King Porus and the people of Pauravas. Manish pressured Rishan to speak publicly regarding the disappearances of the Greek men the night of his flight from Pauravas while Chanakya also advised Rishan to reveal the truth. Rishan ultimately agreed but hesitated elaborating on the specific details; he did not want his dear mother Lakshmi and sister Priya to know. Rishan spoke honestly regarding the events as Manish, Chandragupta, Rajesh, and Chanakya closely listened.

"There were two Greek men at my family's residence. One was named Arkadios and the other man was a Theban named Myron. I overheard a private conversation between them the night I planned to flee Pauravas. Arkadios was a man I had injured during the riot at my father's construction site. I managed to cut Arkadios' hand and he later had it amputated by a doctor. I believe he was sent to the construction site by Peithon or Eudamus, as I heard him say to Myron that he had suffered embarrassment and injury because of their politics. I suspect these men were sent by Peithon or Eudamus to kill me but I am not sure that the plot to kill me and hurt my family originated from Arkadios alone. Both men attacked me and I acted in self-defense, killing Arkadios and then Myron. I tied boulders to their bodies and threw them into a river within ten miles from my family's house. I feared the events of that night would further give the Mehras and the Greeks reason to punish my family despite King Porus' support."

Chandragupta replied, "I understand these events are hard to speak about now but we must reveal the truth because vicious rumors were spread by Kali Mehra and his sons against you and your family. We will spare the public and your mother and sister the explicit details, but we will make a statement on your behalf and send men to retrieve the cadavers of these Greek men. The facts involving your case will help destroy the false statements propagated by the Mehras and will help your family and Chandragupta in gaining support for our war against King Ambhi. We will attempt to avoid war with King Ambhi but I doubt he will submit peacefully—his Greek supporters wish to put an end to Chandragupta's reign. You will be an important part of our war against King Ambhi and in our administration."

Rishan agreed, however he believed the full truth would be revealed after King Ambhi's defeat. As Mauryan forces swept through previously Greek-held territories, Rishan encountered old friends and enemies and uncovered information that changed the dynamics with each of his respective relationships. One of the families that Rishan was curious about was the Kumaris.

Anand had informed Rishan that the Kumari family's residence was west of Alexandria on the Indus. Rishan's former girlfriend Priyanka Kumari had indeed married Kanchanpreet Mehra after Rishan fled Pauravas. Many of the Mehras also escaped the city of Alexandria in the Indus and the coastal city of Alexandria formerly within Satrap Peithon's territory, as Chandraupta Maurya reclaimed former Greek territories. Chanakya's spies discovered that Kanchanpreet Mehra chose to retreat shortly before Chandragupta arrived to Pauravas and his whereabouts were currently unknown. Rishan and Chanakya agreed that Kanchanpreet possibly escaped by ship near the coastal city of Alexandria or possibly travelled north to join King Ambhi and Randeep Mehra. Rishan did not seek to harm the Kumari family; he only sought to gain intelligence regarding Kanchanpreet's location.

As Rishan searched the surrounding cities, Chanakya notified Rishan that they had contacted Kulvir Kumari, who had asked to speak with Rishan. The remainder of the Kumari family was located within a few miles of the city of Alexandria on the Indus. Kulvir Kumari requested a private audience with Rishan and Manish.

Kulvir Kumari was now a tall, slender man who appeared older than his age. Kulvir seemed stressed and embarrassed as he spoke quietly."I come to you ashamed for my family's actions against yours. My father was nervous and believed the best thing was to disassociate ourselves from you and the rest of the Ramankrishna family. My father Padmesh allowed fear to cloud his judgment and he believed my sister Priyanka's marriage to Kanchanpreet Mehra would place our family on favorable terms with Greek leadership. My mother Padma agreed with my father's decision as she only wanted our safety. My sister was attracted to Mehra clan's power and fame and Kanchanpreet's expanding career prospects. I rejected my father's decision and cursed my sister for choosing a man of low character over the moral and honest man that you are, Rishan. Kanchanpreet's behavior worsened after he was wedded to my sister, manifesting into verbal and most recently physical abuse. I suspect my father was aware of this but he chose not to speak against Kanchanpreet. He feared the Mehra family and enjoyed our new supply of wealth. Kanchanpreet was a substandard architect and a poor leader in his various construction projects. However, the Greeks allowed him to continue. Karna and his other cousins advised Peithon to allow Kanchanpreet to continue new projects within Alexandria in the Indus. Satrap Peithon grew tired of Kanchanpreet's failures and only allowed him to construct minor projects within his cities due to the Mehra family's favorable standing with the Greeks. I believe Kanchanpreet privately acknowledged his lack of skills and Manish's prior successes, but his consumption of wine increased as well as his abuse of my sister."

Rishan asked for the location of the remaining Mehra family members and Kulvir replied, "Most escaped north as Chandragupta began to defeat the Greeks along the eastern border of Pauravas. Karna never respected Chandragupta or Rishan and their ability to defeat the Greeks, choosing to join Eudamus in the ongoing Greek Wars of Succession. There was a rumor that Eudamus and the other Greek rulers had perished at the hands of Antigonus but information has been suppressed and the people never converse about foreign affairs in public. Randeep chose to confront Chandragupta and stated he would humiliate the Ramankrishna family. The Mehra family became alarmed as Randeep returned after his defeat along with Kanchanpreet, who revealed his cowardice in leaving my sister with child and our family at your mercy. All I ask Rishan is for you and Chandragupta to show mercy on my family despite our foolish choices. My father is deeply ashamed regarding his past actions and he will submit to you and Chandragupta. He only asks if he can save face in the eyes of the public. I wish that my humble apologies on behalf of my family and my previous good deeds will grant my father's basic wishes in this unfortunate time." Kulvir's voice began to shake as he finished his statements and he struggled to hold back tears as he lowered his gaze, not daring to look Rishan or Manish in the eye.

Manish responded, "I have always respected you, Kulvir, and I enjoyed our bond. You were an excellent student like my son Rishan and I always enjoyed sharing my knowledge with a capable student such as yourself. I believe I speak for my sons and the rest of the Ramankrishna family when I state that I will forgive your family, but I find it hard to forget the actions your father has taken. At the very least, the business taken from me should be given to someone who is capable in the art of construction. The wealth your father has gained through the deceitful acts of Kanchanpreet and the Mehra family should be redistributed to the families they have victimized. If your father has knowledge of any secret designs of the Mehra family or the Greek leadership, I seriously advise him to come forward and openly discuss this with Chanakya and Chandragupta and perhaps they will offer leniency. I will personally ask for a light punishment, as I don't want your father's decisions and your sister's clouded judgment to impact the entire Kumari family."

Kulvir thanked Manish and apologized to Rishan, hoping to reestablish a relationship with the Ramankrishna family through time, despite the negative actions of his father.

Padmesh Kumari was later summoned to speak with Chanakya and admit his past actions against the Ramankrishnas. After speaking with Manish, Chanakya advised Chandragupta to seize Padmesh's wealth gained through the confiscations of Manish's construction projects. Chandragupta distributed roughly fifty percent of the money to Manish and the Ramankrishna family and the other fifty percent was distributed to the victims of violence and deceitful business practices the Mehra family had perpetrated. Chandragupta would officially hold a trial to judge Padmesh's actions after the upcoming war against King Ambhi Takshashila and his forces. If found guilty, Chandragupta promised minimal punishment for Padmesh Kumari if he revealed all the documents, records, and secret plans of the Mehra family and his help in the search of Kanchanpreet and his cousins Randeep and Karna Mehra.

Padmesh was ashamed but grateful that he would not face a maximum penalty; he did not want his past actions to further punish and shame his family. Padmesh was too embarrassed to personally apologize to Manish and requested to do so after the trial. The Mauryan Army was now mobilizing for their march towards the northern territories of Gandhara as Chanakya advised the war begin before the winter snow.

As Rishan prepared to ride north, Manish approached his son. "Rishan, I have some information I struggled to keep from you for some time for our safety and for the safety of those who helped us. Your childhood friend Anupa Jhingan and her family secretly aided us during our turbulent times. It surprised me that the Jhingan family had extended help to me as those who I believed to be our friends turned their backs on us. I was never close to the Jhingan family; their status as a wealthy Brahmin family kept us apart. However, your friendship with their daughter had positively impacted her and she had urged her father to aid us in our time of need. Anupa's father Daha, her mother Surina, and older brother Nakesh provided money and influenced others to shelter your mother and family as they moved east. The Jhingan family also influenced King Parvateshwara into looking at us favorably and remaining neutral in the wider regional conflicts. Daha and Surina frequently inquired about your wellbeing and they anxiously waited for information about you and always wished for your safety. The Jhingan influence began to diminish as King Parvateshwara's health began to decline and his son King Malayaketu took power. We lost communication shortly afterwards, as they understandably did not want to get involved in regional politics and risk their safety."

Rishan was surprised to hear the news and was happy that past actions could become such positive results many years in the future.

The pain Rishan had felt over the betrayal of Priyanka as well as the events that had occurred with Kanchanpreet had lessened. Rishan remembered his first love Anupa. She was beautiful and uncorrupted by politics, greed, or violence as other people were during these turbulent times. She was honest, pure, and the ideal woman that Rishan yearned for, but she was seemingly out of reach. Anupa was of a high Brahmin caste and she was the object of affection for many of Punjabi's wealthiest and most powerful young men. She and Manish had informed Rishan that she remained unwed, possibly in devotion to the gods. However, she had asked frequently about Rishan and wished to see him. Rishan remembered his long friendship with her but he had never been properly introduced to her family and laughed to himself, aware of the fact that his fame had now informally introduced him. Rishan thought that perhaps he would send her a message before he rode north for battle. It was a chance he had to take; he realized through experience how short and precious life was in the life of a warrior.

Manish was concerned for Rishan's personal life and wanted to see his son gain a quality woman. He had wished for his son to pursue a young lady such as Anupa, however he understood that Anupa belonged to the influential Jhingan family—a family which belonged to the Panjatias group of five Brahmin families in the Punjab. Anupa was frequently approached by many young suitors belonging to the other Brahmin families such as the Jaitely, Kumaria, Mohla, and the Trikha.

Manish advised his son before he marched into battle, "First you must focus on your upcoming war against King Ambhi. Although the advantage is on your side, remember you must remain confident but do not make the error of becoming overconfident. After you are successful, then you can begin to concentrate on affairs of the heart. I believe your new knowledge of Anupa's role in helping us in our time of need has awakened your thoughts of her. You should remember that Anupa is of a high Brahmin caste and she rejected your advances before. I do understand that time changes perspectives, but you must conquer your feelings and calmly think about what is best for you. Your brother has chosen a fine woman through my advice and I wish the same for you, Rishan. Ratnavali is a lower caste widow with child and I would advise you to thoroughly ponder the responsibilities you would acquire if you chose her. Ratnavali is of great character and truly loves you. She is also a distinguished warrior and intelligent; I believe she could also be an amiable wife for you. I wish you well and may Lord Krishna guide you in battle as he did with Arjuna."

Rishan's uncle Manu asked to ride along with his nephew and Rishan reluctantly agreed, as he believed the conflict against King Ambhi would end in a quick, decisive victory. Rishan became even more focused when Chanakya informed him of new information that Kanchanpreet Mehra was now with the rest of the Mehra family, which included Kali and his wife Sanjeeta and his eldest son Randeep. With General Eumenes' devastating loss to Antigonus and heavy Indian losses, Karna was possibly dead and Rishan believed this was the best opportunity to defeat King Ambhi and the remaining Mehra family who held significant power. Many of the Mehra family were killed in the battle against Chandragupta in Pauravas, including Kanchanpreet's estranged father Jagmohan Mehra, who died with an arrow in his lungs as he fled along with the rest of his nephew Randeep's retreating forces.

Rishan spoke to Ratnavali before the battle began, whispering, "Thank you for simply listening to my struggles. Your strength and the sharpness in your eyes gave me the will to emancipate you and the rest of the servants. You are a great leader just as my friend Anand. You are a courageous woman and fighter and you are the inspiration for my army in battle. You and your son Atallan deserve the best opportunity in life and I will provide that for you; just promise me to remain safe in battle. It should be a short fight."

With tears in her eyes, Ratnavali embraced Rishan and thanked him for his kindness and appreciation. "You are a great man, Rishan. I am happy that I have met you. If you are in my life in any capacity I will forever be appreciative."

It was a rapid march to the north as Chandragupta urged his generals to initiate the confrontation against King Ambhi before the snows began to fall. Chanakya advised Chandragupta that he needed to initiate an attack on King Ambhi before the elements created mud that would slow the numerous chariots and the wheeled vehicles that provided the food supply for the Mauryan army. Rishan convinced Manish to stay with the rest of their family—Rishan felt his father was too tired to fight in armed combat—while his uncle Manu continued at his side.

King Ambhi's allies had become disenchanted with King Ambhi and the Mehra family, including the Kamboja people. Randeep Mehra had successfully arrived to Gandhara and met King Ambhi at his palace. King Ambhi became enraged at Randeep as he returned in complete failure with nearly the entire Greek and Ambhi army killed in battle against Chandragupta Maurya. Just a few hundred men made the trip back along with Randeep Mehra, who explained the need to stage a final battle with the full force of King Ambhi's military. Randeep requested an audience with the Kamboja leaders but was surprised to learn that they had abandoned King Ambhi shortly before his arrival.

Randeep Mehra became enraged as he stated, "All the wealth my family has given those people to fight along with us and this is the way they repay us. What about the horses and our Greek allies?"

King Ambhi replied, "I advised against your march to Pauravas but you insisted on defeating Rishan and the Ramankrishna family and now Rishan has defeated you backed by Chandragupta Maurya. You never wished to incorporate the Kamboja people in our alliance with the Greeks, just use them—a fact they now have realized.

Perhaps Chanakya has informed them of your family's previous political betrayals. What secrets have Chanakya and the Ramankrishna family uncovered after your family failed to safeguard our correspondence? I believe they have revealed our many years of plotting along with the satraps Eudamus and Peithon. The Kamboja clan has been alerted to Chandragupta's successes and they have been informed that their correspondence has also been found and they have placed the blame entirely on us. Now the Kambojas have retreated into their mountains where I believe they will remain neutral. I have spent the last year trying in vain to hold our alliances together. Now they have attacked us, further diminishing our military, and we will receive little help from the Greeks. They are fighting their own wars. Our main Greek allies— including Eudamus—have been murdered."

Randeep's emotions had turned from anger to fear as he learned that the former great Greek general had been killed. Eudamus had taken more than 120 elephants and close to 4,000 men in support of Eumenes against Antigonus. A massive war in Gabiene between Antigonus the "One-Eyed" and Eumenes had come to a close. Antigonus had the numerical advantage with over 22,000 men in his infantry and close to 10,000 in his cavalry, while Eumenes amassed 17,000 men in his infantry and hoped to even the battle with doubling the amount of elephants in control under Antigonus. The end result was disastrous for Eumenes: he received heavy losses while the famed Satrap Peithon planned a conspiracy against his leader. Fearing death and fueled by his jealousy of Eumenes, Eudamus formed a secret alliance with the leaders of the legendary Silver Shields, Antigenes, and Teutamus.

Randeep asked about the specifics of the fate of his former leader Eudamus and King Ambhi replied, "Eudamus, Antigenes, and Teutamus hoped to gain favor with Antigonus, but we have learned that Antigonus burned Eudamus and Antigenes alive—the fate of Teutamus is still unknown. However, I believe he will also be executed. General Eumenes was starved for three days before he was burned alive, and his ashes were given to his family. Many of the warriors in Eumenes' army, including the Silver Shields, were absorbed by Antigonus' army."

Randeep felt a cold chill as he heard of Antigonus' major victory over Eumenes and the inglorious deaths of Eudamus, Eumenes, Antigenes, and other leaders. Sadly, the defeat for Eumenes had been caused largely by his own subordinates who did not respect him and the Silver Shields who despised him after their baggage train and large wealth was lost. The legitimacy of Alexander's Royal Argead House had received a massive blow with the defeat of Eumenes and now the Mehra family and King Ambhi also received a devastating setback.

Kali Mehra had fled months prior to Randeep Mehra's attempt to defeat Chandragupta Maurya in Pauravas and was returning from the Kamboja territories in the north where he failed in his renegotiations. Kali was informed of the devastating events at the battle of Gabiene and he explained to King Ambhi and his son Randeep that their only advantage would be with the return of Karna Mehra, who was participating at the battle of Gabiene. This hope of Karna's return along with thousands of Indian troops to aid in King Ambhi's battle against Chandragupta was replaced with desperation and despair when unfortunate information was delivered to King Ambhi by his spies.

As the battle against Chandragupta was set to begin, King Ambhi informed the Mehra family of Karna's possible fate at the disastrous battle of Gabiene. "General Ceteus, who commanded your son Karna Mehra, died in battle against Antigonus' forces and the fate of Karna is unknown. What is certain is that Karna and the rest of our men will not arrive to supplement my army and most of our allies have failed us."

Randeep defiantly replied, "I will kill Rajesh and Rishan Ramankrishna before this war is over. If I die in the process then I will die a happy man. I will not let them enjoy a single living day putting our family through shame!"

A light snow began to fall in the hills and mountains

as the battle against King Ambhi began. Rishan, Anand, and Ratnavali led their army now backed by Chandragupta in the right flank, while Sakatala commanded the left flank and Chandragupta led the central forces. Chandragupta's forces outnumbered King Ambhi's forces more than three to one when the fighting began. Chanakya advised Chandragupta to use the cavalry to smash King Ambhi's right flank, however Chandragupta wished to show the world his massive military might as a projection of power to the Greek Hellenistic world and any remaining rivals Chandragupta had within India.

Chandragupta slammed into the center of King Ambhi's army, crushing his center within a few hours and splitting his forces in two. King Ambhi circled behind his left flank as he fled from Chandragupta Maurya and was subsequently forced up a hill towards Rishan's army. Rishan deployed his Dravidian archers, greatly devastating King Ambhi's forces.

Randeep Mehra ordered his cavalry to plunge into Rishan Ramankrishna's line, disobeying King Ambhi's order to take a position in defense of the arrows. Randeep understood the war would quickly turn in favor of Chandragupta's forces and only wished to kill Rishan and Rajesh.

Taking heavy losses, Randeep's forces managed to reach the archers and Rishan's infantry. The blood poured into the snow-covered ground, creating a deep reddish-brown mud which began to slow Chandragupta's reserve forces. King Ambhi grew angry as he realized that the incoming snow and mud would not be used to his advantage as Randeep's own motivations to attack now made this advantage void.

Chandragupta closed in towards the rear of Randeep while King Ambhi retreated with less than 4,000 men in his infantry remaining, leaving Randeep alone in his blind rage and questionable judgement. Kali screamed for his son to retreat but he did not obey; he only listened to hatred.

Ratnavali closed in on Randeep and landed a sword strike to Kali's eldest son, causing him to fall to the ground. As Ratnavali approached, Randeep struck her leg with his sword as Rishan raced towards him, pushing Randeep to the wet earth. Rajesh and Anand encircled Randeep, both trying to be the man to kill their hated rival. Randeep managed to make Rishan stumble in the wet snow, slicing Ratnavali across her chest. As Randeep was about to land a final blow, Anand Agrawal landed a strike upon Randeep's head with the broad side of his sword. Anand continued his assault on Randeep's body and he cried in pain with blood forcing its way out of his mouth.

Anand exclaimed, "Your family is no more, and your king will soon be dead. I will avenge my family and deliver justice myself!" Anand brought down his sword with full force upon Randeep's neck and shoulder, causing blood to shoot up into the air.

Anand then slowly stuck his sword into Randeep's stomach and he yelled in agony as Anand made sure to twist and turn slowly as Rajesh watched. Randeep finally succumbed to his injuries hours later, just as King Ambhi's retreat failed.

Rishan ordered his men to chase down King Ambhi and capture the remainder of his forces as he stayed behind with Ratnavali. Rishan's tears flowed like a waterfall as he anguished over the death of his lover. Chandragupta led the advance behind the retreating King Ambhi desperately trying to catch up to King Ambhi's rear.

Chandragupta anxiously laughed as he spoke to Chanakya. "I must defeat King Ambhi myself or I will risk Rishan Ramankrishna also stealing my victory against him!"

Chandragupta got his wish as he caught up to King Ambhi and his remaining troops. Rajesh reached King Ambhi, striking him with his sword and causing the king to fall from his horse. King Ambhi was now an older man whose last few years had been full of anxiety and stress, which only made him appear older. Surrounded, King Ambhi was astonished at the power of the child he had once met under the protection of Chanakya. King Ambhi once viewed Chanakya as a fool who attempted to lead a foolish rebellion against Dhana Nanda with Chandragupta a young boy who would possibly die in Chanakya's rebellion. King Ambhi once hoped to defeat the mighty King Porus with the help of Alexander and was subsequently saved by Alexander from King Porus' wrath. The once mighty King Ambhi now trembled at the feet of Chandragupta Maurya, the mightiest king in India.

King Ambhi was forced to officially relinquish his crown and the territory of Gandhara was now under Chandragupta's control. King Ambhi's army was dissolved with many executed or absorbed into Chandragupta's forces at the lowest levels. Kali Mehra and his wife Sanjeeta were captured and the fate of Karna Mehra remained unknown, finally ending the Mehras family's dominance of politics in the Punjab. Kanchanpreet Mehra died in deep sadness with the knowledge that his father had perished pleading for his life. Upon finding Kanchanpreet's corpse, Rajesh was informed by an infantryman that Kanchanpreet had soiled himself in fear and had wished to surrender. When the soldiers went to arrest him for questioning, he mistakenly believed they were about to kill him and he stumbled in the wet snow, falling upon his own dagger which pierced his heart.

Kanchanpreet's last words were, "Any information about my son? Give him my apologies."

Later in the day, Chandragupta questioned Ambhi and searched for additional intelligence regarding his previous relationships with the deceased Alexander and the Greeks as well as his involvement with the assassination of King Porus. Ambhi turned against the Mehra family, stating they were behind all the plots against King Porus' assassination. Ambhi revealed, "I was forced to cooperate with this shameful Mehra family by Eudamus and Peithon. I never trusted them previously when they worked with King Porus. They were quick to become allies of mine as soon as the Hydaspes war was completed; how can I trust a family like them? I was a king and my responsibilities were to my subjects. What were the responsibilities of the Mehra family? Their gods are wealth and power! All I ask is for my life to be spared as you did with Malayaketu. I can keep an administrative position and maintain your territory. The remainder of my family perished in this war and all I ask is for my life."

Chandragupta replied, "You will publicly write down your involvement in the plots against King Porus and the Ramankrishna family. You will acknowledge your alliance with the Mehra family and the Greek rulers and you will aid us in our search for further documents. You will also dismiss all false judgements against the Ramankrishna family and publically reveal all political murders committed by you, the Mehra family, and other allies."

For several days, Ambhi partially cooperated with Chandragupta Maurya, however he was untrustworthy and his relationship with the Greeks was a threat to Chandragupta Maurya. Chandragupta Maurya would hold trials and executions of Ambhi and many of his high-ranking officials.

Kali and his wife Sanjeeta were held for trial and Ambhi would later be executed without torture by Emperor Chandragupta Maurya. Ambhi was spared torture due to his cooperation however, he was deemed dangerous to the expanding Mauryan Government. Gandhara would become the northern border of Chandragupta's empire. Rishan did not join in the celebrations as he mourned the death of Ratnavali. Manish advised him to adopt Ratnavali's son Attallan and raise him as his own if that was what would bring joy to his heart. Ratnavali was honored as any military general as tears flowed from Rishan's eyes. That night, Rishan was heavily drinking wine with his brother Rajesh and Anand when Chanakya approached the group. Chanakya noticed Rishan was drunk and upset and stated that even Emperor Chandragupta was not safe from personal loss.

Chanakya calmly stated, "Chandragupta had lost his son Keshnak only three days after his birth. Chandragupta's wife Empress Maharani Durdhara, the daughter of Dhana

Nanda, had died during childbirth when she delivered Bindusara seven years prior. Chandragupta suffered deeply and in silence while we both managed the affairs of his new empire. Now Bindusara is a young strong boy and he may be the next emperor. You must look at the good that sometimes springs from tragedy. Your new stepson Atallan will perhaps bring you joy and fulfillment."

Rishan appreciated Chanakya's thoughtful words, but Rishan was curious about their success in battle.Rishan "Chanakya, how did you know that this battle would be a quick and easy affair?"

Chanakya replied, "The bread, Rishan. The bread is hot. You start at the edges until the center cools and then you can easily eat the rest."

A smile slowly spread across Rishan's face.

CHAPTER 17:
THE BABYLONIAN WAR AND THE FALL OF THE ARGEAD DYNASTY (309 B.C.)

*"Like the generations of leaves, the lives of mortal men. Now the
wind scatters the old leaves across the earth, now the living timber
bursts with the new buds and spring comes round again. And so
with men: as one generation comes to life, another dies away."*
—Homer (*The Iliad*)

Rishan Ramankrishna had served in various battles
in alliance with the Mauryan Empire soon after the defeat
of King Ambhi and now Chandragupta had brought stability
throughout northern and central India. The last few years
had seen a general peace in the land and a cohesive system
of laws had been set in place under Chanakya's direction.
Chanakya advised Chandragupta to initiate large public
work programs to include expanding the roads previously
built by the Nanda Dynasty. The roads were improved and
widened to accommodate heavy traffic and the number of
roads greatly increased from east to west and south to north
with minor interconnected roads to help transport goods
and services throughout the Mauryan Empire. Rishan and
Chanakya were discussing plans to incorporate Rishan
officially as a mid-level leader in the Mauryan Army. Rishan
and Anand were still leading roughly fifty Dravidian men
who had fought with them since the battle against Bramilan

and King Ambhi's Greek-backed forces. They were fiercely loyal to Rishan and Anand. Rishan allowed some of his loyal men and women to retire from their duties of battle and seek new lives in the Punjab where they settled and began families of their own. Although they were not officially part of the Mauryan Army, Rishan encouraged Chanakya to allow them a paid retirement. Chanakya wanted Rishan and his combatants to become leaders in the Mauryan Army and in exchange they would be honored with full pensions in addition to the spoils they had gathered.

Chanakya respected his cousin Manish and the Ramankrishna family. He also recognized the importance of making Rishan a commander in the Mauryan army due to his rising popularity among all castes of people throughout India. Chanakya also recognized the need to increase the might of the Mauryan army and the involvement of Rishan would further spread support for Chandragupta's forces. The Hellenistic Empire was not ruled by one man, but various generals who had continued to carve out their own territories, which left India ripe for conquest.

The third war of the Diadochi had ended five years prior and saw the murder of young Alexander IV and his mother Roxane, ending Alexander the Great's direct line of the Argead Dynasty. Antigonus, who had become the strongest leader, faced the combined forces of Ptolemy, Cassander, and Lysimachus. Antigonus' failure to subdue the Nabataeans of northern Arabia began a series of failures. In the battle of Gaza three years prior, Antigonus' son, Demetrius Poliorcetes, was defeated as Seleucus gained control of Babylon and the eastern portion of Alexander's empire. Antigonus finally agreed to a peace treaty with Ptolemy, Lysimachus, and Cassander named the Peace of the Dynasts.

Seleucus I Nicator, who had been cast out of Babylonia, was provided an army by Ptolemy to counter Antigonus. Antigonus had excluded Seleucus from the treaty to reclaim his eastern territories, so Antigonus the

"One Eyed" entered a war against Seleucus as he tried to retake Babylon. Seleucus had constructed a dam on the Euphrates River, creating an artificial lake. Seleucus purposefully destroyed the dam which released flood waters that destroyed the walls of the fortress which housed forces still loyal to Antigonus. Antigonus' satraps, Nicanor in Media and Euagoras in Aria, had come to his aid with a combined army of over 10,000 infantry and over 7,000 cavalry. Seleucus' numerically inferior army of 3,000 infantry and a 400-man cavalry hid near the marshes close to the Tigris, choosing a surprise attack during the night. Seleucus defeated Antigonus' army, causing the native Babylonians to side with Seleucus which helped Seleucus move through the Zagros Mountains and occupy Ecbatana, the capital of Media. Seleucus then secured Susa, the capital of Elam. By the time of the Peace of the Dynasts agreement, Seleucus had secured Babylonia and much of Antigonus' eastern territories.

Antigonus sent his son Demetrius Poliorcetes to Babylon during Spring 310 B.C. to attempt a recapture of Babylon, which was a drastic failure and ended in his retreat. Antigonus himself tried to recapture Babylon later that year but was outsmarted by Seleucus when he ordered an attack on Antigonus' army while they ate breakfast. The surprise attack defeated Antigonus, who was forced to cede his former territories.

The strength of Antigonus the feared Cyclops had severely diminished by 309 B.C. and he had become the topic of conversation among Chanakya, Chandragupta, and any person interested in foreign affairs. Chanakya understood the power of image and had worked carefully to craft Chandragupta's domestically and abroad. Chanakya also understood the importance of patience and projecting power over time through intricate strategy before striking with military force. Chanakya admired Seleucus, who he viewed as a leader who had used intelligence and strategy to beat Antigonus' power and brutality. Chanakya had utilized strategy to maneuver Chandragupta's strength towards decisive victory while viewing his cousin's son

Rishan as using intelligence and willpower despite his severe lack of resources and limited formal military training. Chanakya always hid his emotions, including the growing sense of pride he had for Rishan and his potential for success in the Mauryan Army.

Rishan had many discussions with Chanakya regarding the daily lives of the Indian poor. Chanakya pointing out the overall decrease of poverty of the lower caste and poor people since he began creating general improvements in the political and economic structure and Rishan agreed that slow progress was better than none. He believed that peace should be fully established with the elimination of any foreign threat to Chandragupta's empire. After these goals were realized, India could rise and utilize their own resources for the good of its people. Rishan also encouraged Chanakya to allow him to pursue study at Takshashila along with full military training. The university at Takshashila was usually reserved for the warrior caste, the Brahmin caste, and Royal Family members, but Rishan had encouraged Chanakya to allow Anand to also study alongside him. Rishan wanted Chanakya to expand the education system within the Mauryan Empire along with the progress made in economics and the judicial system.

Manish had reestablished his career and continued his work on numerous building projects within the Punjab, quickly reestablishing his family's wealth. Rishan was also contacted by Kulvir Kumari, who had reestablished his relationship with the Ramankrishna family in the previous few years. Rishan would encourage his father to slowly allow Kumari to learn the art of architecture so he could pursue his own business and develop a respectable life apart from the errors of his father. Padmesh Kumari had also finally apologized to Manish in a private meeting. Chanakya had confiscated roughly one third of Padmesh's wealth and had levied high taxes upon him and his family as punishment for his previous actions and as reparations to the victims of Greek occupation. Manish had personally intervened to spare Padmesh from a public humiliation that Chanakya had originally planned. Padmesh also provided important information pertaining to the families previously allied with the Mehra family. Priyanka had also approached the Ramankrishna family to offer her apologies, finally meeting her former lover Rishan for a private conversation.

Priyanka had aged far beyond her years due to the stress and shame of her past decisions. Priyanka's son had been born without atman (or breath of life), which devastated Priyanka—a grief that was intensified when she was notified her husband had died in battle when King Ambhi's forces were defeated by Chandragupta. Rishan felt empathy for Priyanka despite her mistakes and shielded her from the details involving Kanchanpreet's cowardly manner of death. Despite Rishan's previous anger and frustration he held towards Priyanka, he could not see the justification in her further punishment due to the actions and influence of her father and advised Chanakya to lessen the punishment for the rest of the Kumari family and separate the punishment from that of their patriarch.

The information uncovered from further questioning of the Kumari family and others revealed that Anjali had possibly accompanied Karna and other Punjabis at the battle of Gabiene—a n observation later confirmed by Kali Mehra under interrogation during his imprisonment. Kali's wife Sanjeeta was interrogated during her initial capture and was now allowed to live with relatives under the supervision of Mauryan authorities.

Chanakya believed that the ancient beliefs of Hinduism provided the basics of law and order and crime and punishment to be interpreted by those who carried out the law to include the king. Chanakya was an avid reader and was well versed in the Laws of Manu and the various punishments to be administered relative to the crimes committed. The punishment should also be of a specific degree deemed fair according to the punishment committed. Kali Mehra and his sons had committed crimes against the people of Pauravas, their political rivals, and King Porus himself while aiding the foreign Yavana, Macedonian, and Greek occupiers. Initially, Kali faced the death penalty but after various conversations with Manish and Rishan, it was determined that Karna Mehra had committed the most heinous crimes. There was concern that if Karna survived the Greek wars, he would continue to commit crimes against the Mauryan Empire. Chanakya believed that Karna would encourage the Macedonians to send Greek armies to attempt to reclaim their former occupied territories.

After years of questioning, Kali did not know the whereabouts of his youngest son Karna. Kali was isolated and his previous political and personal connections had been severed by Chanakya. He remained under strict observation so as not to allow any lines of communication. Rishan questioned Chanakya's thoughts regarding foreign affairs and the possible motives of Karna Mehra.

At a particular event near the Indus River, Rishan and Chanakya discussed a myriad of topics including foreign affairs and the future of the empire. Chandragupta Maurya had taken time from his capital in Pataliputra to observe his western territories and would later participate in a Royal hunt. Chandragupta had arrived with a long procession along with the Royal Family including his son Prince Bindusara. Gold adorned Chandragupta, his elephant, and horses. Chandragupta also had taken the practice of training beautiful young maidens in the art of combat and using them as his personal bodyguard which he liked to display during his Royal hunts.

Rishan and his brother Rajesh accompanied Chanakya into the forest as Chandragupta entered through another location. Chanakya asked Rishan, "Do you not enjoy the hunt Rishan? It is a fun sport."

Rishan replied, "I understand that it is the tradition of kings to hunt but I only hunt to satisfy my hunger. Some of these adventures are rather excessive, however this is my opinion and I do not wish to judge others who find leisure in the activity."

Chanakya listened and after a brief silence answered, "I understand why you hold such thoughts, but the Royal hunt is great for our emperor. This activity aids in exercise and the cleansing of the body through the release of sweat and bodily fluids as you progress throughout the day. This sport also aids in the release of stress in our daily lives—particularly for Chandragupta, who has a new empire to protect from foreign and domestic threats. I understand you have become a great student in the art of combat and have not tasted defeat in many years. It is a sport many do not enjoy but it provides leisure for you as hunting does for our emperor."

Rishan agreed with Chanakya; he did enjoy combat and it did allow him the release of negative energies while further improving his skills. Rajesh, who accompanied his brother and Chandragupta, stated that he had found delight in his family life and felt fortunate to have married a great woman such as Divya. As the three men conversed, Chandragupta ordered the release of his dogs to aid him in the hunt for tigers. Chanakya explained the dogs were raised well and consumed a steady diet of milk from the Royal cows.

Chanakya inquired about Rishan's motivations. "You remain single and perhaps you are happy to enjoy the abundance of women who seek you for your new status as a champion in war. Chandragupta enjoys his relationships with various women as well. After the empress died, he has enjoyed a life surrounded by distractions. It is hard being an emperor. The life of an emperor is not just a life of leisure; it is also a life of numerous responsibilities."

Rishan laughed. "I enjoy the women that have come with my fame, Chanakya. It is a luxury that has come with years of sacrifice and success in the battlefield. The truth is, I would like to get married and begin a family. My previous attempts at marriage failed but I have a few women in my thoughts. The land is large and if you are patient, Lord Krishna will provide."

The men laughed as the hunt continued throughout the day, resulting in two tigers killed by the emperor.

Chanakya was curious to understand Rishan's future goals within the Mauryan Empire and asked him to consider a high leadership position in the Mauryan army after he was satisfied with his ongoing studies at Takshashila. Rishan agreed to join the Mauryan military as long as his best friend Anand Agrawal was allowed the same opportunity. Rajesh was also given the chance to join the Mauryan army and agreed, as he needed a sense of purpose and a steady income for his family. Chanakya also advised Rishan to seek other positions available to him in the years to come. "You are very smart Rishan and have led your inferior forces towards surprising victories. You also seem to communicate well with people, especially the lower castes of our empire. We can use you not only in our military, but possibly as an adviser to one of our governors. Or if you learn administration, you can possibly become a governor yourself. It will be an improvement over your father's glorious career as an adviser for King Porus."

Rishan asked to take time to decide his future. Perhaps after his military career Rishan could pursue architecture instead of politics.

The next day, Chandragupta invited Rishan and his family along with Chanakya and Anand to the Indus delta to sail in his fleet and fish near the mangroves. Chanakya took this time to speak about Alexander's fleet which had been partially crushed by large waves caused by tremors in the earth. When Rishan asked why a large event such as the earth moving was not initially widely known, Chanakya answered, "Alexander did not want his rivals to know that part of his fleet was destroyed for fear that his rivals might exploit his weakness. Alexander projected the idea of being a demi-god and the censorship of information—particularly regarding natural occurences beyond the control of man— is the first thing a man who projects godliness needs to control."

Chanakya's knowledge of past events impacted his policy towards events which had not yet occurred. "To be a powerful leader you need to have access to information as well as control of that information. When I met Chandragupta, he was a small boy from the Maurya family of the peacock Moriya Clan and the son of a regional chief who was a distant relative of the Nanda family. Utilizing the combined dissatisfaction of the upper and lower castes against the Nandas, we were able to wage a successful revolt, installing Chandragupta as the rightful ruler. I managed to use the emotions of the people and focus them in the direction I wanted. If you choose a life of politics, Rishan, you will understand why Anand's proposal for the possible elimination of caste is not possible—at least not in a sudden fashion. You will understand that the power of the ruler has much to do with the power the people *choose* to give him. If the people question their ruler's legitimacy, the empire will begin to rot from within, which is more dangerous than any foreign enemy."

Chandragupta enjoyed his time with the Ramankrishna family and was satisfied with the observation of his western territories and its administration. Chandragupta invited Rishan and his family to the Lion Capital at Pataliputra when he completed his studies and military training. Chanakya wanted to showcase the capital to the Ramankrishna family and the new palace. He also informed Rishan of all the sporting activities in which they could partake. A smile spread across Chanakya's face. "There are chariot races at the capital with oxen and horses. Usually we have two oxen with a horse and in between these beasts we have men fasten a chariot. We then bet on these chariot races while drinking wine and discussing politics and other affairs. We also have animals like rhinos and bulls which are trained to fight each other for sport. As for the hunt, we have more animals prepared for hunting at the Royal jungles near the palace. You are called '"Sera," the Lion of the Punjab.' Your name has traveled by way of the tongue and it is important that you visit our capital. I assure you that many people will welcome you there."

Rishan was curious to see Pataliputra and promised Chanakya and Chandragupta he would visit once his studies and military training were complete.

Rishan began to ponder his future, including finding a woman and a family like his brother. Rishan was now close to thirty years old and felt he should attempt to pursue Anupa, who had begun a correspondence with him. Rishan asked his parents for advice and they approved of the union.

Manish approached Anupa's parents, Daha and Surina Jhingan in an effort to secure a possible union. Daha and his wife agreed with Manish and believed Rishan would be a great husband for Anupa. It was rare for a Brahmin woman to marry a man from the warrior Kshatriya caste, but despite this, Daha had recognized a growing love in Anupa for Rishan as well as empathy for his family's previous predicament.

Anupa had grown dissatisfied by her numerous suitors from the other major Brahmin families in the Punjab. Suitors from the five major Panjatias families including the Kumaria and Mohla pursued Anupa, but her focus remained on Rishan's safe returnRishan. Daha, who had previously advised Anupa to distance herself from Rishan due to the growing tensions involving the Mehra and Ramankrishna family, now openly accepted the possibility of marriage between them.

Rishan began to visit the Jhingan house frequently and almost immediately sparks of love began to grow between him and Anupa. Anupa had apologized for her previous behavior towards Rishan and provided an explanation: her father was trying to keep her safe from the Mehras' political aggression. Anupa also questioned Rishan regarding his adopted son Atallan—she had heard rumors of Rishan and Ratnavali. Anupa held a little jealousy regarding the false tales of Rishan fathering Atallan which had secretly persisted throughout the Punjab, particularly originating from jealous rival suitors who viewed Rishan as being of lower value. Jealousy had arisen due to the fact that Rishan had gained fame even though he was a Dravidian from the warrior caste who was perceived as unsuitable for Anupa. Anupa learned to restrict her own jealousy regarding Rishan's former lover Ratnavali as well as ignore the opinions of others. Anupa welcomed the idea of marrying Rishan and felt the time was right due to the peace and stability now found within the expanding Mauryan Empire. Rishan enjoyed Anupa's intelligence and thirst for knowledge as well as her pure beauty, which was only surpassed by the beauty of her personality. The

Jhingan and Ramankrishna families became close and they began spending large amounts of time together while the love between Rishan and Anupa strengthened and eventually they started to plan their wedding.

CHAPTER 18:
HOUSE OF JHINGAN AND THE MARRIAGE OF RISHAN AND ANUPA (307 B.C.)

"Om! May He protect us both together; may He nourish us both together; May we work conjointly with great energy, May our study be vigorous and effective; May we not mutually dispute (or may we not hate any). Om! Let there be Peace in me! Let there be Peace in my environment! Let there be Peace in the forces that act on me!"
—*The Taittiriya Upanishad*

The Jhingan family had established themselves as a central part of the Punjabi community. They were one of the most powerful Brahmin families and had gained reasonable wealth and respect. Various Jhingan family members had previously advised King Porus but avoided involvement in the increasing internal divisions within King Porus' administration. During Alexander and the Greek occupation of the Punjab, the Jhingan family remained neutral. The Mehra family had influenced many of the prominent Brahmin families in the Punjab as they grew their power while Karna Mehra unsuccessfully attempted to gain the attention of Anupa Jhingan. Karna's aggressive behavior towards Anupa was met with anger from her father Daha, who sought to distance his family from the Mehras and their motives. Although the family continued to maintain their influence and position in society, Daha was opposed to the Macedonian occupation and influence in the Punjab.

Daha was an important priest in his Punjabi community and was usually called to consult on matters of dharma and perform various social rituals. He was predominantly called to advise and perform rituals during major events such as marriages, births, and deaths. Daha was a man of mild temperament who thought before he spoke and he always made sure to control his emotions. His wife Surina was a teacher in Pauravas and their son Nakesh studied law, attempting to pursue a career as a judge in the Mauryan government. Daha respected Manish Ramankrishna and his family's hard work and rise in the Punjab. Daha always spoke with his family and friends about the Ramankrishna family and their impressive rise to the heights within the warrior caste.

Rishan Ramankrishna was also deeply embedded in the Jhingan family's thoughts. The Jhingan family appreciated Rishan's close childhood relationship with Anupa as well as his innate ability and discipline to learn new concepts. Rishan was also deeply intelligent and it impacted his interactions and conversations. Daha was highly impressed with Rishan's skills in the art of war as well as the goals he had for the future. After a long discussion, Daha and Surina agreed that despite Rishan belonging to the warrior caste, he would be a great husband for their daughter.

Rishan and Anupa spent more time together while their families planned the wedding. Rishan convinced his father that it would be best if they were able to bring his grandparents to Pauravas for ceremonies Rishan and had also received information that the Assaka Kingdom had grown unstable under the troubled leadership of King Aruman. King Aruman looked unfavorably at the growing power and influence of the Mauryan Empire and was paranoid regarding the expanding network of Mauryan agents infiltrating other kingdoms. Chanakya had informed Rishan that perhaps the remaining Ramankrishna family within the Assaka Kingdom should seek refuge within the Mauryan Empire. Chanakya advised Emperor Chandragupta that the empire should establish an alliance with King Aruman or pursue relations with other members of Aruman's Royal Family.

Rishan traveled to the Assaka Kingdom and convinced his grandparents Mahesh and Seeta to join the family for the wedding ceremonies. Rishan additionally feared for his grandparents' safety which was the main reason Rishan convinced them to live in Pauravas. Located at the northern border of Assaka, the Ramankrishna house had been under the ownership of relatives until Manish himself moved there. As Manish grew older, he openly discussed with Rishan the possibility of moving south to the Assaka Kingdom if it remained stable.

Through the efforts of Manish and other Mauryan builders, the Ramankrishna house in Pauravas was remodeled and expanded. Chandragupta Maurya was not able to attend Rishan's wedding, however Chanakya had attended on behalf of the emperor and as a relative of the Ramankrishna family. Weeks before the wedding, numerous guests arrived to the Ramankrishna house to enjoy numerous dances and games and enjoy an abundance of food and wine.

Rishan's former Greek captive Pylas was also invited to the wedding. While Pylas was no longer a captive, he remained under the observation of Chanakya's agents and kept under protection of other Greeks who viewed him as a possible traitor. Pylas had grown close to Rishan and Rishan understood the young Greek was previously just following orders. Pylas did not share the same hatred towards the Punjabi or Dravidian people that many of his Greek people did. Even though he was a Greek, Pylas did not view Punjabis and Dravidians with the disdain that Karna and the Mehra family held towards their own people.

Through the teachings of Rishan, Pylas gained a greater understanding of Indian culture. This brought about a respect and with the help of Rishan, Pylas also began learning the various Punjabi languages in the region. The two men frequently shared ideas about spirituality and philosophy and Pylas displayed a general interest in customs within Indian society, including Rishan's wedding.

Anupa was wearing a bright red sari with gold jewelry and the finest gems adorning her beautiful brown skin, complementing her natural beauty and enhancing her already stunning appearance. When Anupa spoke, her beauty shined brighter, making even the sun and stars in the sky jealous. The individual conversations halted as everyone gazed at Anupa's beauty, causing admiration among the men and women and silent jealousy among the insecure. Rishan was draped in the finest linens of blue and red with his dark skin gleaming in the afternoon sun. Rishan's hair was long, clean, and matted as it continued to grow throughout the years.

Rishan stood well over six feet and had grown wise beyond his years as he entered the third decade of his life. The future seemed secure with a possible promotion to high leadership in the Mauryan military. With continued progress and determination, the position of general was within Rishan's grasp.

The wedding ceremony was an opportunity for the Ramankrishnas and Jhingans to discuss the future course of their respective families through the union of Rishan and Anupa. Manish openly spoke with Daha about the possibility of his retirement and relocation to his native land to the south. Daha felt assured that Manish's sons Rajesh and Rishan would succeed in maintaining the Ramankrishna home in Pauravas and he felt confidence in Rishan as a husband for his daughter. Rishan's grandparents were now weak in their old age and would remain in the Punjab under the care of Rajesh and Rishan. The family exchanged gifts in the days before the wedding and the red ceremonial chunni was placed on Anupa's forehead. The festivities went on for several days and Chanakya waited until he could get Rishan alone along with his cousin Manish. Chanakya was eager to share the new information provided by his agents.

Some Punjabi men who had fled the battlefield after commander Ceteus' death had reported that Karna Mehra had survived the Greek wars and had escaped certain death at the hands of Antigonus. The fleeing Punjabi combatants were promised minor punishment if they provided as much intelligence as possible and this intelligence revealed that Seleucus had grown powerful and had solidified his territories while the once formidable Antigonus had lost several battles against Seleucus. The possibility of an alliance between Karna and Seleucus troubled Chanakya due to the possibility that Seleucus might not only wage a war against Antigonus but also attempt to reclaim Alexander's previous territories within the Punjab.

With calm focus, Chanakya related these possibilities. "Rishan, after your studies in Takshashila we request you begin training in the Mauryan army. Kali remains ignorant regarding the possible survival of his son. I plan on informing Karna that his parents are under our custody. Perhaps we can influence Karna's future decisions and influence Seleucus' decisions and redirect his potential aggression away from us and towards his main rival Antigonus."

Rishan replied, "Karna is unpredictable. There is a possibility he might seek recruitment into Seleucus' army. As for Seleucus, his past battle strategies against the numerically superior forces of Antigonus reveal his intelligence and his prior success will encourage him to establish his legitimacy as king. The reoccupation of Alexander's former Punjabi territories would solidify his legitimacy and he will seek to reoccupy these lands."

Rishan attended university studies at Takshashila while construction of his new family home proceeded next to the main Ramankrishna house in Pauravas. Rishan was soon called by Chanakya to begin training within the Mauryan army as the fourth Diadochi war began. Ptolemy, who was seeking to strengthen his position as Pharaoh of Egypt, had expanded his power into the Aegean and Cyprus. Antigonus' son was able to take Athens from its governor Cassander and turned his attention on Cyprus, landing a victory on Ptolemy's fleet at the Battle of Salamis in 307 B.C. Antigonus planned on occupying Egypt but storms had stopped Demetrius and his ships from providing adequate supplies. Antigonus and his son's efforts were able to weaken Cassander and Ptolemy and reestablish Antigonus' strength.

To Chanakya's relief, Antigonus the "One Eyed" once again turned his vengeance upon his main rival Seleucus to the east. Chanakya's major concern was now the capture of Karna and a possible treaty with Seleucus if he was victorious in his approaching war with Antigonus. Chanakya believed Chandragupta's army would defeat Seleucus and his army. A war against both Antigonus and Chandragupta would prove deadly for Seleucus.

CHAPTER 19:
THE SELEUCID–MAURYAN WAR (304 B.C.)

"Life has been compared with a battle and rightly so, as each day comes up with a new set of challenges which we must meet. One can just not shy away from the problems if he has to survive. He has to meet to challenges with courage."
—*The Sama Veda*

The peace brought about by Chandragupta Maurya was broken one night the previous year when Seleucus invaded the Punjab in an effort to reclaim the territory for his kingdom. The fears long held by Chanakya were realized in a surprising offensive launched by King Seleucus. Rishan's personal peace was also shattered when a month before Seleucus' offensive it was confirmed that his main enemy Karna had allied himself with this king. Karna Mehra kidnapped Rishan's young cousin Paraman and Priya's lover Mandeep Duggal and was now leading hostile Greeks and Indians into the northwestern borders of the Mauryan Empire. Upon learning of his father's captivity, Karna sent word of his possible surrender. Near Takshashila, Rishan sent for his father and brother. They attempted to speak with Karna's agents while Chanakya sent Mandeep of the prominent Brahmin Duggal family. During the potential peace, a battle broke between the two parties, which ended in the kidnapping of Mandeep Duggal and Paraman Ramankrishna. In an attempt to save Mandeep and Paraman, Manish was severely injured in a sword fight. Despite Rishan's efforts to continue, Mauryan forces did not pursue Karna into Seleucus' territories without the direct orders of Chandragupta Maurya.

Anupa gave birth to their first son Raghu Ramankrishna two years prior and she was currently with child again. Rishan's adopted son Atallan was nearly twenty years of age and had chosen to serve in the Mauryan military as a young leader despite his lower caste origins. Rishan feared for his family; Karna had already inflicted major damage during the broken peace treaty right before the start of the war. Chanakya and the Mauryan forces were initially caught off guard by Seleucus' offensive; they had believed Seleucus' forces were occupied with the war against Antigonus west of Seleucus' kingdom.

The war continued successfully for King Seleucus on his western and eastern fronts. For an entire year, Chandragupta suffered losses to the surging Seleucus army while Karna Mehra attempted to open another front in the northern reaches of the Mauryan Empire. Using Rishan's anger, Chanakya sent Rishan along with 5,000 additional Mauryan forces that were partially under Rishan's command. Rishan entered the war eager to defeat Karna and prove his leadership abilities in his first major battle.

Upon learning of the deaths of his eldest brother Randeep, his cousin Kanchanpreet, and other Mehra family members, Karna became enraged, aiming his vengeance on the entire Ramankrishna family and all Punjabis that supported them. Karna had married his lifelong companion Anjali and his anger was further fueled by the knowledge that her family members had perished during Rishan's overthrow of King Malayaketu and Chandragupta's capture of Pauravas. Karna had managed to gain the confidence of King Seleucus after the deaths of Peithon and Eudamus. Seleucus was impressed with Karna's will to survive and most importantly, his knowledge of Indian affairs—particularly Chanakya, Chandragupta, and India's hero, the Lion Rishan Ramankrishna.

Ptolemy, Lysimachus, and Cassander had offered a temporary peace treaty for Antigonus and his son Demetrius to save Rhodes. Ptolemy took the title of Soter or "Savior" for his peacekeeping efforts to save Rhodes from Antigonus and Demetrius after the peace treaty. Although Ptolemy Soter I saw it as a victory, the real victor was Demetrius, who was freed to attack Cassander at Greece while his father Antigonus also began to attack Seleucus once again.

During these events, Karna Mehra and a few hundred of his Indian and Greek supporters were approached by some of Seleucus' generals. Seleucus personally invited Karna Mehra to speak with him on political issues regarding Chandragupta and the Mauryan Empire. Karna had persuaded Seleucus to launch a war against Chandragupta Maurya while encouraging his Greek allies to launch a combined attack on Antigonus. Seleucus respected Rishan's intelligence and had studied his previous battle strategies. He believed he could use Karna Mehra as a psychological weapon against Rishan—use Rishan's anger against him. Seleucus could also exploit Karna's knowledge regarding the internal politics of the Mauryan Empire. Seleucus' wife Queen Apama had welcomed Karna on several occasions to the Royal Palace at the new capital Seleucia in Mesopotamia. Queen Apama had grown close with Karna, who spoke pleasantly of Persia and his family's alleged Persian Aryan roots.

The northwestern regions under the control of Chandragupta Maurya were viewed as the rightful possessions of the Persian Empire transferred to Macedonian control at the time of Alexander's triumph over King Darius III. Seleucus viewed the Indus Valley as his rightful territory as the successor to Alexander the Great and the Persian Empire that came before him. With the help of Karna Mehra, King Seleucus attacked one night on the outskirts of the Indus Valley. Karna Mehra was supplied with Greek troops after the kidnapping of a Ramankrishna family member and a prominent member of the Duggal family. With Chandragupta preoccupied with political affairs south of his empire and the Ramankrishnas and various other military families preparing for Hindu celebrations, Seleucus' army managed to have an impressive first year as they continuously advanced hundreds of miles into Mauryan territory before Chandragupta managed to mount an adequate response.

Karna was overconfident as he proceeded towards Lampaka northwest of Takshashila. He had defeated several thousand soldiers of the Mauryan army during his march, easily defeating them in combat. Karna believed Seleucus would defeat Chandragupta within a year despite Chandragupta's numerically superior forces. He also wished to personally engage Rishan in battle by using his cousin and Mandeep Duggal to lure Rishan into full battle in the open field, where Karna believed his better trained Greeks would overwhelm Rishan's Dravidian and Mauryan forces.

Karna was ignorant to the fact that Mandeep Duggal was not only Priya's suitor, but also a personal friend of the Jain religious leader Bhadrabahu I. Bhadrabahu I had heavily influenced Chanakya and Chandragupta in their conversion to Jainism six years prior when Bhadrabahu and Chandragupta traveled to the city of Shravanabelagola during a great famine that had gripped the Mauryan Empire for several years. Chandragupta had taken Chanakya's advice, increasing public works programs as well as allowing some Mauryan subjects to travel outside the empire for temporary work periods. Chandragupta had traveled with Bhadrabahu in a religious as well as political journey to analyze the state of his empire.

Chandragupta and Chanakya had a personal interest in Rishan's success in his northern march against Karna. Chandragupta could not initially supply Rishan with adequate troops to counter Karna, as he had dedicated most of his Mauryan forces further south between Kandahar and Patala. Rishan had continued his march north alongside Anand Agrawal followed by 100 of his most loyal lower caste Vaishya and Shudra Dravidian forces. These fiercely loyal men carried a flag with the Hindu svastika bestowing good luck upon Rishan's forces. Rishan adopted the svastika symbol and viewed this ancient religious icon in the Jain perspective due to the teachings of the deceased Jain monk named Saket who had saved his life and heavily influenced his thoughts on spirituality. Rishan was also given the command of 5,000 Punjabi Mauryan warrior caste soldiers. It was a test for Rishan and if he succeeded, he would be granted a high position as a general in the Mauryan army. The aging Sakatala was now serving strictly alongside Emperor Chandragupta in an advisery role and was retired from military duty.

Rishan, his uncle Manu, and Anand led their respective forces north, where they faced about 8,000 of Seleucus' Greek forces entering the city of Pushkalavati west of Takshashila. Rishan decided that Anand should lead 4,000 Mauryan infantry into the city and engage the Greek soldiers led by Argos, who had earned a reputation for his brutality. Rishan ordered Anand to lead his men into the city to engage Argos' forces where the streets were most narrow within Pushkalavati, while Rishan would lead 500 cavalry and 500 infantry— including his loyal Dravidian troops—through the river and engage the unaware Argos from his rear. It was a desperate maneuver that would place the people of Pushkalavati in danger. Rishan felt he did not have enough time to lead his men in open combat outside the city and he believed a violent conflict within the city would surprise the invading Greeks who had walked in unopposed through previous Punjabi cities.

Anand ordered 1,000 archers to stand above rooftops throughout the inner sections of the city as the Greek commander Argos entered on horseback. At once, Anand ordered his archers to launch a hail of arrows unto the Greek troops as they retreated into their phalanx positions with their shields facing upwards. Another group began launching arrows from their rear positions, killing hundreds of Greek soldiers. Anand screamed at the Punjabi women and children to run into their homes while many of their husbands took any weapons they could find to aid Anand and the Mauryan forces. The archers continued to rain down deadly arrows until Anand ordered his infantry to attack the Greeks from all sides within the tight streets of Pushkalavati. The other 500 archers continued to fire their arrows towards the Greek rear lines, preventing them from aiding the Greeks in front of them which had now separated from the main group. Rishan was crossing the river and entering the city behind the Greek infantry. Greek archers began firing at the Mauryan archers, killing many of them. The rest of the Greeks were now free to join the fight against the Mauryan forces.

Argos could not take advantage of his numerically superior army within the narrow streets as he witnessed Anand lead a successful frontal assault. As the fight raged on, Rishan's cavalry attacked from Argos from the rear, killing thousands of Greeks in the process. As the battle raged, Argos' forces began to reduce to less than a few thousand as they were pinned in the city streets with no additional Greeks arriving to support them. Rishan ordered archers to surround the city, preventing Greek messengers from reaching the rest of Seleucus' forces. The blood flowed into the streets as Argos' forces dwindled to less than 1,000. Rishan had joined in, ordering his men to fight until Argos' surrender and to hold the remaining Greeks captive to gather intelligence.

Argos did not wish to be taken captive by Rishan Ramankrishna, who he considered beneath him, and ordered his Greeks to fight Rishan to the last man. Dreading the embarrassment of defeat, Argos and the Greeks fought throughout the day and into the night, causing major losses to Rishan's forces. By morning, the Greeks numbered less than 100 men while Rishan's forces were reduced to a little over 3,000. Argos himself was found later in the day dead with several sword wounds to his body among thousands of his Greeks. It was an impressive victory for Rishan Ramankrishna as he prepared an attack on Karna Mehra's position. Rishan ordered his men to collect the bodies away from the city while he and his advisers planned his march on Karna's position.

Although he had defeated a numerically superior

force of 8,000 Greeks, Rishan could not celebrate. Rishan had suffered losses numbering nearly half of his troops, leaving only a little more than 3,000 Mauryan forces under his command. Rishan's loyal Dravidian forces suffered minimal losses and about eighty Dravidian fighters remained. Rishan sent a messenger to the Mauryan forces headed by Subandhu in Sagala southeast of Takshashila. Anand spoke with Rishan, informing him Argos' defeat would alert Karna to possibly march on their position or send Greek troops to confront them. Rishan had received information that Karna and a Greek commander named Rhexenor were leading roughly 15,000 Greek troops and had established a base at the city of Lampaka. Rishan needed additional troops quickly and could not rely on Chandragupta, who was leading the majority of his Mauryan forces between the cities of Kandahar and Patala.

After about a week, Subandhu reluctantly agreed to supply Rishan with 5,000 Mauryan troops with an additional 5,000 upon the agreement of Chandragupta Maurya. Rishan was supposed to wait several weeks before the troops arrived to his location at Pushkalavati but he grew anxious as the days progressed. He did not want to face another numerically superior force. The son of Chandragupta, Prince Bindusara, was initiating a campaign south of Kandahar but could not reach Rishan in the northwestern front of the war, leaving his trusted friend Subandhu to regulate the troops to be allocated to Rishan as well as maintaining the northwestern supply lines.

Anand questioned Subandhu's decision, "Rishan, we must demand the troops now because we cannot hold this city without an adequate number of forces. We do not know how many troops Karna will send our way; we should retreat out of this city east towards Takshashila then regroup and come back."

Rishan replied, "Subandhu fears that Karna will take this city and burn it to the ground, but it has already been destroyed in our battle. My agents have informed me that King Seleucus has yet to supply Karna with further troops, focusing on the main front south of Kandahar. I will order our current force to march north into the mountains and try to recruit further support. We will inform our additional troops to follow our route while asking Subandhu for supplemental troops into Pushkalavati. Karna Mehra will not expect us to take this action and we will catch him by surprise."

Anand did not agree with Rishan's plan and feared this decision would isolate them and place their forces in a dangerous situation.

Rishan said, "We will possibly lose our supply lines and this city but we have a chance to defeat Karna Mehra and the Greeks. Subandhu must move the rest of his forces towards Takshashila and reinforce the Mauryan numbers there. By the time Subandhu reaches our position at Pushkalavati we will have already struck Karna. We can land a decisive blow in Seleucus' northern advance within the coming weeks!"

After a few days of waiting, Rishan and Anand sent word to Subandhu of their plans and began marching north into the mountains intent on reaching Karna from the rear of his position at Lampaka.

At once Rishan's infantry and remaining cavalry tried to cross the mountain ranges before the long winter months arrived. The Mauryan forces had collected as much of the food as they could carry and Rishan instructed them to bring wine as well to promote cohesion and a positive attitude despite the circumstances. The march continued despite the cold and some men began to openly criticize Rishan's decisions, advocating for a tactical retreat.

Anand had doubts that the additional troops would follow Rishan's route through the mountains, quietly stating, "The extra 5,000 will most likely try to hold the city of Pushkalavati and Subandhu may order them not to follow us. We may win the war, but we will lose the battle and not survive to see Seleucus defeated."

Rishan replied, "I have already made our decision. We will encourage these local tribes to join us if we can and camp within a few miles of Lampaka. Our move will force Subandhu to support our efforts. Chanakya is backing us and he will overrule Subandhu. First we must be successful in our siege and the support will come."

Rishan had encountered some Kamboja tribes in his journey and asked them for help. Despite the anger shared between the Kamboja tribes and Rishan against Karna Mehra and the Greeks, many of the Kamboja people remained neutral. Out of desperation, Rishan shared his wine and food with them.

One of the Kamboja leaders stated, "What do we gain in exchange for our people's loss of blood in your war effort? We have been independent and do not seek the protection of Chandragupta Maurya. We shall defend ourselves to the death—our men and women are known as great warriors who can defeat any Mauryan or Greek warrior. Our Kamboja women are just as capable as any Greek or Mauryan man."

Rishan thought as he drank his wine. "If your men and women are indeed fierce and capable warriors, then join our efforts to defeat King Seleucus and I will personally advocate that Chandragupta Maurya reward you. We have all heard of your legendary warriors in the Mahabharata and how they swarm like locusts upon the field of battle. We respect your republican government and do not wish to interfere with your people. We will be peaceful towards you after this war is over."

One of the Kamboja leaders named Kamajit approached Rishan. Kamajit was of medium build and was respected for his strength, agility, and skills in combat as well as his intelligence in politics and governance. Kamajit was of average height with small eyes, light brown complexion, and he had black hair which was cut short. Kamajit asked Rishan how he could guarantee this and Rishan replied, "Chanakya is my father's cousin and he will see that your people are rewarded."

There was silence in the camp and some leaders agreed to supply Rishan with the finest horses, promising Rishan additional Kamboja warriors only if the other leaders approved.

Rishan continued his march, meeting some tribal men along the way—many of whom spoke Aramaic. Rishan's uncle Manu had fought valiantly and maintained a positive spirit, and he asked him for help in translating. After spending time with many of these tribes, Rishan was able to gather additional young combatants who were willing to assist due to their fear of reoccupation by the Greek army. Rishan finally descended the mountains of the Hindu Kush as he reached a position near the rear of Karna's army at Lampaka. Some Mauryan spies had reached this area and informed Rishan that Karna was now aware of the Greek defeat at Pushkalavati and had sent 5,000 Greek soldiers to take the city. However, Rishan's forces celebrated—they were also informed that Subandhu had sent 5,000 troops to Pushkalavati as well as 5,000 troops towards Lampaka. Rishan was informed that Karna had roughly 10,000 Greek soldiers at his base in Lampaka without additional support arriving anytime soon. Karna was unaware of Rishan's current position and Rishan believed a surprise attack would devastate his enemy despite his forces more than doubling the Mayuran and native tribe army.

Rishan's scouts had spotted more than fifty war elephants inside Karna's camp and the whereabouts of Paraman Ramankrishna and Mandeep Duggal remained unknown. Rishan understood the importance of saving his cousin and Priya's potential husband. It was a trap designed to draw in Rishan and his Mauryan forces into a battle against Karna's heavily defended base at Lampaka, but Karna was unaware that Rishan was only several miles away—he was expecting him to arrive months later.

Rishan carefully explained the plan to Anand and several other leaders. "We will keep 3,000 men away from Karna's base. Each man will take two pieces of wood and light them on fire upon my signal. Anand will lead 500 men into the elephant holding pen and will stir them up, aiming them into Karna's military barracks, while I lead 100 men into the upper levels where I will try to reach Karna while he is asleep. You will wait for my signal and only when we initiate our attack will the remaining troops light their wood. If we fight hard and fast, we can beat them before the additional Mauryan army arrives."

One young man had crossed paths with Rishan as they began preparations for the siege. The young man admired Rishan and wanted to know how a Dravidian from central and southern India had become such a famed leader in the Mauryan army. The young man had followed the stories of Rishan's redemption and his current military victories under the leadership of Chandragupta Maurya. Rishan stood and slowly began his story, beginning from his childhood all the way up until adulthood and the wars against King Ambhi. The young man sat silently as he carefully listened to every word that Rishan spoke. The young man sat in awe at Rishan's life story as they drank wine and ate until their bellies were full. They went to sleep for the rest of the afternoon until nightfall. During the night, they would assault Karna's base at Lampaka. Many of the men—including Rishan—had trouble sleeping in anticipation of the siege.

CHAPTER 20:
KARNA MEHRA (304 B.C.)

"The gentleman holds justice to be of highest importance. If a gentleman has courage but neglects justice, he becomes insurgent. If an inferior man has courage but neglects justice, he becomes a thief."
—Confucius (551—479 B.C.)

Karna Mehra had adopted the Greek style of dress and had been learning the language as well. He sought a new beginning in the Seleucid Empire as a military leader and perhaps as an adviser to King Seleucus Nicator I. Chandragupta's defeat would clear the Indus Valley for Greek occupation once again, enabling Karna to reestablish his family's presence in the Punjab. Knowledge of the embarrassing capture of his parents Kali and Sanjeeta and the deaths of his brothers and cousins angered Karna and fueled his revenge. Karna was confident that his patron Seleucus would eventually defeat his main enemy Antigonus as well as Chandragupta Maurya. He had successfully convinced Seleucus to open up several fronts but had failed in his efforts to gain the additional troops he needed. Karna had learned about Rishan's impressive victory but believed the 5,000 supplemental Greeks sent to Pushkalavati would crush his rival's forces.

Karna was in his private quarters with his Greek

girlfriend Apollonia. He had left his wife Anjali and his newborn son Krupal in the security of Seleucus' Royal Palace at the capital Seleucia on the Tigris. The previous day,Rishan Karna had learned the details of Rishan's additional forces now confronted by more troops supplied by Subandhu. Karna had also learned Subandhu's position at Takshashila had been strengthened by additional Mauryan troops. However, the location of Rishan Ramankrishna remained unknown and he grew anxious to find the man he hated.

Karna's instability had gradually increased throughout the last few years. He had on many occasions tortured his Punjabi followers who angered him or those he viewed as potential threats. Karna would cut off the limbs of men who had failed him in combat and burned men alive who he believed were plotting against him. His favorite form of torture and execution was letting elephants walk on top of men. His brutality caused Punjabis as well as Greeks to hate him and although Seleucus appreciated Karna's military abilities and knowledge of internal Mauryan politics, he secretly did not fully trust an Indian to lead his forces.

As Chandragupta began to turn the balance of the war towards his favor, Seleucus focused his attention towards Antigonus. Karna had knowledge of Emperor Chandragupta's successes and felt pressure to succeed. He relieved his anxiety by repeatedly beating his captives Mandeep Duggal and Paraman Ramankrishna. When his girlfriend Apollonia spoke out against the beatings, Karna began to beat her as well. He threatened Paraman with death if he did not reveal his cousin Rishan's location and despite Paraman's ignorance regarding the whereabouts of his cousin, the beatings increased.

Several hours after the sun sank below the horizon, Rishan's rested forces woke. They picked up their weapons and exercised in preparation for the siege. Rishan and Anand repeated the strategy to their men as they marched into Lampaka. Rishan and 100 of his most loyal soldiers including over fifty Dravidian men marched towards the side of Karna's compound. Anand led 500 infantry into the elephant holding pen near the main entrance of Karna's base after the guards were killed by a few men who had arrived an hour prior. The elephants were beaten and stabbed then set free, running wildly towards the barracks of the resting Greeks. Anand then ordered flaming arrows be shot into the compound, causing most of the wooden structures to burn. The Greeks were awakened and as they left their barracks they were trampled by their own elephants racing towards them and crushing everything in sight. Mauryan archers climbed the walls and began shooting unarmed Greeks. Anand ordered 1,000 Mauryan combatants to run towards Karna's base as thousands of Greeks battled for their lives. At once the Mauryan forces began cutting down the surprised enemy, killing thousands before they were able to organize.

The Greek commander Rhexenor was not able to fully position his phalanxes as many of his soldiers were killed before they were able to gather their weapons. At once Anand ordered his men to wave their torches to signal 2,000 Mauryan combatants waiting in the reserves. Each man lit three wooden stakes, giving the illusion that they numbered more than 6,000 men—over three times their actual size. Rhexenor ordered over 5,000 troops to leave their base and counter this imminent threat.

Rishan and roughly 100 men were able to sneak into Karna's main building. Rishan sent a few soldiers into Lampaka to notify the men of the city that Karna's reign of terror would soon be over. Karna would let his Greek and Punjabi men rape the women of each Punjabi city he had occupied including Lampaka, personally taking young ladies for himself. Some of the men of Lampaka were encouraged by the sight of Karna's base on fire and began to arm themselves for possible combat against their hated enemy.

Rishan raced through the halls, killing any Greeks he saw. There was a frantic search for Karna Mehra who was noticeably away from his command in front of his troops. Rishan focused his attention on finding Karna and his cousin and friend. As the base began to burn more rapidly, one of the Dravidian troops reported that Karna had been spotted near the rear of the base with a few Greek soldiers. Rishan sprinted towards his location, encountering approaching Greek soldiers as he unsheathed his sword again, striking his enemies with skill, speed, and accuracy. Rishan was a man possessed as he ripped through Greek flesh, disabling his enemies as he spotted Karna with his cousin Paraman and his friend Mandeep.

Many of the Greek fighters were angered with Karna as they witnessed him fleeing, leaving his Greek girlfriend Apollonia in danger. As the fighting became more intense, Apollonia herself could not escape the clutches of death as the fires consumed her. Anand's men secured and defended Rishan from incoming troops as Anand rushed to his aid.

Karna was found in a back room as some Greeks held Paraman and Mandeep. Karna threated to kill them if he was ambushed, which caused Rishan to reply, "Fight me to the death and release Paraman and Mandeep. Fight me and show those you lead that you have at least some honor remaining within you!"

The Greeks who were outnumbered released Paraman and Mandeep in fear that their lives would be sacrificed for Karna, a man they did not respect. At once Anand ran to help the captives, killing one of the Greeks while coming to the aid of Mandeep Duggal. Out of desperation, Karna pressed his sword against Paraman's neck, threatening to kill him. Rishan ordered his advancing troops to stop in an effort to save his cousin and watched as Karna sliced his throat. Rishan ran towards Karna and their swords struck each other at full force, causing a deafening sound.

Rishan shouted, "I will kill Karna just as I have killed the other Mehra cowards!"

Rishan ordered Anand to command the remaining troops as he continued to fight Karna in a fierce and bloody battle. Rhexenor was assaulted by arrows as he engaged

Rishan's remaining troops several miles from Karna's base and hundreds died as Mauryan arrows continued to rain down while the 1,000 man Mauryan cavalry hit Rhexenor's right flank. The Greeks still believed they were fighting a larger force but remained steadfast under the leadership of Rhexenor. As the night progressed, although scoring major victories, the remaining Mauryan forces were in danger of defeat. Several miles away, thousands of Kamboja cavalry led by Kamajit crashed into the rear of Rhexenor's Greek forces, causing devastating losses to Rhexenor's army. Over a thousand men from the city of Lampaka, angry at the abuses and killing at the hands of Karna Mehra, quickly approached Karna's stronghold with vengeance, anxious to be free of Greek occupation.

Karna was eager to kill Rishan and in the process, eliminate the legend that had grown from his previous exploits. Karna felt jealousy regarding Rishan's rise in standing while his family had been put to shame. Karna felt Rishan's power as he hammered his sword down with force, pushing Karna backwards while Rishan's men cheered him on. Rishan's speed was also on full display as he dodged and weaved Karna's attacks. Karna managed to kick Rishan, sending him to the ground as he attempted to strike with his sword. Rishan kicked Karna's feet and made him fall and break his jaw.

As some of his teeth fell from between his lips, Rishan exclaimed, "Your mouth has caused the destruction of many families and perhaps along with your teeth you should lose your tongue!"

Karna laughed as blood poured out of his mouth. "You are unfit to lead and the Ramankrishna family are usurpers who came to the Punjab, displaced our family, and led King Porus towards the unwise decision to fight Alexander. Your father was outsmarted by King Ambhi and if it was not for my family and the stability of Alexander's reign, our lands would've been plunged into war just as it has always been under corrupt Indian kings who only live to gain power and lands through wars against each other. Do you really believe the people will follow a man like you who makes love to lower caste women and who has children with them?"

Rishan replied, "You speak of Indians fighting each other but since the death of Alexander the very same Greeks you fight for have waged a long Wars of Succession. Filled with greed and lust for power, they have eliminated Alexander's Royal Family in their effort to seek power for themselves. The Greeks have taken power now and have made themselves rulers of lands that have existed before Greece became a civilization. My uncle has traveled to the lands of Africa and Palestine and he has taught me from a young age of these mighty cultures. How long do you think these Greeks will call themselves rulers of the world if they continue to wage war amongst themselves? Your brother Janeesh was the best Mehra my family had known but the rest of your family have allowed the Greeks to take our ancient land's wealth for themselves. The Greeks will use you until they have no purpose for you any longer. To the Greeks you are just a monkey in a tunic and himation clothing—a man they can never trust because you wage war against your own people."

Karna and Rishan locked swords again and Karna managed to knock Rishan's sword away from him. As Karna ran to land a blow, Rishan evaded the sword strike and they landed on the ground, the force of which dislodged Karna's sword.

Karna held Rishan's throat, attempting to choke him to death. "You are only leading an army because of Chanakya. Chanakya has helped your family but do you think he approves of Dravidians and lower caste men leading the Mauryan forces? Chanakya is a Brahmin who understands the purpose of laws and the caste system that your lower caste friend Anand wishes to abolish. When Chanakya dies, Anand Agrawal and the Ramankrishna family will not have a high place in Mauryan Society. Even if Chandragupta defeats King Seleucus, I will kill you now and you will not taste victory."

At once Rishan managed to release himself from certain death and began to land strikes as his forces shouted with glee.

Rishan ran to pick up his sword as Karna struggled to get up and fell backwards, his legs betraying him. Outside the voices of thousands of Lampaka men eager to be rid of Greek occupation overwhelmed the Greeks trying to defend Karna's base. The fires spread and reached close to Rishan's position and he tried to breathe through the incoming smoke.

Rishan stated, "You have lost, but I will not kill you. You will provide us with information on the location of Seleucus' other Greek soldiers. After this war is over, you will be placed in jail to be prosecuted under the laws of Chandragupta Maurya as a traitor to your own people!"

With tears in his eyes, Karna reached for his sword and yelled, "You will not embarrass me as you have done with my father!"

Rishan evaded Karna's attempt at his life and struck his rival's shoulder towards his neck, which made him fall to the ground. As Karna lay gasping, Rishan said, "I have shown mercy to your father Kali and would have shown mercy to you. The same mercy you refused to offer to my family, the hundreds of Punjabis you have embarrassed or killed, and the thousands of women and girls you have abused. The same mercy you failed to show King Porus— the king you swore to protect—as you and your family allied themselves with the satraps Eudamus and Peithon."

Karna gasped. "Don't let the Greeks hurt my son Krupal or my wife Anjali. My choices in life should not impact theirs."

Rishan replied, "I will show mercy but I doubt the Greeks you have fought with will provide safety for your family."

Karna shook his head as he tried to breathe, choking on his blood. His eyes rolled back as he breathed for the last time, finally dead as the fires consumed most of his base. Rishan landed one final blow, extinguishing Karna's life.

The Mauryan forces cheered as Karna's body was brought out for public display. Rishan ordered his cousin

Paraman's cadaver to be carried out and burned while Karna's body was placed outside in full view of the fighting men. The people of Lampaka were inspired by the death of the feared Karna Mehra who had occupied their deepest fears for many years as the Punjabi men loyal to Karna surrendered or fled. The remaining Greek forces within the base escaped the burning compound as they clashed with the fierce Kamboja male and female fighters. The battle raged on throughout the night with Rhexenor leading the remaining Greek forces in open battle against a combined force of Kamboja and Mauryan forces. Anand had rejoined the fight against Rhexenor, who managed to break through the Kamboja cavalry in his effort to engage the Kamboja leader Kamajit.

Rishan and his uncle Manu rode down to the main battlefield to fight the remaining Greek troops. During the fight, Rishan's horse was slain as he fell from it. Rishan cut through the Greeks with fury with his matted hair waving widely in the winter wind.

The Mauryan Army began to shout of the death of Karna Mehra, motivating the Kamboja forces and Kamajit, who was valiantly fighting Rhexenor as his forces pinned down the Greeks. At once Rhexenor was able to land a decisive strike on Kamajit, killing the brave fighter as he desperately tried to rally the Greeks to continue fighting. Rhexenor managed to get on his horse despite injuries. Anand Agrawal constrained the remaining Greeks as he clashed with the Greek leader Rhexenor. The fight between the men was violent as both Anand and Rhexenor were famously known for their brute strength. Rhexenor wrestled Anand to the ground as both men tumbled around, enabling Rhexenor to reach for his dagger. Rhexenor managed to stab Anand several times before Anand broke Rhexenor's hand and held him by the head, breaking the Greek leader's skull.

A light snow began to fall and the battlefield became muddy. The Indians cheered the death of Rhexenor and Karna Mehra as the Greek forces began to scramble in a deadly dance of desperation—they were now surrounded. The sun rose as the enemy lay dying with several hundred Greeks captured and used to gather information. The snow stopped the fires but not before they had partially consumed Karna's base, leaving the smoke to rise for several days.

The Kambojas suffered massive losses and only several hundred of them remained to be publicly recognized for their bravery the next day. Rishan was later informed that Subandhu's forces defeated the additional Greeks at Pushkalavati while further Mauryan reinforcements were on the way. Rishan was ordered to hold Lampaka as Subandhu reached Pushkalavati to face incoming Seleucid forces. Everyone praised the efforts of the Kamboja warriors who performed valiantly as their ancestors did in the Mahabharata as well as Anand and Rishan Ramankrishna, the Lion of India.

Subandhu's additional Mauryan forces defeated the Seleucid Greek soldiers as the winter snows fell, forcing Seleucus to abandon his northern front and concentrate his efforts south of Kandahar where Chandragupta was now brining the full force of his war machine. Prince Bindusara and Emperor Chandragupta were now closing Seleucid's numerically inferior forces into a single front as the Mauryan navy began defeating Greek warships that attempted to land additional troops. The war against Chandragupta and the Indians had become a major disaster for King Seleucus as the months passed, causing him to begin seeking the possibility of a peace treaty. King Seleucus wished to concentrate his war effort against Antigonus or risk the possibility of losing both the Indian Mauryan war and the Greek Wars of Succession against his hated rival.

Rishan, under the orders of Subandhu, would march alongside Anand Agrawal in an attempt to retake all of the Indus Valley territory as well as enter Greek territory. Chandragupta and Chanakya understood King Seleucus would seek an end to the war and they wished to take territory to the west in order to negotiate from a position of power. The Indian people celebrated as the final year of the war began and they were free from Greek rule, taking back their ancient lands that had remained under occupation for seemingly countless generations. Chanakya celebrated the fact that the lands would be used by the Mauryan government for the Indian people and not for the exploitation of foreign rulers. Rishan's name became even more famous as he awaited the end of the war to see his family and his father, who was still recovering from his injuries. Rishan's uncle Manu as well as Mandeep Duggal would return to Pauravas until Rishan returned.

CHAPTER 21:
BURN DOWN BABYLON (303 B.C.)

"And a mighty angel took up a stone like a great millstone, and cast it into the sea, saying, 'Thus with violence shall that great city Babylon be thrown down, and shall be found no more at all.'"
—The Holy Bible (*Revelations*, 18:21)

Rishan continued his advance into Greek territory as the Mauryan-Seleucid war began to reach its end. Rishan successfully fought against Seleucid's forces, and each successive conflict was easier than the last. Rishan was tasked with riding south towards Kandahar after months in the north. Subandhu replaced Rishan at his northwest post as the war was coming to a close and Chandragupta Maurya had displayed to the world the power of a unified northern Mauryan India against a respected Macedonian leader in Seleucus Nicator I. Chanakya believed that a united Indian force would have previously defeated Alexander the Great and he had proved his theory true. Chandragupta Maurya displayed his massive forces numbering over 600,000 infantry, 30,000 cavalry, and close to 9,000 war elephants with additional reserve forces ready to continue the war. Seleucus controlled over 200,000 infantry and over 40,000 cavalry with heavy losses of 60,000 of his allied forces including the Bactrianss. Over 30,000 Indians lost their lives in the war with well over 55,000 Greeks and their allies. It was a powerful and important display of power for Emperor Chandragupta Maurya to maintain the security of their lands.

Anand Agrawal passionately disagreed with the negotiations between Greek diplomats and Chanakya to end the war. He wished to take the battle to King Seleucus and destroy Greek Hellenistic cities in an effort to cripple their political centers and the organization of their war machine. In a moment of general euphoria, during several nights of wine drinking and festivities, Rishan also agreed with Anand. India should expand their power and influence beyond their borders to ensure they never lived under the occupation of Persia or the Macedonians again. It was a great message and it resounded with many of the Indians, specifically the lower caste and poorer people who sought a better life with the support of a more powerful India—an India that looked beyond its own borders and could possibly change the negative aspects many believed impacted their society. Issues such as caste division and mistreatment could potentially be reduced with a powerful India that could take the best from other cultures.

Rishan stated the importance of a powerful Indian Empire that would rise just as the Greek city-states were able to rise under the Macedonian King Philip II. Through its unity, Greece was able to surpass civilizations which predated their own. In addition to the war ending, Rishan was excited about the recent birth of his second son, who he named Rajat. Rishan partially agreed with Anand, but he was also satisfied with Chandragupta solidifying his control within India and creating a stable, peaceful society where his children could be raised in peace. Rishan added, Rishan"My eldest son Raghu and my newborn son Rajat will grow up in a land without foreign occupiers with strange customs and languages. They will grow up with a strong ruler and pride in who they are as people. We will talk with foreign people and demand respect and equality. We will receive foreign dignitaries and we will be able to spread our history, culture, and all our beliefs outside of our borders. The knowledge of Hinduism and the *Mahabharata,* the *Ramayana*, the *Upanishads*, Jainism, and Buddhism are part of our beliefs and history and will be seen on equal footing as other belief systems. My uncle has traveled to these ancient lands called Kemet now known as Egypt as well as Palestine—lands now ruled by the Macedonians and Greeks. These lands were once where many of these same Greeks traveled to learn from older civilizations and gave birth to these great Greek thinkers like Plato and Aristotle. India is an ancient land as well and now we rule ourselves. I am glad our children will live and learn in a land where our own people are the rulers and teachers!"

Rishan was celebrated and cheered for his speech as Chandragupta was close to victory.

Anand asked to speak and everyone stopped to listen. "I agree with my best friend Rishan, and after this war is over we should strike at the heart of Greek power. Just as they occupied us while our kingdoms warred against each other, we should attack them while they war against themselves. We can ally ourselves with the native Egyptians who wish to rid themselves of Greek rule just as they celebrated their independence from their Persian rulers. After our victory, the Egyptians and others ruled by the Macedonians and Greeks will seek independence just as we have. We should also eliminate the negative elements of our own society and allow all people no matter their wealth or caste to rise and be judged by the power of their intelligence and abilities. We were led by Rishan Ramankrishna, a Dravidian warrior who fought alongside lower caste men and women who helped him taste victory in the battlefield against the Greek forces. United, we will always be victorious and with allies we will not only have our security and peace but we can have an empire which stretches outside our borders. King Seleucus fears our further expansion into his territory and is sending his diplomats to develop a peace treaty with Chandragupta Maurya. This is the time to urge our leaders to make sure we are in a position of real power."

The fighters cheered Anand and Rishan as they realized their victory was secured and the possibilities for their personal futures were numerous.

The Greek envoy Megasthenes was sent by Sibyrtius, the satrap of Arachosia, into Mauryan territory near Kandahar. Prince Bindusara, along with Rishan Ramankrishna and Anand Agrawal, were there to receive Megasthenes. Chandragupta was marching east of Kandahar alongside Chanakya after the official surrender of Seleucus' forces. The meeting started in the early afternoon and lasted several days. Chanakya helped negotiate the deal with Megasthenes along with several other Greeks who were desperate to agree to a compromise as their leader Seleucus was busy fighting Antigonus' armies. From a position of power, Emperor Chandragupta expanded his territories to include Herat, Kandahar, and areas west of the Indus to include Balochistan and the Hindu Kush. The Greek governors controlling parts of Kamboja and Gandhara officially transferred their rule to Emperor Chandragupta.

Chandragupta requested an official wedding agreement between his son Bindusara and Seleucus' daughter Cornelia, as well as a marriage between himself and a cousin of Seleucus named Helen. Seleucus agreed to the terms and Chandragupta gave him 500 war elephants as a gift, making their peace agreement official.

Anand expressed his dissatisfaction with the Seleucid-Mauryan peace agreement within earshot of Chanakya, who expressed his dissatisfaction with Anand's behavior. "I respect your leadership and the blood that you have shed in the war against the Greeks. However, you are a man who uses his fists to reach your goals. I must use my mind to maintain Chandragupta's empire. Perhaps in the future you will have an opportunity alongside Rishan to work in the Mauryan government and only then will you realize the differences in our perspectives and duties. Chandragupta is the strongest Indian ruler this land has ever seen with an army that can defeat any Greek army. The Macedonian generals have declared themselves kings and none of them want to give up their positions of power. Chandragupta, or perhaps his son Bindusara, will seek to conquer more than sixteen kingdoms in the southern regions of these lands and they will not match our strength. This is our future goal if we seek to become an empire of the world and it will only happen after several generations when we have consolidated power. The divisions that men are born into had been designed long before we came into existence and will persist far after we are gone. We will offer more opportunities to our people but you must remember that a hasty removal of our traditions and customs will cause disorder and we will again fall victim to foreign occupation. We must not let that happen!"

Anand remained upset. He felt that a total defeat of Seleucus Nicator I would strengthen India and further secure it from potential rivals. Rishan would push Chanakya to seek government policies to improve the lives of all Indians despite the position in life they were given at birth. However, the divisions would persist. After several weeks, Chandragupta asked to speak with Rishan privately. When they were alone, Chandragupta thanked Rishan for his efforts and his leadership. Chandragupta was slightly angered at Rishan's failure to follow Subandhu's orders to hold Pushkalavati, but Rishan stated that they had needed to strike quickly to catch Karna and Rhexenor by surprise. Chandragupta advised Rishan not to let personal issues, fear, or anger cloud his judgement, especially in a leadership position in the Mauryan army.

Chandragupta looked Rishan right in the eye. "Your father Manish is Chanakya's cousin and I am Chanakya's adopted son; this makes us family. The passion and determination you have demonstrated throughout your life has been legendary and your story is not over. My story is almost complete and my victory over Seleucus has solidified my name in history. Thanks to you and my army, we have shown the other kingdoms that Indians will be respected as equals—or as this war has shown, as equals in the battlefield. In several months I will name you as general in the Mauryan army and I will give Anand a larger force of several thousand to command. The older Dravidians who fought with you can retire with a pension and the younger

Dravidians who are loyal to you must swear allegiance to my son Bindusara, who will become emperor soon. I will remain as emperor for only a few years but will allow my son more control. I want to enjoy time with my new wife Helen and then follow the ways of the Jain people . I will soon depart south and follow the Jain beliefs taught by Mahariva several hundred years ago. Chanakya has also discussed pursuing the life of a Jain alongside me. We believe the empire will be in good hands under my son's leadership. I will allow you some time to be with your wife and the rest of your family. You will be made a general before I leave the throne and seek Moksha, liberate my soul, and release myself from my physical body." Chandragupta Maurya appeared assured in the future of his empire under the leadership of his son Bindusara and he stood tall and confident in his legacy and the future of his state. Chandragupta Maurya and the other officials sought to leave the northern regions after the negotiations with the Greeks and Rishan subsequently traveled southeast towards the Punjab region where his family awaited him.

Rishan was overjoyed to finally be back with his family and his young boys Raghu and Rajat. Rishan was also proud of his adopted son Atallan and his courageousness in battle against the Greeks. Rishan, who had carried the symbol of the svastika on his clothes and the flags of his Dravidian forces, understood its value in Hinduism, Jainism, and the new belief of Buddhism. Rishan was curious to ask Chandragupta what had made him choose the path of Jainism.

Chandragupta replied, "My teachers and your story regarding your experience with Saket, the Jain monk who saved your life. Also, I had sixteen dreams and all were interpreted by the teacher Bhadrabahu. The first dream was of the sunset and Bhadrabahu stated that all the knowledge would be darkened. The second was of a branch falling from the Kalpavriksha wisdom tree, which I was instructed was the decline of Jainism and the non-initiation of my successors. The third dream was of a divine vehicle falling from the sky and arising once again, which was explained to be that the heavenly beings will not visit Bharat Kshetra. The fourth vision revealed the disk of the moon split in half and Bhadrabahu answered that Jainism would be split into two belief systems. The fifth dream displayed large black elephants fighting and he stated it was lesser rains and poor crops. The sixth was of fireflies shining during twilight and I was informed that true knowledge would be lost with only some sparks shining in the glimmering light. The seventh dream was a lake that had dried up and I was told it was that Aryakhanda will be without Jain doctrines and falsehoods would increase. The eighth dream was smoke covering the air and it was explained as evil prevailing and enveloping goodness."

The two men continued walking alone as Chandragupta continued. "The ninth dream was of a large ape sitting on a throne and Bhadrabahu explained it to mean those who were wicked and undeserving would ascend to power. The tenth dream involved a payasam rice pudding within a golden bowl being consumed by a dog—kings not content with a sixth share of tax would create land rent and increase it on their subjects. The eleventh dream had young bulls performing labor and I was told it signified that the young people would practice religious discipline but abandon them as they aged. In the twelfth vision, warrior Kshatriya boys rode on donkeys and the teacher informed me that kings from elevated origins would associate with people of low character. The thirteenth dream involved monkeys scaring away swans: those of low origin would torment those of high origin and bring them to their level. In my fourteenth dream I observed small calves jumping over a wide sea and I was told that the king would subject the people to poverty by imposing high taxes. The fifteenth dream involved foxes pursuing an old ox—those of lowly character with their hollow compliments would remove those who were good, noble, and wise. The final dream I experienced involved a large, twelve-headed serpent approaching me and Bhadrabahu stated it was a famine of twelve years upon our land."

Chandragupta advised Rishan to find a way to

cooperate with Subandhu, who he assumed would become lead adviser to his son Bindusara. He understood there might be a possible rift forming between Rishan and Subandhu and particularly between Subandhu and Anand. Chandragupta sought to dissolve any possible rifts within his government and military before he renounced the throne. Rishan

"My son Simhasena is now known as Bindusara for his bluish birthmark on his forehead. My wife, the empress Durdhara, died from complications after giving birth to him. The tongue is a more powerful weapon than the sword and there are rumors regarding the death of Durdhara and Chanakya's involvement. Chanakya has served me well and he has made some enemies in helping establish my empire. He is your father's cousin and others may be jealous of your fame and the positon of general that I will soon give you. I want you to be cautious. You should understand my son has a different personality and perception of the world. Bindusara is slow to form relationships with others and may not seem as charismatic as me, but he will only seek to make my empire greater than it is today. If you help Bindusara reach his goals, you will be rewarded. I wish you the best in your career and in your personal life, Rishan. Hopefully you will taste success in your future endeavors."

Rishan travelled quickly on horseback rarely stopping as he raced home to spend much needed time with his family. When Rishan arrived to the Ramankrishna home in Pauravas, he was greeted by his family and many who wished to see the Lion of India. Manish was still recovering from his wounds and contemplated leaving his career for a life of rest. Rajesh would soon take control of the building projects. Although he did not have knowledge regarding architecture, perhaps Manish's grandchildren would learn. The Ramankrishna family mourned the death of Paraman but were relieved to know that Karna Mehra was now deceased. Rishan also displayed compassion by bringing the body of Karna Mehra to his father despite calls to publicly display or keep it as a trophy. The Ramankrishna family celebrated the return of Mandeep Duggal, who married Priya the following year. There was a large celebration and Rishan's grandparents Mahesh and Seeta witnessed their final grandchild wed. It was an enjoyable experience for Mahesh and Seeta, and a lasting joy they would experience for the remainder of their lives.

CHAPTER 22:
INDICA AND TRAVELS WITH MEGASTHENES
(295 B.C.)

"One need not scale the heights of the heavens, nor travel along the highways of the world to find Ahura Mazda. With purity of mind and holiness of heart one can find Him in one's own heart."
—Zoroaster

The battle of Ipsus began in 301 B.C. between Antigonus I Monophthalmus and his son Demetrius I of Macedon against the coalition of Cassander the ruler of Macedon, Lysimachus Ruler of Thrace, and King Seleucus who reigned over Babylonia and Persia. Antigonus commanded a combined force of over 70,000 infantry, 10,000 cavalry, and 75 elephants, while the allied forces commanded over 64,000 infantry, 15,000 cavalry, 100 scythed chariots, and over 500 war elephants. Chandragupta's elephants proved to be pivotal for the allied forces against Antigonus. Demetrius led the right flank with Lysimachus in charge of the center line and King Seleucus' son Antiochus with the weaker left flank for the allied forces. Seleucus ordered about 100 of his elephants in front near the center line of Lysimachus' infantry while Seleucus and Cassander's brother Pleistarchus were stationed on the right flank, keeping the rest of the more than 400 elephants in reserve. At once Demetrius outmaneuvered his cavalry around the elephants, crushing Antiochus' left flank while he retreated in defeat. Seeing his son in danger, Seleucus launched 300 elephants into Demetrius' path, cutting him off from his father's infantry and exposing Antigonus' right flank.

Seleucus dispatched his horse archers towards Antigonus' infantry as his elephants caused panic and made his horses flee, launching their riders to the ground. Allied scythed chariots ripped through Antigonus' infantry forces, detaching limbs from bodies as they began to surrender to the allied Greek forces. Once the most powerful Greek successor, Antigonus the "One Eyed" tried to rally his infantry as he waited in vain for Demetrius' return. As allied forces surrounded Antigonus, Seleucus ordered skilled javelin throwers to launch into the infantry center towards Antigonus. They finally landed two fatal blows into his heart and lungs, leaving the feared leader dead on the bloody ground.

Demetrius managed to flee to Ephesus with 5,000 infantry and 4,000 cavalry, leaving his father and the last chance for a united Greek Empire dead along with Antigonus.

Chandragupta's empire would be secured, and Bindusara would be free to conquer and bring more of India under Mauryan control.

Rishan Ramankrishna had befriended the Ionian-Greek ambassador Megasthenes and they discussed many issues involving Greek and Indian culture. Rishan loved the works of Megasthenes; it was a way to distract Rishan from the constant wars launched by King Bindusara into central and southern India to expand the Mauryan Empire. The Ramankrishna family had lost their patriarch Mahesh during the Battle of Ipsus, which staged the final fight between King Seleucus and Antigonus the "One Eyed." Emperor Chandragupta Maurya renounced his throne and passed away from self-imposed starvation while following Jainism with Chanakya. After which, Seeta passed away as well. The details of Chanakya's death were unknown to a majority of the public, causing various rumors to foment.

Some implicated Subandhu and other advisers in a possible assassination.

Due to the Mauryan-Seleucid war and the birth of his children, Rishan never traveled to Pataliputra with Chandragupta to participate in the hunts and chariot races as he previously promised. However, Rishan had toured on the Royal Road several times with Megasthenes to the Royal Court of Bindusara. Throughout their journeys, Megasthenes shared the maps he had made of India as well as works describing birds, insects, and plants. Rishan spoke of his life and of his friend Anand Agrawal Rishan as well as the fates of others with whom he had crossed paths. Rishan spoke of his former Greek captive Pylas, now living in the Punjab, taking a Punjabi wife, and learning the local language. Rishan was proud of Pylas and Megasthenes was impressed that Rishan could show forgiveness to a former enemy.

As the two men walked the streets of the Mauryan capital of Pataliputra, Megasthenes wanted to share some of his writings about India. Looking into the distance, he glanced at Rishan as he stated, "This land is a beauty to behold, my friend. The soil is rich and fertile, made possible by the irrigation policies set in place by Chandragupta and now his son Bindusara. The irrigation and the cleanliness of waste disposal in the capital are impressive. The people are very content in their duties, particularly pertaining to the respective caste into which they are born. The people also show respect to foreigners and provide them with doctors and other luxuries if they are ever in need. The Ganges River is very important to the Indian people and it is so immense that it cannot be described—it must be seen with one's own eyes. You are well educated in the Greek language and culture, and you have taught me the similarities in our beliefs. I have seen the parallels between Lord Zeus and Indra, Thanatos and Yama, Hephaestus and Agni, and many others. They are very similar and perhaps they are the same."

Rishan replied, "I read the tale of Daedalus, the

master inventor and his son Icarus. Daedalus created wax wings and put them on Icarus, instructing him that he should fly low to avoid the sun and melting his wings. In his ecstasy, Icarus flew too close to the sun, melting his wings and falling to his death. It is a similar tale of Sampati and Jatayu and their father Garuda. Sampati and Jatayu were two vultures who competed to see who could fly higher. Jatayu, blinded by his competitiveness, flew too close to the sun, causing his wings to burn off. As Jatayu fell, he was saved by his brother from certain death. I have also read the story of the Minotaur and the labyrinth of Minos. An agreement was made to prevent Crete from waging war on Athens if every nine years Athens would send nine males and nine females into the labyrinth. The demi-god Theseus finally killed the Minotaur. We also conversed regarding the beast named Bakasura, who lived on the outskirts of Ekachakra. There was an agreement that the people would send a cartload of food to the beast. Bakasura would consume the cartload of food and the man bringing the food until a man named Bhima volunteered. Bhima killed Bakasura just as Theseus killed the Minotaur."

Megasthenes enjoyed his conversation with Rishan and he discussed one of his favorite heroes: Heracles. The story was once shared by Alexander during Rishan and his father's visit to his court in Pauravas.

Megasthenes was excited as he exclaimed, "Dionysus traveled to these Indian lands teaching the people how eat from various plants, methods of cooking, and how to build cities. I traveled to Methora and Kleisobora and saw the navigable river, the Jobares. While there, I encountered an ancient tribe called the Sourasenoi; they spoke of Heracles and his many adventures."

Rishan replied, "Yes, I believe you mean Mathura, the birthplace of Lord Krishna and the capital of Shurasena. Heracles and Krishna share similarities the same way there are similarities between Balarama and Heracles. Balarama was also the nickname of Malayaketu's grandfather and the younger brother of King Porus who once fought bravely against Alexander in battle."

Rishan continued, "The horn of plenty that Zeus removed from the goat Amalthea provided him endless nourishment. We believe in Kamadhenu the sacred cow with a beautiful woman's face and the Akshaya Patra providing endless nourishment to the Pandavas, the five sons of Pandu, and his wives Kunti and Madri. The famed Arjuna, who fought Karna with the aid of Lord Krishna, was one of the brothers. The others were Yudhishthira, Bhima, Nakula, and Sahadeva. Perhaps we will converse about the *Ramayana* and the *Mahabharata* at a later time. They are interesting tales that have taught me and my family valuable lessons. I also learned about the titan Helios and his chariot led by bulls used to pull the son across the sky. It is similar to our deity Surya, who rides his flaming chariot across the sky pulled by seven horses."

Megasthenes was delighted every occasion he spoke with Rishan. Through Rishan, he began to understand just how timeless India was, stretching back countless generations. The dark people of India had a history just like the dark people of Egypt who came from Ethiopia and various other places within that large land. Megasthenes indeed felt fortunate to converse with a man who also lived to distance himself from ignorance. He felt that these conversations with Rishan were what living was about.

Megasthenes would often ask Rishan why he chose the military over a life such as the Brahmin and Rishan would often reply, "It is the path chosen for me."

"Be cautious, Rishan," Megasthenes warned. "Even the great Socrates was falsely accused and made to drink hemlock because of his thinking and questioning of society. Perhaps your wisdom should be tempered and best used in a diplomatic capacity."

However, life would not follow a predestined path for Rishan, as his knowledge and his name had lifted him beyond his position of general. Rishan enjoyed the work that Megasthenes took part in and would seek to choose that career for himself. Rishan wanted to see the world beyond India just as his uncle Manu had. Rishan sought to travel not as a merchant, but perhaps in a diplomatic capacity as Megasthenes suggested. Rishan had to prove himself as a capable general in Bindusara's march into southern India to consolidate all of the land under Mauryan rule.

Disappointed to end his enlightened conversation, Megasthenes quietly stated, "I have lived a long life and will soon retire and seek peace in my death. Perhaps when I am judged I will be sent to the pleasant Elysian fields; or perhaps if I lived an ordinary life I will be sent to the Asphodel Meadows. I have lived a good life and do not expect to visit Hades and will never go to that evil place Tartarus."

Rishan replied, "Yes, I hope to reach our Elysian fields called Svarga and wish to avoid our eternal abode of torment called Naraka. We believe moksha is the true goal, as our afterlife is not permanent."

Megasthenes responded. "Yes, we can also be reborn up to three times then we are sent to the ultimate paradise at the Isle of the Blessed. You are a great man, Rishan. A man who allowed your greatest enemy dignity even after his death."

Rishan answered, "I read about your hero Achilles. His greatest strength was his heroism and abilities in battle and his greatest weakness was his rage. It consumed Achilles and manifested itself in his shameful act of dragging the corpse of the Trojan prince Hector behind his chariot. It was the same action Alexander the Great committed against the Persian commander Batis after the siege of Gaza, although Alexander's horses dragged Batis while he was still alive. The Gods and King Priam intervened in an attempt to quell Achilles' anger and allow Hector proper funeral rites. Wars are brutal but that does not mean we should let ourselves become the embodiment of brutality. Best of luck, my friend. We learned many things from each other but now I have to perform my duties as general."

Megasthenes laughed as Rishan quoted King Priam in his conversation with Achilles, "'Think of thy father and this helpless face behold. See him in me, as helpless and as old! Though not so wretched, there he yields to me. The first of men in sovereign misery! Thus forced to kneel, thus groveling to embrace. The scourge and ruin of my realm and race, suppliant my children's murderer to implore, and kiss those hands yet reeking with their gore!'"

It would be the last time Rishan and Megasthenes conversed.

CHAPTER 23:
BINDUSARA, "THE MAN WITH NO ENEMIES"
(290 B.C.)

*"Just because you do not take an interest in politics doesn't mean
politics won't take an interest in you."*
—Pericles

Rishan had to report to the Royal Palace to speak
with Emperor Bindusara regarding the southern strategy to
occupy more than sixteen kingdoms not fully integrated
into the Mauryan Empire. The Royal Palace now held a
growing Mauryan family to include Bindusara and his
wives Cornelia and Subhadrangi. Subhadrangi was
Bindusara's Indian primary wife while Cornelia was of half
Greek, half Persian origins. Subhadrangi was also named
Dharma and had given Bindusara two sons named
Vitashoka and Ashoka. The eldest brother was named
Susima Maurya and he was the only son Rishan had known
and befriended. Bindusara was also taking care of his father
Chandragupta's widow Helen and their son Justin, who at
seven years old was the same age as Susima. However,
Justin could not ascend to the throne because of his Greek
blood. Rishan had visited several times but had only grown
close to Susima, a smart, quiet boy who was to take the
throne after Bindusara's death.

Anand Agrawal had recently married a woman

named Jamena and had a son named Jagdesh. He had confided in Rishan that he would probably renounce his leadership position in the Mauryan army and perhaps retire after a few more years. Anand harbored growing tensions with Subandhu and did not fully support Bindusara's attempts to conquer southern India—h e still believed that Chandragupta should have continued the offensive against King Seleucus. Rishan had informed him that the constant Greek Wars of Succession would secure the Mauryan Empire for many generations. Anand would agree with Rishan eventually, however he had lost the appetite to fight other armies within India.

The Greeks called Bindusara the Slayer of Enemies and that name was earned through the tip of Rishan's blade. Rishan had been fighting for the previous two years with little break as he advanced through central and southern India. After Sakatala's death and Rishan's numerous successes, Rishan began gaining more power as general of the Mauryan army. The kingdom of Assaka had been under indirect partial control of Chandragupta Maurya. However, King Aruman began to demand complete independence from King Bindusara to avoid paying taxes to the Mauryan Empire. It was also confirmed that King Aruman of Assaka had previously threatened the Ramankrishna family within his kingdom. King Aruman's minister Ashva was now secretly allied with King Bindusara in an effort to overthrow his king to avoid war. Rishan was also informed that the rumors of a previous secret agreement between King Aruman and the deceased Bramilan the Butcher were true due to evidence provided by Ashva. King Aruman and Bramilan the Butcher were rumored to be distant cousins and Bramilan had previously provided woot steel weaponry as well as intelligence regarding the affairs of the kingdom of Kalinga.

As King Aruman's paranoia increased, he began threatening Rishan's cousin Rupesh— who was currently in charge of the Ramankrishna house and affairs in Assaka—with imprisonment. Rishan now led a force of roughly 10,000 Mauryan soldiers into Assaka, expecting a quick battle and eventual overthrow of King Aruman. As Rishan entered the kingdom of Assaka, King Aruman's army put down their weapons and proclaimed their loyalty directly to Emperor Bindusara with the help of Ashva's secret plot. However, King Aruman's vanguard was fiercely loyal and Ashva's plot was uncovered by the king himself just as Rishan began entering the capital city of Potali. King Aruman moved quickly to seize his adviser and purge all traitors within his kingdom.

King Aruman mobilized his vanguard against the approaching Mauryan Army as a violent clash ensued. The continued battles Rishan had faced the last two years had only added to the experience of the professional army he now commanded. As Rishan's forces defeated King Aruman's elite guards despite their valiant efforts, Rishan asked his most loyal Dravidian forces to capture King Aruman, who fled the battlefield into his palace. Rishan's most loyal Dravidian veteran forces now numbered less than fifty as they entered Aruman's Royal Palace carrying Rishan's flag which displayed a black lion above a black svastika with a blue background. The black signified the Dravidian people and the dark skin of Lord Krishna as well as the richness of the fertile soil of India. The blue symbolized the depth of knowledge and stability found within the mind of a good leader—a standard Rishan tried to live and lead by. The lion represented Rishan Ramankrishna and his bravery. The svastika stood for various ideas from different faiths. In Jainism, the four arms of the svastika represented the forms in which a soul could be reborn: svarga or heaven, naraka or hell, manushya or humanity, or tiryancha as plants or animals. It was a flag that had developed over time and was finally presented during the Seleucid-Mauryan war. Rishan's flag was instantly recognized by the palace guards, causing some to flee in fear.

As General Rishan entered the upper floor of the palace, he found King Aruman unprotected and his adviser Ashva freed from his former captivity. As he entered, King Aruman's eyes burned with anger as he exclaimed, "I gave you gold and gems so you could fund your campaign in the Punjab and this is how my graciousness is repaid? Now you have become a powerful general in the Mauryan army, leading men to depose other kings and disrupt other societies. Should I stand here and let you kill the innocent and perhaps my own family? Will your King Bindusara trust Ashva, who is a traitorous man who was sworn to protect me and my family?"

Rishan replied, "I will pay you what you gave me and will add extra money for your help. My duty as general is to follow my king's orders and to lead his army towards victory. I have been informed of your secret deals with Bramilan the Butcher, a brutal and merciless killer who once held me in bondage. There are rumors you were also related to Bramilan and you used him to terrorize the people of Kalinga and provide you with cheap supplies. I was also informed by my grandparents that in the last years of their lives here in Assaka you sent agents to terrorize them and possibly steal from my family. You also tormented my cousin Rupesh Ramankrishna, who has been the caretaker of my family's estate here within this kingdom. Even with your past transgressions, I will not kill you. All I ask is that you step aside and renounce your throne."

Rishan handed King Aruman Mauryan coins, paying him almost double what King Aruman had given him as a young man.

The former King Aruman said, "I was not aware of the brutality of Bramilan. His relation to me were rumors created by my enemies in Kalinga and Ashva, who will now become Emperor Bindusara's puppet. But will Bindusara trust Ashva the usurper? It was believed that the Ramankrishna family in Assaka was working with the Mauryan army in a possible invasion but I did not wish to harm the Ramankrishnas. I simply sought to protect my kingdom. Enough blood has been spilled in the streets; please allow me to leave in peace and protect my family."

Rishan agreed as Ashva was installed as governor of Assaka under the Mauryan Empire. Rishan was directed to occupy the former Assaka Kingdom for a month before marching back north towards the capital. Anand Agrawal was farther south near the Tamil Kingdoms, reluctantly leading Mauryan forces in wars of subjugation.

Anand had made the mistake of openly criticizing Subandhu's advice to King Bindusara which urged the conquest of all southern India. The last few years of wars had begun to cast a different perspective into General Rishan's mind. Rishan started to see the horrors of war from a different perspective as a middle-aged man with young children who might grow to join the army in the futre. Rishan was appalled by the bloodshed in the streets of Assaka caused by the men he led and he began thinking of what Anand had personally told him. Anand had felt disgusted fighting other Indians—especially the Dravidian Tamils. Rishan informed his closest friend that he would seek retirement within the next several years after these last battles in central and southern India and that Anand should do the same, particularly because of rising tensions between him and Subandhu. Rishan would seek work as an adviser to Bindusara or perhaps he would become an envoy similar to the work his old friend Megasthenes performed for the Seleucid Empire.

As Rishan began to march back towards Pataliputra the following year, he received information that Megasthenes had passed away. Megasthenes lived the remainder of his life learning about different cultures other than his own and Rishan felt he should also pursue a similar path. Rishan discussed his thoughts with his wife Anupa and his sons before he would decide to approach Emperor Bindusara with his retirement proposal. Rishan's close friend Rishan Anand would march towards the southernmost Tamil Kingdoms of the Pandyas, Cholas, and Cheras.

CHAPTER 24:
ECHOES OF AJAX (288 B.C.)
*"He who attends to his greater self becomes a great man, and he
who attends to his smaller self becomes a small man."*
—Mencius

Ashva assassinated the deposed King Aruman and
most of the Royal Family of the former kingdom of
Assaka, angering the local population and placing his own
life in danger. The Feudal Republic of Kalinga and the
Tamil Kingdoms of southern India now remained as the
strongest states outside of Mauryan domination. The Chola
Dynasty had become the most powerful of the three Tamil-
Nadu Dynasties and southern India. King Ilamcetcenni had
denied accusations that his armies directly inflicted death
on hundreds of Mauryan soldiers exploring southern India.
Anand Agrawal was leading a few thousand soldiers near
the Chola border when his men were ambushed and cut off
from the rest of the Mauryan forces. It turned out to be a
violent and bloody clash, resulting in hundreds of losses to
the Mauryan army with Anand Agrawal lost in the battle.

Emperor Bindusara sent a search party to locate
Anand's body among the dead as Rishan and Anand's
family grasped onto any remaining hope. After several
weeks, Anand Agrawal's body was finally found near the
Chola border among the other dead soldiers and Rishan and

Anand's wife Jamena were filled with grief and despair. Rishan asked to personally bring Anand's body to Jamena in order to prepare it for funeral rites. It was devastating for the fifty year old Rishan, who had planned to live out his retirement with his closest friend as they watched their children grow and hopefully achevie more than what they had. Anand had frequently questioned the constant wars against other Indians and the possibility of war with the Tamil Kingdoms. The politics of Pataliputra and particularly the politics of Subandhu had further disappointed Anand as he sought retirement. Rishan also began to wonder about his own fate as the endless politics of Subandhu caused disillusionment within his mind.

After spending time with the Agrawal family, Rishan had entered the capital of Pataliputra to ask the emperor to provide Anand's retirement funds to his widow Jamena and eight year old son Jagdesh. Rishan believed Anand's son should receive the same advantages other young children of higher castes received, especially because of the sacrifices Anand had made for the Mauryan Empire. As he entered the Royal Palace, he was confronted by Subandhu. Rishan asked that the government provide for the Agrawal family, which angered Subandhu.

With fire in his eyes Subandhu responded, "The Mauryan government provides for retired military. The Agrawal family will be compensated for Anand's sacrifices. Anand will be compensated beyond what his caste would have ever afforded him. You must remember Rishan that your friend caused many problems as he criticized the policies of Mauryan expansion into southern India. As a military leader, Anand should not have questioned the policies determined by his superiors and the emperor himself, which causes the seeds of dissent within the empire to eventually sprout. If the emperor's wishes are not respected, our enemies both internally and externally will notice this weakness and attack us. Furthermore, Anand supported the establishment of natural divisions within our society which proved problematic. You are a smart man, Rishan, and can easily be mistaken for a

Brahmin. You understand the differences between managing a government and managing a battlefield. I suspect Anand never did. He caused problems since Chanakya first initiated the peace treaty between the Mauryan and Seleucid government."

Rishan replied, "Subandhu, you have made a career out of politics. However, men like Anand are concerned with simply what is right and what is wrong. As a politician, you divide the world into rich and poor, high and low caste, Royal and common blood. Anand only wished to provide for his family so they could live a life better than himself and his parents before him, who were brutally murdered due to the politics of the Macedonians and wealthy families like the Mehras. My father treated Anand like his own son and upon your advice to the emperor, you sent Anand into a fruitless expedition knowing full well the power of the southern Tamil Kingdoms. Anand only wanted people in this new Mauryan society to rise in status because of their hard work or intelligence; he did not wish to weaken this empire. He did not wish to hurt Chanakya's peace treaty with Seleucus and he never trusted the Macedonians and Greeks because of what he witnessed as a young man and in the various wars he fought alongside me. Many of the Dravidians that carry the blue and black lion flag also followed Anand loyally. All I ask is that you allow these remaining men to succeed in the Mauryan army or retire with full benefits just as any Punjabi of higher caste would."

Subandhu was surprised at Rishan's honesty. "Are you accusing me of placing Anand in danger? I am not a killer—despite the rumors accusing me of wrongdoing in your cousin Chanakya's death. Your fame among the people and your kinship to Chanakya has long shielded you from trouble, Rishan. Although you have never publicly created discord like Anand, you have disobeyed a few orders in your military history including those of my own. You must understand Rishan that no one remains safe when a new generation comes to power—not even me, and I am one of the most powerful men in the Mauryan Empire."

Rishan came closer. "Are you threatening me, Subandhu? Please don't speak in riddles. Speak directly."

Prince Susima of the Mauryan Empire interrupted the tense conversation. "Why do you two continue to fight even regarding the death of Anand, a warrior that gave his life for my father's empire?"

The prince separated the men, preventing a potential argument and choosing to speak with Rishan privately. Prince Susima escorted Rishan to a private area of the palace reserved only for the Royal Family and he stated. "I heard some of what you had to say and I agree with you. You were like a brother to my grandfather and I look at you as a great-uncle. Tales of your heroism have inspired my brothers—including my younger brother Ashoka, who always mentions your battles. After you speak with my father I will make sure Anand's family receives his full pension, retirement, and an additional payment be made for his young son Jagdesh until he is fully capable of leading his own family. As for your adopted son Atallan, I will make sure he has the ability to rise within the Mauryan army despite his lower caste as long as he is qualified to do so. I agree with your ideas, Rishan. A man's hard work and intelligence should be the only factors involved in improving his station in life, not caste or wealth. I will also extend women's rights just as my father and grandfather have. You must admit, we have not progressed as far as your friend Anand wanted, but we have still progressed. I understand you wish to become a diplomat and represent the Mauryan Empire in foreign kingdoms. When I am king I will welcome you back and ask you to become my adviser. My father's wars are almost over and we have taken control of India, leaving only Kalinga and the Tamil-Nadu Kingdoms outside of our control. As king, I will seek diplomatic relations first and put an end to the wars."

Rishan was impressed with the young Prince Susima and felt the empire would prosper under his leadership. Although rumors continued, the Mauryan Empire could not provide adequate proof that the Tamil King Ilamcetcenni was directly responsible. However, Emperor

Bindusara realized that war against the Cholas would not be reasonable after prolonged yet successful warfare. Emperor Bindusara sought to organize recent kingdoms he had acquired under the Mauryan Empire.

Emperor Bindusara was in good spirits when Rishan finally met him in his throne room. Rishan formally asked about his retirement and requested to work within a diplomatic capacity in Egypt.

Emperor Bindusara replied, "I have a good relationship with Egypt. I do not need a representative there at this moment; perhaps I can send you to the lands of the east. However, if you really wish to travel and follow your uncle Manu's footsteps, I will assign you to Egypt if you can extend your service as general. I also believe it is a great idea so I can avoid a conflict between you and my adviser Subandhu but remain vigilant and careful as the Greek Wars of Succession are still ongoing. After assassinating Cassander's son Alexander V, Demetrius remains on the throne of Macedon despite rebellions against him. Ptolemy, King Pyrrhus, and Lysimachus are now threatening Demetrius I and we do not know how this war will develop. I request that you continue your work as a general for a period of a year and then I will grant you several months to get your affairs in order before you travel to Egypt. I will make sure you remain safe in your travels."

Rishan had a great meeting with the emperor and his mood was finally lifted—at least temporarily. Rishan wanted revenge, but he did not want emotion to cloud his judgement. It was war and this was what happened in war. Rishan thought of his own life and the wellbeing of his family; he wished to live a long life like his grandfather Mahesh.

As he left the Royal Palace and was ready to leave Pataliputra, he encountered Ashoka. Ashoka was a year younger than his brother Susima but appeared larger and overflowed with confidence. He came up to Rishan and said, "I am sorry for the loss of your friend Anand. He was a great warrior. I believe we should avenge him and conquer the remaining Tamil Kingdoms, the Pandyan, the Cheras, and specifically the Cholas and King Ilamcetcenni. I understand the Cholas are the strongest at this time but if we do not fight them now perhaps we will fight them when the Tamils fight amongst each other. I have heard of your heroism and perhaps I can convince my father to organize an attack. We can have Mauryan chariots with our white flags waving triumphantly as they enter the Chola Kingdom. Perhaps you can lead this war and raise your famed blue and black flag with the lion and svastika. I will advise my brother Susima when he takes the throne to avenge our losses as well as your personal loss."

Rishan slowly responded, "Ashoka, you have so much youth and energy but you still do not understand what it is to fight. In war you may face evil men or simple men who are just like you, however the only difference is that they serve a different king or a different purpose. When you stare into the eyes of a young man drawing his last breath who never experienced the joys of a woman or a family, you will suddenly develop a hole which you may never fill. Some men drink wine until they cannot remember, other men continue to kill until they themselves perish, while only a few are able to face themselves at the end and begin to build a new life when their old life decays right in front of them. I understand Susima will become viceroy of Takshashila and you will become the viceroy of Ujjain. Emperor Bindusara informed me that your brother Susima will rule over Takshashila—an important location where my youngest son Rajat is currently attending university. Ashoka, you will lead men into battle so remember to remain humble even as you gain power. Remember my words. Wars with no purpose rot the soul of a man and sometimes it is hard for you to regain your own life. Are you familiar with the Greek hero Ajax and how he met his fate after the Trojan Wars? Allow me to explain this story and perhaps you can remember it during your life."

Rishan told Ashoka the tale as he prepared to leave the capital of the Mauryan Empire.

The following year, Rishan left the Mauryan army. He received a pension and retirement as well as continued benefits for his family. Rajesh had retired a few years earlier due to physical problems with his leg that had worsened while he served. Rajesh had taken control of Manish's projects while Manish pondered moving back south with the rest of the Ramankrishna family after the Assaka Kingdom was fully under Mauryan control. Rishan advised his father to remain until Assaka was secure, and his advice would prove to be beneficial for his father: Ashva was later assassinated by agents loyal to the former king. The Mauryan Empire took full control of Assaka and more than sixteen different kingdoms soon afterwards, finally bringing peace to the Mauryan Empire.

Rajesh's son Raahi Ramankrishna served briefly in the Mauryan army but was now helping Rajesh with Manish's building projects. Rishan's eldest son Raghu was now eighteen years old and training as a young leader in the Mauryan army, while Rishan's youngest son was currently away at the University of Takshashila studying architecture. Raghu had recently arrived to the Ramankrishna home in the Punjab to see his father as he prepared to leave for Egypt. Priya, now forty-eight years old, and her husband Mandeep Duggal also came to congratulate Rishan on his new career. Priya's daughter Sulehka was fourteen and studying to be a religious teacher while her thirteen year old son Mahandeep hoped to become a judge just like Anupa's brother Nakesh.

Several months passed while Rishan prepared for Egypt when he began hearing rumors regarding the death of Kali Mehra, who was suspected of taking his own life. Kali had become a shell of his former self. A disgraced man in his seventies too proud to show his face in public and display any weakness, he was found by his wife Sanjeeta face down on the floor. The cause of death was confirmed to be consumption of poison and Rishan's family was never implicated. Manish had previously visited Kali to try to gain closure from the once dangerous man but Kali rarely looked directly into his eyes, usually bowing his head in shame. Rajat questioned his father Rishan about Kali and his children and the stories of the dispute between the Ramankrishnas and Mehras. Rajat also asked Rishan about his visit to Pataliputra. Rishan described his disagreement with Subandhu but warned his son to stay away from political arguments yet be aware of Subandhu and politics within the Mauryan army. Rishan also mentioned his meeting with Emperor Bindusara and Prince Susima and spoke about the interesting young prince named Ashoka and the advice he had given him.

Rajat stated curiously, "I do not know of the fate of the hero Ajax, Father."

Rishan explained, "Homer, the great teacher of the Greeks, had taught that Ajax was the son of Telamon and grandson of Aeacus, the king of Aegina. Ajax was also a cousin of Achilles and a descendant of Zeus. Ajax was known for his heroism, intelligence, and great physical strength particularly during the Trojan War. The Trojan Prince Hector challenged any brave Greek warrior to face him in combat. After being chosen at random, Ajax fought Hector valiantly for an entire day, wounding Hector with his spear and knocking him to the ground with a large stone. A draw was called and the two heroes exchanged gifts. Hector gave Ajax his sword while Ajax gave Hector his purple sash. There was a second fight between Ajax and Hector after Hector infiltrated the Mycenaean camp and fought the Greeks on their ships. Ajax nearly killed Hector with a large stone and with a long spear was able to defeat many Trojan warriors mostly by himself. Hector disarmed Ajax in their last battle and Ajax retreated only because Zeus favored Hector. When Achilles was killed by Prince Paris, Ajax and Menelaus fought off the Trojans while Odysseus helped bring Achilles' corpse to Ajax's chariot to be returned for funerary rites."

Rajat listened carefully as his father Rishan continued, "Ajax believed he deserved the honor of claiming his cousin Achilles' armor because of his bravery during the war and in combat against Hector. However, Odysseus proved more eloquent and claimed the armor. Ajax fell into despair and killed himself by falling on his sword. Sophocles retold this story, stating that Ajax felt extreme anger towards Menelaus and Agamemnon after Achilles' armor was awarded to Odysseus and Ajax sought to kill them. The Goddess Athena clouded Ajax's vision, causing him to murder a flock of sheep because he was fooled into thinking they were Odysseus and Menelaus. When Ajax awoke covered in blood he experienced great mental anguish as he realized what he had done. Believing he had diminished his honor, he took his own life with Hector's sword, preferring death rather than living in shame. Ajax's half-brother Teucer stood trial in front of his father for failing to return Ajax's body and armor and was later disowned by his father after being found guilty of negligence."

Ragni explained the story of Ajax as a way to teach his son about the violence of war, the isolation and depression a person felt, and the misunderstanding that others had about the warriors who participated in war and the lifves they led. Raghu listened to his father's words as the sun began to set in the beautiful Indian sky.

CHAPTER 25:
THE INDIAN SAMSON IN SELEUCIA &
PALESTINE (285 B.C.)

"This is what the Lord says to his anointed, to Cyrus, whose right hand I take hold of to subdue nations before him and to strip kings of their armor, to open doors before him so that gates will not be shut."
—The Holy Bible (*Isaiah*, 45:1)

Rishan remembered his journey through the Seleucid Kingdom and the personal invitation of Seleucus to meet him in his capital of Seleucia. It was an enjoyable trip for Rishan and his uncle Manu, who had agreed to join him as a translator. Seleucus had continued his battle against Antigonus' son Demetrius, who was forced to leave his throne in Macedonia three years prior after facing a rebellion and the combined forces of Pyrrhus, Ptolemy, and Lysimachus. Demetrius initiated an unsuccessful siege of Athens but was repelled by forces aided by King Pyrrhus, who also held a personal grudge due to Demetrius' marriage to King Pyrrhus' former wife Lanassa. Demetrius had some success in attacking Lysimachus' territories, but soon lost a majority of his army to famine and disease. Demetrius attempted to establish relations with King Seleucus but later surrendered as the remainder of his army abandoned him.

King Seleucus anticapted his meeting with Rishan would maintain his relationship with the Mauryan Empire and he desired to learn about Emperor Bindusara and his policies from Rishan. King Seleucus was also curious to gain information about Rishan's mission in Egypt.

Rishan conversed with King Seleucus and witnessed the hated Demetrius as he had been imprisoned in an annex within the palace complex. In a pathetic state, Demetrius appeared dirty, slender as opposed to his previous robust appearance, and his eyes were not focused. Seleucus hated Demetrius more than his father Antigonus the "One Eyed" and he personally commented that the only thing he respected was Demetrius' tenacity and thirst for maintaining power. Although Seleucus won the war, his own son Antiochus was overrun and defeated by Demetrius during the Battle of Ipsus. Demetrius was married five times, producing various children—including the current ruler of the Antigonid Dynasty named Antigonus after Demetrius' father.

Seleucus privately stated to Rishan, "I wish my son Antiochus had the thirst for conquest that Demetrius had— in the military and especially with women. I had to pair my son with one of my former wives Stratonice almost ten years ago because he could not secure a wife for himself. I have always secretly believed my son felt as if he was inferior among the other Macedonians and Greeks because he is of half Persian origin. What I do respect about my son is his loyalty and honorable character traits that Demetrius severely lacked. Demetrius was ambitious to a fault and his greed and lust for power became a problem. What a scandal Demetrius caused when he lusted after a young man named Democles the Handsome who continuously refused his advances and eventually jumped to his death into hot water after Demetrius cornered him at the baths. Another shameful act of King Demetrius involved the waiving of a fee of fifty talents from one man for the favors of the man's son named Cleaenetus. Various despicable acts committed by the lustful, and extravagant Demetrius turned his Macedonian subjects against him and led him here, where he lives in shame and captivity. Demetrius' son is nobler than his father and has offered me all of his riches—including his own life—but I cannot grant freedom to a man such as Demetrius."

King Seleucus I Nicator continued, "Demetrius reminds me of Karna Mehra. I must apologize for his actions and him murdering of your cousin Paraman Ramankrishna. Karna was ambitious and fueled with hatred; I believed he could have aided in my victory over Chandragupta, however the Mauryan army was large with intelligent leaders such as yourself—the one they call the Lion of India. As for the son of Karna, Krupal Mehra, he briefly joined my army, serving in the infantry after I offered protection to his mother Anjali. Krupal was undisciplined and had hatred for you, yearning to avenge his family's honor. He tried to motivate other Greeks and Persians to attack the Mauryan Empire and personally planned to kill you upon your entry into my kingdom. In his desperation, he attempted to join Demetrius' army but was himself murdered by other Greeks. The failure of Karna Mehra to defeat you and the deaths of thousands of Greeks was blamed on Karna, who was despised because he was an Indian. The hatred continued towards his son Krupal soon afterwards, culminating in his death less than two years prior. Anjali has re-married now to a Persian man and lives a private life away from men of power and influence."

Rishan was surprised when he was informed of the death of Krunal Mehra but he was relieved that the last of Kali's descendants were now eliminated.

King Seleucus continued, "I remember meeting your father and you as a young boy after the Hydaspes War. Your intelligence was apparent from a young age. You were soft-spoken and I never believed you would turn out to be such a fierce, capable warrior. I hope you have found a place in your society and have come to terms with the events of the past. I am now an old man of seventy-three and I have seen many things in my life. I have defeated my main rival Antigonus the "One Eyed" and hold his son in captivity. I rule over a large kingdom of Greeks, Persians, and people native to these lands. My capital has surpassed the glory of Babylon and now rivals other Hellenistic capitals such as Alexandria. It has been a pleasure to meet such a fabled adversary and hopefully a new friend and I wish you the best in your new capacity of diplomat and in life. I wish you and your uncle Manu a pleasant journey and stay in Egypt."

As Rishan subsequently entered Palestine, he remembered the conversations with King Seleucus and was impressed with his intelligence and the way he ruled his kingdom. Palestine had been carved into Seleucid and Ptolemaic regions after the death of Antigonus the "One Eyed." Rishan enjoyed the city of Gaza and was able to communicate easily with the aid of his uncle. Gaza was called the prized city by the Egyptian Pharaoh Thutmose III over 1,000 years prior. One of the oldest cities was Jericho and afterwards the region of Gaza became the land of the Canaanites. Canaan had served as the administrative capital of Egypt in this region with a sitting Egyptian governor for over 350 years until the arrival of the Philistines.

Rishan, Manu, and the rest of the Mauryan dignitaries were welcomed to Gaza by Ptolemaic officials who had secured Gaza under the rule of Egypt. There had been previous skirmishes between King Seleucus and Pharaoh Ptolemy but it was relatively safe by the time of Rishan's arrival.

To Rishan's surprise, the people of Gaza recognized him by name and were also able to identify him by appearance. His long matted hair and dark skin roused some attention amongst the crowd as many came to speak with him. The Mauryan defeat of the Seleucid Kingdom was widely known and secretly celebrated among the Hebrew people. Many of the Hebrews came to greet Rishan near a Ptolemaic administrative building where Rishan and Manu planned to rest for a few days before embarking towards Egypt. The Hebrews nicknamed Rishan "Samson" (or the Indian Samson), creating curiosity in Rishan as to why they chose that name.

While walking towards a large statue of Zeus, he was approached by a Hebrew of medium build with tan skin, dark eyes, and black hair. "Hello, my name is Bar-Nabha. I am an economist and adviser to the Greeks on the business of Gaza."

Barn-Nabha spoke Greek and Aramaic and was surprised to see that Rishan spoke fluent Greek and a little Aramaic. Manu had learned to speak Aramaic fluently from his previous work as a merchant in Palestine.

Rishan was curious about the Hebrew people and he asked questions regarding the history and culture of the region. Barn-Nabha replied, "After the Canaanites arrived, different civilizations ruled over Palestine, including the Amorites, the Egyptians, and afterwards the Israelites. The Israelites formed the kingdom of Israel over 700 years ago in the north and Judah in the south over 600 years ago. The Assyrians conquered Israel while Judah became a client state until Babylonian occupation, which enslaved and relocated many of the Hebrews to Babylonia. Cyrus the Great liberated the Hebrews and allowed some of my people to return to Judea, including my ancestors who returned to Jerusalem, creating the Persian Province Judah or "Yehud Meditana" in Aramaic. There were only a few thousand Hebrews in Jerusalem and its surrounding areas and then we began to repopulate this region, writing down our beliefs and making Yahweh our only God. Also, it is worth noting that Alexander the Great had a personal residence in Jericho after he conquered Persia and spread Greek power throughout most of the kingdoms."

Rishan and Barn-Nahba briefly paused their walk as they continued to speak regarding the history of the Hebrew people and their relationship with other cultures. Rishan asked about the Greek influence in the region and Barn-Nabha replied, "Greek influence has been minor as compared to others due to constant battles between Seleucid and Ptolemaic forces, leaving us to develop a little independence throughout the last few decades. Government affairs and business are conducted in Greek, but we mostly speak Aramaic in common, everyday personal affairs. Judea is under the direction of the Hebrew high priest and he has power over the religious and government affairs in Judea. There is a class of Hebrew priests who do not pay taxes and have great political power similar to the priest class in Egypt. Under the direction of these priests, we have created a unique culture and belief system distinct from the Persian culture that stated the Persian kings were the gods of the four corners of the earth. During Cyrus' reign, we were allowed to practice our religion freely, but I fear that the Greek rulers who have adopted the Persian style of divine rule will hurt us now under the Greek Pharaohs of Egypt. Pharaoh Ptolemy is now old and we will wait and see how his son, Ptolemy II Philadelphus, will rule as Pharaoh."

Rishan spoke about the unique monotheistic aspect of the Hebrew religion, comparing it to Zoroastrianism which was once the state religion of the Persian Empire. Barn-Nabha replied, "Ahura Mazda" is the supreme creator according to Zoroaster's teachings, which has influenced Judaism. We have also been influenced by the Greek religion as well but the Laws of Moses anchor our faith and culture. The Hebrew priestly class has designated our religion unique and the Hebrews as a people unlike others. I have secretly been against the growing power of the priests in Judea since I was a young man. My family followed the Hebrew priests somewhat blindly while ignoring elements of corruption among them. Many of the traditionalists like my father support the Hebrew priests while the Hellenized Hebrews support Greek culture and Pharaoh Ptolemy. Other Greek-supporting Hellenized-Hebrews prefer King Seleucus. These divisions in our politics have created cracks in Hebrew society. Some of the young Hebrews admire you, Rishan, and have wanted themselves to revolt against Greek occupation. Many of the young people are also opposed to the traditionalists and priestly class because they are ignorantly supporting elements of corruption."

Rishan and Manu listened carefully as Barn-Nabha continued, "Our priests have created a new religion after rebuilding the temple and restoring the glory of King David and Solomon. The conquest of Palestine by various empires such as Assyria and Persia and the occupation of Egypt have created an effort within us to distinguish ourselves from the occupying forces. We are brown and black people and some of us also originate from various regions including Persia; we have mixed throughout hundreds of years. Through these cultures and societies intertwining, I believe we may have changed our own culture and our history in the process. It has also impacted how we view the world, ourselves, and our perspective on our future."

Manu responded, "I agree. I traveled here as a young man and much has changed. I am in my seventh decade of life while my nephew is in his fifth. In my previous travels to Egypt and Palestine, I was informed that there were no hostile relations between the two during the time when the native pharaohs ruled. I was taught about the black nubian pharaoh Taharqa and the king of Kush who was the son of the nubian King Piye of the state of Napata. Pharaoh Taharqa was able to defeat the aggressions of King Sennacherib of Assyria and saved the Hebrew people. Pharaoh Taharqa also improved the Egyptian economy and the standard of life."

Barn-Nabha laughed as he replied, "Manu, you are a man of great wisdom. Now I understand why your nephew became such a great man! Our current society has an increasing anger regarding Greek control and their occupation of Palestine. We have often walked freely to and from Egypt during their periods of prosperity while other lands suffered great famines. We had some political disputes, but we were free to leave if we did not find Egyptian life suitable. Many Hebrews remained in Egypt and began new families there."

Palestine had Ptolemaic Greek and Egyptian soldiers patrolling the streets, but it was relatively safe while Rishan was there. Pharaoh Ptolemy had encouraged Greek soldiers to marry local Hebrews to encourage unity as he attempted to follow Alexander's policies within his empire.

Burning with curiosity, Rishan finally asked, "Why

do the people call me the Indian Samson?"

Barn-Nabha replied, "Samson, the man of the sun, was a man who had been bestowed with supernatural strength by Yahweh. Samson was one of the last Judges—men who had a special interaction with Yahweh and acted as military leaders for the Hebrews. Yahweh was punishing the Israelites by allowing them to come under Philistine's power; during this time an angel appeared to Manoah, a man from the tribe of Dan, and his wife Hazelelponi, who was barren. The angel advised the couple to abstain from alcohol and the child was not to cut his hair. He would be born a Nazirite, and this child was Samson. Samson killed a lion on his way to seek marriage with a Philistine woman from Timnah. Upon his return, Samson observed that bees had settled on the carcass of the lion and made honey. Samson ate the honey and brought the remainder to his parents. At the wedding feast, Samson challenged thirty Philistine groomsmen with a riddle. The riddle was, 'out of the eater, something to eat; out of the strong, something sweet'—an account of the lion and the honey. If they answered correctly, they would receive thirty pieces of linen and if not, Samson would receive it. When the Philistine groomsmen could not answer the riddle, they threated Timnah and her family if she did not reveal the answer. Samson later stated to the Philistines, "'If you had not plowed with my heifer, you would not have solved my riddle,'" and soon after Samson killed them. An enraged Samson killed more Philistines after they burned alive both his wife Timnah and his father-in-law."

Barn-Nabha continued, "Samson was so powerful he killed 1,000 Philistines, but then he fell in love with a woman named Delilah. Delilah was approached by Philistines trying to find the root of Samson's' strength, offering her 1,100 coins if she could aid in their efforts. Delilah eventually realized his long hair was Samson's strength and called a servant to cut his seven locks. The weakened Samson became blinded and forced to work in Gaza making milk by turning a large millstone. Philistine leaders gathered to worship Dagon, one of their major gods. With his hair and strength restored, Samson asked to be taken to a pillar where he collapsed the temple and killed all the Philistines as they ran in fear.

"Many of the Hebrew youth view your long matted hair, your bravery, and strength to be the same as that of Samson's. This region is embroiled in various conflicting political perspectives but you are a wise man, Rishan. Enjoy your stay in Gaza and in Egypt."

Rishan stayed for several weeks, later visiting Samaria and speaking with many Samaritans before departing for Egypt. Rishan saw the similarities between the Hebrews and Samaritans as well as their differences. Samaritans seemed to follow the Laws of Moses more strictly but still had elements of Judaism from which the Hebrews had distanced themselves. Rishan would speak with his uncle about these Hebrew people and their ancestors including Abraham, Ismael, Isaac, Jacob the Patriarch of Israel, Joshua, and other figures.

CHAPTER 26:
EGYPT (280 B.C.)

"Then a king will come from the south, Ameny, the justified, by name Son of a woman of Ta-Seti, child of Upper Egypt. He will take the white crown, He will wear the red crown; He will join the Two Mighty Ones. Rejoice, O people of his time, the son of man will make his name for all eternity! Asiatics will fall to his sword, Libyans will fall to his flame, rebels to his wrath, traitors to his might, as the serpent on his brow subdues the rebels for him. One will build the Walls-of-the-Ruler, to bar Asiatics from entering Egypt."
—The Prophecy of Neferti

Rishan Ramankrishna and his uncle Manu had arrived at the city of Memphis— the former capital of Egypt before Pharaoh Ptolemy moved the capital to Alexandria— five years prior. They were welcomed by the Savior, Pharaoh Ptolemy I, who ruled along with his son Pharaoh Ptolemy II Philadelphus. Rishan marveled at the large obelisks of polished stone rising high and gleaming in the African sky as well as the people and history that spanned thousands of years which had given rise to their great wisdom shared around the world. Pharaoh Ptolemy I improved agriculture and irrigation techniques which were neglected during the earlier wars of Greek Succession. Ptolemy also developed the Egyptian navy, mastering the great sea and controlling his empire from Alexandria. Ptolemy welcomed Rishan and quickly brought him to the site of Alexander the Great's tomb.

The Pharaoh was glad to see Rishan as he remarked, "I am blessed in my old age and see the young boy become a man of such intelligence, bravery, and distinction before me. I remember seeing you and your father Manish in a conversation with Alexander so many years ago and even as a boy your knowledge astonished me."

Alexander's sarcophagus was a work of artistic excellence that was observed by most dignitaries visiting Egypt. The body was fitted in a gold casing and the sarcophagus had a magnificent quality and color. In a previous conversation with King Seleucus, Rishan had been informed that Alexander the Great wished to be buried at the Siwa Oasis in Egypt to lie in rest with Zeus Ammon. After Alexander's death, it was decided that his body would be taken to Macedonia but instead it was taken by Pharaoh Ptolemy in Memphis over thirty-five years ago.

The Pharaoh remarked, "Shortly before his death, Alexander asked for his corpse to be taken here to Egypt. However, some of the other generals decided to bring his body to Macedon possibly to be placed next to his father Philip II. Alexander loved this land and its people because this is where the oracle confirmed his subsequent victory over the King of Kings Darius III and the Persian Empire. I have secured my empire and have not involved myself in costly wars in many years. I will only enhance this land and its people and encourage learning and the arts. I have funded a large museum to include a growing library in my capital of Alexandria. Alexandria is also where I will relocate Alexander's body for public display next year. This library will serve as a grand location for learning and for scholars to add their own knowledge. It will also be a place for schools and intellectual discussions—something which I personally enjoy. You will accompany me to Alexandria, where I will show you my own writings displaying my various intellectual pursuits."

Ptolemy conserved much of the native political

structure and boundaries, keeping the regional territories called sepat (or "nomes" in the Greek language) intact with their own governors called heri-tep a'a (or nomarchs) Ptolemy had promoted the production of cotton and wine within Egypt as well as Egyptian products for export which had helped increase the status of living within Egypt. The Greek-drachma within Ptolomaic Egypt strenghted as the state currency as the Greeks now controlled the riches of Egypt.

Ptolemy remarked, "Near Nubia I have also promoted Greek settlements and have created another capital city named Ptolemais Hermiou in upper Egypt. Perhaps you would like to visit sometime during your stay. My loyal Macedonian veterans who fought so valiantly in bringing about peace were given land grants across Egypt to help promote Macedonian and Greek settlement. I also encourage Greeks to learn the native Egyptian language to improve social cohesion as Alexander once had." Pharoah Ptolemy wanted Rishan to explore the city of Alexandria, which represented Greek power within Egypt. After a short stay and a visit to the Ancient Giza pyramid complex, Rishan would travel to the city of Alexandria. Alexandria was to become a center of Hellenistic education and culture and was initially built by Alexander the Great in 331 B.C. next to the Egyptian city of Rhacotis which now served of the Egyptian quarter of the larger city of Alexandria. Pharoah Ptolemy escorted Rishan throughout the city in the hopes that Rishan would later inform Emperor Bindusara of all he had seen and learned.

During Rishan's travel towards Alexandria, he noticed Macedonians and Greeks were indeed the privileged class in Egypt and the future children of the Greeks or between Greeks and Egyptians would remain a class above native Egyptians. Rishan pondered whether the people would continue to support a foreign Macedonian or Greek pharaoh and the fate of Ptolemaic Egypt.

Rishan's curiosity compelled him to later ask Pharaoh Ptolemy questions regarding the fabric of his society. Ptolemy replied, "There is a difference in being a general, as you and I were in our previous occupation, and being a leader of a civilization. There is also a difference in the way in which you lead in times of war and peace. I have studied this culture since I was a young man and have followed the same principles that Alexander once held. Alexander was successful because he believed in unification through mutual assimilation of different cultures and beliefs in the empire he ruled. Alexander was welcomed in Egypt as a liberator for releasing the people from Persian rule. As you remember, the Persians ruled these lands hundreds of years before and were overthrown only to return once again. I rule directly within the land of Egypt, not from a distant capital, and I respect the religion here, which is why I have secured the support of the Egyptian priests. I also allow freedom for the Egyptian people to practice their own faiths and continue their customs. The Macedonian veterans have been rewarded for their efforts just as I assume Emperor Bindusara has rewarded his Indian veterans such as you and your brother Rajesh. I have built schools for Greeks and Macedonian children so they may also learn our Greek teachings in our Greek language. Native Egyptians are welcome to learn Greek language and culture just as the Greek people will be encouraged to learn the language and culture of Egypt. I have built numerous Greek and Egyptian temples of worship with the support of the Egyptian priests. Temples have been constructed for the various gods including Zeus, Dionysus, Isis, and others including those for myself—as pharaoh, I am the physical representation of god in this world."

Manu also questioned Ptolemy. "I worked in Palestine and Egypt when I was a young man and I remember the last native Pharaoh Nectanebo II after he fled towards upper Egypt due to his overthrow at the hands of Persians aided by the Greek mentor of Rhodes and his Greek supporters. I believe these lands in Egypt and Nubia have created some of the oldest societies where men have cultivated language and science. I was once promised to marry a beautiful Aksumite woman named Saba but had to leave the war that Alexander had brought to Palestine. I sometimes ponder Saba's fate and hope that she found happiness and perhaps a family. She explained to me that when the Greeks previously arrived in Egypt and Nubia they learned from the customs of these lands. The Greeks were divided and subject to invasions from Persia just as the Indian people were in the time of my childhood, divided under numerous kingdoms and under foreign rule. Alexander was a strong force and he was able to unify the people at least temporarily. However, we believe he would have been defeated if he faced a united Indian force. I respect the peace in which Egypt exists now. Perhaps the division of Alexander's empire will benefit some kings such as yourself, as you have ruled Egypt wisely."

Pharaoh Ptolemy seemed slightly annoyed at Manu as they reached his capital of Alexandria. "When you visit our grand library, you will see our vast Greek contributions to the world which we now rule over and how I have maintained Egypt safe and secure under my rule. I am a man who loves learning and I have invited the best Greek thinkers to Alexandria, including Philetas, Callimachus, and Apollonius of Rhodes, who shared his poetic compositions."

Pharaoh Ptolemy continued, "I have also had the pleasure of hosting Aristophanes of Byzantium, Aristarchus, and Eratosthenes of Cyrene and his advances in chronology and geography. Manetho is a great historian who has been documenting this land. Euclid has made many advances in mathematics and has given us access to a new world of understanding. He is currently awaiting my arrival along with my son Ptolemy II Philadelphus. Every land has great thinkers and as a leader I am here to uphold Egyptian society and improve upon it. The Greek people were divided once before, and we are divided now. However, we each rule our own kingdoms today just as your emperor rules India. We have arisen from our humble beginnings and have now spread our culture and influence throughout the farthest regions. There is a new order and my responsibility is to foster greater education along with safety and security."

On their way to Alexandria, Rishan witnessed the Great Pyramids and was stunned by these majestic structures of human ingenuity. Rishan learned about the oldest world wonder as a young boy from Manu's previous travels and observing them proved to be far more impressive. The Pyramids' white polished limestone surface was smooth to the touch and glimmered in the African sun. They could be seen from far beyond the cities to which they belonged. The Pyramids were the largest structures Rishan had ever seen and served as tombs which kept the Pharaoh's body and permitted them to pass into the afterlife. The structures were sloped at five and a half seked in Egyptian units with a benbenet stone and a layer of gold as a capstone on top. The pyramidion (or capstone) was inscribed with different religious writings and symbols representing the pharaoh who built them.

Pharaoh Ptolemy commented, "Greeks arrived here many centuries ago to study these pyramids which were probably built by hard slave labor. I have requested slave labor from Greece and my territories to aid in building construction."

Rishan replied, "I was informed by Manu and a Hebrew about the misinformation of the usage of slaves in Egyptian history. The Pyramids were constructed by members of Egyptian society and they were provided incentives and wages."

Ptolemy laughed. "It is hard to believe a Hebrew that has a different view from the historical accounts. Hebrew religious texts state that the Hebrews themselves escaped from Egyptian bondage at the hands of Pharaoh Ramses the Great. It is ironic that your friend disagrees with my statements as well as those of his own people. Under my rule, the Hebrew people enjoy vast religious freedom and can cultivate their own culture within Alexandria and our other cities."

Rishan said, "I understand slavery has been part of many societies including during Greek and Persian rule. I do not believe slavery was part of Egyptian society just as it has not been a part to our Indian society. Although we have inflicted levels of debt bondage to those of lower castes, we provide a wage for our lowest servants."

Ptolemy replied, "There are always divisions. You need them to maintain a stable society. Not everyone can be a citizen and participate equally in government affairs. The role of government is an important one and it is an occupation which few can perform or be allowed to undertake."

Rishan disagreed with Ptolemy's views on society, however he kept many of his harshest criticisms to himself to maintain a stable relationship. Rishan's primary mission was to sustain a working relationship with Pharoah Ptolemy and build a relationship between Ptolemaic Egypt and the Mauryan Empire. Alexandria was Ptolemy's capital city and where Rishan would reside during his stay. Alexander's body had now been placed in Alexandria for public viewing and many dignitaries came to see the leader's final resting place. At Alexandria, Rishan met the son of Pharaoh Ptolemy, Pharaoh Ptolemy II Philadelphus. Philadelphus was a man of academic leanings who sought to translate many works into Greek. He stated he was encouraged by his father, his mother Berenice I, and his childhood tutor Philotas to study and become a great pharaoh.

Philadelphus stated, "My childhood tutor Philetas of Cos was a slender, fragile man who is now in the final stages of life and has recently moved back to the Greek island of Cos in the Aegean Sea. Philotas' beard was large and the only robust feature of his anatomy while his small eyes revealed a man of great intelligence. He devoted most of his life to academic pursuits and had written great works such as *Demeter* and *Disorderly Words*, which he contributed to the Alexandrian Library."

At the Royal Palace, Euclid and the Royal Family awaited the arrival of the Egyptian rulers. Rishan was informed of the great works in mathematics of Euclid. The pharaoh observed Rishan's thirst for knowledge and the interest he had in meeting many of the world's greatest thinkers. He sought to introduce Rishan to many of the famed thinkers now residing in Alexandria including Euclid

Upon Rishan's arrival to the Roual Palace, he was introduced to Euclid. Euclid of Alexandria was an old man with a long greying beard and focused eyes. Euclid was excited to speak about his works and meet Rishan. Euclid enjoyed speaking with guests from foreign civilizations and his pace quickened as he walked towards Rishan while stating, "I have heard of your life, Rishan. Our Pharaoh spoke of you when you were just a small boy in India. I understand you are also a man of great intelligence and wisdom and a man who seeks knowledge from others. I am currently writing observations and discoveries I have made in mathematics into a series of books called *The Elements*. I write about axioms, mathematical statements which can be used to reach other statements through the process of deduction. For example, in my first book I wrote about the parallel postulate where if the sum of two interior angles of a triangle adds up to less than 180 degrees then these lines will intersect if continued indefinitely. I speak about tangents and methods of finding the square root of a number as well as magnitudes which can measure distances, areas, volumes in our world around us, and angular magnitudes."

Eager to prove his knowledge of the subject, Pharaoh Ptolemy had made incorrect statements on various theorems. In an effort to hide his embarrassment, he said, "Euclid, I believe you should search for a better method of explanation regarding your observances in your book."

Euclid turned towards Pharaoh Ptolemy, stating, "There is no Royal method or road in learning geometry," causing some of the guests to quietly laugh."

Rishan asked for Euclid's mathematics books as well as those of other Greeks upon their visit to the Library of Alexandria. Rishan had learned mathematics and science from many of the teachers of his homeland. "In India, we have had many books written regarding mathematics which have been applied to the observable space around us, including astronomy and construction. In construction we use math to measure and cut precise bricks. We use numbers in relation with each other in order to mass produce them in different geometrical shapes for specific projects. We have writings that detail mathematical principles that are said to have existed for over 400 years. It details certain ideas such as the diagonal rope of an oblong rectangle produces a specific sum of what the vertical and horizontal produce separately."Rishan " "

Euclid replied, "Yes, this I believe is a mathematical discovery by a Greek named Pythagoras who lived a little over 200 years ago. He described that in a triangle containing an angle of ninety degrees, if you can measure the distance of two sides, you will be able to find the length of the third. "

Rishan replied, "This has also been understood by the Babylonians and several other societies under the Persian Empire. I have read some Persian mathematical and scientific principles. I had a privileged upbringing in the Punjab despite my family's ancestry to the Dravidian and Tamil peoples of central and southern India."

Rishan continued, "Our thinkers have discussed human mentality and our physical bodies, the relation between both, and its application towards the salvation of our inner soul or Moksha. This also includes the relation to the ultimate reality which is Brahman. In our Vedic traditions we speak of the concept of Rta, which is the pure truth or the Universal Order. Baudhayana also wrote about the study of triples that are the same triples that Pythagoras wrote about. "

Manu replied, "Babylonian mathematicians also stated Pythagorean principles centuries ago and this knowledge was spread into India through the Persian Empire. They have written examples of these triples and recorded vast sums of numbers."

Rishan was intrigued by these scholars and he would often participate in intellectual discourse and pursuits at the Museum of Alexandria, where he would spend the majority of his time during his work in Egypt. Rishan was also entertained by reading Apollonius' work in progress named Argonautica, which told the tale of Jason and the Argonauts and the quest for the Golden Fleece. During his stay in Alexandria, Rishan made sure to meet with many great thinkers and explore their teachings and writings as they were being written. Rishan also enjoyed learning about the various disciplines from the great thinkers of the past and the minds presently living within the city.

      The following year, Ptolemy I Soter passed away, leaving his son Ptolemy II Philadelphus as sole pharaoh of Egypt. Manu had devoted himself to traveling throughout the various cities as he enjoyed his life as a single man, while Rishan spent most of his time speaking with politicians and scholars that had arrived at Alexandria from the surrounding kingdoms. Pharaoh Ptolemy Philadelphus focused his attention on his book collection, the arts, and expanded the splendor of his court. Philadelphus increased the power and expansion of Egypt with his only concern and threat to his rule being his half-brother Magas of Cyrene, who was the son of Berenice I.

      Philadelphus spoke with Rishan while they walked through the Alexandrian Library, admitting the potential trouble brewing in the region. "I have enjoyed your conversations, Rishan but I face some foreign disputes. The empire my father fought to secure is now being threatened not only by King Seleucus but now my own brother."

      Rishan asked, "What is your opinion on the Roman Republic? Do they also pose a problem?"

      Pharaoh Philadelphus replied, "Alexander could have defeated them and the other Italic tribes including the Latins, Etruscans, Samnites, and Romans while they were at war with each other but he decided to go east and confront the Persian Empire. The Romans had a bloody war over fifty years ago with the Latins but after their victory they were able to incorporate the Latin culture and make it their own while also granting the remaining Latin people Roman citizenship. The Romans were also involved in other wars including the Roman-Samnite Wars and the Roman-

Etruscan Wars. The Romans have been smart politically but they have their own conflicts with other Greek states and increasing hostilities with the Africans of Carthage."

Before his death, Philadelphus'father had advised him to be cautious of Rishan due to his relationship with Seleucus and Antiochus. The late Ptolemy I had been annoyed with Rishan's questioning of his society and rule and had advised his son to monitor Rishan's activities within his kingdom, as Rishan could possibly arouse tensions with the native African population with his ideas.

During the last two years of Rishan's stay in Egypt, Pharaoh Philadelphus began to exclude Rishan from important meetings, leading Rishan to believe that Philadelphus did not trust him with sensitive information. Rishan thought war would erupt and discussed with his uncle a possible early return to India. Rishan spoke with Philadelphus regarding setting up a residence in the city of Ptolemais Hermiou and Philadelphus agreed.

Rishan and Manu traveled to the city of Ptolemais Hermiou and observed the settlements of Hebrews and the Thamud people, who were referred to as Arabian by the Greeks. The Hebrews were a growing minority and there was a sizeable Arab population as well. Macedonians and Greeks were given land grants and encouraged to settle in Egypt; they were continuously immigrating. The Hebrew people living in Egypt were quick to assimilate to Greek culture and strived to learn the language of the ruling classes.

Manu engaged in social gatherings and interactions which allowed him to meet a beautiful Egyptian and Nubian woman named Shai-Nefer. Shai-Nefer was a tall, slender woman with smooth, dark skin the same as her Ethiopian ancestors before her. Shai-Nefer was a divorced woman approaching thirty-five with an adult daughter named Amisi who was twenty. Shai-Nefer had married young to a wealthy Egyptian merchant before they both agreed to go their separate ways nearly ten years prior. Shai-Nefer and Manu became inseparable despite their age and cultural differences; Manu's knowledge of Egyptian culture and language helped bridge the gap between them. During their stay in Ptolemais Hermiou, Rishan would frequent Greek plays along with Manu and Shai-Nefer, enjoying many of them—particularly Oedipus the King and Oedipus at Colonus while Manu enjoyed Antigone. Rishan also enjoyed Egyptian wine and beer and often remarked on its quality over intellectual conversations with Manu, Shai-Nefer, and her cousin Menmet-Ra.

Menmet-Ra was a strong Nubian man of thirty who resided in the city of Naucratis. He was a teacher in various disciplines including mathematics and Egyptian history. An intelligent man, at a young age he hoped to use his physical capabilities and intelligence in a leadership role in the Egyptian military. However, Pharaoh Ptolemy I and his son Pharoah Ptolemy II restricted native Egyptians from joining the Greek-Egyptian army, but they did allow the native Egyptians to serve minor roles in the navy and as auxiliaries. Menmet-Ra was allowed to serve in the Egyptian army as an auxiliary due to his intelligence and physical strength.

Rishan asked about class and Egyptian society and its military, to which Menmet-Ra replied, "Egyptian society has prospered with Ptolemy I and now under Pharaoh Philadelphus. The dominant class is exclusively Macedonian and Greek and they have made the Greek language the dominant one. We are a secure society, but the other Greek Kingdoms, particularly the Seleucid Kingdom to the east, will be our major rivals in the future. Carthage is engaged in conflicts of their own in the great sea against Rome and with King Pyrrhus of Epirus. Pharaoh Philadelphus' growing navy and influence in the great sea may also cause a greater conflict between Rome, Carthage, and other Greek Kingdoms. There are many native Egyptians that are secretly and sometimes openly opposed to Greek rule and occupation of our lands; they oppose the political alliance between the Ptolemy family and the priests. Potential wars against other Greek Kingdoms will require a larger Egyptian army and native Egyptians will be required to increase the numbers. The Ptolemies fear a widening division between the Greeks and the native Egyptian people so they need to promote assimilation as well a healthy economy. The Greeks are also nervous of the Kushite Kingdom and their relationship with the native Egyptians."

Menmet-Ra continued, "Egypt is called Kemet by the native Egyptians and has been documented for thousands of years on papyrus within our own libraries. Pharaoh Ptolemy I elevated the economy and promoted education. Although he has incorporated Egyptian culture in the Royal House, he still documents Greek culture as the dominant culture in his library. Publicly the Ptolemies promote our culture, even performing the Egyptian rites of mummification on Pharaoh Ptolemy I Soter. Our first Greek leader, Pharaoh I Soter is also rumored to have married a daughter of our last native Egyptian leader, Pharaoh Nectanebo II—all in an effort to legitimize Ptolemy's rule and Greek rule over our ancient civilization. A segment of our native population secretly aims to restore a native Egyptian pharaoh to the throne and free ourselves from our occupation no matter how pleasant Ptolemaic rule may seem. The Greeks and the Mycenaeans previously arrived into Egyptian lands to learn about our mathematics, sciences, politics, and society before their oldest Greek philosophers came into existence. Greeks once served as mercenaries fighting for our armies and now they call themselves pharaoh. Egyptian thinkers such as Imhotep, the high priest of Ra and adviser to Pharaoh Djoser of our Third Dynasty, helped create the Great Pyramids you see today. Imhotep was a doctor who, along with Merit-Ptah and Hesy-Ra, influenced the Greeks who have researched their writings regarding surgeries and diseases in the teeth, eyes, and other specific regions. The Greeks have made him into a divine figure due to his importance in different disciplines and identify him as Asklepios."

Rishan enjoyed the conversation with Menmet-Ra and invited him to India along with his cousin Shai-Nefer. Manu had found love once again and asked Shai-Nefer to marry and return with him to India; she accepted after speaking with her family and daughter. Menmet-Ra also agreed with his cousin's blessings, as he believed she could start a new family in India as well as live a more privileged life with the Ramankrishna family. Rishan was overjoyed and agreed to attend the wedding after he had a final meeting with Pharaoh Ptolemy II Philadelphus.

Rishan was asked to meet the pharaoh at the Canal of the Pharaohs, an important waterway the pharaoh wished to renovate and extend. The canal was initially constructed by Pharaoh Necho II over 300 years prior but he did not fully complete the project. The Egyptians desired to open up sea lanes between the Nile River and the Red Sea to facilitate travel to the land of Punt farther along the Nile into Africa.

The Pharaoh was proud of the progress of his canal which some native Egyptians referred to as Necho's canal. Menmet-Ra had also informed Rishan that this canal may have belonged to Pharaoh Senusret III, who had reigned over 1,600 years prior.

Philadelphus was glad to see Rishan and exclaimed, "I hope you have enjoyed your stay at Ptolemais Hermiou. It is one of our great Greek cities in the land of Egypt. I am also building a magnificent lighthouse in the island of Pharos near Alexandria that will illuminate all trade and military ships arriving and departing the great city of Alexandria. This project, along with the successful completion of this canal, will be a great feat of human ingenuity which will be as great as the Great Pyramids of Egypt. I will make Egypt better than it has been and unify the cultures and people of this land. The Hebrew religious books are now being translated into Greek as well as all Egyptian and Arabic writings. My half-brother Magas has currently been trying to take control of Cyrenaica, as he desperately wants to be king and harbors resentment that I became Pharaoh of Egypt. My major concern is the possibility that Magas can destabilize certain African societies with his arrival depending on who offers him support. Your friend Seleucus and his son Antiochus I do not fear their military power and my navy is the most superior in the great sea so it appears to be a potentially minor problem. You will be rewarded greatly for your stay here and I apologize that you have chosen to leave Egypt earlier than intended. Please send my regards and gifts to Emperor Bindusara and thank him for the gifts he has sent me throughout the years. I wish you a quick and safe return to India."

Rishan attended the wedding of his uncle and Shai-Nefer and remarked on the nature of the Egyptian ceremony and courtship. The Egyptian people placed an importance on love within a relationship and marriage which was usually a practice enjoyed by the Brahmin or warrior castes. Rishan also learned that the Egyptians married early and prized family life and stability. Marriage in Egypt usually concentrated on monogamy with the exception of the Egyptian elite and there was little importance placed on the region from which the bride and groom originated. Throughout Rishan's life, he had observed Greek men and their views regarding women as being beneath the man and oftentimes Greek men would marry later in life primarily to fulfill their duties of family creation. Rishan observed the great freedoms allowed to Egyptian women under Egyptian law that he seldom witnessed within other societies. Women could divorce and retain what they owned and they could work independently from men and participate in politics. Greek men would often keep other women as well as young boys for their own pleasure while Egyptian men would marry and honor their wedding contract, fostering their relationships. Rishan was also informed of women that had previously served as pharaoh of Egypt such as Hatshepsut and Nefertiti over 1,000 years prior. Manu and Rishan made a sizeable monetary gift to Shai-Nefer's family and promised her safekeeping in India. Rishan also asked the direct permission of Pharaoh Philadelphus for the relocation of Manu's bride to India, which he approved.

Rishan was curious about the kingdom of Kush after his numerous conversations with Menmet-Ra and had convinced Manu to partake in a brief journey there before they returned to India. Menmet-Ra was aware of Rishan's legendary capabilities in martial arts and wished to fight Rishan in a short contest. He had informed Rishan of the extensive history of martial arts in Egypt, Kush, and other regions of Africa which had sparked Rishan's curiosity. Rishan had not participated in unarmed combat for many years but did not hesitate to test his abilities. Rishan was proud of his hundreds of victories and less than five defeats throughout the last four decades.

The men participated in combat for the period of half an hour until the aging Rishan eventually lost to the younger and faster Menmet-Ra. However, the victor was surprised and full of admiration witnessing the great strength of Rishan Ramankrishna. Both men laughed and drank beer, promising they would meet again when Menmet-Ra journeyed to India.

The following day, Rishan and his uncle Manu travelled to the Kingdom of Kush.

CHAPTER 27:
THE KINGDOM OF KUSH AND THE CITIES OF AKSUM (280 B.C.)

"The humble man flourishes, and he who deals uprightly is praised. The innermost chamber is opened to the man of silence. Wide is the seat of the man cautious of speech, but the knife is sharp against the one who forces a path, that he advance not, save in due season."
—The Instructions of Kagemni

The Kingdom of Kush had a long history with male as well as female rulers. These Nubian lands were rich in mineral resources which provided a main source of wealth for Egypt. The villages were abundant in resources and operated semi-independently from the central government. The people of Kush provided a percentage of their wealth to the central government in their capital named Meroe, where the king resided. As Rishan and Manu approached the capital, they observed large majestic statues of their former kings rising high into the African sky. King Sabrakamani ruled Kush while his son Prince Arakamani was currently being groomed to rise to the Kushite throne.

There were numerous statues depicting their queens called Kandake (or Candace) and their kings called Negus. The people were dark skinned like Rishan and other Dravidians of southern India. The kings had short cropped hair with round faces and dark black skin as well. The region was very hot and water was an important part of society. The Kushites created great infrastructure and irrigation systems for their crops which were given to the state to be redistributed to the less fortunate and prepare for famine and economic troubles. Manu understood some of the Meroitic language and writing. There were two forms: one similar to Egyptian hieroglyphs and the other in cursive. The Kushites wrote from right to left and top to bottom with the exception of certain monuments which had left to right writing. Manu understood some of the Kushite language which was similar to Aksumite and the various Arab and Hebrew languages. Rishan spoke with some of the Nubian people as he and Manu rode their horses towards Meroe, taking time to learn the extensive history of Kush.

For thousands of years, Kush and Egypt shared a long history and sometimes engaged in warfare with each other. The people of Kush moved down the Nile and settled into Kemet, now known as Egypt, creating the civilization's foundation. Some of the Nubian kings had unified Nubia and upper and lower Egypt as well regions in Africa. One of the Nubian kings named Alara consolidated Nubia and Egypt. The Nubian Dynasty established their capital in the Nubian city of Napata and uplifted all facets of Egyptian society while expanding Egyptian territory and power. The Nubian Pharaoh Taharqa also protected the Hebrews from Assyrian military aggression and he was heavily celebrated in Kush, tales of his deeds recorded in the Hebrew religious texts. Rishan admired Taharqa's persistence in the face of initial failure and how he managed to retake Egypt against the Assyrian Empire.

As Rishan and Manu approached the capital city, they observed the prosperity of Kush. It was the land of gold and they traded it to the east with the people of Aksum. Rishan saw an array of jewelry made out of gold, silver, and colored glass, which were fitted together by master craftsmen. Rishan was particularly interested in the naturally occurring alloys found throughout the kingdom. King Sabrakamani was not present in Meroe during

Rishan's visit, however government officials were aware of Rishan's his presence and allowed Rishan a brief stay.

Meroe had smaller, steeper pyramids than Egypt. These pyramids far outnumbered those found in Egypt and they were also used to bury the Nubian kings. The city of Meroe was majestic and the sheer size amazed Rishan and encouraged him to explore. Temples lined the Royal streets and the inscriptions that were placed on the walls and interior of the various temples and monuments told the stories of Nubian history and the greatness of their people, culture, and kings. The Nubians called themselves the true children of the God Amun and Nubian priests poured libations of water and milk to the Nile god named Hapi, depicted in numerous statues inside and outside of temples. The walls were perfectly fitted with bricks and the floors were pieced together with carved stone sanded over until they were smooth to the touch. Numerous colors decorated the Nubian buildings and shone brightly in the hot sun with the help of numerous lights. Mathematical and astronomical discoveries were observed and documented and the names of the kings were surrounded by an oval with horizontal lines at the end called a "cartouche" to protect and identify them.

Rishan and Manu made their journey towards the Aksumite cities to the east that bordered a much traveled sea that the Hebrews named the Yam Suph and the Greeks called the Erythra Thalassa. This was the famous sea that seasonally turned red and once supplied trade to the land of Punt. It was a major waterway for Egypt, Kush, and other Aksumite cities. The Aksum were an intelligent and ancient people which constantly shared their culture and natural resources with the Semitics of the kingdom of Saba on the eastern side of this Red Sea. During their stay in Aksum, Manu inquired about Saba, the woman he'd loved as a young man. Manu needed to know the fate of his old lover and he began to ask local officials regarding her place of residence.

Rishan was amazed by the Nubian women; the men within the city remarked on the beauty of the black women with round hips that commanded power and respect. Rishan did not want to surrender to his desire as he did once during his stay in Egypt. One night, he had met a beautiful Arab woman named Ameena. Ameena was a settler who'd arrived with her family just a few years earlier from the western Arabian region of Hejaz. While drinking beer and speaking with this Arabian woman, Rishan had fallen for her dark brown skin and majestic eyes and had awakened the next day glad to have met her. Ameena shared the story of her land and people, but their meeting was cut short as Rishan had to depart to attend to his diplomatic duties. Rishan decided to halt any further meetings with Ameena and to ease his conscience, he promised himself never to give in to temptations.

Towards the end of their journey, Manu was informed of Saba's location. Saba's family had successfully escaped Alexander's wars in Palestine and she now enjoyed numerous grandchildren and a large family. Manu was able to briefly converse with his long-lost love and they shared the tales of their lives. Saba was overjoyed to know that Manu had finally found a wife in his old age and they shared a joyous final embrace.

Rishan and Manu journeyed back towards Egypt where Manu's wife Shai-Nefer awaited their arrival and subsequent departure to India. They spoke about the great monuments in Aksum's cities as well as the cities of Kush. They were impressed by the scholars in Egypt and the Greek and Egyptian plays involving the gods Horus and Osiris. They spoke of the legal codes of Egypt and the Goddess Maat and compared them to the Babylonian Code of Hammurabi. The Goddess Maat, as observed in *The Egyptian Book of the Dead*, would measure the hearts of the deceased against a single feather to determine the person's fate. Rishan pondered these laws. Did Maat truly determine the fates of men or was fate determined by those who held power? Rishan observed the laws applied more favorably towards Macedonians and Greeks and applied less favorably towards the native Egyptians and Nubians.

During their trip towards the Seleucid Kingdom,

Rishan was determined to improve his own life and purpose. Rishan would attempt to discuss his perspectives with his family when he was back in India.

When Rishan arrived at Seleucia, he was welcomed by the new leader, King Antiochus I Soter and was informed that Demetrius had died in captivity. Rishan was also informed that King Seleucus I Nicator had previously traveled to Thrace, where he defeated and killed Lysimachus in the Battle of Corupedium. King Seleucus I Nicator was killed soon after by Ptolemy Keraunos, the half-brother of Pharaoh Ptolemy II Philadelphus and eldest son of the deceased Ptolemy I Soter. Ptolemy Keraunos' reign had been brief and he was captured and killed by the invading Gaul armies of Bolgius. The Gauls could not settle before they faced the professional forces of Antigonus II Gonatas, the son of Demetrius I—who had drunk himself to death during his captivity.

Rishan was surprised by the details of the Greek wars. He was effectively kept ignorant of them through the efforts of Pharaoh Philadelphus. Rishan thanked Antiochus, who supplied Rishan with many gifts for Emperor Bindusara. Rishan was promised the position of adviser by Prince Susima, once he took the Mauryan throne of India. Rishan promised King Antiochus I renewed relations between India and the Seleucid Kingdom if he became adviser to the next King Susima. As Rishan approached India, he received information of unrest and rebellion in several cities within his homeland. Rishan revealed his doubts to his uncle regarding the stability of India and the impact it might have on the Indian Royal Family and the political stability of the Mauryan Empire.

CHAPTER 28:
SAMRAT ASHOKA THE GREAT & THE FALL OF THE VICEROY (268 B.C.)

"A man is seated on top of a tree in the midst of a burning forest. He sees all living beings perish. But he doesn't realize that the same fate is soon to overtake him also. That man is fool."
—Lord Mahariva

After spending a few years with his family, Rishan was asked to advise the future heir to the throne, Prince Susima, who was governing the territory of Takshashila. Prince Susima had become the head of the Provincial Administration and was a representative of his father Emperor Bindusara. Rishan had improved his relationship with the emperor but tensions between Rishan and Subandhu continued to rise. The emperor believed the best way to alleviate political turmoil between Rishan and Subandhu was to approve Susima's request and allow Rishan to become his adviser. Rishan would reside in the provincial capital of Takshashila.

Rishan's son Raghu was now thirty-eight years of age and a mid-level commander in the Mauryan army. Rishan's youngest son Rajat, now thirty-five, had become a skilled architect and mathematician and had taken full control of Manish's construction projects in the Punjab with plans to expand towards other regions of the Mauryan Empire. Rajesh and his family had moved down with their parents Manish and Lakshmi towards the Ramankrishna's ancestral home in the former Assaka Kingdom (now part of the Mauryan Empire). Priya had remained in the Punjab with her husband Mandeep Duggal and their daughter Sulehka, who was now thirty-eight as well, and a religious teacher with a family of her own. Priya's son Mahandeep was thirty-seven with a successful career as a judge and had a family. Rishan's two sons had married and given him grandchildren during the years Rishan had resided in Egypt. Raghu married a Punjabi woman named Jasaleen and had a ten year old boy named Radhesh and an eight year old daughter named Manpreet. Rishan's youngest son was also married to a Punjabi woman named Harleen and they had a six year old boy named Rajul and a four year old girl named Jaspreet.

Rishan was now a seventy year old grandfather who hoped to work as an adviser for Prince Susima until he became emperor. After which, he would seek retirement and live his last days with his family. Susima's ministers at Takshashila had fallen into corruption and the local populace began to rebel. Rishan strongly advised Susima to punish his ministers and raise the standard of living—the local ministers believed Susima was arrogant and their concerns were not being addressed. Rishan urged Susima to be more aggressive and address the problems of the people in a more direct fashion, as it seemed his ministers were already against him. Rishan's efforts did not improve the situation. A large rebellion began in Takshashila, but was eventually suppressed by Emperor Bindusara. Prince Susima had advised his father to decrease the political influence of the local ministers and the aggressive Ashoka, opposing Rishan's advice. In response, Ashoka had left for Kalinga for a few years but returned with the support of various ministers and military officials.

Ashoka later suppressed a revolt at the provincial capital of Ujjain and gained increasing military strength. Although Susima was the viceroy and would soon become emperor, he found it increasingly challenging to govern Takshashila as a new rebellion erupted. Rishan believed Subandhu secretly supported Ashoka as well as a younger, more influential adviser named Radhagupta. Rishan strongly advised Susima to crush the rebellion at Takshashila and eliminate the ministers against him while Rishan traveled to the capital at Pataliputra in an effort to speak against Subandhu's actions. Rishan's attempt was doomed to fail, as Emperor Bindusara died before Rishan began his trip and he was forced to return to Takshashila as Ashoka began to move towards the city.

Rishan had learned that Subandhu assassinated the deposed ruler Malayaketu while he was in Egypt as well as many other political figures who might have posed a regional threat or who publicly supported Susima. With Emperor Bindusara dead, Susima was in a dangerous situation. Rishan did not fear for his own life but he did not want to place his son Raghu, who was a commander under Ashoka's forces, in danger—a civil war seemed to be an approaching reality.

When Ashoka reached Takshashila, he quickly crushed the rebellion, exposing Susima as a weak leader as Susima's ministers openly showed support for Susima's younger half-brother Ashoka. Rishan repeatedly advised Susima to forcefully assume his father's throne, take full control of the Mauryan Army, and purge any ministers who disrespected him. As Ashoka departed Takshashila, he left many of his agents within Susima's administration. Rishan, who had briefly returned to Takshasila, now requested to retire from his duties. Rishan was old and did not want his own politics to put his son's military career in jeopardy. Susima strongly suggested Rishan remain by his side and asked him to initiate an assassination plot against Subandhu and Radhagupta. Susima also offered Rishan a position in the Mauryan army after the elimination of his political rivals. Rishan desired to leave Susima's palace in Takshashila as he secretly believed that Susima would fail to become emperor and he did not desire to place himself or his family in political turmoil once again.

Susima angrily stated, "Ashoka is beginning to move against me and he is using other ministers—including your enemy Subandhu. I will give you a greater role in my government as chief political and military adviser. I understand your son Raghu is directly under my brother Ashoka's command and that he cannot defect to our side, but after I crush Ashoka he will be forgiven. I need your presence, Rishan. Your fame inspires the people and will inspire our forces against Ashoka, but if you choose to retire I will grant you your retirement. You have served the Mauryan Empire faithfully throughout your life."

Rishan replied, "I wish to retire within a year. However, I do not trust Subandhu most of all and I will seek to kill him if he threatens any member of my family. My only advice to you is that you strike first and you strike before Ashoka's power rises or you will be a victim. If you can claim your rightful place as emperor, I suggest you do it with as little conflict as possible. This civil war might place my son Raghu who fights for Ashoka and my adopted son Atallan who fights for you in danger."

Within a few months, Ashoka initiated a first strike against his brother Susima and a civil war began.

After about two years the civil war quickly shifted towards the side of Ashoka, who began regaining all key cities as Susima retreated towards the capital at Pataliputra. Rishan believed his decision to retire was a wise one, as he did not want his previous affiliation with Susima to put Raghu's life in danger. Atallan remained in extreme danger as Ashoka's forces began to overtake Susima, causing Rishan great stress. During the final year of the war, Ashoka had claimed most of the territory but had trouble taking the capital. The end would be negotiated by Susima and Ashoka at Pataliputra.

To Rishan's disappointment, Susima and some of his other brothers were soon assassinated by some of the ministers. The rumor was that Ashoka was behind the assassinations, possibly personally killing Susima himself. Rishan also suffered with the death of his adopted son

Atallan, who fought bravely to preserve Prince Susima's rightful claim to the Mauryan throne. Atallan had fathered a son who he named Rishan Ramankrishna—a true honor for Rishan. Ashoka's brothers and cousins were placed as governors or military leaders as Ashoka Maurya became the most powerful man in India.

Rishan had referred to Ashoka as the Chanda Ashoka—the fierce Ashoka. Rishan secretly disliked the new emperor and his method of governance as well as Rishan the vengeful acts of Ashoka against his enemies and their families. Ashoka also built a jail that people referred to as "Ashoka's Hell" due to the types of torture that took place within its walls. Ashoka's most infamous torturer was a man named Girikaa, who would develop different methods to punish and extract information from political prisoners.

Subandhu, who had turned on Susima after Bindusara's death, only lasted a year after Ashoka took control of the Mauryan Empire. Rishan had feared Subandhu, who he believed would influence Ashoka and would endanger him and his family. Subandhu would also die under mysterious circumstances after Ashoka became emperor. Subandhu was rumored to have spent his final days secretly in Ashoka's infamous jail. Although Rishan disliked Ashoka, he was relieved to know his last political enemy was now dead.

Ashoka declared himself emperor in an elaborate celebration in Pataliputra. His ministers had invited Rishan Ramankrishna, who respectfully declined. Rishan was moving south to be with his older brother Rajesh and his aging parents, who were now approaching 100 years of age. Manu and his wife Shai-Nefer also moved south with Rishan to live in peace the rest of their days.

Manu now had a son with Shai-Nefer named Ra-Hotep Ramankrishna who spoke Tamil as well as Egyptian and was showing a talent for mathematics. Rishan was a wealthy man now and the Ramankrishna family had amassed greater wealth than before. They had become a powerful family with no major rivals—the Mehra family had little political power. Kali's wife Sanjeeta had died quietly under the care of her family members while the remaining Mehra clan continued to distance themselves from the actions of Kali Mehra and his children.

Emperor Ashoka had increased the size of the Mauryan Empire and there was no threat from the Greeks, as the Macedonian and Greek kings could not match the strength and power of Ashoka's army. Rishan mourned the death of his adopted son Atallan but was happy with the security and peace within the empire. The peace would soon be broken by Emperor Ashoka, who sought to bring all of India completely under his control.

CHAPTER 29:
ROAD TO TARTARUS: THE KALINGA WAR
(261 B.C.)

"I am death, the mighty destroyer of the world, out to destroy.
Even without your participation all the warriors standing arrayed
in the opposing armies shall cease to exist. Therefore, you get up
and attain glory. Conquer your enemies and enjoy a prosperous
kingdom. All these have already been destroyed by me. You are
only an instrument, O Arjuna."
—Lord Krishna (*The Bhaghavad Gita*, 11: 32-33)

Emperor Ashoka increasingly gained power, as he sought further territorial expansion. He and and his wife Devi were traveling throughout the southern regions of their empire while their son Mahendra and daughter Sanghamitra remained in the capital of Pataliputra. Rishan was enjoying his retirement with his wife Anupa. Rishan's love for her had grown every year and he believed he was fortunate to find such a great, understanding woman. Although he had made his mistakes in the past, Rishan was a good husband and strived to grow closer to Anupa and make sure she enjoyed their final days together. Lakshmi, Anupa, and Rajesh's wife Divya had become the most honored and respected women in the Ramankrishna family. As the matriarch, Lakshmi was happy to attend the various weddings of her children and grandchildren. It was a grand blessing to watch her great-grandchildren growing up to be intelligent, capable young men and women.

Emperor Ashoka had requested to meet Rishan to speak to him personally about the possibility of an attack on Kalinga. King Kharasala had ruled Kalinga for most of his life along with his chief minister Manoj, and now Kalinga was ruled by King Kharasala's grandson King Anantha Padmanabhan. Under King Anantha Padmanabhan, the Kalinga state enjoyed larger participation of their citizens in government. Kalinga grew rich and powerful and their navy had set up colonies and outposts throughout the islands of the east whichalso approached the Chinas people of the orient.

Emperor Ashoka was finally able to speak to Rishan. "I am sorry for the death of your adopted son Atallan. He was a strong and proud warrior. This is a war we must fight now. Kalinga grows stronger and hinders our internal trade as well as trade with the eastern islands. How can I call myself great and stand fearless against any Greek army yet not call myself the ruler of all of India? My grandfather and my father were renowned conquerors, yet I have not engaged in any major battle and Kalinga remains as a rival to my empire after three generations? Join your son Raghu and help lead our army against King Anantha Padmanabhan. You have served my family throughout your life and our warriors will be motivated simply by your pressence upon the battlefield. I understand you supported my older brother Susima and I recognized the existence of enemies in my administration. I eliminated Subandhu because he believed he would manipulate me. This is why I did not choose to move against you, Rishan. I recognized your primary rival was Subandhu as well."

The two men continued to walk near the Ramankrishna house as they conversed about various issues.

Rishan replied, "I am an old man about to enter my eightieth decade of life and I cannot fight or lead men into battle. I supported your older brother Susima and have been disappointed in the politics of Pataliputra. I respectfully disagree with the idea of war against Kalinga. However, if you choose to persue this path, my son Raghu will follow your orders and lead your army into battle. It will be long and violent. The people of Kalinga are fiercely prideful and loyal to their leaders and culture. Kalinga is proud of being independent. They are currently establishing their trade routes throughout the eastern islands and have built a formidable navy."

Ashoka responded, "It is for this reason we must strike. If they continue to grow in strength, they will impact our trading routes. When we are victorious we will unite India, inherit the eastern sea routes, and expand upon them. This will greatly benefit our economy and people. If you wish to have a position as military adviser once again, you are welcome to come to the battlefield. I will be leading my army from the front and will conquer Kalinga, who has defied me, my father, and my grandfather Chandragupta Maurya!"

Emperor Ashoka was angered by Rishan's opinions and disagreed with him. He sought to gain Rishan Ramankrishna's support and wanted to use his fame as the Lion of India to encourage the Mauryan army against the formidable army of King Anantha Padmanabhan of Kalinga. Ashoka's wife Devi and the Royal train continued to Pataliputra, where they began planning for war.

Rishan and Anupa feared for Raghu. Anupa did not want her eldest son to be used in a war she viewed as unnecessary and had tried to convince Rishan to dissuade Emperor Ashoka from initiating war against Kalinga. Rishan had felt fear before, but he had never felt this type of fear. It was for this reason that he sought his father's advice.

Rishan now understood why Manish was careful while serving as adviser to King Porus. Rishan disliked the decisions his father had taken as opposed to the more aggressive Harbir Marawar.

Manish spoke softly as he addressed his son. "Now you understand the fears of a father. My first responsibility was the safety of my wife and children. Therefore, I did not engage in open hostilities with Kali Mehra. He was hungry for power and influence and my own success had blinded him with jealousy. Janeesh Mehra was the only son of Kali's who would have led that family down the right path and he was killed during the Hydaspes War. The rest of the Mehra family was of low character like their patriarch with the worst qualities manifested in Karna. I supported and respected Harbir and I was honored that he believed Rajesh was the best man for his daughter, but I did not believe we should have openly created a political rift between our family and the Mehras. However, in my caution I made mistakes and my family was placed in danger. I am proud of you, Rishan. You were a sensitive, quiet boy more interested in learning and books, yet you became a legendary warrior. You must understand that your own son will have a different opinion and might want to step out of the large shadow you have cast. Every generation has their differences.Rishan You must learn to shift your perspective and see the issues through the eyes of others. I will not live long and I hope Raghu remains safe. I am proud of my family and most of all, I am proud of you, Rishan."

Rishan replied, "Thank you, Father. I also apologize for my actions as a young man. I only sought to keep you and my family safe and I agreed with you and Harbir. I was afraid but my fear was overshadowed by my hatred for Karna Mehra. This is what motivated me to seek victory over the Mehra family and participate in overthrowing the Macedonian and Greek occupation. I only wanted you to feel pride in me as your son and also provide safety and security for my family."

Both men had a long conversation throughout the night.

Within a few months, Ashoka would launch the most violent, bloody war India had ever experienced.

Ashoka's initial offensive was met with stiff resistance and the first battles resulted in victory for Kalinga. Ashoka continued to escalate the war and sent hundreds of war elephants against Kalinga, surpassing the number the enemy possessed. He had lost the first battles but repeatedly stated that he would not surrender his offensive against Kalinga as his father Bindusara had. King Anantha Padmanabhan took command of the Kalinga forces and continued the strike against Ashoka. After several years of fighting, Ashoka overwhelmed Kalinga, who continued to fight bravely.

Raghu was involved in the last major offensive in the Kalinga war, which sent Rishan and the Ramankrishna family into a state of great anxiety and stress. Anupa advised Rishan to encourage Ashoka to call an end to the war. Rishan rode his majestic black horse named Yama (after the Hindu lord of death) to the battlefield in Kalinga. The horse had been a gift from Emperor Bindusara.

During Rishan's travel, his father Manish passed away. As the family mourned his death, they continued to worry about the fate of Raghu. Rishan was later informed of his father's passing and was saddened but was glad to know Manish would never witness what he was about to see at the battlefield of Kalinga. Ashoka's army of over 400,000 men had devastated the Kalinga forces of over 60,000 and killed more than 100,000 civilians. Ashoka had lost over 100,000 men and Kalinga's losses were upwards of 150,000. The lands of Kalinga were drenched in blood and full of weeping widows, mothers, and children. Rishan was overwhelmed at the amount of lives lost and he believed the dead numbered much larger than the official reports stated. Never in his entire life of battle and war had he seen a landscape filled with so much death. Rishan wandered throughout the land seeking the fate of his eldest son Raghu.

The Daya River flowing next to the battlefield ran red with the blood of the fallen and a horrible stench filled the air. There were many more thousands of people shambling across the land, missing various body parts and releasing groans of death. King Anantha Padmanabhan of Kalinga was also dead and found beneath the bodies of his vanguard with two arrows through his chest shot by Mauryan archers.

Rishan was able to locate Ashoka, who directed him to his son Raghu. Ashoka had fire in his eyes and was still raging with fierce determination which would soon give way to contemplation and sadness. Raghu valiantly commanded his men into battle but was now lying on the earth wounded with various injuries. Tears began to flow from Rishan.

Raghu said, "Father, I only wished to be a great leader like you were. I only wished for you and my family to be proud. I followed my king and fought bravely in battle."

Rishan replied, "I am very proud of you, my son. You have lived a greater life than me. If you leave your earthly family, you will join your grandfather Manish. This life was never meant for you."

Rishan held his son, begging him to stay alive as he closed his eyes and drew his final breath. Rishan cried in a way he had not cried for many decades.

Emperor Ashoka tried to comfort Rishan, tears in his eyes. "I am sorry for the loss of your son. He was a great leader and warrior just as you have been. I am sorry that this has been the price of war—a price we all have to pay. Kalinga was growing in strength and threatened to ally themselves with the southern Tamil Kingdoms."

Rishan said, "You have won the war, but you have also won the tears of widows and fatherless children. You have won the tears of mothers without sons or daughters and that price will be charged upon your own conscience for the rest of your life, Ashoka."

Rishan went back to the Ramankrishna house, where his family finally learned of the dreadful accounts of the battle and the fate of Raghu. The journey home was the longest Rishan had ever taken. A slow journey filled with sorrow and disappointment as Rishan began to believe he had not done enough to prevent Raghu's death. He was filled with the unbearable weight of thousands of questions with no answers and a search for the simplest, easiest way to explain the hell on earth that had occurred during the war against Kalinga.

CHAPTER 30:
CONVERSATIONS WITH XIAO QIANG AT THE LION CAPITAL OF ASHOKA (250 B.C.)

"This is the land of the gods. The people should revere them. In my essence I [Amaterasu] am the Buddha Vairocana. Let my people understand this and take refuge in the law of the Buddhas."
—Shinto (Revelation of the Sun Goddess to Emperor Shomu)

The Mauryan Empire was now divided into four regions with four provincial capitals: Tosali in the east, Ujjain in the west, Suvarnagiri in the south, and Takshashila in the north. The Mauryan Empire was now at peace. Rishan mourned his eldest son's death and was overwhelmed with sadness. His mother Lakshmi had also passed away five years after the death of his father, causing great sorrow within the Ramankrishna family. Rishan found some solace in the respect that the people of India and even the conquered people of Kalinga had for him, despite the fact that Raghu had led Ashoka's forces in combat against them. Saket's grandnephews had served in the Kalinga war against Ashoka and they spoke about Saket and Rishan's relationship before Rishan became a general of the Mauryan army under Emperor Bindusara. Rishan traveled to the Tamil Kingdoms of the south as far as the island kingdom of Lanka. Rishan's voyage back to India ended in a shipwreck where his fellow voyagers perished during torrential monsoon rains while Rishan was able to swim over fifteen miles back to mainland India. After this near-death experience, Rishan cut his hair and chose to follow Jainism.

Rishan remained angry at Emperor Ashoka for most of his early reign, but now he began to shift his attentions towards his wife and family. Rishan and Rajesh were now the eldest and most respected men in the Ramankrishna family. Raghu was survived by his widow Jasaleen, their son Radhesh, and daughter Manpreet Ramankrishna. Radhesh had become a respected diplomat who had learned the language of the Chinas people of the far-east. Several years prior, Radhesh had been invited to Pataliputra to welcome diplomats from the eastern kingdoms and partake in the same intellectual conversations his grandfather Rishan once had. Radhesh's success convinced Rishan to travel to Pataliputra one last time, where he once again spoke with Emperor Ashoka. This was the first time Rishan and Emperor Ashoka would speak since the end of the Kalinga war.

The Imperial Capital of Pataliputra was a magnificent wonder to behold during the reign of Ashoka. The city which had been the capital for many rulers and their families had now become the seat of power for an empire respected far outside its borders. Emperor Ashoka had now earned the title of Ashoka the Great, as he brought about great peace in India, converted to Buddhism, and decided against a potential war with the southern Tamil Kingdoms. Rishan, who had remained skeptical of Ashoka, began to believe the sincerity of the emperor during his conversations with him. Emperor Ashoka had found peace in Buddhism and his growing family. He was now blessed with several wives, including his first wife Empress Devi, and their children. His son Mahendra and daughter Sanghamitra were Buddhists as well and were preparing to spread their knowledge of Buddhism to the east. Ashoka's second wife Karuvaki from the former Kalinga state had provided Ashoka a son named Tivala. Ashoka's other wife Rani Padmavati gave birth to a son named Kunala, who was second in line to the throne after Mahendra Maurya. Emperor Ashoka also brought a beautiful young dancer and maid named Tishyaraksha to Takshashila who was not yet in her second decade of life.

Rishan respected Ashoka and many of his new Dharma policies, which created a positive shift in the quality of life among all castes within the Mauryan Empire. Rishan also supported Ashoka's efforts to loosen the rigid caste structures inherited from his father Bindusara. Rishan believed in these new policies and informed Ashoka that his friend Anand Agrawal would have also supported them if he were still alive. Chandragupta had chosen Jainism, Bindusara had chosen Ajiviksim, and although Ashoka focused on Buddhism in his private life, he allowed religious freedom for his subjects while defining sets of social norms to be followed by everyone regardless of caste or religious beliefs.

Ashoka proudly stated, "I have begun placing my edicts in various locations to include Dhauli, Jaugada, Amaravati, Sopara, Kausambi, and as far as Mansehra and Kandahar. I understand you have chosen to leave the Punjab and live out your final days in your ancestral homeland towards the central and southern regions of my empire. It will be my honor to welcome any members of the Ramankrishna family to continue to serve the Royal Family as I have welcomed your grandson Radhesh."

For the first time in many years, Rishan felt pride in the Mauryan Empire and its leader. Rishan enjoyed his visit to the Mauryan capital city and enjoyed the various visitors and diplomats who were invited to Emperor Ashoka's court.

Various diplomats and military members representing various civilizations were present at the Mauryan capital and Rishan was introduced to some of the foreign dignitaries. The Greek diplomat Dionysius, representing Pharaoh Philadelphus of Egypt, was in Pataliputra as well as a far eastern diplomat named Xiao Qiang, who was accompanied by Radhesh. Rishan smiled, curious to know the affairs of Egypt and the mysterious lands of the east. Rishan had become interested in diplomacy through his friendship with Megasthenes and had briefly met the Greek diplomat Deimachus. Dionysius stated that Pharaoh Ptolemy II Philadelphus' two half-brothers, Ptolemy Keraunos and Meleager, were both killed as Rishan left Egypt on his return trip to India. Philadelphus' other half-brother, Magas of Cyrene, had assumed kingship of Cyrenaica in northern Africa. Pharaoh Philadelphus' fear became a reality several years after Rishan's departure when Magas invaded Egypt from the west while King Antiochus I Soter of the Seleucid Kingdom invaded from the east. An internal revolt in Cyrenaica halted Magas' offensive against Egypt and Egypt was able to defeat both.

King Pyrrhus of Epirus had defeated the upstart Romans twice and although Pyrrhus suffered massive losses, he continued his reign and his relationship with Carthage. At the battle of Beneventum, King Pyrrhus and his Samnite allies fought the Romans led by consul Manius Curius Dentatus, which resulted in a stalemate. King Pyrrhus left and the Romans later defeated the Samnite people and captured the Italian peninsula, including Magna Graecia of Greek-occupied southern Italy. He also attacked Antigonus II Gonatas at the battle of the Aous, seizing the Macedonian throne. He would later face a long struggle during the siege of Sparta after he was invited by a hated Spartan of Royal blood named Cleonymus who wished for King Pyrrhus to place him on the Spartan throne. King Pyrrhus facing large resistance retreated from Sparta where he lost his first-born son named Ptolemy.

At Argos, King Pyrrhus faced the advancing army of Antigonus II Gonatas while also facing hostile armies within the narrow streets. While King Pyrrhus engaged an Argive soldier in combat, the soldier's mother threw a tile from a building rooftop and paralyzed him. Defenseless, the king was decapitated by a solder named Zopyrus and his cremated body was later sent back to Epirus and given to his surviving son Helenus. The Greek city of Tarentum subsequently fell to the Romans as they began to gain more power.

The Greek Wars of Succession had mostly ended, marking a period of peace. It was a peace the Greeks had not experienced since the death of Alexander the Great. Rishan stated, "So I assume the Romans have increased their power in the absence of King Pyrrhus."

Dionysius replied, "The Romans are now in a violent struggle against Carthage in northern Africa and although they have grown more powerful, they will be preoccupied with their Carthaginian wars. The Romans are not powerful enough to launch a major offensive against the Greek Kingdoms and Egypt still maintains superiority in the Aegean Sea." Rishan was deeply involved in conversation with the fellow diplomat. Rishan enjoyed his life as a diplomat himself—more than his role as a Mauryan commander during wartime.

Ashoka celebrated the peace and had promised to send ambassadors of Buddhism throughout the various Greek Kingdoms. Rishan laughed at the irony— just ten years prior he had initiated the bloodiest conflict in India's history. Radhesh and Xiao Qiang finally arrived and joined in the conversation. Rishan was curious to learn about Xiao Qiang and his people and spoke to him while his grandson served as translator. Qiang was wearing fine silk clothes that were only seen on the wealthiest Punjabi people like Kali Mehra who once paraded around in exotic clothing.

Qiang stated, "Our lands and history are vast and rich just as the history of the Indian people. I am from the state of Qin on the western regions of our lands. Our location has created easier communication between our people and those to the west of us. The Zhou Dynasty collapsed and a war between our states continues. The Zhou emperor had become simply a figurehead and there was a lack of centralized power. Qin is currently the strongest state and our leaders believe we can one day unify our entire land just as Ashoka has. I was informed that King Zhaoxiang of Qin has died and now his son King Xiaowen rules. I have come to India to learn from your culture and your beliefs. I have also come to learn about the history of India and how Emperor Ashoka rules. We will soon become a united land if the state of Qin succeeds and we must start laying the framework for future relationships between our people."

India under the Mauryan Empire had full control of its trade and resources and now possessed the extensive trade routes Kalinga had already established.

Rishan believed Jainism, Buddhism, and Hinduism would spread throughout the far eastern lands. Ashoka was eager to share the culture and beliefs of the people of India with particular focus on Buddhism.

Xiao Qiang continued, "Our political beliefs have been partially based on the teachings of Confucius, who lived over 250 years ago. Confucius' teachings are contained in five books and his ethics have been used by our rulers. The concepts that Confucius taught were ren or humaneness, li or proper rite, zhi or the importance of knowledge, yi or justice, and xin or integrity. The five constants that have been written down by the followers of Confucius are zhong or loyalty, xiao or piety or respect for elders and teachers; jie is self-discipline, and yi or righteousness. Confucius believed leadership began within the leader himself before the leader could successfully guide his subjects. These beliefs set values within society between ruler and subject, father and son, husband and wife, elder brother and younger brother, and between friends. "

After a brief pause, Xiao Qiang stated, "The Qin state has also applied another political way of thinking with a focus on pragmatism and the importance of laws and government. Throughout the constant wars that continue to rage in our lands, we focused on creating a set of legal rules which reinforce our state and our laws to establish an efficient, just society. Many of these beliefs were influenced by Taoist thinkers like Guan Zhong and Huang-Lao. Laws based on these ideas have facilitated a strong central government and should be our road to success in the future. Shang Yang helped our political structure by weakening the feudal lords and strengthening our central government as

Ashoka has done in India."

Rishan was interested in Taoism, which influenced the culture of these far eastern people. Taoism was aided by the teachings of Laozi and Zhuangzi and instructed followers in the ways of wu-wei (or action through inaction) and the beauty of simplicity. Taoism also valued compassion, moderation, and humility.

Rishan shared the teachings of Hinduism and Jainism and the importance of the *Mahabharata* and *Ramayana*. Rishan spoke of the *Mahabharata* and the account of the Kurukshetra war between two sets of cousins—the Kauravas and Pandavas—that were locked in a war of Dynastic succession.

Rishan explained, "The blindness of the older Prince Dhritarashtra caused him to be passed over by the younger Prince Pandu to become king after their father's death. Then a curse prevented Pandu from fathering children. Pandu's wife Kunti asked the Gods to help father children in place of Pandu. The God Dharma fathered Yudhishthira, the wind fathered Bhima, Indra fathered Arjuna, and the Ashvins fathered the twins Nakula and Sahadeva with Pandu's second wife Madri. Jealousy later forced the Pandavas to leave the kingdom when their father died. The five Pandava brothers married Draupadi, who was born out of a sacrificial fire and who Arjuna won after shooting an arrow through a row of targets. The brothers returned to their kingdom only to be exiled once again for twelve years after Yudhishthira lost everything to Duryodhana and the Kauravas in a dice game played with loaded dice. The Kauravas attempted to embarrass Draupadi by disrobing her but Lord Krishna prevented this by creating extra lengths of cloth. The Kauravas and Pandavas were later involved in a great war at Kurukshetra. Arjuna and the Pandavas and Karna and the Kauravas helped lead their respective sides in battle. During this battle, conversations between Arjuna and Lord Krishna took place and are called the *Bhagavad Gita* or the *Song of the Lord*."

Rishan continued, "Arjuna was a man of great

knowledge and was taught disciplines including science, mathematics, and the ways of a warrior. He was considered the strongest warrior representing the Pandavas. Karna held the same respect as a warrior and displayed this when he ripped through the defenses of the Pandavas in an effort to defeat Arjuna with Lord Krishna intervening to save Arjuna's life. By the sixteenth day, Karna was made the Supreme Commander of the Kauravas and on the seventeenth day Karna was decapitated by Arjuna when his chariot wheel got stuck in the mud. Lord Krishna advised Arjuna to strike Karna, as he reminded Arjuna about the death of his son Abhimanyu when he was in a similar situation without a chariot or weapons. Lord Krishna and five Pandava brothers survived while all the Kauravas were killed. Lord Krishna died when a hunter named Jara confused him for a dear and shot an arrow through his foot. Krishna left his physical body as the world fell into Kali Yuga or the Dark Age in 3102 B.C. The Pandavas along with Draupadi sought Indra's heaven. The family was later reunited in svarga, a good plane of existence, where they lived serenely without the pains of the material world. Yudhishthira was then crowned king of Hastinapur, ruling for thirty-six years and after renouncing the throne, Arjuna's grandson Parikshit becomes king. Parikshit died after he was bitten by a snake and his son Janamejaya decided to perform a snake sacrifice when the story of his ancestors was revealed to him."

The story appealed to Dionysius and Xiao Qiang—particularly Dionysius, who observed the parallels between Lord Krishna's interventions with mortal men in war and the interventions of Zeus, Apollo, and other Greek gods during the battle of Troy as well as the other stories.

Rishan remained in Pataliputra for several months while Emperor Ashoka erected a large stone monument he called the Lion Capital of Ashoka on top of a fifty-foot pillar. It had four lions with various animals below including an elephant, a bull, a horse, and another lion above an inverted lotus flower and Chakra wheel. Ashoka would build Lion Capitals and place them throughout his empire and along his Royal Road connecting east to west and later other roads connecting north to south and all major regions of the Mauryan Empire. Each pillar also had an Ashoka edict inscribed at the base in different languages depending on the region for the benefit of the population. Ashoka had admired Rishan Ramankrishna during his youth almost as much as he admired his legendary grandfather Chandragupta Maurya. The lion was a powerful symbol for Ashoka and represented Rishan and the importance of Buddhism. Emperor Ashoka would not seek war with the three major Tamil Kingdoms of the Cheras, Cholas, and Pandyas, and promoted peace through his personal beliefs of Buddhism.

Rishan Ramankrishna remained in Pataliputra during the Third Buddhist Council under the Buddhist monk and scholar Moggaliputta Tissa with a focus on purifying the Buddhist religion and its opportunistic factions. Rishan would move back towards his ancestral home of Assaka with the rest of the Ramankrishna family with the exception of his sister Priya and grandson Radhesh. Radhesh would later attempt to translate the sixty-four Hexagrams of Taoism as a gift for his grandfather. Rishan would live his final days with his wife Anupa and his family, finally at peace. His long hair had been cut and with that came a rebirth and separation from his former unhappiness and strife aided by the love of his family and Jainism. Rishan said goodbye to Dionysius, Xiao Qiang, Radhesh, and Emperor Ashoka, wishing to leave the politics of Pataliputra behind. During his journey back to his ancestral home, Rishan's uncle Manu had passed away, leaving behind his beautiful Egyptian wife Shai-Nefer and their son Ra-Hotep Ramankrishna.

CHAPTER 31: THE LION OF INDIA (242 B.C.)

"In those days Solomon was King in Jerusalem, and Mâkĕdâ was Queen in Ethiopia. Unto both of them were given wisdom, and glory, and riches, and graciousness, and understanding, and beauty of voice (or, eloquence of speech), and intelligence."

"I am above the earth, and I am at the ends of the world, and I am Master of everything. I am in the air, my place of abode, and I am above the chariot of the Cherubim, and I am praised everlastingly by all the angels and by holy men. And I am above the heights of heaven, and I fill everything. I am above the Seven Heavens. I see everything, and I test everything, and there is nothing that is hidden from me. I am in every place, and there is no other god besides Me, neither in the heaven above nor in the earth beneath; there is none like unto Me, saith God; My hand hath laid the foundation of the earth, and My right hand hath made strong the heavens; I and My Son and the Holy Spirit."

—Kebra Nagast

Rishan awoke right before sunrise and gazed lovingly at the face of his wife, the woman who had supported his family during his long adventures away from home. Rishan proclaimed that his great love for Anupa had grown greater than ever before. Anupa had made a curry dish with a larger portion of turmeric for Rishan before he quickly fell asleep the day before. Rishan enjoyed a deep sleep so his sudden awakening slightly surprised Anupa. After listening to her husband's loving words, Anupa

419

wiped his tears and proclaimed her love for Rishan—a love that would last beyond this world. Rishan tried to explain a strange dream he had before he suddenly fell asleep once again. It was the last time Rishan would be awake as he mumbled the words he heard in his dream. Rishan closed his eyes as he remembered the Egyptian Bennu bird living for 500 years, building its own funerary pyre before rising from its ashes. The Greek historian Herodotus was influenced by the story of the Bennu bird explained by Egyptian priests at Heliopolis. This was the great Bennu bird which gave rise to the Greek Phoenix. As he closed his eyes, a small smile appeared on his face and a deep sense of rest enveloped Rishan and Anupa. As Rishan slipped into the warm embrace of sleep, a small but powerful voice perhaps from Makhan Chor enveloped Rishan.

"I am in you and you are in me, a good life you have yearned to seek. You have lived as you have loved, your soul shall be set free like the birds above. I came before and I will come again; many forms I have taken and many more when I rise again. I was within Zoroaster, within Siddhartha, within Mahariva, within all sages throughout countless ages. Within the wise dark teacher in him I will exist, the Lion within that man in Bethlehem. Through my words you will awaken from the worldly miseries you have seen. You will enter another abode of wisdom and experience the pleasures you seek. In death you will be pleased, for in life your descendants will be blessed as I have foreseen."

Inspired by the many love songs and poems of India and Egypt, Rishan had written a poem for Anupa just a few weeks prior to his death. It was a poem Anupa would keep until she passed away just five years later. Rishan also had been given silk gowns by Xiao Qiang during his stay at Pataliputra, which he gave as gifts to his wife and daughters. The Ramankrishna family and many others from around India came to see Rishan's body as they performed his funerary rites. Emperor Ashoka had traveled down to see the Ramankrishna family along with his last and youngest wife Tishyaraksha, who had gained considerable influence in the Royal Family. Rishan's son Rajat was now sixty-eight and came with his wife Harleen and Rishan's grandson Rajul who was thirty-two with his own wife and family. Raghu's widow Jasaleen was now sixty-four and was there along with her son Radhesh, thirty-six, and his sister Manpreet, who was thirty-four and married to a man named Vijay with a young daughter named Sajni. All of Rishan's grandchildren were married with families of their own.

Rishan's older brother Rajesh had passed away just six years prior with his wife Divya also passing away two years ago. Rajesh's son and Rishan's nephew Raahi Ramankrishna was now seventy-five years old had continued working in architecture in Assaka but he was also in addendance at Rishan's funeral. Long ago Raahi had married a woman named Garima and had a son named Mahabir who was an astronomer with a family. Priya also came to see Rishan. She had been gravely sick for the last few months and her family stayed in the Punjab.

Manu's widow Shai-Nefer and their son Ra-Hotep, who was now in his mid-thirties and had established a great career as a teacher of mathematics and astronomy, were also with Rishan for his funeral rites. Ra-Hotep Ramankrishna married a Tamil Indian woman named Avira and his children became teachers in various disciplines. Anand's son Jagdesh Agrawal and his family were there to celebrate the life of his father's best friend. Priyanka had passed away several years prior and never married again, while her brother Kulvir married, had a family, and became a successful architect. Pylas remained in India, enjoying his older years among his family and friends. Menmet-Ra was never able to visit India and his descendants later participated in the great native Egyptian revolt against Pharaoh Ptolemy V Epiphanes and Macedonian and Greek occupation.

Ptolemy V was victorious suppressing the native Egyptian revolt and inscribed his decree and legitimacy as pharaoh to God in various stones including the stone stele of the Rosetta Stone.

Mahendra, the oldest son of Ashoka and his first wife Empress Maharani Devi, decided to pledge his life to Buddhism and become a Buddhist monk. Mahendra was the heir to the throne but he did not wish to rule and left for the island kingdom of Sri Lanka along with his Buddhist sister Princess Sanghamitta. Prince Kunala, the son of Empress Rani Padmavati, was next in line to Ashoka's throne but was blinded by Ashoka's youngest wife Tishyaraksha. Radhagupta, the powerful minster of Ashoka, wanted to punish Tishyaraksha but she was believed to have committed suicide before her apprehension. Ashoka became old and was under the care of his daughter Charumati, who later married Prince Devapala. Emperor Dasharatha Maurya succeeded his grandfather Ashoka to the Mauryan throne, ruling for ten years until 224 B.C. when his cousin and Kunala's son Samprati took over.

Radhesh Ramankrishna continued his diplomatic work at Pataliputra and taught his son Raamraj the languages of the Qin state of the far-east. Raamraj later worked for Emperor Samprati Maurya as they extended diplomatic relations with the Qin Dynasty of the first united Chinese Empire under Emperor Qin Shi Huang and his son Emperor Qin Er Shi. Emperor Qin Shi Huang conquered the surrounding states, all of China, and began building and uniting great sections of an east to west northern Chinese wall to stop the invasions of northern nomadic tribes including the Xiongnu. Emperor Qin Shi Huang destroyed the walls which had been built hundreds of years earlier to separate the once warring states.

Under the rule of Emperor Samprati, Rishan Ramankrishna's name received fame once again. He built many religious temples for Jainism and had worked to spread the beliefs across India and beyond his borders just as Ashoka had done for Buddhism, earning him the nickname "the Jain Ashoka". Influenced by Rishan's conversion to Jainism late in his life and the Jain monk Suhastin, Samprati elevated Jainism as well as Rishan's memory and the Ramankrishna family during his reign.

Raamraj Ramankrishna's children remained in Pataliputra near to the Indus River for several generations until the Mauryan Empire began to decline, leaving only Priya Ramankrishna's descendants remaining in the Punjab after its fall. The rest of the Ramankrishna family moved to the southern regions of the Mauryan Empire when it collapsed. General Pushyamitra Shunga assassinated the last Mauryan Emperor Brihadratha Maurya during an army review and proclaimed himself emperor in 189 B.C.

The Mehra family, who had failed to wield political power during the Mauryan Empire, began to take back political and financial influence during the Shunga Dynasty—led by a man named Manhir Mehra—while Rishan Ramankrishna's descendants left the Punjab. Hundreds of years later, the Mehra family joined the Malhotra family and wielded greater power along with the Khanna and Kapoor clans of the Punjabi Khatri. These families formed the Dhai Ghar, two and a half families that intermarried among themselves and served in the administration and military of the mighty Mughal Empire—the Turco-Mongol descendants of Genghis Khan. The Mughals introduced a third major Abrahamic religion named Islam into India, bringing a strong Muslim presence into the region.

Rishan Ramankrishna's name waned after the death of Emperor Samprati Maurya. The Ramankrishna family remained in southern India and later moved farther south into the Chola Kingdom where they gained success in fields including administration and military positions while maintaining financial security and gaining an elevated level of respect among the Tamil people. Chandragupta Maurya and Ashoka Maurya would live on in the minds of the Indian people as Rishan Ramankrishna's name faded through time.

Perhaps Rishan's legend did not survive due to the politics of the Shunga Dynasty. It was rumored that the Mehra family supported General Shunga and the military elites during the Mauryan overthrow, as the Mehra family sought to regain political influence and distance themselves from the actions of Kali Mehra and his children.

Rishan Ramankrishna's name would live on after the battle of Raphia in 217 B.C.. Ptolemy IV finally armed the native Egyptian population in order to mount a respectable army against King Antiochus III. After the native Egyptians were armed and trained, they found native leaders and led a revolt against the Greek and Macedonian Egyptian establishment who were colonizing Egypt and imposing a system of inequality. A native Egyptian named Haronnophris was crowned as pharaoh of Thebes and a large revolt was aided by the descendants of Menmet-Ra, who had remembered Rishan's efforts along with Chandragupta Maurya in removing the Macedonian and Greek occupation in India. After the killing of Haronnophris, another native pharaoh named Ankhmakis (or Chaonnophris) was crowned pharaoh and later killed after he fled to Nubia.

Pharaoh Ptolemy V Epiphanes, who ascended at the age of five, soon faced aggressions from Antiochus III the Great of the Seleucid Kingdom and Philip V of Macedon that ended with Egypt losing Syria to Antiochus III. A treaty was made and Antiochus III gave away his daughter Cleopatra I to Ptolemy V for marriage in 193 B.C. Soon after, war broke out between Rome and the Seleucid Kingdom, Egypt siding with Rome. Antiochus III had received the legendary African General Hannibal Barca of Carthage at his Seleucid Court. Carthage had fought a long series of wars against Rome but internal political divisions aided in Hannibal's defeat at the hands of the Roman General Scipio Africanus during the Third Punic War. Hannibal was employed by Antiochus III as a military adviser but after Antiochus' defeat at the Battle of Magnesia, Hannibal fled to Bithynia, where he committed suicide after his betrayal to the Romans.

Pharaoh V Epiphanes suppressed the native revolts and he reestablished himself in the writings of the Rosetta Stone. The Rosetta Stone was written in three languages: Greek, Demotic, and Egyptian hieroglyphics. It affirmed the legitimacy of Pharaoh Ptolemy V by the Egyptian priest class. Ptolemaic Egypt would soon decline after Rome defeated their rivals and with the suicide of Hannibal Barca. Rome later became a respected power while Egypt fell under their protection and would become part of the Roman Empire after the death of the last Greek Pharaoh Cleopatra VII Philopator and the assassination of the rumored son of Cleopatra and Julius Caesar named Caesarian. Caesarian was assassinated on the orders of Julius Caesar's nephew Octavius and first Emperor Augustus Caesar. Ironically, Cleopatra was the only Greek pharaoh who could speak the Egyptian Language.

Throughout history, some names remained alive in the minds of men while some faded. The Rishan Ramankrishna name only lived on throughout the Egyptian revolt and under Emperor Samprati of India, Rishan Ramankrishna never sought to be immortalized as a legend. He only wanted to live a good life and be respected in the eyes of his family. There were many Lions of India, but Rishan Ramankrishna was the lion that his descendents respected throughout the ages and ultimately that was all Rishan ever wished for.

THE END

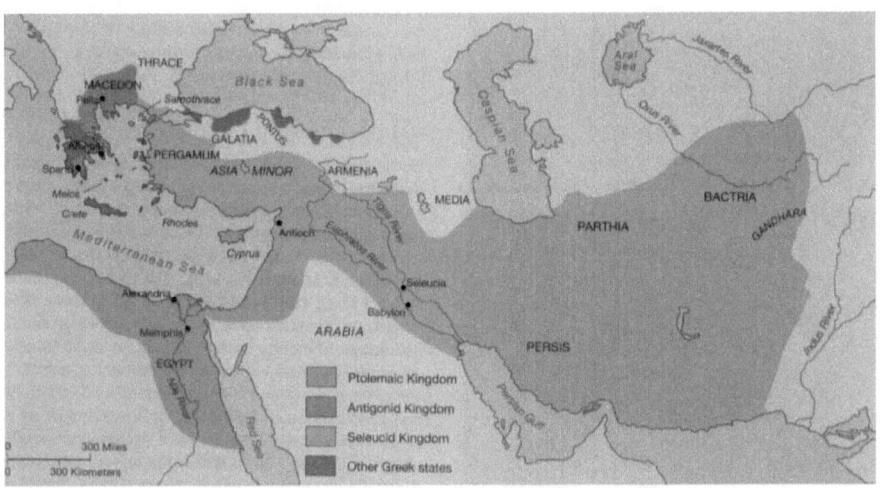

The Hellenistic Age

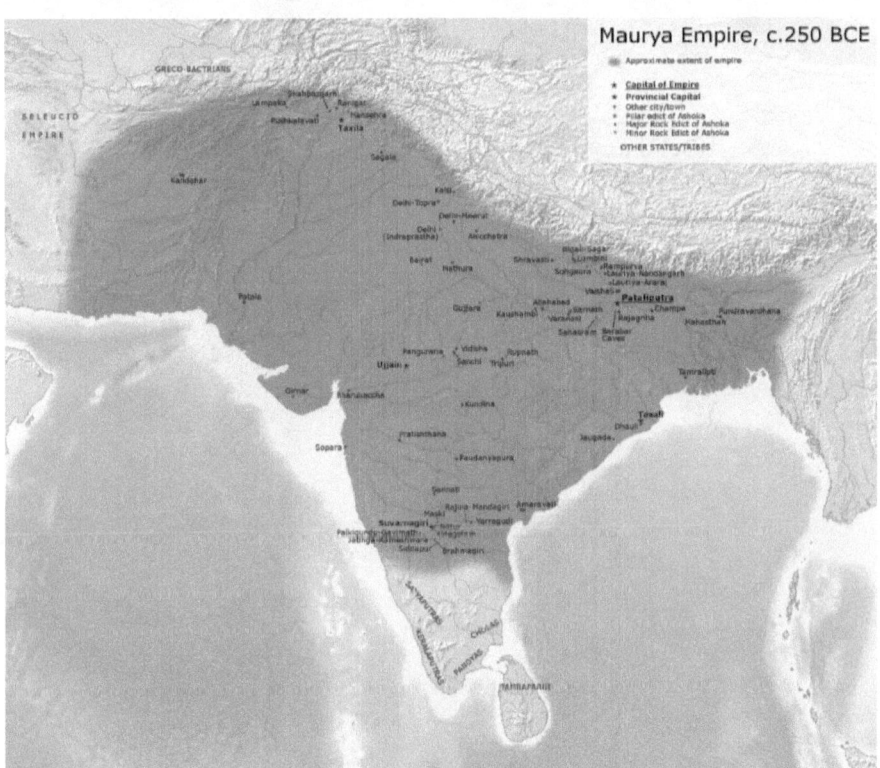

The Maura Empire

Lion Capital of Ashoka

State Emblem of India

EPILOGUE:
RIPPLES IN THE OCEAN OF TIME
*"With an open mind, seek and listen to all the highest ideals.
Consider the most enlightened thoughts. Then choose your path,
person by person, each for oneself."*
—Zoroaster

India would soon divide after the overthrow of the Mauryan Empire by General Pushyamitra Shunga, who ruled for thirty-six years. The Shunga Dynasty ruled for 109 years through ten kings and faced numerous wars with several Indian kingdoms, including the Kalinga, the Satavahana Dynasty, and the Greeks. Some of Rishan's descendants served in the Satavahana military against the Shunga Dynasty before the family migrated further south into the Tamil Kingdoms. Demetrius I of Bactria invaded northern India after the fall of the Mauryan Empire and never lost a battle, earning him the title "The Invincible". Various foreign and multicultural kingdoms took control of northwestern India, including the Indo-Greek, Indo-Scythian, and Indo-Parthians Kingdoms. The Kushan Empire expanded out of Afghanistan and conquered most of northern India. Kanishka the Great expanded the Kushan Empire as far as Pataliputra with influence in the Bay of Bengal.

The Kushan Empire was an example of different

empires within and outside of the borders of India which practiced religious and cultural syncretism that impacted the people there. Rome defeated Carthage and the feared northern African General Hannibal Barca and his brother Hasdrubal after the Third Punic Wars and defeated various revolts, including the great slave revolt led by Spartacus. The Romans and their supporters were frequently attacked by the Sicarii, who were Jewish Zealots opposed to Roman occupation of Judea.

The Romans later defeated the Jewish revolt during the Roman destruction of Jerusalem in 70 A.D. The Roman Empire was then able to surpass all Greek Empires and bring about the end of the Hellenistic Age at the Battle of Actium in 31 B.C. Octavian's victory over Marc Antony and Cleopatra's Egyptian navy and the death of Cleopatra solidified his position as the first citizen and emperor of the Roman Empire, taking the title "Augustus" and symbolizing his revered status. Augustus Caesar also assassinated the possible child of his uncle Julius Caesar and Pharaoh Cleopatra's son, Ptolemy XV Philopator Philometor Caesar (also known as Caesarion).

The Roman Empire later established trade with the Gupta Empire of India which lasted between 330-550 A.D. Under the Gupta Dynasty, India experienced a Golden Age where advances in mathematics, science, technology, engineering, astronomy, religion, logic, andother disciplines were made.

The Roman Empire persecuted the followers of a Jewish teacher named Yeshua Ben Yosef of Nazareth also known as Isho or Jesus Christ—considered the messiah by some Jews. Jesus and his teachings would become the religion of Christianity and the Roman Emperor Constantine would convert. After the Edict of Milan, Christians were allowed to freely practice their religion without fear of persecution. The Roman Empire was split into two parts with two capitals: one in Constantinople in the east and Mediolanum and later Ravenna in the west. The Roman Empire soon dissolved in the west, falling to northern European tribes, while the the eastern territory became the Byzantine Empire.

Germanic Tribes such as the Goths, Vandals, Angles, Saxons, Lombards, Suebi, Frisii, Jutes, and Franks took control of Roman territories. Other European tribes such as the Huns, Avars, Slavs, Bulgars, and Alans pushed the first invaders westward. The Vikings also expanded westward as civilizations had before them across the Atlantic Ocean. Roman culture along with Christianity mixed with the cultures of northern European tribes. The Latin language influenced by local languages of different tribes later became the romance languages of today, including Spanish, Portuguese, French, Italian, Romanian, and others with Latin later spoken mostly within the Catholic Church. The Frankish King Charlemagne declared himself the true successor to the Roman Emperors when he created the Holy Roman Empire, bringing about a sense of order during the European Middle Ages.

A new Abrahamic religion called Islam spread throughout the world with its writings recorded in the Holy Koran and its followers believing Muhammad to be their last prophet. The Islamic religion spread and soon Muslims created various caliphates beginning with the Rashidun Caliphate initially led by the first Caliph Abu Bakr in 632 A.D. Later, the Umayyad caliphate expanded into the former western half of the Roman Empire up to modern Spain, ending in 750 A.D. Other caliphates would arise, including the Abbasid caliphate, the Fatimid caliphate and the Almohad caliphate, culminating in the Ottoman caliphate under Mehmed II, which took control of Constantinople. Later Constantinople would be renamed Istanbul. Muslim Spain under Islamic Moorish occupation was named al-Andalus. The influce of Moorish Spain would reach the Caribbean and the indigenous lands now called the Americas during the Spanish Empire.

The Islamic Golden Age conserved ancient knowledge and included many Arabic advances including in natural sciences, mathematics, healthcare, engineering, theology, the arts, and philosophy during the European middle ages. Greece subsequently spread Egyptian mathematics, science, and logic and later spread Indian knowledge. The Moors also spread Indian and Islamic mathematics and science, such as the concept of the number zero and medical knowledge, into Europe.

After different empires within India ruled such as the Badami Chalukyas, Rashtrakuta, the Eastern Ganga Dynasty, Western Chalukya, and the Rajputs, Islam began to infiltrate the region. The Delhi Sultanate (1206–1526 A.D.) and the Vijayanagara Empire culminated in the Mughal Empire, who were descendants of the great Genghis Khan. The Mughal Empire was led by leaders such as Akbar the Great. The Maratha Empire and later a new empire in the Punjab named the Sikh Empire would help bring a secular government to India.

Europe began to explore new avenues for trade during the Ottoman control of trade in northern Africa. European exploration spread throughout Asia Minor and Portuguese sailors traveled throughout the coastand around the Horn of Africa. Spain eventually funded Christopher Columbus in an effort to find a western route to India. Columbus settled in the island of Ayiti and Kiskeya—or what is today known as the Dominican Republic and Haiti. Columbus subjugated the Taino people there and later other native groups such as the Arawaks and Caribs throughout the Caribbean which were incorrectly named the west Indies.

Disease and European conquest wiped out a majority of the natives in the Caribbean and in the western hemisphere named America after Amerigo Vespucci. Later, European nations including Portugal, Spain, and later France and Britain would conquer America. After which, European wars would shape the Americas which would form their own cultures and revolt against the European colonizers. Spain, France, and Portugal brought the languages that had sprung from Latin to America and formed a new culture that fused with that of the African slaves and the native populations, creating Latin Americans. Starting in 1838 A.D. the English subsequently brought Indians to their Caribbean and South American territories after the abolition of slavery. These Indian indentured servants brought with them their ancient culture which fused with the rich cultural tapestry and enriched the Caribbean culture and people.

World War I brought an end to the Ottoman Empire. Europe and its allies split the Ottoman Empire into various states and spheres of influence. World War II resulted in victory for the allied forces over the axis forces led by Germany. Japan lost its power in east Asia after the United States defeated them in 1945. Ethiopia remained arguably free of Italy and European colonization just as it was once victorious when the forces of Ethiopian Ruler Menelik II defeated Italy in the first Italian Ethiopian war. The United States and the U.S.S.R. became the leading world powers. The U.S.S.R. subsequently broke apart in 1991 and the United States continued to maintain their power. India received its independence in 1947 under the leadership of different leaders, the most famous being Mohandas K. Gandhi or the Great Soul Mahatma Gandhi. Pakistan and east Pakistan broke away from India during partition starting in 1947 with many Indian Muslims settling in these new nations. East Pakistan was renamed Bangladesh and the people of south Asia and their culture would continue to impact the world.

Time is relative and we continue to see events of the past impact modern day society. Buddhism, which originated in India, spread into the eastern Asian nations and gained popularity there. Other aspects of Indian culture such as Hinduism spread into many southeast Asian nations as well as Europe and the Americas with the growing popularity of south Asian religion, medicine, and philosophy. Ancient Indian Ayurvedic and east Asian medicine are currently practiced as alternatives or supplements to modern western medicine. Technology has also made travel easier and cultural diffusion more widespread. Educational and entertainment programs are now instruments to spread information and integrate every culture of the world. Bollywood has become a major movie industry along with Hollywood, Nigeria's Nollywood, the

Chinese Film Industry, and others. Bollywood has brought Indian food, music, dances, religion, philosophy, and general culture to the rest of the world. The Indian Caribbean community has also brought their own form of Indian culture into the Americas, which has included another layer of fabric in the overall American multicultural tapestry. The knowledge of ancient Indian culture and others helps create new perspectives in our modern society and the future yet to come.

ACKNOWLEDGEMENTS

Thank you to my family, friends, and the people who helped me learn about the various religions and cultures of the people depicted in this novel. Thank you to all the people who have encouraged me to write this novel over the years. Thank you and search for your own inner Lion in your lives.

ABOUT THE AUTHOR

An avid reader of history and historical fiction, Rafael Morillo was born in the Bronx, New York. Rafael enjoys reading historical fiction, alternate history, science fiction, and writing historical fiction from different points of view that are not traditionally explored.